"It was the signal of the chief who wore the great feather head-dress"

THE HORSEMEN OF THE PLAINS

A STORY OF THE GREAT CHEYENNE WAR

BY

JOSEPH A. ALTSHELER

Author of "In Circling Camps," "The Last of the Chiefs," etc.

Illustrated by
Charles Livingston Bull

1910

CONTENTS

CHAPTER		PAGE
I	Friends in Need	1
II	In the Wilderness	16
III	The Shadow in the Dusk	33
IV	The Dog Soldiers	47
V	The Snowy Pass	68
VI	The Precipice	85
VII	In the Bearskin	96
VIII	The Midnight Meeting	113
IX	The Sunken River	126
X	The Return by Land	142
XI	The Coming of Carver	155
XII	The Great Laugh	171
XIII	The Departure	182
XIV	In Cheyenne Hands	197
XV	A Modern Mazeppa	212
XVI	The Island in the River	232
XVII	Little Thermopylae	256
XVIII	The Charge of Roman Nose	274
XIX	The Amazing Flight	291
XX	A Light in the Dark	308
XXI	A-Horse with Custer	320
XXII	The Battle of the Washita	338
XXIII	The Lone Search	357
XXIV	A Miracle	370
XXV	The Final Settlement	380

LIST OF ILLUSTRATIONS

"It was the signal of the chief who wore the great feather head-dress" ....Frontispiece

Facing Page

"They're Utes from the other side of the mountain".. 90

"A great bear sprang up from the thicket"........... 104

"As it shot through the mouth of the pass it took a foaming fall" 145

"As it was, Bob heard the bullet singing a little warning in his ear".................................163

"The great figure was tense and drawn, ready to lash out like lightning with those sharp hoofs"....... 230

"They bore the body between them"................ 290

"The buffalo, hurt and weak, no longer tried to move" 377

THE HORSEMEN OF THE PLAINS
CHAPTER I
FRIENDS IN NEED

A boy sat in a little room in the frontier town of Omaha. It was a poor and cheap place. A flimsy table stood in one corner, an equally flimsy bed in another, and one or two pictures from newspapers were tacked on the bare, pine walls. There was no carpet on the floor. Nothing showed quality, except a rifle that lay across the foot of the bed.

The weapon was a fine breech-loader, advanced in type for the time, and a skilful hand had carved initials and several graceful little decorations on the stock. Any one would surmise that it was highly prized by its owner.

The boy himself was a match for his rifle, a stalwart youth, seventeen years old, with the stature and strength of a man. His brown hair, cut short, curled just a little, and his blue eyes were set wide apart, as they usually are in those of large minds. His face was brown with tan, but, at the edge of the collar, his fair white skin showed.

A comely boy, and a strong and brave one, as the most casual observer would have inferred. But he was dressed poorly, and the look upon his face, just now, was not cheerful, although his was a nature disposed to see the better side of things, and he had all the flush of early youth. The window was open, and he gazed out of it, but saw little, because his thoughts, for the moment, were turned elsewhere.

What the blue eyes did not see was an expanse of new wooden houses, built hastily for shelter, and not for beauty, unpaved streets, with sidewalks of boards, and, beyond them, the circling eddies of a great brown river that flowed from regions yet largely unknown.

But a sky of an extraordinary, brilliant blue curved over the new town. The same intense vivid light that showed all the crudeness of the houses and streets, surcharged the air with buoyancy and hope, and made the world itself seem very beautiful.

The wind was blowing steadily out of the west, and it was a remarkable wind. It swept over two thousand miles of clean land, as pure as the sea, but it was touched with a faint odor of coming spring, of the young grass beginning to appear on the boundless plains, and of the buds breaking forth in the mountain forests.

The note of the wind at last reached the boy. He raised his head a little, and the indefinable perfume, faint in fact but powerful in fancy, entered his nostrils, and all his senses were keenly stirred. The blue eyes turned toward the west, and they began to see at last. But they did not see the rough wooden houses and the muddy streets. They saw the vast West, that lay beyond the white man's plow, the land of the unknown, of mystery, of the shaggy buffalo herd, and the pitiless Indian. It was an enchanted region, none the less so because of its dangers, and just now it was calling to the boy in a voice that he must hear.

He bent his head a little toward the wind, and gradually the gloom went from his face. The blue eyes grew bright as became his years and his mind roamed far in pleasant lands, through great adventures.

He left the window presently, and, going to the bed, took up the rifle, which he handled with affection. It had belonged to his father who fell three years before, in the great Civil War, at the Battle of the Wilderness, and he had left little but this fine weapon and his memory, to his son.

The war was over a year and Robert Norton, without either father or mother or any near relative, had wandered into this frontier town, not knowing what he was going to do. He had no plan. He had spent a little time with an emigrant train; he had helped farmers to break horses, but, passing from one task to another, he had been moving steadily westward.

He did not realize until now the direction in which his course had taken him, but when he saw it he also understood it. It was the Great West, the Mighty West, the West of mystery and romance that always beckoned him. Since he could remember he had heard of it, the wonderful tales of the Forty-Niners, the plains, the mountains, the wild animals, the wild Indians, the gold, the furs and the danger.

Now, with the feel of the rifle in his hands, he

took his resolution. He would go into this vast and yet wild West, and fend for himself. One could not go alone, but he might find comrades, and there was no better place than this town of Omaha, the point of departure for the plains, in which to look for them.

All his confidence returned. The tide of early youth was at the full, and, rifle on shoulder, he left the house, going into the fresh, perfumed air, which still blew strongly from the great regions of mystery. Many people were in the unpaved streets, and, like himself, they were occupied with thoughts of the West. Their faces were seldom turned Eastward.

The fact that a boy was carrying a rifle attracted no attention. Nearly everybody carried either rifles or pistols and often both, and there was abundant need of them. Before a man went many miles west of Omaha his life depended solely upon his own skill and courage.

The crowd in the street interested the boy greatly. It was a cheerful throng, thinking little of the dangers it was about to face. An emigrant train would start for California by the Santa Fe route in the morning, some gold-seekers would leave a few hours later for the mountains of the far Northwest, and a pony express was just going.

Robert looked at both the emigrant train and the gold-seekers, but he decided that he would not apply for membership in either party.

His walk took him toward the river, and he stood looking at the brown stream, his face turned towards its source. His feeling of mystery and fascination was deepened by the Missouri, which was not in itself a beautiful object. But it came from the unknown, the lands that he longed to enter.

While he looked, a half dozen boats, flat and broad, manned by perhaps thirty men, appeared, floating on the muddy current. The men were clothed partly in white garb and partly in skins. Their faces were almost as brown as those of Indians, and their hair grew long. Every one was well armed, and the boats were filled with large bales.

The boy knew that they were fur hunters, returning from a successful expedition, probably lasting two or three years, into the Rocky Mountains. They appealed to him more than either the emigrants or the gold-seekers, and he regarded them eagerly. What wonders they must have seen and what deeds they must have done!

"Looks as ef they had been somewhere, don't they?" said a cheery voice beside him.

The boy turned abruptly. He had not noticed the approach of any one, but the voice was so deep, it had such a round, full and hearty tone, that he knew an honest heart must have inspired the speech.

He beheld a man of middle height, but uncommonly big of bone and very powerful. He had thick curly hair, rosy cheeks and a magnificent set of large, white teeth. All of his dress was civilized but a raccoon skin cap, with the short tail hanging down behind. He was fully armed, carrying a fine rifle on his shoulder and a revolver and knife at his belt. But he had a wonderfully ingratiating smile, and the heart of the lonely boy warmed to him at once.

"Trappers comin' back," said the stranger, nodding toward the men in the boat, "an' they've been in luck. They've got somethin' worth sellin'. Took a long time though."

"Wish I was with a party like that, going instead of coming," said the boy. "I'd like to be a fur hunter."

"Good trade," said the man, "an' it ain't dead yet, by no means. Has its dangers, though. Injuns, lots of 'em. Look out for 'em. But do not be a pessimist, my boy. It's a habit."

Robert stared and the man smiled back at him in a gratified way.

"I'm always hopin' for the best. It's comfortin'," he said. "My name is Sam Strong an' I come from Kentucky, but I've been a hunter an' trapper more than ten years. What's your name?"

"Robert Norton," replied the boy, not at all offended by the question, which was natural on the border.

"Robert, h—m! That's long for Bob. Bob's better, and Bob it will be."

"As you like," said Bob smiling.

"Now, Bob," said Sam Strong, "I saw you standin' here lookin' at them fur boats, an' I knew what you was thinkin'. You was wantin' to be out in the wilderness yourself takin' furs."

"That is so," said Bob frankly, "you read me right."

"An' you was lookin' tre-men-je-ous lonesome, but

there's a good time comin' for you. Now Bob, you want to go fur-huntin', an' fur-huntin' you shall go."

"What do you mean?" asked Bob, his whole face beaming. Sam Strong of the twinkling eyes already inspired confidence in him.

"Didn't I just tell you I was a trapper an' hunter? I'm one of a little band that's just startin' out, an' we need another. You want to go, an' we take you. So we kill one bird with two stones."

Bob smiled at his mixture of the proverb, but he was happy. His heart had cried for a friend, and he was finding one.

"I'll go with you," he cried, "I'll go anywhere with you, and I'll do my part of the work."

"An' your part of the fightin' too, I take it, if any is to be done. Well, variety is the salt an' pepper of life, an' you an' me, an' the rest of the fellers ought to see some lively times together, Bob. I'm takin' you on faith, an' you're takin' me the same way. Come along."

They left the river, and went back toward the center of the town, the minds of both intent upon the business ahead. The crowd was still lively, and, in one or two places, it had become turbulent. The cause of the turbulence was obvious. The trapper looked at the offenders in disgust.

The eyes of Sam Strong, usually so benevolent, snapped with disapproval.

"Fools! Little children!" he said. "Seems strange to me, Bob, that anybody should want to get that way with bad liquor, when this air itself fills up with wine."

He too lifted his head, and inhaled the perfumed wind that blew from the great clean West.

"I reckon I'm a good deal of a wild man, Bob," he continued. "I like to come into a town now and then, to see the sights and have a good time, but for a reg'lar life give me the wilderness. Now this party of ours ain't a big one, an' we don't go by water. We ride across the plains."

"I haven't any horse," said Bob, with a sudden sinking of the heart, "and I haven't money enough to buy one."

"Ain't that too bad?" said Sam Strong. "He ain't got any horse an' he ain't got money 'nough to buy one. Now he's invited to join a trappin' outfit, everybody expectin' him to do his share of the work, an' his share of the fightin' if need be, an' he thinks nobody will grubstake him."

His playful little satire was so obvious that the boy blushed. It was a long time since he had met so much kindness, and his heart warmed more than ever toward stalwart Sam Strong.

"I'll pay you back out of the very first money I earn," he said earnestly.

"Don't I know that?" said Sam. "Did you think I'd take you, if I didn't know you was the right stuff? Here's our shanty. I'll introduce you to the boys, an' make you one of the gang."

He led the way into a large wooden house that served as a hotel. The lobby was crowded with all the types of the border, and the air was thick with smoke, but Sam did not stop there. He ascended the narrow staircase that led to the second floor,

Bob by his side. Two men, to whom he had given glances that Bob did not notice, detached themselves from the crowd and followed.

Sam Strong went down a narrow hall, opened a door and entered a large room. The two men who had followed came in also, and then he closed the door. Three others who were already in the room rose to their feet and one of them said:

"Hello, Cap, what's this critter that you've brought us?"

Bob blushed again, knowing that five pairs of inquiring eyes were upon him, but Sam Strong laughed.

"This," he replied, "is the camp baby; that is, he's goin' to be. We thought we needed one more feller for our trip, an' a likely chap like this can be a lot of use. Boys make things lively around a camp, an' he can wait on us, when he ain't got anythin' else to do. I ketched him down by the river, an' brought him in."

All the men laughed and Bob was embarrassed. But he knew that word and laugh were kindly. While Sam Strong was giving his name and pedigree, and introducing him in his easy Western fashion, he looked carefully at them all, one by one.

They were a marked lot. Second to Sam Strong was a tall, lank Missourian with a scarred and weatherbeaten face, called Bill Cole. Then came two younger men, Tom Harris and Porter Evans. Harris was from Michigan and Evans from Tennessee. They had fought on different sides in the Civil War, and that fact now made them the closest of friends, although they never agreed in anything about the late great strife. Then there was Louis Perolet, a little French-Canadian, compact and strong like a coil of woven steel wire, and Obadiah Pirtle, a slow spoken man from Maine, completed the list.

All were dressed in a mixture of wild and civilized garb, and their faces showed many signs of life, far beyond the fences that the white man builds. Every one seemed to the boy to speak, by his very appearance, of the mountains and the plains. Their rifles leaned against the wall, their pistols were at their belts, but their voices were gentle, and no hostility was in the glance of any one of them.

Bob was seized with a mighty sense of intoxicating joy. He had found suddenly, and, without the least hope, that for which he longed most. He, an inexperienced boy, was going to be admitted to a most glorious company. No young squire, about to become a knight, was ever more enthralled. He resolved, if he passed the ordeal of trial successfully, to devote his last breath to the common good, if need be.

"Well boys," said Sam Strong, "havin' looked him up an' down an' studied his p'ints, what do you think of the colt?"

"Strappin' big youngster," said Porter Evans. "We had a lot like him at Shiloh when we give the Yankees such a terrible beatin'."

"Give us a beatin', did you?" exclaimed Tom Harris. "I could live and grow fat on such beatin's as that. Why, we chased your whole army right into the middle of the Tennessee River, an' for all I know it's there yet."

"That'll do for you two," said Sam genially. "If you are bound to fight the war over again, go out an' do it in the hall. Now, Louis, what do you say?"

"Heem all right," said the shrewd little Frenchman. "He look all of us ver straight in the eye, an' that enough. He one of us, he help me wiz ze cooking."

"An' you, Bill Cole?"

"Looks smart to me."

"An' you, Obe?"

"I reckon he'll do."

"Then it's settled," said Sam Strong, clapping a heavy hand upon the boy's shoulder. "You're chose, Bob. You're a member of this here band. Our secrets are your secrets, an' we stand together, every man for the lot. Shake hands with your new pards."

Bob shook hands, taking them in turn, and his feelings almost overpowered him. But he was duly silent, as became a tyro, and, taking a chair, he listened, with consuming attention, to their talk. It was all of the wild places where they had been, and to which they expected to return. The six were veterans. Both Harris and Evans had been on the plains, when they were boys, before the war, and as soon as the struggle ceased, they had returned to their old life.

It surprised and delighted the lad to find himself fully accepted into fellowship. Now that he had been made a member of the band they kept nothing from him, but discussed their past lives and their plans, with the utmost freedom, in his presence.

After an hour he went with Porter Evans, the Tennesseean, to his boarding house to pay his bill, and to obtain his few belongings. The afternoon was well advanced when they stepped out, and the western wind was growing colder. Bob shivered, just a little bit, but would not let the Tennesseean see it. He would have been deeply shamed to show lack of endurance at the very beginning of his career. But the thoughts of Evans were elsewhere.

"I was right, Bob," he said, somewhat anxiously, "when I told Tom Harris that we beat the Yanks at Shiloh. We had 'em well thrashed when Buell came up. What happened after that don't count. Tom was there on the other side, an' he knows, but he won't admit it."

Bob laughed from sheer exuberance of spirit.

"You are surely right, Mr. Evans," he said, seeing that his comrade wished to be confirmed by his opinion.

But Evans suddenly stopped and faced him.

"What did you call me?" he asked.

"Why, Mr. Evans, of course."

"Now, see here, I'm Mr. Evans only to them th don't like me, an' that I don't like. To them t run with me I'm Porter, or Port. Which do mean to be, a friend or an enemy?"

"A friend, surely, Porter."

"That's all right. Now we'll go on an' g things of yours."

Bob had little to take back with him—merely a large old-fashioned valise, filled with clothing—and, in a half hour, he was at the hotel again with his new comrades. The big room, in which they were staying, had several beds, and he was to sleep there with the others. When he put his valise down by the wall Harris drew him to one side, and said in a whisper:

"I know Port told you again about the Battle of Shiloh an' claimed that they licked us, but don't you believe a word of it, Bob. We drove 'em right into the Tennessee."

"Of course, of course, Tom," said the boy.

He meant to be no arbiter of history, nor did he make the mistake of calling Harris "Mister." He began in this case with "Tom."

The cold was increasing as the prairie night drew down, and a negro brought in logs for the big fireplace, at one end of the room. Soon a fine blaze was crackling and roaring, and they sat in their cane chairs in a loose circle about it. Bob had little to say, but he still listened, all ears, although a pleasant, drowsy warmth was creeping over him.

They went down to the main dining-room presently, and ate supper together. Then they returned to the rear room, lighted by the fire, and the men brought forth their pipes. The smoke rose, and deep content permeated the air. Outside a chill wind screamed over the prairie.

"Them ham an' eggs was mighty good," said Bill Cole, "an' they've filled up a big hollow right in the inside of me, but I've knowed buffalo steak to taste better, 'specially when Louis here cooked it.''

"Have you really lived on buffalo steak, Mr. Bill?" asked Bob eagerly.

Bill Cole took his pipe out of his mouth, and blew a beautiful ring of smoke to the ceiling, where it broke.

"Have I lived on buffalo steak?" he replied in tones of deep satisfaction. "Well, I should say! For whole months at a time, an' I lived tre-men-je-ous well. You just wait till Louis there cooks one for you. You could live on them kind for a whole year, an' then ask for another year of the same."

"We'll have 'em soon," said Obadiah Pirtle.

Bob's eyes glowed with admiration.

"We've got to advance the boy enough money to buy a pony," said Sam Strong. "'Twon't take much, an' I reckon we can clear out of here in about another day. They say that the battle ain't to the swift nor the strong, but I reckon that it often is. I mean, Bob, that some places in the Rockies are much better for trappin' than some other places, an' we want to get to the best first."

Then they began to run over the tally of their resources, the rifles, the pistols, the ponies, the steel traps and the provisions. Bob gathered from their talk that they were well supplied with money, and that they had obtained the best of everything. As he listened his eyelids grew heavier, and the lids pulled down hard. The warmth made him dreadfully sleepy. He tried to hide it, but Sam Strong caught him at last.

"Don't be ashamed, boy," he said. "Tumble over into bed there at once. The wisest thing that a man can do is to go to sleep when he is sleepy, if the place allows."

Bob obeyed without demur. For a few minutes he saw the fire and the men smoking their pipes, and then he was dreaming a mighty dream, in which single-handed he was slaying buffalo herds, and fighting Indian tribes.

CHAPTER II

IN THE WILDERNESS

When Bob awoke, dawn was coming in at the uncurtained windows. All his comrades were up but the two young soldiers of the great war. Not willing to be last, the boy sprang out of bed, and began to hurry on his clothes.

"That's right, Bob," said Sam Strong cheerily. "You've beat both them lazy generals the very first mornin'. Good start for you."

Harris and Evans opened their eyes at the same time, and, at the same time, both sat up.

"What kept me asleep," said Harris, "was dreamin' about that time we whipped the Johnny Rebs so bad at Chickamauga. I was just helpin' chase 'em into Chattanooga, when I heard your disturbin' voice, Sam."

"You beat us at Chickamauga!" exclaimed Porter Evans. "Why, we give you the worst lickin' of the whole war then, an' when you woke up we were chasin' you, not you chasin' us."

"Shut up," said Sam Strong. "The war has done been dead an' buried a whole year, an' I guess we'll go down to breakfast. We'd better post Bob here, an' tell him not to say anything about our plans."

While the laggard two were dressing, Strong told the boy that it was necessary for them to keep their expedition and all its plans secret. The only good trapping grounds left were deep in the Rocky Mountains, and trappers would stalk one another in order to discover a choice reserve. Men in Omaha now were watching Strong and his comrades, believing that they might follow them and profit by it.

"If anybody asks you questions, Bob," said Strong, "just tell him you don't know anything, an' you'll be tellin' the truth, too."

Bob promised, and nothing could have made him break the promise. They ate breakfast and dispersed about their errands, having agreed to meet again at the hotel late in the afternoon. Bob's business was to buy a pony with money loaned him by Sam Strong out of the common fund. He was a good judge of horses, and, as they were for sale everywhere, he soon selected a strong young animal from a group in a corral at the edge of the town. Several spectators stood by, as the boy bought his horse, and one of them, a tall man of strong build and dark skin, said in the most casual manner:

"You seem to have a good eye for a horse, my lad. That's a fine one you bought just then, and you didn't let them make you pay too much."

Bob flushed with appreciation at these chance words of praise, evidently so sincere, and replied:

"I hope you're right, sir. I've need of a good mount."

"Going across the plains, I presume," said the man in the same casual tone. "It's dangerous, but it's a great thing for a youngster like you."

Bob was about to reply, but checked himself suddenly, remembering the warning that Strong had given. However, there was nothing in this man's appearance to cause apprehension. His smooth, slightly foreign face was well cut, and his eyes had the look of benevolence. His English was modulated correctly, and without accent. His manner was decidedly attractive, but Bob was already devotedly loyal to his comrades, and he was resolved to be on the cautious side, even at the risk of seeming churlish.

"It's a long ride to California," continued the man, "unless you're stopping somewhere in the Rockies, and one has to be a member of a strong party, too, as the Cheyennes, both northern and southern, are out, and are taking scalps."

"So I've heard," said Bob vaguely, and mounting his new pony he rode away. He found the others already at the primitive hotel, making all their things into packs for the start. He thought at first that he would not say anything about the stranger, but the manner in which the man had continued his inquiries, or rather suggestions, caused him to be suspicious as he thought it over. So he told Strong of the circumstance. The leader was at once alert.

"Now I always think the best is goin' to happen," he said, "but it won't happen unless you help it to happen, an' it seems to me somebody else wants to put a finger in our pie. What kind of lookin' feller was he, Bob?"

"Tall, strong, smooth face, dark skin, hair and eyes."

"Look like a preacher?"

"Yes, he did, and there was something foreign about him, too. It showed mostly in his voice."

"Hear that, Obe?" said Strong. "I'm always hopin' for the best, but who do you think that fellow was?"

"Juan Carver."

"An' you, Bill? You ain't a bad hand at guessin'."

"Juan Carver, an' it ain't no guess, neither."

"An' our two generals here, an' Louis, think the same way," said Sam Strong. "Still hopin' for the best, I know it's Carver, an' he means to follow us. He was tryin' to pump you about us, Bob."

"Who is Juan Carver?" asked the boy, his nerves tingling with curiosity.

"Juan Carver is a bad man," replied Sam Strong. "I like to think the best of everybody, but there ain't a doubt of it. He's the son of an American father an' a Mexican mother—that's where he gets that touch of the foreigner—and they do say that he ain't got the virtues of either, though full of knowledge an' cunnin'. He's a trapper with a band of his own. Some say he's independent, an' some say he represents the Hudson Bay. If a few fellers like ourselves were to find rich trappin' grounds an' streams he'd foller along, drive us away, an' take 'em himself. Like jumpin' a claim, don't you see?"

Bob saw very well, and he was glad that he had not let the man draw him on in regard to their plans. His news stirred his comrades greatly, and they held a council in their own room. It was agreed that they should make a night start as soon as the moon rose. Their horses and supplies were on the other side of the town. Bill Cole was to slip away first and have everything ready. Then the others would come.

"We want to shake Juan and his crowd clean off," said Sam Strong, "an' if we get a good start they'll never find us."

"We can be forty miles from here by dawn," said Obadiah Pirtle.

Bill Cole left at eight o'clock, and then the others followed about nine, every one armed with a rifle and revolver and knife. Bob's revolver and knife, like his pony, were bought from the common fund. The night was dark, which favored their wishes, and it was but ill lighted by a few flaring gas lamps.

People, mostly men, were still in the streets, but so far as they could see, no notice was taken of the comrades, and they sped to the other side of the town, where at one of the corrals, used by outfitting expeditions, Bill Cole was waiting for them.

"Haven't seen anybody watchin' us," said Bill, tersely. "B'lieve they think we're not going for several days yet."

"Hope you're right, an' it's good always to hope for the best," said Sam Strong.

Besides their own mounts they had fifteen pack horses, all trained to follow without being led, which was a valuable quality, when their owners wished to be free for action. These horses were well loaded with supplies besides carrying a number of extra rifles and revolvers, several fine breech-loading shotguns, and great quantities of ammunition.

Bob mounted his horse and they rode out. Every nerve in the boy thrilled with a vast and vivid delight. Here he was, embarked upon his great adventure, and, from the first moment, they were in the thick of it. He sat his saddle firmly. His rifle was strapped across his back and he looked straight ahead at their leader, Sam Strong, whose figure had become dim, as the dark deepened.

They passed, with the rhythmic sound of hoofs, out upon the prairie into the land which belonged to him who could take it. Bob looked back. The light of the last flaring street lamp was gone, and the night had blotted out everything. Overhead, the stars were hidden by drifting clouds.

A horse and rider rose out of the prairie.

"Which way, friends?" asked a voice, and it was that of the man who had accosted Bob when he bought his pony.

"None of your business, Juan Carver," cried Sam Strong.

Bob was startled by the change in his leader. All the gentleness was gone from his voice which had the sharp, fierce crack of a pistol-shot. Without an instant's hesitation Strong rode his horse directly at Carver, whose own horse went down under the impact, carrying with him his rider who uttered an angry cry, as he fell.

Strong's horse leaped clear and his rider called out: "Come on, boys!" as he swung away at a swift gallop. The six followed at the same pace, Bob's heart beating loud and fast, as he galloped over the swells. They heard the faint sound of a shot behind them, but Sam only laughed.

"That's Juan," he said, "but he's only wastin' a good bullet. His horse will walk lame for some days, an' the rest of his band are too far back to catch us. I'm always hopin' for the best, an' I don't think Juan Carver will have the chance to raid our fur village."

They galloped on over the low swells, and the supply horses in a close group thundered after them. Bob kept his place next to Sam Strong, riding with an easy but firm seat. His heart was not beating so loud and fast now, and pride began to take the place of excitement. He had been under fire! That shot might as well have been aimed at him as at anybody else.

Sam let their pace sink to a hand gallop, but, even then, they ate up space at a great rate, never veering from a course that led due west. Bob trusted everything to his pony, knowing that he was keen of sight and sure of foot. The night darkened further, but he could see that the country was free from obstructions, just the low swells, succeeding one another, at almost regular intervals.

He felt once more that singular penetrating thrill, giving a pleasure so keen that it was almost a pain. He was now well into his magic world, and the first of his wishes had come true. About midnight they stopped and Strong and Cole, taking the boy with them, rode back a hundred yards or so.

There they listened intently, but could hear nothing, not a single sound of pursuit. Bob heard instead a low moaning, but he knew it to be the wind sweeping over the swells. Sam Strong dismounted at last and put his ear to the earth.

"Nothin', Captain?" said Bill Cole after a wait of two minutes.

"Nothin'," replied Strong with conviction. "We've shook 'em off. There can't be a doubt of it an' Juan, whether he stands for himself or Hudson Bay, will have a hard time in findin' us."

They rejoined their comrades, and rode at a walk about three hours longer. The sky was then beginning to lighten, the clouds having gone away. The great stars were coming out, and they danced in the blue in what seemed to Bob a friendly way.

They came to a dip, deeper than the rest, at the bottom of which flowed a shallow creek, and Sam Strong gave the word to dismount. "It's a sheltered place, as good as any we can find," he said, "an' we'll camp here, but there are to be no lights. We'll just roll up in our blankets and go to sleep."

Bob, stiff from the long, hard riding, was glad enough to dismount, and he did not delay about following the second part of Sam's directions. After the horses were tethered he picked out the softest spot on the ground that he could find, folded his warm blanket about him, and in five minutes was sleeping soundly.

He awoke when the first bar of gray was just appearing in the east. He saw, with sleepy eyes, that Strong and Cole were on watch at the edge of their little camp. Most of the horses had lain down, and all were still. Three recumbent forms near him showed that the others were yet asleep.

Bob himself was only half awake. He was in the dreamy, delightful state when one neither remembers nor plans. He lay there, still looking toward the east. He saw through filmy eyes the great red rim of the rising sun that seemed to come bodily out of the earth, pouring a brilliant light over the gray prairies. He saw one of the sentinels moving on noiseless feet, and, although he knew the day was at hand, he fell asleep again.

When he opened his eyes once more it was to awake completely, and to find that all the others were up and moving. He threw off the blanket and sprang to his feet, ashamed of himself, but he was greeted only with laughter, full of good nature.

The sun was a full three hours high, and over a fire of sticks some broiling birds gave out a fine odor.

"Yes, you've slept late," said Sam Strong. "I believe in takin' rest when you need it, an' can get it, without payin' too high a price, so, as last night was most likely the first of the kind you ever had, we let you snooze on so sound that you didn't wake, while Tom and Porter were fightin' the battle of Gettysburg over again for a full hour. Ain't that so, generals?"

The two young soldiers grinned and nodded. The broiling birds were prairie chickens that Bill Cole, an uncommonly good marksman and hunter, had shot. Bob was invited to help himself, and, broiling one on a sharpened twig, he ate the whole of it. The morning air, with the wind blowing, as it usually does on the prairies, was sharp and crisp, and he could never remember to have had such an appetite before.

After breakfast he went down to the shallow stream and drank. The water was not very clear, and it had a slightly bitter taste, but he did not mind it. Again that wonderful air made everything seem good. Then he began to work with the horses and the packs, and to look after as many details of the camp as he could, resolved that he should justify the confidence that had been placed in him.

Sam Strong watched Bob out of those benevolent blue eyes of his—eyes that were shrewd, eyes that could become as cold as steel—and he was pleased. The lonely boy by the river had appealed to him, but he never would have chosen him for their party had he not judged him the possessor of qualities that would prove valuable. Now he was justified, and he turned to Bill Cole.

"He's the right stuff, ain't he?" he said, nodding toward the lad.

"True blue, all wool and a yard wide," replied Bill, sententiously.

Then they held a brief conference. They were about thirty miles from Omaha, and already in No Man's Land, but they knew the locality well. Nevertheless they must choose their route, and proceed with great caution. Both the Northern and Southern Cheyennes were raiding the plains, and many terrible tales, most of them true, had come into Omaha.

"We've got to watch sharp for warriors," said Sam Strong. "If they're only a few when we see 'em we'll stand 'em off; if they're a lot we'll run."

It was now past eleven o'clock, and they rode away again, the mustangs proceeding at a long, easy walk that they seemed able to keep up forever. Bob rode now by the side of Obadiah Pirtle, who pointed out to him how spring was approaching. He called his attention to the tiny shoots of green, almost hidden under the dry grass of last year. They saw here and there also a modest little flower just raising its head.

"Spring will come runnin' now," said Obe. "She'll just bust out. This ain't like the country in which I was born. Up in Maine there are big forests, an' heaps of rocks, an' lots of clear water tumblin' down the hills. Here there ain't any forests, nor rocks, an' mighty little runnin' water, but I love it all the same."

"So do I," said Bob with so much earnestness and emphasis that the Down Easter smiled.

That night they reached another shallow creek, and encamped in the fringe of cottonwoods on its banks. Strong permitted them to build a fire, as he believed that they had thrown Carver off their track, and that no Cheyennes were near. It was still cold at night, and the blaze was grateful. Several of the prairie chickens were left, and they a' them, preferring to save their stores.

That night Bob at his own request helped w

the watch. He was to keep the first half and Porter Evans the second, and he felt the weight of his responsibility. But he was proud of it also. He saw the men lie down in their blankets, and then become still. The wind moaned across the swells and a restless horse moved now and then, but the boy was not lonely.

The darkness thinned away, as his eyes grew used to it. He saw the cottonwoods, not yet in spring foliage, swaying back and forth in the wind, and he clearly saw the outlines of the horses tethered near. He walked for a long time in a half circle about the camp, the creek forming the segment. He trod softly lest he awake any of his comrades, and he never ceased to watch. Doubtless no camp on all the plains that night had a more vigilant sentinel.

It was about midnight, when he heard a low wailing cry, far off on the prairie, and it made a little shiver run through his flesh. He thought at first that it might be a Cheyenne signal, but it was only the howl of a coyote, scavenger of the plains. He shook his rifle a little scornfully, and walked on. He would not let wolves annoy him.

But, as the moon faded and the night grew colder, and the wind stronger, Bob was glad to keep a little closer to his comrades, his half circle narrowing perceptibly. He felt now the full immensity of the wilderness and its desolation. The coyote howled again, a dismal weird howl, full of ghostly suggestion, and Bob came a little closer to the fire, glad to see that some coals were left yet, sparks of living red in the grass.

Despite his occasional attacks of goose-flesh, the boy never shirked his task. He made it a test for himself, subjecting his own body and mind to stern discipline. He was to go off duty about one in the morning, but he purposely waited an hour later before he awakened Evans.

The Tennesseean yawned prodigiously, as he came from his blanket.

"One o'clock, is it, Bob?" he said.

"Yes," replied the boy.

But Evans had a watch and there was light enough for him to see its face.

"Why, it's two o'clock," he said, "an' you've watched an hour over time! What did you do it for?"

"I forgot," said the boy in some confusion.

Evans eyed him keenly and with suspicion.

"You didn't do anything of the kind," he said. "You gave me an extra hour on purpose. I won't forget it, Bob."

They rode on two more days without event. They saw antelope in the distance, several times, but they did not turn aside for a shot, and once Bob beheld on a distant slope huge, shaggy forms that he knew to be those of the buffalo. They were all sorely tempted to try for such big game, but the leader finally ruled to the contrary.

"What we want to do," he said, "is to cover ground, not to shoot buffaloes."

But, as they continued their journey and saw no signs of Indians, they turned aside for buffalo and antelope, the game still being plentiful. Both Sam

Strong and Bill Cole argued from its abundance and comparative tameness that neither white men nor red had passed recently through that region. Bob helped at the killing of a fat cow and they enjoyed a great feast, Louis Perolet cooking the steaks with the skill and delight which perhaps only a Frenchman knows in such pursuits.

"Eet ees good," he said, "this buffalo steak, an' eet belongs to America. The Old World have hees triumphs, an' the New World have hees too."

The next day they saw a long blue line under the horizon which Bob mistook for a haze. But he was soon set right by Sam Strong.

"That's a range of hills or buttes," he said, "an' they're a good place to stay away from. The Sioux an' the Cheyennes keep lookouts, posted on the highest summits, an' when they see an emigrant train or any other white party passin' they signal to the warriors on horseback below. We'll sheer off."

They turned from the blue haze, but Bob saw the low line for a long time. The air was so wonderfully clear that it refused to disappear in the plain, and the faint blur did not go until sunset came.

That night it was again Bob's turn to keep the first half of the watch and, for precaution, Sam Strong was sentinel with him. The night was light, with a good moon and plenty of bright stars, and the boy found himself looking, nearly all the time, toward that point on the horizon, where the unseen line of buttes lay. His eyes were drawn in that direction by a sort of terrible fascination. The idea of the savage warriors, watching on the crest of the buttes to signal an ambush, made his flesh creep once more.

When he had been on watch about two hours, and, while his eyes were turned toward the haunted horizon, he saw a light, faint and very far. He thought at first that it was some star hanging low, but its motion and radiance were unlike those of a star, and, when he saw it swing slowly from side to side, he knew that it was a signal. He touched Sam Strong on the arm and pointed to the light.

"It's a Cheyenne talkin' from the top of one of the buttes," said the leader. "Now I wonder what he's sayin', but anyway some friend of his will be answerin' him soon. There, look! See the other fellow talkin' back!"

A second light appeared on the horizon to the right of the first, and it too swung slowly back and forth. It ceased and the first took up the talk again. The second made a vigorous rejoinder and then both disappeared like the blowing out of a candle.

"What do you make of it?" asked the boy.

Sam Strong shook his head in doubt.

"Nothin'," he replied, "except that there was never a better time for us to be watchin'. The Cheyennes are full of tre-men-jeous-ly bad medicine, an' they've got two chiefs, Roman Nose an' Black Kettle, as bold an' cunnin' as they ever make 'em. I'm goin' to wake up the rest of the boys, Bob, an' we'll move on in the night."

He shook the sleeping men one by one, and they sat up.

"I know you both were dreamin' that you won Antietam, or some other of them big battles," he said to Evans and Harris, "but if we don't look out we may have a battle of our own not so big, but jest as dangerous to us. Me an' Bob have seen Cheyennes talkin' to each other, a long way off, it's true, but it's time for us to scoot."

The men asked no questions, knowing that Sam Strong would not act without good cause, and in fifteen minutes they moved away with their horses in the dark, advancing at a rapid gait, but as before into the west.

The country was now slightly more broken. At intervals, they skirted shallow oblong depressions, which Bill Cole told Bob were buffalo wallows. Some of these basins still held water from melting snows, and twice they stopped for their horses to drink from them. Once they heard a snort, and the hasty tramping of heavy feet. Bob saw dusky forms disappearing, and he knew that they had disturbed resting buffaloes.

They did not stop until nearly daylight, camping in a little grove of cottonwoods that grew between two high swells. Strong and Cole watched and awakened the others at the first upshot of the dawn. The day came on, gray and lowering, and every one scanned the entire circle of the horizon with anxious eyes. No fire was lighted, the breakfast being of cold food, and Bill Cole, who went on scout around the grove of cottonwoods, returned with the report that he had seen the hoofprints of unshod ponies.

"'Bout a day old, near as I can guess," he said, "an' Cheyennes were ridin' them ponies. There can't be a doubt of it."

"Which means that Cheyennes are somewhere near us, may be to the right, may be to the left," said Sam Strong. "I am always hopin' for the best, which I believe a man should never fail to do, but jest now I think we ought to get ready for the worst."

CHAPTER III

THE SHADOW IN THE DUSK

All their journey hitherto had been made in fair weather, but now was a promise of foul. The wind that nearly always blew across the plains, shifted to the northwest, with great rapidity, and its touch made Bob shiver, with sudden cold, clear to the very marrow. The horses seemed to feel apprehension, and all of them—whether for packs or for riding—crowded close together.

"Looks like a blow," said Obadiah Pirtle, "and maybe rain or hail with it, too."

"I'm always hopin' for the best," said Sam Strong, "but I think you're right. After all it may not be a bad thing for us, as a storm may hide us from the Cheyennes."

They decided to move at once from the cottonwoods, as a fierce wind might send the trees crashing upon them, and they advanced into the open plain, here rising and falling in gentle swells. The whole sky was now leaden, and the whistling wind, out of the northwest, steadily grew colder. Even the horses shivered, and, when they reached the deepest dip that they could find, the riders dismounted and arranged them in a ring, some tethered and others held by their lariats. The men stood in the center of the ring.

Before these brief preparations were completed,

solemn thunder began to growl on the horizon, and lightning flared in the same direction. Then both thunder and lightning ceased, and the wind died. After two or three minutes of intense stillness, both lightning and thunder began again, but in a wholly different way. There was a crash, so tremendous, that it made the boy jump a foot into the air, and then came the stroke of lightning, cutting the heavens across with a dazzling flash and blinding every one, for a moment or two.

As soon as Bob recovered from the glare, lightning and thunder came again, surpassing anything that he had ever heard or seen further east, and frightening him, despite every effort of the will to control himself. It was, perhaps, fortunate for him that he, as well as the others, soon had occupation. Some of the horses, terrified by the storm, were pulling at their lariats, and it was hard work to hold them all. Yet this must be done. Their horses were like boats to sailors, and they did not wish to lose a single one.

The men, knowing what was to come, had wrapped blankets about themselves, and Bob did likewise. Soon the thunder sank, and the lightning faded. Then the cold wind from the northwest sprang up again, and with it came the rain in slanting sheets, that soon deluged the earth. But in ten minutes the rain changed to driven hail, and then they were glad enough to have the ring of horses about them as shelter.

Bob wore a cap, the brim of which he pulled down to protect his eyes, and cowered against his pony.

But the hail beat upon his blanketed back and shoulders like bird-shot. He was cold, partly wet, miserable physically, but he would not complain, although several of the men whose characters as plainsmen were already established, did not hesitate to grumble.

While the hail was still falling, they heard a rumble, and saw a dark, moving mass to the right of them, but several hundred yards away. It was a buffalo herd stampeded by the storm and fleeing before it. Bob was glad they were not in the path of the mighty beasts, whose numbers ran into the scores of thousands. They were over an hour in passing, and their line extended further than he could see. For the full hour their hoofs kept up a steady rolling thunder.

When they were gone Sam Strong looked significantly at Bill Cole, and Bill Cole gave back the same significant look.

"Frightened by the storm," said Sam, "but something else may have been after them, too."

"Cheyennes been huntin' them most likely."

"I'm hopin' for the best, but I guess you're right. The hail is about stoppin', an' we'll move on again."

The hail ceased entirely in five minutes, the clouds marched away in battalions, and a brilliant sun began to pour down warmth. All the hail quickly melted, and the earth would soon be drying. The men threw off their blankets, saddled their horses anew, and once more sped into the west. It was Strong's idea to travel in a course exactly opposite to that taken by the buffalo herd, in order that the distance between them might widen as fast as possible.

The day seemed bent on atoning for the storm in its early hours. Not a single cloud was left in the sky. It was a vast arch of blue, shot with the gold of the sun, and the wind, which now came from the south, was laden with warmth. The earth, drying fast, showed new green where the bunch grass was appearing.

All of them recovered their spirits, and the two soldiers, in the utmost friendliness, began to whistle "Dixie" together. Several of the horses raised their heads and neighed, showing that they, too, appreciated the change.

"Here we are, all right and not a Cheyenne in sight," said Louis Perolet. "Our General Sam Strong ees like ze great Napoleon. He lead us out of danger every time."

"Don't you bank too much on that, Frenchy," said Sam. "The time may come when you'll have to fight your way out of danger, or stay in it."

Beyond a doubt Strong was still anxious, and his apprehension was reflected in the face of Bill Cole, the next best plainsman, and second in command. Both of them looked anxiously for hilly country in which they could escape observation, but there was no promise of it. In fact, it could not be expected, unless they cut across the course of some considerable stream.

"I'm hopin' for the best," said Sam Strong, "but the bands of Cheyennes are certainly somewhere about, an' maybe old Roman Nose himself is **near.**

I think we'd better turn south. I know of a stream that we'll strike ten or fifteen miles from here, an' we can travel in its bed where we won't be seen."

"Like ze great Napoleon who use everything, the earth eetself, to help him," said Louis Perolet, admiringly.

They rode rapidly on their new course, and, in a half hour, they saw far to the north of them a thin column of smoke, rising into the heavens like a spire. Presently another rose to the same height, but several miles to the eastward.

"Cheyennes talkin' again, an' now they are talkin' in the day time," said Sam Strong. "The sooner we hit that creek bottom the better."

They reached it in about an hour, a wide, sandy bed with a depth of about five feet or so and a width of thirty or forty feet, a narrow stream of cold water flowing down the center.

They led the horses into the channel, although they were reluctant, having some fear of the sand, and then all dismounted.

"We're hidden here from anybody at a distance," said Sam Strong, "an' now we'll go down stream, leadin' our horses, an' lookin' out for quicksands."

It was not the best method of traveling, but it was the safest, and they trudged along in the shadow of the banks until nightfall, several times narrowly escaping the quicksands.

Sam Strong breathed a mighty sigh of relief when the darkness came, and then every one in his turn breathed a similar sigh. They emerged from the shelter of the stream into a pleasant little valley, where oaks as well as cottonwoods grew. They secured their horses with lariats to the trees and bushes, not hobbling any of them, as they might wish, at any moment, to make a speedy flight.

They ate cold food in the dark, and Bob slept through the first watch. He was awakened about one in the morning to relieve Perolet, and had as his comrade Bill Cole, who had relieved Sam Strong.

Bill took the northern side of the camp, and most of the time walked back and forth in a semicircle. Bob had the semicircle on the south, and they met at each side of the circle which the two made complete. Then they would exchange a word or two in a whisper and pass on.

Bob felt his responsibility, and he appreciated to the full the great trust that these men put in him. Throughout their journey and flight he had watched the plainsmen, studying their craft and precaution, and now he imitated them. He felt the fine rifle that he had inherited from his father, and saw that the cartridges were slipped in just right. He loosened the pistol in his belt that it, too, might be ready on instant call. And he was careful as he stepped to make no noise whatever. It had become a matter of pride with him that no footfall should be audible, and that no one should hear him brushing against the bushes.

The night was peaceful. The wind did not keep up its usual moaning across the swells, and the branches of the oaks and cottonwoods were still. The horses seemed to be at rest. Bob apprehended no danger, but he was glad whenever he and Bill

Cole met. The gaunt but friendly face of the trapper cheered him, and the few words that he spoke were a comfort to him in his loneliness.

Two hours passed and it seemed to Bob that the watch might well be relaxed. The stars twinkled and danced in the most friendly fashion, and the wind was yet still. He met Bill Cole, they exchanged the usual friendly word or two and the boy passed on, describing the southern arc of the circle. His path led through the thickest clump of oaks, and just beyond them in a close group were the horses.

Bob's eyes, good at any time, had become used to the darkness, and he could see very well. He saw clearly the outlines of the horses, nearly all of them lying down, but two standing on the side nearest to him. A peculiar spell or intuition caused him to remain there, well hidden in the clump of trees, and look at the horses, especially the two that were standing.

One of the horses raised his head with a quick, jerking motion, and at the same time the other stamped with restless foot. Both motions seemed unusual to the boy, and he leaned a little forward, staring with all the power of his eyes. Was it a shadow that he saw just beyond the first horse? and if a shadow, was it caused by a bough or trunk of a tree?

Bob's heart rose up in his throat. The feeling assailed him with overwhelming power that here was an alien presence. His hands clasped his rifle lightly, and it was cold to his touch. He trembled ever so slightly, and then was quite still. He knew his responsibility and accepted it. He must save his comrades as well as himself. The danger was here on his side of the circle, and he would detect it.

The boy took a step forward, holding his rifle in front of him, but he was yet hidden in the cluster of oaks. There had been no sound since the stamping of the uneasy hoof, but now one of the horses moved again, and Bob believed that he heard a soft hiss, so very soft that it was scarcely more than the whisper of the wind in the grass.

But he knew. He had heard it. It was not fancy. He sprang forward and a shadow appeared from behind the horse, the shadow of an Indian, fully armed and in all the panoply of war-paint. The warrior with a sweep of his knife cut the lariat of the horse, struck him on the side, and uttered a loud, thrilling shout. Bob fired at the same instant and cried, "Up! up! the Cheyennes have come!"

Bill Cole rushed down from the northern segment of the circle, Sam Strong was on his feet in a moment, thoroughly alive and awake, and the others were but little behind. The center of the trouble was obvious at once.

"Look out for the horses!" cried Strong and Cole together. "They are tryin' to stampede 'em."

Bob sprang forward, seized a flying lariat and checked the impending flight of a pony. The two soldiers hurled themselves into the group, and they seemed to be all hands, grasping at least a half dozen ropes. Louis Perolet was just behind them, calling upon the name of the great Napoleon as his patron in war, and, at the same time, acting with speed and decision.

Strong and Cole ran toward the edge of the grove and fired twice each. Scattering shots came in reply, and then the long, fierce yell of the Cheyennes, which the plain beyond took up, and then sent back in a quavering under note, like the savage whine of some wild beast.

But the cry was not repeated, and there was no other sound in the grove just then but that of the struggling horses. These, too, were soon reduced to silence, and, although they stood quivering, they made no further effort to get away. Not one had escaped, so quick and resourceful had been the trappers, although the lariats of half of them had been cut. Across the shoulder of one of them was a long, red streak, where the Cheyenne had drawn his knife in order to add pain to fright. Sam Strong growled deep when he saw it.

"I try to think the best of people," he said, "but I'd like to get hold of the Cheyenne who did that." He walked to the edge of the grove, took a long look, came back and said:

"You saved us, Bob, my boy, an' we didn't make any mistake when we picked you up. The Cheyennes, the ugly snakes, came on your side and you saw 'em in time. If they'd stampeded the horses we wouldn't have been much better off than sailors in a sea without a boat."

Bob flushed in the darkness with pride. It was, as Louis Perolet would have said, like having the approval of the great Napoleon, and he was ready, at that very minute, to lay down his life for his leader, Sam Strong. But he said nothing, as Strong was already in conference with Bill Cole. Instead he stood guard by the horses, holding three lariats in one hand, and his rifle in the other.

Strong and Cole, masters of all the wiles and arts of the plains, considered their situation extremely dangerous. So far, only one Cheyenne had been seen clearly, but many more were probably near. Strong had no mind to be besieged in the grove. They were largely hidden by the trees at night, but by day it would be a different matter when the Cheyenne sharpshooters swarmed on every side of it. They must steal away now, not so difficult, perhaps, for the men to do, but the horses would make noise.

"It's got to be tried, though," said Strong, in a grim whisper, "an' Tom, maybe you an' Porter will have a chance to be in a better fight than the one at Gettysburg you talk so much about."

"Suppose we go back into the creek bed," said Obadiah Pirtle.

"We might be penned up there."

"If we were we could shoot from the shelter of the banks, an' if they ain't watchin' close on that side, it'll give us the better chance to get away unseen."

The plan carried and they began to move, leading the horses slowly and very cautiously. Fortunately it had turned a little darker, the moon being gone, and many of the stars ceasing to twinkle, and there was a chance that their movements would be completely hidden by the oaks and cottonwoods.

Strong and Cole stayed fifteen or twenty yards in the rear, and Bob was at the head of the troop, by the side of the Maine man. It was a hundred yards to the bed of the creek, but it seemed a mile to the boy. His head was throbbing with excitement, and the soft footfall of the horses fell on his ears like thunder. He heard a rifle-shot behind him, and the horses jerked on the lariats. A second shot followed and then several more.

"Keep movin'," whispered Obadiah Pirtle. "They've sent scouts forward, an' Sam an' Bill are drivin' 'em back. It's all right. It'll make them Cheyennes think we're still stayin' in the grove. There's the creek bank."

They led the horses down with the greatest caution, and luckily none of them slipped. Then they paused, huddled close together in the thick shadow of the bank, and Strong and Cole leaped lightly down beside them.

"I think I nicked the shoulder of a warrior," whispered Strong, "an' they are likely to be cautious. They won't find out that we've gone for a half hour yet, an' that half hour will be worth an ordinary year to us."

They advanced southward, the soft sand drowning the tread of the horses. Ten minutes passed and they heard no alarm. Fifteen minutes and yet there was none. Twenty came, and Strong led them out of the sand upon the hard plain.

"We can mount an' gallop for it now," he said. "Of course, when daylight comes they'll find our tracks in the sand, but we'll have a good start then, an' we may stave 'em off.''

Bob, his heart exulting, sprang into the saddle. It seemed to him that they had already made their escape complete, and he settled himself firmly, while he waited for Sam Strong to give the word of command. In the few seconds of pause a long cry, piercing and full of anger, came from the grove that they had left.

"They've stalked the place, found out that we've gone and they're mad about it," said the leader. "Now boys, hold firm to the lariats of your led horses, and away we go."

All swung into a gallop, and in a group they swept toward the southwest. Bob felt the cold night air rushing past him, and before him he saw only a misty, undulating world. He did not know where he was going, but all the little pulses in his head were throbbing with excitement, and he had unbounded confidence in these brave comrades of his. The men seldom spoke. The wiry mustangs seemed to show no weariness, and mile after mile fell behind them.

Just before day they stopped, changed the packs on seven of the horses, and took fresh mounts. Then they increased their speed somewhat, but soon the great red sun sailed out of the east, and the dazzling morning came. They stopped their flight and looked back. The keenest eye could discern nothing on the plain. It merely rolled away, in swell after swell, touched lightly with the green of early spring.

"We've shaken 'em off," said Bob, triumphantly. "Those Cheyennes will never find us."

But Sam Strong shook his head.

"I'm always hopin' for the best," he said, "but when Indian warriors want your scalp, an' want it real bad, you don't shake 'em off so easy. I'm jest tellin' you this, so you won't be disappointed if somethin' happens."

It did not seem possible to Bob. The plain was so empty; and surely the warriors could not trail them fast enough to overtake them. Strong announced that they must rest a while, whether or not the Indians still pursued. It would not do for them to be overtaken when their horses were broken down, and all dismounting, they sat upon the ground. The horses began to nibble the young grass, and they, at least, were content.

"What do you think of it, Bill?" asked Strong.

"Six of one an' a half dozen of the other," replied Cole. "They may ketch us, or they may not, but, if they do ketch us, I'm thinkin' that they'll have a hard time to hold us."

"We have come for the trappin', but, eef we must, we'll do the fightin', too," said the valiant Louis Perolet. "The great Napoleon not fight until the time come, but then he fight most terrible."

"Seven Napoleons, like ourselves, can make things hum," said Obadiah Pirtle, dryly.

They rested about three quarters of an hour, and Bob noted that the day was going to be one of the most brilliant that he had ever seen. The air was absolutely transparent, and distant objects came very near. It was this effect that caused Sam Strong, just as they remounted, to notice dim, moving specks under the horizon. He took a second glance in order to be sure, and then he announced quite calmly:

"Boys, the Cheyennes have followed our trail. See 'em comin'."

His long forefinger pointed them out.

"Louis," he said, "I think you can soon prove that you're another Napoleon, an' Tom, you an' Porter can fight Gettysburg all over again, but you've got to be on the same side now."

CHAPTER IV

THE DOG SOLDIERS

Strong, like a good general, sought a field of battle to his liking, and he observed a slight, sandy elevation in the plain, a few hundred yards further on. The sandy nature of the hill caused him to hope for something else, and, when they reached it, his hopes were fulfilled.

The hill had a slight crater, and in this crater were a dozen deep buffalo wallows, where the herds had rolled and scratched themselves for generations against the grateful sand.

"It's a fort! A real fort!" exclaimed Strong, joyfully. "We'll stand 'em off here!"

"He ees the great Napoleon," said Perolet, admiringly. "He has found the best place to fight."

They rode the horses into the buffalo wallows, tethered them together, and then took their own position in the deepest of all the depressions. They were so well protected that only the head of an animal showed now and then over the hill.

"Makes me think of Little Round Top at Gettysburg," said Tom Harris.

"If it hadn't been for that blamed hill we'd have beat you," said Porter Evans.

"See how fast they come!" said Strong, pointing toward the eastern horizon, "an' there's a lot of 'em, too."

Bob was by the leader, and he was tall enough, standing at his full height, to see over the crest of the hill. Now the wild horsemen of the plains were in full sight, fifty or sixty strong, galloping straight toward the hill.

"They make a fine sight," said Sam Strong, impartially. "Them must be the Dog Soldiers."

"Dog Soldiers!" said Bob, "what does that mean?"

"The Cheyenne warriors are divided into bands like societies, and the band that comes first is the Dog Soldiers—Hotamitaneo is their Indian name. They generally lead the battle, and they are most to be dreaded. They picked up our trail somehow, an' I reckon they think our goose is cooked."

Strong pressed his lips tightly together, and his blue eyes were full of resolute fire. It was evident that if the Cheyennes thought their "goose was cooked," he did not.

The approach of the warriors on their trained mustangs was spirited, and not without poetry. They were still far away. Only the extreme purity and thinness of the air made them seem near. But Bob saw the feathers in their hair waving, and the short rifles in their hands. They rode without reins, letting them fall free if they had them, and urged on their horses with a pressure of the knee.

They formed a line, curving slightly outward, and the horses were eight or ten feet apart. They were coming at a full gallop, but, when they were within a third of a mile, every man raised his rifle in his right hand above his head, as if by signal, and altogether uttered their war-whoop, a long thrilling cry that was repeated in echoes across the plain. Then they filed suddenly to the right like cavalry men, trained at drill, each horse keeping his regular place, and they galloped about the hill, at a uniform distance of a third of a mile.

"It's the Dog Soldiers sure enough," said Sam Strong, "an' maybe old Roman Nose himself is there. How do you feel Bob?"

"I feel that we can beat 'em," replied the boy with spirit.

"That's the way to talk," said Sam Strong. "Still I wish that this hill which ain't much of a hill after all, was higher an' that these wallows were deeper. But I'm hopin' for the best."

Bob, in spite of the fact that they sought his life, had admiration for the Cheyennes, who rode about them with savage grace, their sinuous brown forms shining in the crystal air. They stopped presently, and, some of them dismounting, walked near their horses, seeming to ignore the presence of any enemy.

"They're tryin' to show us how little they think of us," said Sam Strong. "They're pretendin' that they've nothin' to do when they get good an' ready, but ride right over us. It's an Indian's way. He wants to rub it in before he sends you to the happy huntin' grounds."

The Cheyennes took no action for at least half an hour, sitting their horses or walking about the plain as if they had all the time in the world. It was Bob's guess that they wished to worry the besieged, and make their nerves unsteady, and probably he was right. But he was soon to see the methods of Indian warfare, as usually practised on the plains.

"They'll be feelin' for us in a few more minutes," said Sam Strong.

A dozen warriors, mounted on fine ponies, rode out a little distance from the group and began to gallop up and down, and these men carried lances, as well as rifles, which they shook in a threatening way at the little white band. They began to shout also—cries of many kinds.

"Do you know what they're saying?" asked Bob of the leader.

"I can understand some Cheyenne," replied the leader, "an' I ketch a word here an' there, enough to tell me what they mean, an' they're sayin' to us, Bob, that we're mean, low down, cowardly white people, that we're thieves, robbers, skunks, coyotes, that our grandmothers an' grandfathers ain't what they ought to be, an' that our grandsons an' granddaughters, if we should live to have any, which we won't, would be worse, an' they say that we've lived as long as we ought to, or are goin' to, an' they're promisin' to dissect us most beautiful, an' then to have the precious remnants scattered wide among the tribes. These are a few of the things they're sayin' about us, but don't you be scared, Bob; most of them descriptions ain't true, an' not many of them promises will come to pass."

"I'm not scared," replied Bob, stoutly.

He told the truth. The situation had not yet impressed him with the full sense of danger. It was too unreal, too much like a play, a great spectacle of the open air. The gentle wind of the morning was merely the breath of peace. The brandishing of the lances added color and life to the scene, and while the shouts of the warriors might contain taunts, they came musically at the distance.

The galloping warriors presently cast their lances from them, and came closer. The speed of their horses increased, and the riders lay flat upon the backs and necks of their mounts.

"Keep close all!" suddenly shouted Strong in sharp warning. Even as he spoke he pulled Bob down, and the others ducked.

Four Cheyennes had suddenly dropped down on the far side of their horses, and fired under the necks, leaving only a clinging hand and foot exposed, targets too small for the distance. Two bullets sang over the heads of the crouching trappers, and two more buried themselves, with a nasty little spit, in the sand bank.

The prologue was over. The play had begun in real and deadly earnest. Bob saw it and knew it. Sam Strong's eyes narrowed.

"That's an old trick of theirs," he said, "to shoot from the other side of the horse, an' under his neck, an' it's worked often with greenhorns, but we know a trick or two ourselves, don't we, Bill?"

"Reckon we do," answered the saturnine Missourian.

More bullets made the sand fly up about them.

"Take the first horse, Bill," said Sam.

"I hate to do it, but I'll get him," said the Missourian.

The shouting warriors swung a few yards nearer. The Missourian rested the barrel of his rifle on the sandy bank, aimed with great care, and pulled the trigger. The sharp report, and the rising puff of white smoke followed. The foremost pony made a half leap in the air, and then ploughed forward, falling upon his side. The Indian, who had been hanging to his far side, sprang clear, alighting on agile feet, but at that instant Sam Strong, too, pulled the trigger.

The deadly bullet sped, and the warrior, his protection of the living pony taken from him, fell prone upon the plain and lay still. A shout of rage came from the other Cheyennes, but now they galloped away from the hill instead of toward it.

"People have got to pay for their fun," said Sam Strong, as he reloaded. "I think that a lot of foolishness is over. At least I'm hopin' for the best."

The retiring Cheyennes fired several shots, but all of them fell short, and then two, riding with their ponies between them and the hill, began to approach the dead warrior.

"They come for their slain comrade," said Perolet.

"That's so, Frenchy," said Strong, "an' while they're doin' it we won't fire on 'em."

The two warriors cautiously approached the fallen figure, but as no bullet came, they seemed to feel that they were safe in their task. They leaped

THE DOG SOLDIERS

down, quickly lifted the body across one of the ponies, remounted as quickly and galloped away.

"I wonder if they feel any gratitude because we didn't shoot at them," said Bob.

"'Tain't likely that we'll ever know," replied Strong.

The Cheyennes, now out of rifle range, gathered in a group, and seemed to take counsel. Meanwhile, the defenders waited patiently.

"Makes me think of the time when we stood on the ridge at Gettysburg, while Pickett and his men were gettin' ready to charge," said Harris.

"I saw 'em go," rejoined Porter Evans, "an' if there had been more of them Virginians you wouldn't be here, Tom Harris."

"Thought that war was finished," said Obadiah Pirtle. "Seems it's ragin' 'bout as bad as our own with the Cheyennes."

Sam Strong took food out of their packs, jerked buffalo meat principally, and gave a share to every one. Then he showed his method and his coolness under fire. Buffalo "chips" were lying about near the wallows, and, throwing several of them together, he lighted a fire on which Perolet boiled coffee.

"Tastes good, Bob, my boy, don't it?" he said.

"Fine," replied the boy, drinking two cups.

"The great Napoleon say that an army crawl on eets stomach," said Perolet, "an' he ees right, as always. It fight on eets stomach, too."

A long time passed without any further hostilities from the Cheyennes, and it was very trying. Spring seemed to have melted suddenly into summer, and a great sun, poised in the center of the heavens, poured down millions of fiery rays. It grew extremely hot in the shallow depressions, and they felt the want of water. The horses, too, moved restlessly, and had to be quieted now and then. Bob's lips became parched and his tongue lay hot and dry in his mouth.

"What do you think will be their next move, Sam?" asked Porter Evans.

"Hard to say," replied Strong, "but most likely a charge. There are no clouds, and no promise of a dark night, so they can't creep up on us without our seein' 'em. My eyes, but it's hot!"

They had water in canteens, and every man took a sip, but there was none for the horses. Bob being so young, and not yet toughened by experience, suffered the most. But he refused to complain. It seemed to him that the hot air was burning into his brain, but he lay with his face pressed against the sandy bank, and said never a word.

The boy held his rifle in both hands, and the barrel of it was hot to his touch. All the time he was staring out upon the plain at the group of Cheyenne warriors. The heat rose in waves and shimmered before his eyes. By and by the figures of the Cheyennes, some on horse and some on foot, moved further away, and became unreal. Millions of black specks danced before his eyes, and the tint of the air was blood red.

"Here, boy, take a drink of this!" exclaimed Sam Strong.

The sharp voice of the leader called the boy back to earth, and he drank mechanically from a little flask that Strong held to his mouth. It was unpleasant, burning stuff, but his mind and brain cleared instantly.

"Too much strain an' too much sun," said Sam. "Shake yourself up a bit, Bob! Roll around in that wallow, if you want to, while the rest of us watch."

The boy did rise and walk about a little, shaking his head, as if he would clear away the mists and vapors, and flexing his muscles. In a few minutes he felt much better.

"It's pretty hard on a new hand," said Porter Evans. "The terriblest thing about the Civil War was always the long waitin', lyin' on the ground, before we marched up an' whipped the Yankees."

"You never—" began Harris, indignantly, but Sam Strong raised his hand warningly.

"Stop that old, dead war, boys," he said. "Here's our live one. The Cheyennes are about to move, I think. See 'em spreadin' out."

Bob ran back to the bank. He could look now with clear eyes and a clear head, and once more the figures of the warriors were sharp, distinct and real. They were dividing into three bands. One remained where it was, and the others filed to right and left.

"They mean to charge from all sides," muttered Sam Strong, "an' with this poor place to fight behind, it's only a matter of how much they'll stand."

He posted his men in a thin circle about the hill, cautioning them all to lie deep in the wallows. He divided their little territory into two half circles, with himself in command of the northern half, and Bill Cole in charge of the southern. He had Bob and Obadiah Pirtle with him and Bill took the other three.

"Now, Bob," he said, "you've heard Porter an' Tom talkin' about all them big fights east of the Missip, in the Civil War, but this is our own special scrap, an' you want to take partic'lar notice of the order of battle which will be somethin' like this: they'll come on in three bands, jumpin' their ponies from side to side, screechin' an' yellin' somethin' terrible. But don't you be flustered, an' don't you fire too soon. They'll be dodgin' behind the necks an' sides of their horses an' plunkin' bullets into our hill here, but jest you wait, an' when you get a good thing to aim at, hit it."

The three bands of Cheyennes hovered a while just out of range. The sun was growing more intense than ever, and the heat floated in waves across the plains.

Bob heard a Cheyenne who wore a great feather head-dress, a magnificent war-bonnet, utter a long, thrilling whoop, which was taken up, before it died, by the others. Then the three bands charged their horses at the hill. But they did not come on straight and direct, like white men. Instead, they made their ponies career from side to side. They never ceased to shout their war-cries, and often beat with lances upon the heavy buffalo skin shields that many of them carried.

Some of the exhibitions of horsemanship were splendid. A warrior, hanging it seemed by his foot only, would fire under his horse's neck, and the bullet always struck near the defenders. The blood began to surge to Bob's head, and his finger crept down toward the trigger of his rifle. The Cheyennes were yet at long range, but the temptation to fire was overwhelming. A bullet sang a little song within two inches of his nose. The blood flew to his head, and his finger touched the trigger. But the firm hand of Sam Strong pulled it away.

"Jest a little longer, Bob," he said; "I know it's hard to wait, but we can't waste lead. They'll be near enough mighty soon now."

The weird shouting grew louder, and the rifles of the Cheyennes began to crack fast. Gusts of smoke rose and floated about the plain, and Bob distinctly heard the trampling hoofs as the Cheyennes drew nearer. It was well now that they had the buffalo wallows in which to crouch. A bullet grazed Bill Cole's head and another nipped Porter Evans's arm. But neither man made any outcry.

The shouting of the Cheyennes ceased quite suddenly, and then a single cry arose. It was the signal of the chief who wore the great feather head-dress, and, when they heard it, the warriors of all three divisions ceased their gyrations, and made straight at the little white band, every man bent down almost flat upon the neck of his horse.

"Now, Bob," exclaimed Sam Strong, "pick your man an' let him have it!"

The boy saw through a red mist, but he aimed at

a coppery face, just showing over the head of a mustang, and pulled the trigger. Then he saw the mustang galloping away riderless, and he felt, with a kind of a shuddering horror, that he had not missed. But that feeling quickly passed, and was succeeded by another. The desire of combat took hold of him. He lifted his rifle and fired again and then again.

All around the circle the rifles of his comrades were flashing, and they were fired by men who knew how to aim true. The Dog Soldiers, most valiant of the Cheyennes, faced a rain of bullets. Both men and ponies were down, and confusion seized them. They had not expected a fire so fast and deadly, and the rising cloud of smoke caused them to gallop into each other, adding to the confusion.

Ponies, wounded or frightened, reared, threw their riders and galloped over the plain. Others, made riderless by bullets, followed them, and then, above the sound of the shots and the shouting, rose the clear, high-pitched cry of the chief. He was calling his men away when they were yet thirty yards from the wallows, and the Cheyennes were admitting repulse.

The warriors, lifting their dead upon the ponies, fled across the plain, and out of rifle-shot. The defenders turned to their own wounds or needs, all except the valiant little Frenchman, Louis Perolet, who stepped out of his wallow and called after them:

"Ah, you red Indian! You have start to us. Then why you not come? We have the banquet ready. But you stop when you half way an' go back. Then we invite you the second time. We treat you most hospeetable. Or ees eet that you have enough already?"

He waited for an answer, and, as none came, he grew more bitterly sarcastic.

"Ees it that the famous Dog Soldiers of the Cheyennes, of whom the whole world has heard, are afraid of our guns? Do you retreat when the battle has just begun? It was not the way of the great Napoleon. He would go to the feenish, an' the feenish with him was victory."

"Set down there, Frenchy," called Sam Strong. "One of them fellers might reach you yet with a bullet."

"Then I die in a grand cause," rejoined Perolet.

But he came back to the wallow and at once began a congenial task.

"I still remember the saying of the great Napoleon that an army fights on eets stomach," he said, "an' now I feex the stomach while we rest between the mighty battles."

Several buffalo chips were left. In five minutes they were lighted and the coffee was boiling over them. Bob could not eat much, but he found the coffee soothing, and he was very grateful that they had escaped so well. Nobody on their side was killed. Three had received slight wounds to which, after the manner of veteran plainsmen, they paid no further attention when they had been bandaged. But several of the choice Dog Soldiers of the Cheyennes had been slain, others were severely wounded, and the first combat had been clearly in favor of the little band in the buffalo wallows.

"What do you make of it, Bill?" asked Sam Strong, looking attentively at the Cheyennes.

"Nothin'," replied Cole, "'cept that they've had enough of rushin' us for the time, an' mean to wait."

"I size it up the same way. Wish we had a stream of nice fresh water runnin' at our feet, Bill."

Strong looked uneasily at the horses, which were shuffling about restlessly. Only the fact that they were roped together had held them during the firing.

"It's so," said Bill Cole. "They'll want water tre-men-jeous bad before long. We've got enough to last ourselves three or four days, but none for them."

Sam Strong did not answer, but looked up at the blue sky, in which some great, black birds were now wheeling on slow wing. Staunch hunter and borderer though he was, he hated the sight of those birds, and they gave him a little shudder. But he would not let the feeling go far. He summoned up all the courage of his brave heart, and, in his own language, resolutely hoped for the best.

"Think you could sleep a while, Bob?" he said in his most kindly tone to the boy.

"Sleep!" exclaimed the boy, "why how could I at such a time?"

"Sleep, of course you can!" exclaimed Tom Harris. "Why, I slept a full hour at Antietam, jest before we made the last charge that licked the rebels, an' I was right in front of that charge, too."

"You didn't lick us at Antietam," exclaimed Porter Evans, indignantly. "We licked you till we got tired, an' then we walked away, leavin' to you the ground that we didn't want any longer."

"Never you mind these two bull dogs, Bob," said Sam Strong. "They make me think of a fat fellow in a play by Shakespeare that I saw in St. Louis once, though I admit that Tom and Porter here are good men in a scrap when it comes off. Now, Bob, you just try to sleep. You'll be surprised how easy it'll come, an' it'll do you a lot of good. If the Cheyennes come up here an' have an engagement with us we'll wake you up, don't worry."

Bob concluded to try it. It seemed to him the part of a veteran campaigner, and he wanted to do the proper thing. He lay down in one of the wallows, put his folded blanket under his head, and then his cap over his eyes to shade them from the light.

It was a little after noon, and the sun was amazingly bright and hot. From under the edge of his cap brim the boy saw the heat waves rolling up again. He also saw wheeling in the heavens the same great, black birds that Sam Strong had noticed, but he did not draw the same inference from them. They were birds to him, and nothing more.

Bob, still resolute to do what a veteran should do, exerted all the power of his will over his muscles and senses. He lay perfectly still, and tried to imagine that he was in a bed, and that no danger was near. Circumstances helped him. The camp grew quite quiet. The horses ceased their restless shuffle, the men sat quite still. Three of them had lighted pipes and were smoking. Bob, remembering his earlier youth, began to say the multiplication table to himself. It seemed so amusing to him that he should do such a thing, at such a time and place, that he laughed under his breath.

The laugh was soothing. Gradually his pulses ceased to beat so strongly. The fever went from his brain, his whole figure relaxed and Sam Strong's words were coming true. It was easier to sleep than he had thought.

The wheeling birds became dim and were lost in the sky. The figures of his comrades sitting near him, and of the horses, floated off into space. His eyelids drooped, shut entirely, and there upon the great plain, fresh from the battle, with the Dog Soldiers of the Cheyennes yet about him, the overtaxed boy slept. His regular breathing soon rose, and was noticed by the men. Sam Strong walked to him and pulled the brim of his cap a little further over his eyes.

"Good stuff, ain't he?" he whispered, with something of a father's tenderness in his tone. "We made no mistake when we picked up that Bob boy, did we?"

"Not by a long sight," replied Bill Cole. "But he's got baptized mighty early. He's come right into the middle of a terrible hot thing."

Bob slept soundly a long time, and he would have slept longer, but the hand of Sam Strong was on his arm, and a voice said in his ear:

"Wake up, Bob, somethin's goin' to happen."

The boy sat up instantly, wide awake and grasping his rifle with his hands.

"Are the Cheyennes about to charge again?" he asked.

"No," replied Strong, "they're not. Somethin' else is comin' into this little affair of ours. Look there, Bob. Look out into the east!"

The boy followed the long pointing finger, and beheld an immense dark cloud that came on fast. But this cloud, although it banked against the horizon, was not of the air. It clung close to the earth, and it filled the entire east.

"It's a buffalo herd," said Sam Strong, "an' most likely it's the same one that we had the run in with the other day. It's been wanderin' aroun' in search of grass, an' two to one its been scared ag'in by the Indian hunters. But, boys, whatever the cause, an' whatever be runnin' through them there heads of theirs, that buffalo herd, a million strong, has come just in time."

"Why, how can it help us?" asked Bob.

"It ain't meanin' to help us, but it will, an' it will help us a heap. Just you wait a few minutes, an' you will see."

But by waiting Sam did not mean that the time should be spent in inactivity. He issued short, swift orders, and they were obeyed with the same speed.

"Untie the horses!" he said. "Fix the packs! Look to your arms! Have everything ready to march at an instant's notice."

Bob sprang to the work with the others. He led his own pony from one of the wallows, and he held the lariats of two more. Meanwhile, the mighty buffalo herd was still rapidly approaching. Sam was probably right in his surmise that it was the same herd that they had seen a few days before, but it seemed to have increased in numbers, perhaps others had joined it, and they could not see anywhere a break in the dark line that spread from the northern horizon to the southern.

"It will carry everything before it," said Sam Strong. "While I was hopin' for the best, the buffaloes have come an' saved us. Look, the Dog Soldiers are tryin' to shoot a way through them."

The Cheyennes, all mounted now and in solid mass, were firing into the herd with the evident purpose of making it break in half, and pass to right or left. Usually such an effort would have been a success, but this herd was so immense, and it was driven on by such a powerful impulse, that the dark line remained unbroken, others closing up where their brethren had fallen.

"They'll have to run for it," said Bill Cole. "an' so will we."

"But we run willingly," said Sam Strong. "There, look! the Dog Soldiers have broke, an' see that long tongue of buffaloes streamin' by the side of 'em on the south. They've got to gallop to the north, an', boys, we'll gallop to the south, while a million buffaloes come in between. To your saddles!"

Every one sprang upon his horse, holding firmly to the lariats of the led animals, and with Sam Strong at their head they galloped out of the wallows, turning due south.

Behind them the whole plain shook with the tread of the mightiest herd that Sam Strong had ever seen, pushing forward in irresistible columns between the Cheyennes and the little white band that they had regarded as their sure prey. Wider and wider grew the separating current, until a full five miles of buffaloes flowed between.

Southward rode the comrades at a good pace, and they were joyous now. They knew it would be long before the Cheyennes could pick up their trail again, probably never, and they might regard themselves safe, at least for the time. Moreover, the sun was setting, the pleasant coolness of the twilight was coming, and the brisk air gave new life.

Porter Evans suddenly began to laugh.

"Now, what under the sun is the matter with you, you Johnny Reb?" asked Tom Harris.

"I was just thinkin', Tom, that while you an' me don't agree much about the Civil War, you claimin' that you whipped us, an' we knowin' that we jest eternally wore ourselves out whippin' you, that none of them big battles, in which you an' me was such important figgers, was ever stopped by a herd of wild cattle buttin' in between the two armies."

"That's mighty true, even if it is the first true word that you've ever spoke about the Civil War, Port," said Harris.

The sun went down like a plummet behind the hills, the twilight turned into the night, clear and cold, and Strong checked their speed. From the north came the faint rumble of the marching million.

"The Cheyennes might as well try to ride their

ponies across the Missouri in flood as get through that herd," said Obadiah Pirtle.

"Well spoke, Obe," said Strong, "an' bein' as the best that we've been hopin' for has come to pass, we might walk our horses a while. 'Pears to me what we need most now is water for our animals, an' we must keep on until we find it. Scratch your head, Bill, an' see if you can rec'lect any spot on this piece of land where it can be found."

Bill Cole took the suggestion literally. He removed his cap and ran his finger nails thoughtfully across his head.

"I've hunted buffalo 'roun' here more'n once," he said, "an' there is a sunk place where the water oozes out of the ground and makes a big pool that drains away into the plain, an' then is lost farther on. But it is tre-men-je-ously hard for me to locate it as there ain't no sign posts that I can see, an' I don't see no guide comin'."

"Rub your head real hard, Monsieur Bill," said Louis Perolet, entreatingly. "It is massage. It make the brain act queeck, an' maybe it bring you the intelligence you need."

"All right, Mossoo Looey," said Bill, good-naturedly. "I'll do it. I guess it's what the great Napoleon always did when he wasn't sure about things."

He rubbed his head with great vigor, and then spoke up triumphantly.

"It does work, Frenchy," he said. "Now I remember. As certain as I'm sittin' here on top of this horse, that spring lies off there, the way my finger's p'intin'."

They rode without hesitation toward the southwest, where his finger pointed, and the further they went the more confident Bill became. In an hour the horse that he rode threw up his head and uttered a whinney of pleasure.

"That settles it," said Bill. "He smells water. Don't I know this horse of mine? Don't I know every neigh of his? He's got one for water, one for grass, one for feelin' good, another for feelin' bad, and so on. This is his water neigh, an' it's comin' straight from his heart."

The other horses pricked up their heads also, and without urging increased their speed. Before long the ground softened a little, they saw ahead of them a thin fringe of trees, and then, shining between the trunks, a blessed silvery surface that they knew to be water.

They rode straight into the pool, and every horse, standing with the water to his knees, drank deeply.

CHAPTER V

THE SNOWY PASS

Bob had never before in his life felt so deep a thrill of happiness. They had escaped from a great danger. He knew now how providential was the intervention of the buffalo herd, and they had found the water, without which they could not live, even after slipping from the grasp of the Cheyennes. He sat on his pony, and listened to its gurgling as the good beast drank. The same gurgling sound was all around him.

"I guess these horses of ours are plum glad," said Obadiah Pirtle, "an' it makes me glad to see 'em glad."

"Same here," said Sam Strong, "but we mustn't let 'em drink too much right at the start. Lead 'em out of the pool, and we'll let 'em have another try at it in half an hour."

The horses were ridden out of the water, although they required much urging, and then they sought a likely spot for a camp. The pool, which was on the southern side of a swell, steeper than usual in that region, was forty or fifty yards in diameter with an average depth of about three feet. At the southern edge was the outlet, a tiny brook that soon lost itself on the plain. To the right of the pool was a hollow, dry and well enclosed with cottonwoods.

"Of course the Indians come here at times to drink and to water their horses," said Sam Strong, "but we've got to risk that chance, an' camp here to-night, an' what's more, after all we've been through have warm food and warm coffee. What say you, Louis? Are you ready to fix them for us?"

"Eef you keep off the rascally Cheyennes an' don't let them fire any bullets into my camp-kettle or coffee pot, I give you food and coffee that warm not only your body, but your soul," replied Perolet. "I am the great culinary arteest, an' it is at such times that I shine. The cook is greater when he cook under fire. What a great arteest the cook of the great Napoleon must have been!"

Strong knew that the fire might serve as a guiding hand to the Indians, but he knew also the great value of warmth and comfort to his band. Moreover, the danger could be minimized. They dug out a place in the soft side of the hill with one of the shovels that they carried in their packs, and then they filled in the space with dry fallen wood which they coaxed into a fire. The hole was like an oven and no breeze arose, but a great heat was thrown out. Soon a mass of coals was formed, and Perolet cooked food, and boiled coffee in abundance for them all.

Bob felt an immense relief. The night was chill, but he had drawn a blanket about his shoulders, and sat with his face to the coals. He was very tired, but it was a happy weariness, and he thought that God had been very good to them. It seemed to him that the buffalo herd had been sent to save them.

"Sam," he asked, "do you think the Cheyennes will try to follow us again?"

"Not that crowd, anyway. It will be too hard for them to pick up our trail a second time, an' bein' at war with our people, they've got more important work to the eastward. Now, boys, we'll just smother up the rest of this fire, and most of us will go to sleep."

They threw earth on the coals, and, after securing the horses, all lay down to sleep except Sam Strong and Louis Perolet. Bob secured a promise that he would be awakened for the second watch, saying that he ought to stand sentinel as he was the only one who had slept in the afternoon.

The difference was very great, as he sought slumber for the second time in twelve hours. Then the hot sun was burning down upon him; now it was dark night, and the cold had come. But the heavy blanket, wrapped around him, fended off the chill, and made him feel all the snugger because of it.

He did not linger long at the border of sleep, but the events of the day passed rapidly before him. Most vivid of all was the charge of the Cheyennes, and its confused and terrible medley of men and horses, of fire and shots and shouts. He saw the whole red picture before him again, then it passed like a shadow on a screen, and he fell quietly to sleep.

But Bob did not stand sentinel any part of that night. About one o'clock in the morning, when the watch of Sam Strong and Louis Perolet was finished, Sam looked down at the sleeping boy. There was not much light, but the eyes of the two were trained to darkness, and they could see Bob very well. Although breathing regularly and steadily, his face was quite white. He showed plainly to the experienced men the terrible strain through which he had passed.

"Am I going to wake him, Frenchy, for his turn of the watch?" asked Sam Strong in a low, almost solemn voice.

"No, Meester Strong," replied Louis Perolet, "you are like the great Napoleon, who, finding the exhausted sentinel asleep, took the rifle from his unknowing hands, an' did the watching heemself."

"Sometimes I think you're a great man, Louis," said Sam Strong. "You've read my mind most terrible exact. Now you wake up Obe, there, an' in an hour or two I'll make Bill take my place."

When Bob awoke, the coffee was boiling again for breakfast, and they only laughed when he asked, with some indignation, why they had not awakened him.

"Why didn't we wake you up?" replied Perolet at last. "Why, we couldn't. First Sam shake you until he get tired, then I shake you until my two arms ache. Then we wake up the others an' all together shake you, but you just snore on. Then we think of bringing up the strongest horse an' let heem keeck you, but Sam Strong say no. We cannot afford to have our best horse lamed."

They laughed again, and Bob, seeing that he could get no satisfaction out of them, turned to his breakfast, which he ate with the keenest appetite.

"Aha, Meester Bob is heemself again," said Perolet, contemplating him with satisfaction. "Like the great Napoleon, he is nearly ready now for another battle with the Cheyennes."

Bob laughed.

"I think I'd rather wait a day or two for that," he said.

After he had eaten, Sam, Bill and the boy ascended the hill, from the base of which the water trickled, and studied the entire circumference of the plain. They could see nothing but a few scattered buffaloes, grazing at a distance of a mile or so, although the eye ranged many miles in the thin, clear air.

"It's pretty sure that the Cheyennes either lost the trail or did not hunt for it again," said Strong. "At any rate I'm hopin' for the best, so we ought to stop a day at the pool, and renew our supplies for the long march that's ahead of us."

The suggestion seemed good to all, and they spent some busy hours. Sam and Bill rode out, shot a buffalo cow, and brought in fresh meat. Tom Harris and Porter Evans, both capital men with horses, looked after bruised shoulders or sore feet among the ponies. Now and then sounds of wordy strife over some battle in the Civil War arose, but they worked on in the utmost harmony and good comradeship.

"Funny," said Louis Perolet, "two men shoot at each odder for four years, an' then be such friends that each would die for the odder."

Obadiah Pirtle was working among the stores.

He had all a Yankee's cleverness and ingenuity, and he was reducing the size of the packs without throwing anything away. Bob helped Perolet with the cleaning and cooking of the buffalo meat.

"Eet ees one great science," said Perolet, "an' we French who have ceevilized the whole world, an' paid for it, teach it. Many a man has starved to death on the plains and in the mountains with food at hees hands."

Bob also took turns at the watch on the hill, but the day passed on, and they saw nothing hostile on the horizon. It was brilliant and hot, like the one just before it, and Bob felt as if the pool with the cottonwoods about it was an island, and that, when they left it, they were about to venture upon a trackless sea.

Everything was ready, and they departed just after nightfall, both Strong and Cole feeling that it would be safer for the present to travel in the darkness. But as there was no sign of danger that night, nor any the following day, they soon resumed the natural mode of progress, the night for sleep and rest, and the day for riding.

Now ensued a most wonderful journey. They were marching straight into the Golden West, although their gold was to be taken in traps, and was not to be dug from the ground. Every hour of it was full of variety and delight for Bob. He saw spring, with magic touch, transform the plains. He saw the young grass springing up everywhere, and many a shy little wild flower almost hidden in its roots. Now and then, they saw far blue hills but they always kept away from them. Buffalo and antelope were abundant, and the prairie chickens whirred near the camp. Water was more plentiful than usual. Many pools were standing from the spring rains, and they crossed two or three shallow rivers, clear cold streams, flowing in wide sandy beds.

Gradually the picture of the fierce Dog Soldiers and the charge, when white and red came face to face, faded from Bob's mind. Again it had become a peaceful world through which he was traveling.

As they advanced far into the west the grass became thinner and the game scarcer. Now and then they crossed stretches of country which were desert, but always the air was pure, and had a snap to it. It rained only once or twice, and, although they had two tents with them, they always slept in the open. Bob thrived wonderfully in this wild life. Already a strong, dexterous boy, the men could almost see him growing, and no one was handier with the horses, or at any kind of work. One evening in a wrestling match he threw both Porter Evans and Tom Harris, and pinned their shoulders squarely against the ground.

"You're comin' on, Bob," said Sam Strong, as he puffed at his pipe. "To down General Grant and General Lee in the same evenin' is a pretty big thing."

"It was more trick than anything else," said Bob, modestly.

"Good trick to know," said Obadiah Pirtle. "May need it some day."

More days of peace and easy marching followed. The great plains fell behind them, and one afternoon a dim blue line showed along the entire horizon in front of them.

"The Rockies!" exclaimed Bob.

"That's right," said Sam Strong. "We've been climbin' the slopes of the Rockies a long time, slopes so gentle that you don't notice it, but them's peaks you see there."

But to Bob it was his first view of the Rockies, of those famous Rocky Mountains of which he had been hearing all his life, mountains filled with danger, mystery and treasure.

"Our trapping grounds are in there somewhere, are they not?" he asked of Sam Strong.

Sam pointed vaguely toward the southwest.

"Down there," he replied, "among the high ranges, but we've got a good deal of rough travelin' yet."

"All right, we can stand it," exclaimed Bob, joyously. "We're to have a little experience with the Rockies."

Sam Strong smiled. He knew the value of enthusiasm, and he would never discourage it.

"That's the right spirit, boy," he said. "I've always tried to hope for the best, an' I'm glad to see that you're doin' it, too. It helps a heap. There'll be work an' danger in them mountains, but we'll do the one, an' conquer the other, won't we, Bob, my boy?"

"We will," said Bob, stauncher than ever in the respect and admiration that he felt for his leader.

There were yet four hours of daylight after the first sight of the mountains, and they rode until nightfall, but the ranges did not seem to come any nearer. Sam told the boy that they were yet a great distance away. They had seen them because they were so high, and the air was so clear. They would be riding all the next day, and the mountains would yet be a mere blue bank on the horizon.

The country, after a stretch of almost desert, began to improve again. The buffalo grass was abundant, and the horses throve on it wonderfully. Nor had Strong and Cole allowed them to be pushed, knowing how necessary to them these animals were. So it was a fat and sleek expedition that encamped that night on the plain. No longer having fear of the Cheyennes, they built a fine fire of buffalo chips, and ate plentifully of game that they had killed by the way.

Bob walked out a little distance from the camp later in the evening. There was a good moonlight, but he could see the mountains only in his fancy. Nevertheless, to see them thus impressed his imagination as much as the reality. He was eager to be up there among the peaks and ridges, where their work lay. He had seen enough of the plains for a while, and he longed for the crests, white with snow, the slopes and the valleys, green with great forests, and the rushing torrents of ice cold water of which his comrades had talked so much to him. They would find there the beaver, their special treasure, the elk, the bear, and the wolf and the mighty grizzly would not be absent. It appealed powerfully to him, and once more he vowed that he would never spare any effort or any risk to help these comrades who had been so good to him.

When he came back to the camp-fire, Louis Perolet looked at him quizzically.

"You have been staring at the mountains that you cannot see, Meester Bob," he said. "That ees right. The mountains have the majesty, the grandeur. Wait until you see them closer, with the white snow on their heads. They seem to reach up to the great God, and to be silent and awful like Heem."

The Frenchman had begun in a light vein, but he ended with the greatest gravity, and as Bob nodded, he added:

"You can never make fun of the mountains."

Bob watched the blue line all the next day, as they rode toward it, but when night came it was still a blue line, though heavier and darker than before.

"If we start bright an' early we'll strike the first slopes about to-morrow night," said Sam Strong, "an', if I ain't greatly fooled, we'll pitch our camp in the first belt of pines. It will feel good to me to smell the pines again."

They were on the march at the first start of dawn, and now when Bob saw white crests soaring far up into the air, he felt all the emotions that Louis Perolet had predicted. Sometimes clouds or mists hid the lower slopes, and then the snowy heads seemed to float in the air, adding to the sense of mystery and solemnity.

When the clouds and vapors floated away, the

ridges and peaks began to take shape. Irregular lines were disclosed, and here and there appeared openings which, at the distance, looked as narrow as knife blades. As they rode on Bob also saw the green tint made by the evergreens.

The plain, watered all the year around by the melting snows, was now high in grass, and big game was plentiful. They could have shot enough in a day or two to feed a regiment. But a herd of wild horses, the first that he had seen, interested Bob the most. They were at least a hundred in number, fine, clean animals, and from a distance of only three or four hundred yards they watched the trappers riding past. Presently they threw up their heads and galloped off in a file toward the south.

"Happy critters," said Porter Evans. "Nothin' to do but eat an' see the world."

They rode rather faster than usual that day, and as Sam Strong had foretold, they reached the first gentle slope, where the pine was mingled with the ash and the oak. Here was a creek taking it somewhat easier after its rush down the slopes, but ice cold, as Bob's comrades had told him it would be. In fact, everything they had said was coming true. There was the keen balsamic odor of the pines which Bob inhaled gratefully, and the wind that blew now did not come over empty space. It whistled down through great forests.

The wind was cold, too, and Bob found his blanket very welcome. So was the fire built from fallen boughs of oak and ash, and as they sat around it they discussed the second stage of their great campaign. Bob learned that they were now at one of the high passes of the highest Rockies, known only to Indians and wandering trappers, and that their march through it would be slow and risky.

"Will there be any danger from Indians?" he asked Sam Strong.

"Not from Cheyennes, but some wandering Utes might take pot shots at us. That's a chance that we must risk."

They rested three days before undertaking the arduous passage of the vast ranges. The horses, already in good condition, cropped the rich grass and grew fatter.

Bill Cole shot a splendid elk, Porter Evans and Tom Harris caught trout in the creek, and they had a great feast. The remainder of the meat, according to their custom, they packed, ready to be carried on the horses.

There was another overhauling of clothing. Sam Strong told Bob to wrap himself up as warmly as possible.

"Maybe you won't think it's going to be very cold," he said, "but you'll find it out by the time we rise a mile or two. It ain't yet full summer on the mountains, an' there's snow an' ice in plenty."

The third day being completed they packed their horses and began the ascent of the pass. The trail was narrow, but for a long time it was good, though it rose rapidly. Before noon the men dismounted and led all the horses. Bob was near the end of the file, and it seemed to him that he had come into another world. Vast forests were about him. He looked down into a deep chasm on one side, and up to a mighty peak on the other. He saw great fields of ice and snow, and he heard the sound of rushing waters. Once a bear crawled through the underbrush, and again the elk were whistling on the slopes.

The wind grew keener and colder. Coming down from the snow-fields it had an edge of ice, and Bob was thankful for Sam Strong's advice about the clothes. But he was vastly interested, enjoying every moment of the march. He wished to see everything, to note every kind of tree, and to remember the slopes of the ridges and peaks, as far as his eye could reach.

They stopped about the middle of the afternoon and took a rest of an hour, much needed by men and horses. Bob looked back, and he was surprised to see that the plains were yet so near. There they were, rolling away in faint green swells toward the east, and the distance between him and that waving expanse did not seem to be more than a few hundred yards. They had been traveling at such an angle that they had not achieved distance as much as height. Obadiah Pirtle saw him looking back and he remarked tersely:

"It's goin' to be a tre-men-jeous climb, but we'll make it all right."

At three o'clock they began to ascend again. The ponies now proved troublesome. The steepness of the climb, the increasing thinness of the air and the cold seemed to terrify them. Four of the party now went before, holding the lariats, and three came behind armed with stout sticks, ready to beat the stubborn, or the sluggish, back into the path of duty.

They talked for a while, but after the first hour fell into complete silence. The steepness was telling on both man and brute, and the wind from the peaks was blowing with increasing strength and coldness. Already they had reached the region of snow, and Bob saw ravines and chasms in which it lay many feet deep. But the white heads seemed to tower as far above as ever.

His own riding pony, which he led with two others, stopped suddenly, made a desperate effort to catch the stony soil with his front hoofs, and, failing, was about to plunge downward five hundred feet, but Bob, with great presence of mind, released the other two, and pulled with all his might on the single lariat.

The descent of the pony, sustained a little also by his own efforts, was checked, but Bob could not hold him long.

"Help!" he cried loudly. "Quick! quick!"

The two soldiers, who were nearest, releasing their own horses, sprang forward and seized the lariat. The three pulled together with a mighty jerk, and the pony helping, he was drawn back into the path, where he stood weak and shivering, just like a human being saved from imminent death.

The other ponies had been thrown into fright by the plight of their comrade, and might have stampeded down the pass, but the three men behind them closed up and restored order. It was at least a quarter of an hour, however, before the animals were soothed sufficiently to go on without resistance or trembling.

Night came early on these eastern slopes of the heights. The sun was soon gone beyond the high peaks, and cold darkness advanced. Strong and Cole conferred anxiously, and it was evident to Bob, who saw them looking about, that they sought a place for a camp. They found it at last in a comparatively level spot, of half an acre or so, studded about with dwarf pines. Near the center of it was a lakelet perhaps twenty yards across, but apparently deep, and they tethered all the horses near its edge. Brute beasts though they were, they neighed their gladness, and when the men built a fire of unusual size from the fallen timber, they drew as near to it as their lariats allowed.

It was their first mountain camp, and for a while all felt the cold and desolation. Having no fear of Indians here, they threw on wood until the fire fairly roared, but it was yet desolate and chill beyond the circle of the firelight. Bob, from where he sat, saw to the right and above him a vast field of ice and snow, glittering and unearthly in the moonlight.

Before their supper was over snow began to fall in huge flakes, whirled lazily here and there by the wind. They unpacked their two canvas tents and raised them as a protection, but it was not the whirling flakes, at this stage of the ascent, that worried Sam Strong. It was the omen of what might be when they approached the crest of the pass.

"It looks bad," he said to Bill Cole. "We've got to expect wind an' snow, an' lots of both."

Bill Cole nodded.

But Bob, with his heavy blanket wrapped about his shoulders, was not feeling any apprehensions. He had an abiding faith that they would triumph over everything. He walked to the edge of the pine grove with Louis Perolet, and stood there looking out at the cold world. The plains could not be seen now in the gray of the night, and apparently there was a bottomless gulf at their feet. But above them, just where the moon hung over the highest crest, it was brighter.

Directly between him and the moon, Bob saw the outline of some animal, thickset, and with horns. The intense moonlight made it stand out sharply and seem very near. It was perched on a rock, gazing downward at the light in the pine grove.

"A mountain sheep," said Louis Perolet, "but too far away for a shot."

"I shouldn't want to shoot at him, even if he were near enough," said the boy. "We do not need him."

"You are right," said Perolet. "Why should we keel the monarch of the cliffs when he does not hurt us an' we do not wish to eat heem?"

The animal turned back from the projecting rock and disappeared. Presently a low sound, distant and rhythmical, came to Bob's ears.

"Do you hear that, Louis?" he asked. "What is it?"

"Eet ees a snowslide," replied Perolet, "an' eet

ees maybe a mile away. The snow has been loosened by the warmer air of spring an' eet plunges down the mountain in mighty masses. Eet ees lucky that we are not in the path of any snow-field here."

"It is so," said Bob. "It would be a pity, wouldn't it, if our great expedition were suddenly blotted out here by a hundred thousand tons of snow?"

Perolet nodded, and the two walked back to the fire.

CHAPTER VI

THE PRECIPICE

When Bob and Louis Perolet were in the full blaze of the firelight, Sam Strong signed to them to sit down, and they did so, warming their hands at the welcome blaze. It was evident to Bob that the others had been talking about a matter of gravity, and he waited for Sam to speak.

"We've been turnin' things over a bit," said the leader, "an' we want the whole gang to agree, so if things go wrong nobody can say 'I told you so.' I'm always hopin' for the best, but there's no use tryin' to hide from ourselves the fact that the weather is goin' to be bad, mighty bad, while we're travelin' across the mountains. It ain't goin' to be no summer picnic. Do any of you want to turn back an' wait until the warm weather has melted the snow more? If so, let him speak up."

He waited and there was a dead silence. Bob, watching him closely by the firelight, saw a faint smile flicker for a moment in the eyes of the plainsman.

"I don't hear anybody shoutin'," said Sam. "Now, whoever is in favor of goin' on, snow or no snow, ice or no ice, storm or no storm, let him say 'I'."

"I!" shouted six voices together.

"An' I'll add another 'I'," said Sam Strong.

"Of course we'll go on," said Porter Evans. "The Yankee army would have turned back at these mountains, but the Confederate army would have gone straight ahead, hittin' only the high places."

"You got used to hittin' the high places, when we were after you," rejoined Tom Harris.

Bob kept the first watch with the leader, and as the night deepened and the fire died down, he felt to its full extent the mighty desolation of the cold wilderness. The settled East seemed inexpressibly far, so remote that it never could be reached again, and he was glad enough to have Sam walking beside him. Twice more they heard the sound of snow slides, and once the long, whining cry of a wolf.

"That's the mountain kind," said Sam. "Big, gray fellows. I've seen 'em six feet long, an' I wouldn't want to meet one, I can tell you, unless I had a gun along with me."

Bob watched only until midnight, and then he made his preparations for bed very carefully. He crawled into the tent, already occupied by Harris and Evans, spread one blanket carefully on some leaves that they had gathered, wrapped another around him from his neck to his toes, lay down on the first blanket, and composed himself for slumber, although he was situated so he could see through the open flap of the tent. He awoke at some hour of the night and saw that it was snowing, not a snow driven by the wind, but heavy flakes dropping straight down. They were so thick that he could not see the surface of the lakelet, but in his half dreamy state he was not disturbed. The warmth and comfort of his blankets only soothed him soon to deeper slumber.

They found the pass the next morning more formidable than before. The snow had ceased to fall, but it lay a foot deep on the ground, hiding the bad places of the pass and making the good ones slippery. Every man drew the flaps of his fur cap about his ears, tied a woollen comforter about his neck, and put on buckskin gloves. Strong led the way, and all the morning they climbed, choosing the trail with infinite care, and proceeding very slowly. Once they heard the roar of a coming snowslide, and uncertain whether to go forward or turn back they stood still, all except the horses which shivered with fright, although they did not try to break from the hold of the men.

The avalanche passed two or three hundred yards to the right of them, bearing trees and bushes upon its crest. It made a tremendous, crashing roar, but in a few moments it was gone, and they could hear it thundering far down the mountainside.

"Feels just as if you were at Gettysburg an' a hundred pound cannon-shot had whizzed by your head, just tippin' your left ear, to let you know that it was passin'," said Porter Evans.

The wind did not blow until nearly noon, and then it cut deep. Bob's hands grew cold, despite his buckskin gloves, and he was forced to take them out two or three times and rub them with snow to drive away the numbness. But the fine particles of snow, driven into their eyes by the wind, troubled them most. It was like hail, and it became so strong at last that they were forced to stop and turn their backs to it.

"We're goin' to have a blizzard, an' there's no use denyin' it, even if one does hope for the best," said Sam Strong, "an' what we want is shelter."

"An' we want it terrible queeck," said Louis Perolet. "It's a time when the great Napoleon himself would stop."

Strong and Cole, being the strongest, went on ahead a little distance to look for a camp, while the others held the horses. They returned presently, giving a shout of triumph as they approached. They had found a big hollow or cave-like opening in the rocks, three or four hundred yards ahead, where they would be protected from snow and wind alike.

They urged the horses forward anew, but they were a long time in traveling those three or four hundred yards. Several of them had to be beaten with sticks before they would face the stinging sleet.

But when the place, described by Bill and Sam, was reached, it proved a genuine haven, a great recess in the rocks, with an arching stone roof and a comparatively level floor. It was open on only one side, that toward the east, and the wind was blowing from the west.

The horses might not have been willing to enter such a place at any ordinary time, but now they went in willingly, and cowered against the stone wall for protection. The men felt an equal relief. They were no longer blinded by the driven snow, and the wind beat itself out against the stone wall.

But secure as they were for the present, Strong felt great apprehension lest the wind shift. If it turned about, and came out of the east, they would be protected only in part, and he was in a great hurry to fix the tents so firmly that they could not be blown away. They were tied to every available corner of stone, and then the edges were held down by other stones. Thus secured, it would take a mighty blast to tear them from their moorings. The horses were tethered also, lest they take fright and dash over a cliff.

A fire would have been cheerful, but no wood was to be found at that rocky height, and all of the men sought the shelter of the tents, where they sat wrapped in their heaviest clothing and blankets. But Louis Perolet, not daunted at all, brought forth a little alcohol lamp and lighted it. Then he cooked buffalo strips, made them hot coffee, and they were reasonably happy.

"Eet ees not so bad," said Perolet, cheerfully. "Eet ees like the great Napoleon, crossing the Alps to achieve the gran' victory of Marengo. Monsieur Strong ees Napoleon, an' we are the marshals."

The wind did not abate, but it still blew from the northwest, and shrieked over their heads. Although they heard it well, they felt its force but little. Evans and Harris now and then went among the horses, and soothed them with a touch or a word.

"It's wonderful what a gift them two generals have with horses," said Sam Strong. "Some men are that way. I guess they know how to talk horse talk to a horse."

Dark came very early, and, while it was yet twilight, Bob and Sam stood at the edge of the alcove, looking out at what had been their trail. The wind, loaded with snow, screamed past them, but Sam, who was looking up the sharp ascent, pressed his hand upon Bob's arm.

"Don't move or speak!" he whispered. "See who's coming."

A hundred yards above them, two Indians, wrapped in blankets and thick leggins, were staggering down the trail. Their heads were bent in the effort to secure firm footing, and they seemed to have neither eye nor thought for anything else.

"Unless they know of this place they won't see us," whispered Strong. "It's hid too much by the dark an' the snow. They're Utes from the other side of the mountains, an' they're no friends of ours."

Bob could not keep from asking one question.

"Suppose they do know of this place," he said, "and attempt to turn into it?"

"I don't like to think of it," replied the leader. But one hand in its buckskin gauntlet slipped down to the breech of his rifle. Bob's heart began to beat fast. He devoutly hoped that the Utes would go on. They were strong, determined men, and they carried rifles, but they would have no chance if they turned aside into the fatal alcove.

Nearer they came. Now they were level with white men, and it seemed impossible to Bob the two warriors should not see the wide mou' the stony alcove. But he forgot the dusk an

"They're Utes from the other side of the mountain"

and, just before sunset, they stood on the backbone of the pass, ten thousand feet or more above the sea. On either side of them, and, before them, towered other peaks nearly a mile higher, all white with snow.

It was to Bob a scene of indescribable majesty and solemnity. He was lifted far above the earth. Not only were the peaks white, but so was everything else, the ridges, the slopes and the far dim plains, except in the west, where a setting sun of supernatural brightness tinted half of the world with reddish gold. It was like some vast primeval planet, to which man had not yet been born.

The boy was awed, and, when he looked at his comrades, he knew that the same feeling was strong within them. They were not cultivated men in the ordinary sense, but the tremendous spectacle made a deep appeal to them. Sam Strong was the first to speak.

"I ain't a gushin' man" he said, "but I reckon it was worth the climb up here to see this. I've seen it twice before, but it's finest now."

Almost as he spoke, the sun dropped behind a vast range much further west, and the red gold of the sun, that fell across the snow, turned to a pale silver gray. Cold night came down swiftly, and all turned to the work of making a camp.

They could not find a place so suitable as that of the night before, but they were able to secure a fair degree of shelter behind some immense bowlders, where they threw up a wall of smaller stones, facing towards the northwest, in case the wind that they dreaded most should begin to blow again. But the night passed, without trouble, although it was intensely cold, and, in the morning, they began the long descent, which would be extremely broken and irregular. In the valley they had cut grass for the horses which they brought on the packs, and, before starting, they served a liberal portion to them.

By the time they had been marching two hours, great masses of clouds floated in between them and the valley and the world was blotted out again. From the northwest came a mutter and then a whistle. The dreaded wind was blowing again. It was in their faces now, deadly cold, and they made many stops. Strong and Cole, as usual, led the way and they had to exercise extraordinary precaution lest the horses slip forward upon them.

Bob was put in the rear. He wished to be at the front with Strong and Cole, but he was assigned to his place, and he accepted it, without a protest. He was still resolute in his determination never to complain, always to do, as best he could, the duty assigned to him.

As the hours went on, the day steadily grew worse. They were now exposed to the full force of the wind, which never abated for a moment, and the cold was intense. The utmost precaution had to be taken against freezing or frost-bite. Bob began to think they never would succeed, but he put the thought away from him, calling up all his courage for the great work.

They struggled on bravely until night came again, and once more they found refuge in a corner of the cliff, aided a little by the fact that the wind had lulled somewhat. But it was still so strong that it required their united efforts to set the tents, and one of them was blown away before they could fasten it down. They put the horses, as usual, between the tents and the side of the cliff, and now they tethered them together, lest they be thrown into a panic and attempt flight.

They were all roused at dawn, but it was a misty yellowish day, the sun barely showing through great clouds, and before they could start again the snow began to fall heavily.

Bob went forward a little to look at the trail. Clothed thickly, and with his rifle over his shoulder, he made but little progress. Moreover the snow, coming straight into his face, blinded him, and he did not notice that he was stepping from the path, toward the edge of a precipice.

He heard a shout behind him, a shout of warning, uttered at once by Strong and Cole, and he uttered a cry himself, wrung from him by the suddenness of a great peril. He felt the snow yielding beneath his feet. He tried to step back, or to grasp at something. But he clutched only snow, and it slipped from his fingers.

He heard another cry from his comrades, and the roar of a mighty mass falling. He fell down, down with it, he knew not where, enveloped in a great white cloud, and his senses left him.

CHAPTER VII

IN THE BEARSKIN

When Bob recovered consciousness, he was coughing violently, and what caused him to cough was snow that insisted upon entering his mouth. But he cleared his mouth, and undertook to move. He found the operation difficult, but he only struggled the harder, whereupon he righted himself, and found that he was standing in snow to his chin. Moreover, it was still snowing, coming down in great flakes, and they were so thick that he could not see twenty yards from where he was. What he did see was snow, snow, only snow.

He remembered, although there was not much to remember, the sudden terrible sinking sensation, the warning shouts of the others, and then the white darkness. It was impossible to say how far he had fallen, but he had landed feet foremost in an immense drift, where it was well packed, a fact that kept him from going over his head. He had also been helped by the rifle, strapped on his back. It had crossed like a balancing pole, and impeded his sinking.

By cautiously treading the snow beneath him, Bob managed to raise his body up as far as his arm-pits. Then he felt himself, because he was quite sure at first that he was only a fragment of a boy who had fallen off a mountain two miles high.

But he was whole, and even more, no bones were broken. There was a cut across his left arm, where his coat had pulled away from his buckskin glove, but the snow had stopped it from bleeding. He felt no especial pain, as he moved and hence there could be no internal bruise of importance.

He was sure that he could not have been in the snow long or he would have suffered frost-bite, and he was devoutly grateful that he had fared so well thus far, but he realized that he was still in a terrible plight. He looked up, and saw only the blank, white wall of a drift, for a hundred yards or so, and then the cloud of falling snow. The cliff was not perpendicular, but a steep slope. That doubtless had broken his fall and saved his life.

He raised his voice, and began to shout for his comrades:

"O Sam!"

"O Bill!"

Thunderous echoes came back, and he knew that he must be in a deep canyon, but nothing else came. There was not a reply either to the "Bill" or the "Sam." He called them over again. The same echo came back again and that alone. Then, moved by desperate fear, he called them all in turn:

"Sam!"

"Bill!"

"Obadiah!"

"Louis!"

"Porter!"

"Tom!"

Not one answered, and the boy's sense of desolation was so terrible, so overwhelming that, for a moment or two, he felt as one already dead. But he had great courage, fed by a strong body, and once more he took count of himself and his situation. He still had a chance, so long as his limbs were whole, and he had his weapons and ammunition.

He began to move forward slowly, finding the snow so well packed that he did not sink much above his knees. He did not know where he was going, but movement itself brought a new circulation of the blood, and fresh hope of life. He advanced about a rod, when instinct this time warned him. He felt a slight sliding of the snow, and he turned in abruptly, toward the face of the cliff. Ten yards to the right of him the white bank dropped away and he heard the familiar roar of the snowslide.

The boy was appalled, but he drew inferences, nevertheless. He must be standing upon a shelf about twenty yards wide, and as long as he stood close to the cliff, he was in no imminent danger. But if he remained there, he might as well have dropped to death at once, and he continued, still hugging the side of the cliff.

He had no idea of the direction in which he was going, but, at intervals, he shouted again with all the might of a voice that was by no means weak. Still no answer but the echoes. Then another idea came to him. He took the rifle from his shoulder, and fired twice. The reports were sharp and clear, and the echoes rose far above the wind, but there was no answer.

He strapped the rifle upon his back again, and moved on. If only that blinding snow would cease he might discover where he was, and know what he ought to do. He had one advantage. He was more sheltered here from the wind than he had been before his fall, and he was fairly warm. He pulled himself along the edge of the cliff at least an hour, stopping at times to rest, and then the falling snow began to thin. He could still see nothing above him but white wall, but, below him, he saw the dim white floor of a chasm, apparently a thousand feet down. He was right in his surmise. He stood on a shelf which had broken his fall into the main canyon. He could only hope that the shelf would descend gradually, until he might reach the canyon, and, as he continued, there was evidence that the hope might come true. Another hour, and the valley was much nearer, a third and it was not two hundred yards away. Then the shelf ended in snowy rocks and a sheet of ice, which Bob thought must be a miniature glacier.

Further advance seemed impossible, but the resolute and resourceful boy did not yield. His hunting knife was always in its sheath at his belt, and he began to cut steps in the ice. It was slow work, and he had to be careful lest he break the blade, but sometimes there was a stretch of rough rock, not covered with ice, and then he descended more rapidly. It was a delicate task even then, and a slip might send him headlong. He was able to save himself, until he was within ten yards of the bottom. Then his feet flew from under him, and he shot downward into the deep snow.

The boy alighted on one shoulder, and again the rifle served partially as a sort of life belt. He did not sink far, and, when he righted himself, he found that he was unhurt. His first object was to see what kind of a place it was into which he had come. As far as he could make out, he was now standing in a valley, perhaps several hundred yards wide, maybe more, but containing only snow. He had not expected to find trees, as he knew that he was above the line of vegetation, but he did hope that the valley might contain a few shrubs, anything but that eternal snow.

Although the snow was still falling, he could see a faint yellowish sun, and, by taking observations from it, he knew in which direction the west lay. The great ravine led that way, and he moved along slowly, sinking into the snow above his knees, but in no fear of a fall over a precipice. At intervals of a half hour, he fired his rifle, hoping that his comrades would hear, but no reply ever came.

He was not especially cold, but a deadly weariness oppressed him. An increasing darkness in the pass showed him that night was now coming, and that he must rest and sleep. Fortunately, before beginning the ascent they provided for emergencies. Every man carried his blanket in a light roll on his back, food in his knapsack, and a little stimulant for dire need.

The boy found a place under a shelving rock that was free from snow. He pushed himself back into it, not caring for, or not noticing the animal odor that it exuded, and took the strips of dried buffalo meat from his knapsack. He ate them greedily, almost like an animal, and then he took a drink from the emergency stimulant. A pleasant warmth and drowsiness crept through every vein. The driving snow did not touch him here, and he must sleep. But he knew the treachery of the night that was coming, and he did not forget, in the luxury of the physical senses, to take every precaution. He wrapped the blanket about his body with the greatest care, enclosing the feet as usual, drew it up around his neck and face until it met the flaps of his cap, put the knapsack under his head, and then fell asleep as gently as a little child in its bed.

It was a vast cold world that looked down upon the lone boy, deep in a canyon of the Rocky Mountains, and lost to his comrades. His face was pale, and he showed signs of the terrible hours through which he had been, but his breathing was peaceful and regular, and his dreams were happy. Nothing disturbed him. The animal that had slept there before him had known enough to flee at the coming of the snows, and did not return. Bob slept all the night and far into the next day. He was so thoroughly exhausted that nature kept him in what was, perhaps, as much a stupor as sleep. When he awoke, half the forenoon was gone, the snow had ceased and the sun was shining. He was somewhat stiff, but he had not suffered any frost-bite, and he came out from the shelter of the ledge into the open space of the valley.

The valley or canyon was at least a quarter of a

mile broad, but above it towered the cliffs to a great height, steep, white and apparently inaccessible. It was obvious that any attempt to climb them would fail, besides, in all likelihood, bringing down upon his head a snowslide that would end his fur hunting expedition then and there. Nothing was left for him to do but to keep straight on for the west, and trust to happy chance.

The boy judged that he had fallen from the cliff at some point much lower than the present walls or he would have been killed, despite his plunge into the snow. The great heights above him made him shudder.

He inferred from the position of the sun that it was at least ten o'clock when he awoke, and feeling strong and much encouraged, he traveled at least four hours before stopping. He was hopeful that his comrades were marching along some fairly parallel path, but it might be only a hope.

His canyon turned somewhat to the right, and then he saw before him a vast valley, far beneath his feet, and shut in on the horizon rim by other mountains lower than those on which he stood, and probably a hundred miles away at least. He could tell nothing of the nature of this valley, whether plains or wooded, as it, like everything else, was deep in snow and presented only a white expanse.

As his view had widened greatly on every side, he was hopeful that he might see his comrades, but not a single black dot was in sight. He used another valuable cartridge with the usual result, and then, resolved not to repine, he resumed the descent.

He saw great quantities of ice on the western side of the range, sometimes in vast sheets, and at other times in frozen torrents which would unlock when the summer was more advanced. He believed that he could now make out the tree range below him. There was a white tracery which must be the boughs of pines and cedars, and the sight filled him with gladness and courage. Trees mean life, not only living earth, but life for man as well.

Bob traveled all that day down a fairly easy slope, and at nightfall reached the first trees. He felt an immense sense of delight and victory when he was able to reach forward and touch the first scrub pine. He was like a shipwrecked sailor who had swum until his feet touched land, and, moreover, a single bush even was a relief from the everlasting snow.

Despite the danger from the snowslides and precipices, he pushed on a little further in the half darkness until a place was found where the pines were larger and denser. Here, in the center of a dense clump, he made a burrow like a rabbit. He scooped out the snow with his hands until it formed a little circular wall, buttressed by the trees, and, curling himself up in the hole, he lay down to sleep. He was hungry, but the last shred of food was gone, and he must make up his mind to do without it for the night at least, hoping to forget his pangs in slumber. He was warm enough when he lay in his blanket, and he would have been thoroughly comfortable if he could only have stopped that aching sensation in the pit of his stomach.

He did not go to sleep at once. His nerves, somewhat overstrained, would not let him, and he looked up at the sky from his burrow as from the bottom of a well. He saw, therefore, a circular expanse of cold blue, with cold, white stars dancing in it. It was so distant, and he was so alone, that he began to wonder vaguely whether he would ever see his comrades again.

But, while he was wondering, he fell asleep, and, when he awoke the next morning, he was assailed by a hunger so fierce that it could scarcely be endured. He made up his mind to abandon the descent of the range for the time and hunt. He might find a rabbit in the brush. He must find something if he would live.

The slope upon which he now stood was not very steep and it was forested well. It was extremely likely that in such a region, where man was practically unknown, game could be found, and Bob sought vigorously here and there in the snow, looking carefully under the pines and cedars, in the hope of stirring up a rabbit.

Thus passed over an hour without result, and he became very faint and weak. He was compelled to realize that he was reaching the end of his powers. Courage alone could not overcome starvation. He poked a stick that he had found into a clump of cedars, holding his rifle in the other hand, ready to shoot in case a rabbit jumped up.

A roar so thunderous followed that the boy leaped back five feet. It was well that his impulse carried him so far, as a great bear sprang up from the

"A great bear sprang up from the thicket"

Bob had just finished toasting his eighth strip when his attention was drawn by a sound, half a growl and half a whine, but wholly unpleasant and menacing. He saw beneath a pine a pair of fiery red eyes and a long, lank gray body. It was a wolf, not the common creature of the plains, but the great mountain savage, almost as strong, and fully as fierce as a cougar.

The wolf had come to share in Bob's trophy, the bear, and the boy shuddered. This was an animal of unusual ferocity, and more might be behind him. He did not hesitate. He raised the loaded rifle that lay beside him, took quick aim at a point midway in the space between the eyes, and fired. The wolf bounded into the air and fell back in the snow.

Bob did not move, but presently he heard a snapping and snarling in the bushes and he knew that the slain wolf was being devoured by his comrades. He shuddered again, and, foreseeing the danger that might come, began at once to take precautions against it. The bear was too heavy to be dragged to his alcove in the rocks where the fire was burning, but he cut off as much of the flesh as he could possibly carry in his journey, put it in the rock and left the rest to the wolves. They cautiously approached it a little later, and as he did not fire upon them, they fell to work. They stripped it clean in an incredibly short space, and seeing their skill and speed in such a task, Bob was devoutly thankful that he had his rifle with him. The boy took the heavy bearskin down from the tree, pounded the inside surface with stones, and rubbed it with snow. He worked so hard that the perspiration came, despite the great cold, and he was forced to rest his aching arms. But he wanted that bearskin, and he wanted it to be in shape for use. He had an idea that he would need it badly before he reached the valley and the warm country.

He spent all that day dressing the bearskin and dragging up wood for his fire. He knew by the feel of the wind and its sharp edge that the fiercest stage of the blizzard was coming, and he meant to see it through in his present camp. He cooked enough of the bear meat to last several days, built up the fire in front of the warmest and snuggest place in the alcove, and lay down there with the great bearskin around him, the inside turned outward. It was a magnificent robe, and the fur felt very soft and warm as he drew it around his face. He had not felt so warm, so splendidly comfortable in a week, and he lay there, watching the flames of his fire, which were dancing before the rising wind. By and by, he saw red eyes and shadowy, dark figures beyond the flames, and he knew that the wolves, not content with the larger part of a big silver tip bear, had come back for the bear's slayer. But he knew, too, that they would not dare to pass the fire, and that they were intelligent enough to have a healthy fear of his rifle.

He was really but little afraid of the wolves now, and soon they slunk away. All the time the wind was rising, and it had the edge of a knife. But the boy, wrapped to the eyes in the bear's robe, felt like a bear himself, gone into winter quarters. The great cold could not get at him. His food lay within reach of his gloved hand, and what more could he ask?

The day passed, night came and the wind whistled straight out of the northwest like a cannon ball. It brought with it now, not snow, but hail, which rattled among the trees like shot. It came at such an angle that the stone ledge, against which Bob lay, turned it like a shield, and by and by the regular rattling sound became pleasant and soothing. He was conscious that his fire was dying before the wind and hail, but he did not care. He did not believe that the wolves would seek him in such a storm, and, as for the storm itself, it might rise to any height, but it could never penetrate the great bearskin, in which he was enfolded as snugly as its original owner.

The boy, his rifle enclosed in the bearskin also, slept on, and all through the night the great blizzard raged and tore at the flanks of the immutable mountains. The fire was out long since and the charred sticks were covered with frozen snow. Once the mountain wolves, a dozen in number, gaunt, ferocious, and ready, in their fellowship, to attack anything, came back to the place where they had eaten so much good food. No red flame or glowing coal was left to frighten them, but the strange odor, that of a human being, came to their nostrils, and they knew its origin to be a rocky alcove that they could see.

They could have attacked and torn the boy to pieces before he had a chance to defend himself, but the wolves remembered. Their leader, the king of them all, had been slain at a distance by something in the hands of this boy. There had been a sharp crack, a gush of fire, and then the great mountain wolf was dead.

They were drawn by hunger, still unappeased, but shuddering fear, fear of the mysterious death, held them back. Hunger and fear fought, but fear conquered. They slunk away over the frozen snow, and the boy, wrapped in the bearskin in the rocky alcove, still slept, warm, and dreaming beautiful dreams.

After midnight the blizzard increased in violence and ferocity. It was the testimony of wandering Utes and Arapahoes that not another such storm had been known on the mountains in a decade. Now the hail came like a vast rifle-fire, then it was only the wind itself, but with a breath that froze at its touch.

The mountain wolves gave up all thought of the human being who lay in the bearskin under the shelter of the rock. Hardy as they were, they were fleeing now to their own lairs to save their lives, and all the bears, up to the biggest and the strongest, sought their dens, unable to face the cutting sleet. The forest was full of wild creatures by day, but that night none stalked abroad.

The blizzard did not pass until daylight, and it was late when Bob awoke. It was a slight sense of suffocation that caused him to sit up, and he found that he moved with difficulty. Snow had packed in front of him, and, on either side, everywhere except at his back, where the rock thrust up, the surface of this snow was a sheet of packed hail. Only in front of him, where he had been breathing, it was moist around the edges. He was like a seal, with his blowhole in the ice.

Bob's first task was to make his den a little wider, to trample down the snow on all sides, and then to eat up his frozen bear steaks. He found his muscles somewhat stiff at first, but with exercise they soon recovered their elasticity. Again he was devoutly grateful to the bear which had saved him, first from starving and then from freezing.

The snow was not much deeper than on the day before, but the frozen crust of hail and ice made the traveling much harder. Nevertheless, he faced it with a bold heart. Heavy as was the bearskin, he rolled it up and packed it on his shoulders, adding the food to his burden, and then he set out.

Circumstances, which had been so long against the boy, now began to favor him. The slope became steep, though not dangerous, and he rapidly descended to a warmer air. The sun came out, bright and inspiring, and the temperature rose fast. The forest was thick, and he found many easy paths leading through it. At noon he stopped and managed to build another fire under some cedars. Here, while he warmed his body and ate, he took thought with himself and tried to plan the best way to reach his old comrades. They must be somewhere in the great valley before him, and they would follow the easiest trail to the next range of mountains, as he knew that they were yet far from their destination. He must also choose what he thought to be the easiest trail, and follow it as fast as he could.

He could see the valley now, and the greenish tint showed that no snow had fallen there. He surmised that it was much such a country as that which he had left behind him, on the other side of the range. He thought that he would reach the valley before dark, but it was further than it looked, and he was yet a long distance from it when night came. But he was below the snow line, and he had no difficulty in building a fire, by the side of which he slept well.

He deserted his beloved bearskin the next morning. He had come into a warmer zone, and it was too heavy to carry when not needed. But it had served him so well that he was unwilling to have it torn by wolves or other wild animals, and, making it into as small a package as he could, he tied it into the fork of a tree.

He now found clear, cold streams running down the side of the mountain, and he drank plentifully from them. He had used snow water so long that the streams were a relief, although they came from melting snows themselves.

The forest was thick all along the slopes, and as he descended, the trees, chiefly ash, oak and cedar, increased in size. There was beautiful springy turf here, and he knew from the nature of the country that game must be abundant. The sight was so exhilarating that he gave a shout of joy, and set off with renewed courage at an increased pace.

CHAPTER VIII

THE MIDNIGHT MEETING

The boy still had plenty of bear meat with him, and he decided not to seek game for the present. Instead, he luxuriated awhile under the trees and on the grass. The warmth was very generous and satisfying after so much snow and cold, and while Bob still admired the great white peaks and ranges, he felt that he had endured enough of them for the present.

He bathed in one of the streams, finding the water extremely cold, and then descended the last slope. As he was about to emerge upon the plain he saw many hoofprints in the soft earth, and his heart gave a great bound. He had experience enough to know that the tracks were made by shod animals, not by wild ponies, and surely good luck had brought him at once upon the path of his comrades.

The trail was broad and plain. A child could have followed it, and Bob hurried forward, his heart still leaping. He judged that the trail could not be more than an hour old, and it was likely that he could overtake them in two hours, at the furthest.

The footprints led straight away, through a fine forest of oak, without undergrowth, but with a soft turf in which the steel shoes sank deep. He came presently to a place at which they had evidently stopped. Fragments of food were scattered about, and the turf had been cropped close by the horses. Clearly they could be only a short distance ahead, and he increased his pace, eager to see them again.

In ten minutes he heard the neigh of a horse, and he began to run toward the sound. It was perhaps Providence itself that caused him to trip on a vine. He did not fall, but it brought him up with a jerk, mentally as well as physically. Then, remembering Sam Strong's injunction that in the West caution, caution, caution was the quality upon which life most depended, he sank down among some bushes and approached more carefully.

The bushes ended and the ground dropped off into a sequestered little valley, in the center of which men were resting and smoking, and horses were grazing. But they were not his comrades nor their horses. He beheld instead a band of at least a score, dressed like hunters, and with hardened, evil faces. As they talked they swore great oaths, and although they were white men, Bob felt instinctively that he had exercised caution none too soon. The Cheyennes had not inspired less aversion.

His eyes from his covert roamed over the men and alighted at last upon a face that he remembered. He could never forget that dark countenance, the black eyes set close together, and the cruel strength of the pointed chin. It was Juan Carver, trapper, free lance or representative of Hudson Bay, or something else still worse. Bob had listened well to Sam Strong and he never doubted that this band of men would try to rob his comrades of their furs,

THE MIDNIGHT MEETING 115

if they obtained them, or be ready to do any other deed of wickedness that was to their profit. They were men for him to avoid, and he thanked God for the kindly bush that had checked his headlong speed.

Bob surmised that they had found an easier pass over the range than the one chosen by Strong, as they did not show much trace of suffering. Luck seemed to have favored them so far, and with a sigh of regret that it was so, he turned away.

He surmised that the Carver party would remain some time in their resting-place, and he wished to be so far out on the plain that they could not see him when they started. He felt apprehension when he left the cover of the last line of bushes, but it must be done.

The plain, as he had foreseen, was much like that on the other side of the range, waving, treeless, and with grass now turning to green. He did not think it probable that men had passed that way lately, as three bunches of antelope were grazing in the distance, and for a little while Bob was in great depression. It indicated that he was on the wrong trail, and could not overtake his comrades. But he dared not go back and hunt for the right trail. There were Carver and his men whom he must avoid.

He pressed forward all through the day, never stopping long at a time, but often looking back to see if he was followed. He did not see any moving dots on the plain behind him and he was greatly encouraged thereby. It was hot, and he suffered now from the sun, longing, as he thought he would never long again, for the snow of the high mountains.

He crossed one shallow brook from which he drank, and at nightfall came to another, fairly well wooded along its banks, by the side of which he decided to sleep.

He chose his place, well hidden in the bushes, lay down his blanket for softness, as the weather was too warm now to fold it about him, and fell asleep.

The boy was awakened in the middle of a dark night by the sound of voices and the tread of horses. All his faculties were alive on the instant. Carver and his band had come, and he lay perfectly still under the bushes. The moonlight was so thin that he could not see any one, although he heard them distinctly.

The sounds grew louder. They seemed to be coming straight towards him, and the boy, in spite of all his courage, had some minutes of nervous thinking. He decided to creep out of their path and deeper into the bushes. He made a yard or two silently, and then a twig snapped.

"Here! Hold up! What's that?" some one cried.

"A slinkin' coyote, I guess," replied another, and Bob Norton fairly leaped into the air at these two voices. It was Sam Strong who had asked the question, and it was Bill Cole who had replied.

"Sam! Bill!" shouted the boy, rushing through the bushes. "I'm here! and I've found you!"

The six men were all there on horseback, the pack horses following, and they had stopped short when

THE MIDNIGHT MEETING 117

he cried out. Now they sat motionless on their horses, staring at him, all except Louis Perolet who dropped his reins, crossed himself and began to patter out a prayer of his church.

Sam Strong at last uttered a great gasp, and exclaimed:

"Well, if it ain't the youngster, after all, riz right up from the dead."

"It must be him," said Bill Cole, still half in doubt. "He don't look like a ghost."

In another instant they were all off their horses, shaking hands with him, punching him in the shoulders and chest to see that he was real, and showing as much delight as frontiersmen ever permit to themselves. Bob himself was overflowing with exuberance, and shook every rough hand in return as hard as he could.

"I've always hoped for the best," said Sam Strong, "but I never dared to hope that you'd come back to us, shakin' your grave clothes off, so to speak. If you hadn't hollered out loud I guess we'd all have rid on, takin' it for granted that you wuz a ghost ha'ntin' us."

"I could have believed it," said Tom Harris. "I remember a fellow killed at Chancellorsville when we was chasin' the rebels—"

"Why, you never chased us at Chancellorsville," exclaimed Porter Evans, indignantly. "That was our greatest victory, an'—"

"Well, you two generals shut up," said Sam Strong. "We ain't got time to fight the Civil War all over ag'in to-night. What we want to do is to camp here, an' hear the story of the youngster who has been right down into his grave, but who has come right out ag'in."

They had been making a night watch, but they tethered their horses and camped, lighting no fire, however. Then Bob told the story of his fight for life in detail, broken now and then by expressions of wonder from his comrades.

"I'll hope for the best more than ever after this," said Sam Strong. "You came through in great style. Tenderfoots, breakin' all rules, often do the right things, when the men that have seen an' done everything begin makin' mistakes right at the jump."

"It was not chance," said Louis Perolet, gravely, "eet ees because Bob is the bright, smart boy. Why did the great Napoleon, when he was not much more than a boy, whip all the Austrian generals in Italy who were so much older than himself an' with so much experience? Eet was because he had the great min', the genius, an' when he saw he remembered. Meester Bob be the genius, too, in his own way."

"Now you shut up," exclaimed Bob, blushing. "It was luck, just as Sam says."

But Louis would not be denied his assumption. He insisted that Bob was a genius; that he had proved it, and that he was destined to become the greatest of frontiersmen, the superior in time of the redoutable Sam Strong himself.

Strong was somewhat apprehensive over the news of Carver's presence in the valley, but a careful examination showed that he and his band were not in the neighborhood. Then Sam told their own story. They had thought Bob lost when he fell down the snowy cliff, but nevertheless they had descended into the valley and searched two days for him. The falling snow, of course, had covered his footprints. At last they had given him up as dead —certainly the chance of his escape was most remote—and they had gone sadly on. They had suffered much from cold, but they had managed to get themselves and their horses that far into the valley. Their long search for Bob had caused them to arrive later than he.

"But we found you,—or you found us," said Louis Perolet, triumphantly, "an' eet ees the good omen. To escape so great a danger proves that we will find all we seek an' more. Our fortune has been good, an' we'll push it."

"I reckon you're about right, Frenchy," said Sam Strong. "The best has happened an' we'll hope for it ag'in, though I don't like the presence of Carver here."

Strong did not fear an attack by Carver, as the man would have no object in making it now, but he did not like the way in which this band had hung upon his trail. It was the later days of the fur trade, and valleys, rich in furs, were hard to find. Battles often took place for their possession, and the powerful company north of the British line had poached more than once far down into the American mountains.

"We can fight Carver an' his crowd if we have

to do it," said Strong, "but we don't want to waste ourselves that way. What we want to do is to get furs, an' we've got to hide ourselves from both the Indians an' land pirates."

"I move," said Bill Cole, "that we make double quick time to the next range of mountains an' then lay by in some thicket till Carver passes on. We can mark the course he takes, an' then choose another for ourselves."

The suggestion seemed good to them all, and they advanced rapidly for three days until they reached the second mass of mountains. There they found good refuge among dense pines and cedars, where they stayed two days, kindling no fire. On the second day Strong, Bob and Perolet, lying close in a covert, saw Carver and his band go by. They followed them until they saw them high up in a pass, going almost due west. Then they returned to camp, satisfied that Bill Cole's suggestion had been a happy one.

Sam Strong immediately turned his own expedition southward, marching along the flank of the mountain. Bob once more rode his own horse. He had suffered somewhat from fever, brought on by exposure and his great sufferings, and he had collapsed when they stopped to let Carver pass, but the rest had restored him entirely. Traveling now on one's own horse was a luxury, after his struggles in the snowy pass.

They kept a good watch for the Utes and Arapahoes or wandering Apaches who sometimes strayed far northward, but saw none. The slopes, along which they were traveling, seemed to be wholly neglected by the tribes, as game was plentiful, and not especially wary.

After three days of the southern march at good speed they stopped to refresh their horses, and to renew their stock of provisions. They pitched a camp in one of the pleasantest places that the boy had yet seen, an open grove, with a clear little brook running through it. They stayed three days there, and killed several deer, including a splendid elk. Trout were caught in some deep pools of the stream, and proved to be of fine quality.

While they were resting, Strong revealed to Bob more of their plans. When they crossed the second range, a great mass of mountains tumbled together, they would advance southwestward, and enter once more the region of mountains, a huge system that extended with larger or smaller breaks almost to the Pacific. Hidden in these ranges were the beaver streams, some of which no white man had yet reached, and, along these, they expected to find a rich reward.

It was all one to the boy. He did not care where they went, as long as they retained him a member of this chosen band. His devotion to the six men, who had treated him so well, grew as the days passed, and he took fresh resolutions to repay them no matter what the cost.

It was now midsummer, but they did not hurry, as furs would not be in good condition until October. They frequently made stops of a day or two, and, in one wide valley, they chased a herd of mustangs. Sam Strong and Bill Cole succeeded in catching five with their lariats, and they were skilful enough to break them to their service.

"They'll come in handy," said Sam. "Each of 'em can carry back five hundred pounds of smooth, soft beaver skins."

"We'll get 'em," said Bob, with enthusiasm.

Sam smiled benevolently. The boy's freshness and enthusiasm had added new life to the little party.

"It will be a full two weeks yet," he said, "before we're at the beaver streams, an' then we've got to spend some time in locatin' an' makin' traps."

The maze of mountains deepened. Now and then they rode up great canyons, with cliffs a thousand feet high, on either side, and small streams trickling down the center of the canyons over masses of rough bowlders. The wilderness seemed to Bob so vast and so little peopled that he wondered how anybody could ever find anybody else in it. Apprehension in regard to Carver and his band disappeared from his mind, and apparently it was forgotten by the others also.

When the summer was well past, they came to a ravine, and deep valley, through which flowed a creek, emptying about ten miles further on into a river. The creek could be followed thirty or forty miles back into the mountains, and, for the full distance, it was thickly lined with trees and bushes. Many of the trees had been cut down as neatly as if it had been done with an axe, but Sam Strong explained to Bob that the weapon used was the teeth of the beaver.

"This is the best of the beaver streams that we had in mind," he said, "an' we're goin' to trap along here an' on others not far away, all through the winter."

They went up the creek about twenty miles further, until they came to a point where the valley widened out somewhat, and here Sam Strong chose the camp. He could not have found a more favorable spot. On either side of the creek, between the trees and the steep slope of the mountains, was a meadow, several acres in extent, covered with deep rich grass. The horses would find ample grazing here, and the trees and the mountains together would give them protection in winter. As for water, there was the creek.

On the northern side, the meadows made a little bay into the mountain, and here, in a smooth spot, with a clump of oaks circling about it, they selected their camp. They pitched their tents, and turned the horses loose in the meadow.

"It will be fine, here in the tents," said Bob.

Sam Strong smiled.

"It's fine now," he said, "but it won't be fine, when winter comes. No, Bob, we are goin' to build our house. Trappers, who expect to stay a long time in one place, must have a house."

They began the task with great energy the very next day. They were well supplied with axes, and seven pairs of strong arms soon felled the requisite number of trees. These were cut into even lengths, and squared at the ends. The bark was left on.

Then they built a large log cabin, with a lean-to in the rear. The space between the logs was chinked up with mud and chips. It was provided with a puncheon floor, a stone fireplace and a stick chimney. There were two windows, with swinging board shutters, and the roof was covered with shingles of their own splitting. All the men had had plenty of experience at this kind of building, and the work was done in a week.

"There she is," said Sam Strong, triumphantly. "Rain tight, wind tight, snow tight, an' cold tight."

They marked off on the inside seven spaces, one for every man. There he was to spread his bed of blankets, fur, or whatever he wished, and that space was to remain his own. But they slept, for a while, outside under the tents, and the cabin would remain without occupants, until the cold weather began.

They devoted nearly two weeks to the making of traps, embracing all the varieties known to the skilled hunters of furs. They had steel traps with them, but the new ones that they made of wood were far more numerous. Then they explored for miles around, seeking the best places in which to put them. Bob went on most of these expeditions, and invariably he was with Sam Strong. His sense of locality and his trapper's eye developed amazingly. In a very short time he became almost the equal of Strong in noticing the "runs" and other signs of wild life, and no matter how complicated the plexus of the mountains, it was almost impossible to lose him.

About thirty miles up the creek, which flowed almost due west, there was a rift in the mountains opening to the southward. Following it they came to another narrow creek which flowed, on a parallel line with this one, toward the river. This also proved to be stocked with beaver, and they set traps here as well, building another and a smaller log cabin on its banks, a necessity to them, as it could not be reached in a day's journey from their first house.

The foliage began to turn red and brown now with the first touch of October. Everything was ready and the trapping began.

CHAPTER IX

THE SUNKEN RIVER

The days that followed were full of activity and interest for Bob and all his comrades. The trapping was the best that any of them had ever found, and before the winter began, they were packing the beaver pelts in bales. They also took skins of the grizzly and silver tip, but they devoted themselves chiefly to the beaver.

"All kind of pelts are good," said Sam Strong, "but our big market is St. Louis, an' it's a long way from here to St. Louis. So we've got to consider the question of transportation an' carry the thing that weighs the least to the pound, an' that's beaver."

"It counts in more ways than in trappin'," said Tom Harris. "If we hadn't had to take so many provisions into the South with us we'd have licked the rebels in one year, instead of taking four for the job."

They were sitting before the fire in their cabin, when Tom made this speech in a tone of finality. Porter Evans at once sprang to his feet.

"If you hadn't been lucky you never would have won!" he exclaimed. "Besides, you didn't really win. As I told you before we got tired an' reckoned that we ought to go home, an' look after our crops."

"Shut up," said Sam Strong, "I'm always hopin'

for the best, an' I'm hopin' that some day you fellows will forget the war."

A few minutes later the two were industriously scraping the inside of a grizzly bearskin.

It was announced to Bob, late in November, that he would have a full share in the trapping, that there would be seven equal portions, one of which was to be his. He demurred, saying that he was entitled only to a half-share, but the others insisted. He had done his full part in every respect, and so he was compelled to acquiesce.

The year waned and cold gales began to roar up the valleys and canyons, although much red and brown foliage was yet left on the slopes. All the horses had grown fat on the grass of the meadows, and Harris and Evans now built them a shelter among the trees. They made, on three sides, a windbreak of thick, woven bushes, and carried it slightly overhead in the form of an arch. When completed it was a really admirable shelter for their hardy mustangs, both Harris and Evans being skilful at such work. It would protect entirely from the wind, and, in a great measure, from snow also. The ponies soon learned its advantages, and, as the nights increased in coldness, entered it, without being driven.

About ten days after the completion of the stable, as the two builders proudly called it, the party sat late by their cabin fire. The day had not been a hard one and Evans and Harris, who were in fine form, were telling stories, more or less highly colored, generally highly, of the Civil War, with Sam

Strong, as a discreet umpire, to prevent verbal encounters between them.

The fire was a good one. The dry logs crackled, and cast up merry flames. Genial warmth filled the cabin, and the roaring of the cold wind without made it all the more pleasant inside the log house. Bob was lying upon a grizzly bearskin, his chin upon his hand, listening, with all his soul, to the stories. It seemed wonderful to him that these two comrades of his should have been through such great battles. He ran over the names to himself, Chancellorsville, Gettysburg, Shiloh, Chickamauga, The Wilderness, and the others.

"But though them was tre-men-jeous big battles," said Tom Harris, "you was safe after you was captured. Porter, here, knew that when I told him he wouldn't get hurt—that's right, Sam, make him keep still till I get through. As I was sayin', if you lived long enough to be captured you was all right; so it's safer fightin' white men than it is Sioux or Cheyennes. When you're captured by them your troubles are just beginin.' Why I—"

Every man of the seven leaped to his feet, as a scream of pain and terror, the like of which the boy had never heard before, rose above the roaring of the wind. Bob's blood ran chill in his veins. The scream was repeated, and Sam Strong exclaimed:

"It's one of our horses, an' like as not a grizzly bear is among 'em. Come quick with your rifles!"

Every man seized his weapon and rushed for the door, Sam Strong leading. The night was dark, but a terrible commotion came from the stable. The horses were plunging and rearing, and as they ran forward two, wild with terror, dashed past them. Bob kept just at the heels of Sam Strong, and as his eyes grew used to the darkness he saw a huge, dusky figure at the entrance to the stable, and then another.

"It's the grizzlies!" cried Sam Strong. "A whole tribe of 'em! Shoot as fast as you can, but look out for the horses!"

He fired at the first of the bears, and the huge brute, turning instantly, charged straight at him. That would have been the last night of Sam Strong, great hunter, trapper and Indian fighter, had not a boy, whom he had befriended, been just behind him, eager and ready with a loaded rifle.

Bob poked the muzzle of his weapon past Sam's shoulder, and fired point-blank into the eyes of the raging brute.

A grizzly bear has great vitality, but he cannot live with a bullet in his brain. Sam Strong felt the hot breath of his foe on his face, he saw those long, iron claws reached out to destroy him, and he may have felt, for a moment, that he was lost, but the great bear fell at his feet, stone dead. He turned and said only three words:

"Good boy, Bob!"

But they were the sweetest words that had ever sounded in Bob Norton's ears. He had saved the life of his chief, and that chief had given him praise. Meanwhile another huge, snarling form was charging, but Cole, Perolet and Obadiah Pirtle poured bullets into it, and it fell near the first. Two smaller ones ran, but the men followed and slew them at the banks of the creek.

"Now, Bob," said Sam Strong, "you run back to the cabin an' bring us a torch, an' we'll see jest what's been done here."

The boy, still trembling with excitement, obeyed, but by the time he returned with the light, the men had succeeded to some extent in quieting the horses, that is, all that were left in the stable, four being on the missing list. When Bob held up his torch he disclosed a genuine field of battle. Four grizzlies lay dead, two there and two at the creek, and one horse had deep parallel gashes along his shoulder. Sam Strong read all the signs with an unerring eye.

"It was a family of bears," he said, "father, mother, an' two boys. They smelled them horses, an' them horses smelled mighty good to 'em. They crept up an' old pa grizzly here made a jump. He meant to light on old Baldy, the strongest an' fightenest of the lot. He missed just what he was aimin' for, but he did give old Baldy a rake, an' then the flood turned loose. Mustangs, like ours, can kick fast an' powerful hard, but if we hadn't come so quick a lot of our best horses would have been chawed up."

It was indeed a providential rescue, as they relied upon the horses to get both themselves and their furs back to civilization, and it was a danger that might occur again.

"The care of the horses belongs mainly to Porter

an' Tom," said Strong, "an' they've got to fix up somethin' that will keep any more bears away, long enough for us to come. Now, Bob, we'll help skin the lot, 'cause their hides are worth havin'. Besides, Louis, here, can get some pretty good steaks off the young ones."

They spent nearly the whole night skinning the grizzlies and cutting them up. Fierce mountain wolves, attracted by the odor, came down and prowled so near that they were forced to shoot several of them. The horses were continually uneasy, and the best efforts of Harris and Evans could not quiet them.

The two "generals" the next day entirely closed the fourth side of the "stable" with thorny brush which they removed every night and morning for the horses to pass in and out. They attached this brush rather strongly with bark, and Sam Strong gave his full approval.

"You've done well, boys," he said to Harris and Evans. "Not even a grizzly could butt through that without makin' a noise, an' by that time we could be on the spot."

Strong had said nothing more to Bob about the shot that saved him from the bear, but the boy noticed that the leader showed a great increase of confidence in him. He took him with him on nearly all his expeditions, and often these lasted several days. Strong did not work steadily at the details of trapping. He left the bulk of it to the others while he explored for new beaver streams, or for signs of other game wearing furs that would be of value in the great markets. He had a wonderful "scent" for beaver, and found many new dams along these unknown little mountain streams. Bob was now his comrade, and made two or three discoveries on his own account which elated him mightily, and increased his confidence.

Despite the growing cold, Strong and the boy, when on their expeditions, frequently slept in the bush along the slopes. They discarded their blankets, and made for themselves sleeping bags of fur, somewhat like the sleeping bag of the Arctic, and with these they practically defied cold.

On one of their journeys they went down the creek to its mouth. It was a clear mountain stream, emptying itself into a river, which also came from a mountain, and was clear. Strong sat down on a rock and looked meditatively at the larger stream.

"Bob," he said, "do you know what river this is?"

"No," replied the boy, "I don't. Perhaps not enough people have seen it to name it."

"Yes, they have," said Sam Strong. "This is one of the headwaters of the Colorado, an' we'll call it the Colorado. Maybe you never heard of the Colorado, Bob, but old Spaniards saw it more than three hundred years ago, an' Indians an' hunters say it's the funniest river on earth."

"How so?" asked Bob.

"It runs along for a spell as if it didn't mean more than any other river; specially these of the mountains, dodgin' 'roun' hills, dashin' through rock-cuts, foamin' over bowlders, an' cuttin' up such didos. Lots of rivers do that, but with this river the hills keep gettin' higher, the rock-cuts deeper, an' the bowlders bigger. Then the river itself runs faster an' faster. An' the faster it gets the deeper it sinks into the earth. Down, down it goes until you just see a ribbon of sky overhead, an' it goes on that way, they say, for hundreds of miles, rippin' an' roarin' an' dashin'."

The brown face of the trapper was illuminated as he spoke. The look there was not that of one who sought gain, it was the gaze of the explorer, gazing into vast, vague regions, and seeking by some power of the mind to penetrate their mystery. Some such look as this must have been in the eyes of Columbus when he faced the Western Ocean.

"Does the river keep on that way forever?" asked Bob, catching his leader's spirit.

"Nobody knows," replied Strong. "It's one of the mysteries of the earth. This river goes right on, cuttin' right through mountains, not turnin' their flanks, but slashin' the solid stone right across, same as if God had done it with a sword-blade. I've heard tales that 'way off into the southwest it sinks down into the earth so far—well, so far it ain't worth while to tell it, 'cause you wouldn't believe it, an' then again I've heard that it runs clean underground, comes out maybe a thousand miles further on, an' goes into the Pacific."

"Which do you believe?" asked Bob.

"I don't know, but I do know that this is the riproarin'est, strangest river on top of this ball of ours, an' I want to know more about it. I want to satisfy my curiosity, an' I think there must be lots of beaver on the streams runnin' into it. We mean to stay 'roun' in these parts about two years, Bob, an' business an' pleasure can go together. Next year I mean to go down the Colorado, lookin' for beaver streams, an' if you want to go with me, Bob, all you've got to do is to say so."

"Of course I'll go, and thank you for taking me," exclaimed Bob, eagerly.

"Then it's settled, but don't say anything about it now to the boys. Jest put it in the back of your head, an' keep it there."

Strong made no further mention of the subject even then, but he sat long staring at the mysterious river, and the boy, whose eyes followed his, shared the spell. They were deep in the wilderness now, but this stream would carry them into regions yet wilder and grander.

The two slept that night within sight of the river, and in the morning the first snow came. They were back at the cabin by the next sundown, and found the rest of the party there. Strong hoped for an open winter, but no one could tell what was coming, and they made ample provision against every emergency, laying in great quantities of food and firewood. Despite the skim of snow, the grass was still fresh on the meadows, and the horses were fat and full of life. There had been a second alarm of bears, but the thorn fence served its purpose, and they fled in the darkness before the trappers could get a chance at them with their rifles.

The winter, to their great satisfaction, proved to be a mild one, and the trapping could be carried on with only a few breaks. Twice there were blizzards, but on each occasion they were present at the cabin, with the stout door shut and a big fire roaring on the hearth.

"Just think," said Louis Perolet, when the second blizzard was at its height, "it was in such weather as this that the great Napoleon an' hees French soldiers retreated from Moscow. Only French soldiers can stand such a wind an' such cold."

"As I've heard it, Frenchy," said Porter Evans, "not many of Napoleon's soldiers ever got back."

"That's what I've heard, too," said Tom Harris. "Now, we licked the rebels like thunder at Gettysburg, as Porter Evans there knows, though he won't admit it, but if Napoleon an' his French had been in their place we wouldn't have left a grease spot of 'em."

"Bah," said Perolet, "eef ze great Napoleon had been at Gettysburg he would have taken the Yankee army by one ear, an' the rebel army by the other ear; he would knock their heads together an' then he would say, 'go away an' play, leetle boys, mebbe when you grow up you can fight'."

Sam Strong laughed.

"He had you there, boys," he said, "an' what's more, he believes it."

But there was no animosity. Perolet, a few minutes later, was serving both "generals" with especially delicate pieces of beaver tail. The blizzard died down, passed, and they renewed their trapping. Christmas came, was celebrated duly, and then they went far into the New Year. Fortune was certainly good to them. All agreed that they had never known such trapping before. The furs were not only abundant, but of the highest quality, and if the second season proved as good as the first, they would return eastward with all their horses could carry.

But Sam Strong did not forget the Colorado. He was a man who looked far ahead. He knew that beaver streams were soon trapped out, and he wanted to have others in reserve. Partly for that reason, and partly because the mystery of the river called to him, he kept it continually in mind. When the winter began to break up he spoke of it to the entire party.

"We are goin' to stay here all of another year," he said, "an' not only that, after this trip's finished we're comin' back ag'in as long as the furs last. Now it is important for us to know where to find beaver, an' to know it before anybody else. Summer's no good for trappin', so it's my idea as soon as the spring is well opened out to go down the river on a boat, spyin' out the country. I want Bill, Obe an' Bob to go with me. T'other three can stay here, look after the horses an' furs, an' fight off Carver if he comes."

The agreement was soon made, and as soon as the weather admitted they began the task of building a strong boat. Trappers often carry their furs by boats, and they had provided iron spikes and other suitable materials for such a contingency.

Seven pairs of strong and skilled hands built fast, and their craft was soon ready.

The boat was somewhat clumsy perhaps, but it was exceedingly strong. It was about twenty feet long, and a tarpaulin of skins was stretched tightly over the deck, as Sam Strong foresaw much rough water. It was shallow, and there were two pairs of heavy oars. All the provisions were packed under Sam Strong's direction in tightly closed skin bags. The ammunition and two extra rifles were protected in the same way, and a small supply of medicines was also placed aboard.

"There'll be a lot of rough goin'," said Sam Strong. "Falls an' currents an' eddies an' such like, an' mebbe, if our boat should turn over, we could get a lot of our things out, still dry an' useful."

The warm weather had fully come when they were ready for departure. The boat had been built at a point on the creek about four miles from its mouth, and the two "generals" and Louis Perolet were there to see the four adventurers leave upon their great trip. Strong and Bob were forward, and Cole and Obadiah were near the stern.

"Good-by," said the three on the bank together, and reaching down they gave every one in turn a hearty grip.

"I don't know how far we'll go an' I guess we'll have to walk back," said Strong, "but we'll be here again before the summer is over."

The signal was given, and all four pulled at the oars. Their boat, which they had aptly named

"The Columbus," glided smoothly down the stream. Bob had been eager for the great adventure, but he could not help feeling a deep regret now as they left behind them their three comrades and their pleasant camp. They might never return. No one had allowed himself to speak of such a thought, but the possibility was there.

He gave the three who still stood on the bank a long look, and then, taking off his fur cap, waved it to them. They waved in reply, and a few moments later, trees and a curving bank hid them from view.

"Good fellers," said Sam Strong, in a tone of strong approval, "but some mighty battles will be fought back there at the camp while we're gone. Porter an' Tom will go through the whole Civil War, never agreein' on a thing, an' then Louis will step in with the great Napoleon an' show that both are always wrong."

Bob laughed, and homesickness did not then tug quite so hard at his heart. They reached the mouth of the creek, rowed into the middle of the river, and let the boat drift with the current, Bill Cole, with little effort, keeping it in the right course.

They drifted all that day, the strength of the current increasing perceptibly. Every one of the four took his turn at steering, but they did not yet have any trouble. The water flowed smoothly on between shores not yet very high, although on either horizon were lofty mountains, dark with pines on the slopes, and white on the crests with snow. Towards night the river widened somewhat, and passed between cliffs about six hundred feet high.

At the highest point on the right bank, a great silver tip bear stood looking down at The Columbus. Bob gazed straight up at the bear, and it was rather a singular fact that no one of the four, hunters and trappers though they were, wanted to shoot at him.

"I wonder what he thinks of us," said the boy.

"Mebbe he has seen white men before," said Bill Cole, "but it's the first time that he's ever seen 'em goin' down this river in a boat."

It was twilight when they passed the gorge, and running the boat into a little cove, they made it fast to some bushes for the night. All four were glad to step ashore, and stretch their cramped limbs, although the place was not particularly attractive, merely a sandy beach, clumps of dwarfed bushes, and back of them high and steep hills. The wind, blowing down the stream, was quite cold at the coming of the night, and Strong decided to build a fire. Plenty of dry driftwood, thrown up by floods, was scattered about, and in five minutes a big fire cast its welcome glow over the gloomy cove.

"We'll cook here," said Sam Strong, "but I think we'd better sleep in the boat. You can never tell in these regions when Indians will come, an' in that case we'd have nothin' to do but cut the rope an' get away. Still I'm hopin' for the best, an' I don't think they'll come."

Desolate howls came from the peaks, but the four only laughed. They knew the mountain wolves too well to pay any attention to their lament. They took watches of three hours apiece, and were off again the next morning at the first flush of dawn. Before noon they were further down the river than either Strong or Cole had ever been before, and the current was growing decidedly strong. They passed the mouth of another river, equal in size to their own, and the two streams united were now of great volume and power.

The second and third day passed, and they were now in regions incomparably wild and grand. The river, yellow with soil washed in its rapid flight, grew swift and turbulent. The four always sat with oars in their hands watching for rocks, whirlpools or falls. Often the spray and foam dashed all over them, but the skin tarpaulin kept their precious stores and ammunition dry.

It was tiring work. The sharp point of a rock might sink their boat at any time, or they might be dashed in pieces down a fall. The inattention of a single moment could prove fatal. But Bob, though his bones ached, felt all the wild thrill of their mysterious journey. None was readier at the oar than he. None had a quicker eye, and the blood raced through his veins as the river moved on in its steadily deepening channel.

They plunged sometimes between banks two thousand feet in height, again the banks sank to low hills, and blacktail deer scurried away at their approach. The cliffs were generally bare, but now and then early flowers bloomed brightly in the crannies. Evergreens were abundant on the crests, and on the beaches, where they camped, they always found an abundance of driftwood for fires. Then followed long nights of deep sleep, and in the morning Bob's aching bones would be well again.

The fourth camp was made at the mouth of a small creek, flowing in from the east between banks a thousand feet high, and as steep as the side of a church. Strong examined the creek carefully, and decided the next morning to go up it as far as they could in the boat.

"We're lookin' for beaver streams," he said, "an' this seems a likely one to me. Leastways I'm hopin' for the best."

Their boat was of shallow draught, and they were able to row it at least ten miles up the creek. On the way they found that it received two or three small tributaries and that the mountains were much lower here. Strong's surmise about beaver proved correct. They found fine colonies along all the streams. It seemed to be absolutely virgin territory, so far as trappers were concerned, but they touched nothing. They had no way to carry out the furs, as they could not row back against the stream, and after they had taken careful note of the country they returned to the river.

"We'll come here some day by land with plenty of horses and mules," said Sam Strong, "an' then them beaver had better look out."

CHAPTER X

THE RETURN BY LAND

All four enjoyed the rest on the beaver stream, as explorations even were a relaxation after the rush and strain of the river, but they re-embarked with a willing spirit, first replenishing their supplies with a blacktail deer that Bill Cole shot.

The Columbus swung once more into the yellow stream, and it seemed to Bob, looking down a vast chasm, that they were going to enter the very bowels of the earth. All around them now were great heights of black lava, and back of these, snow-capped mountains. But nothing interrupted the rush of the river. That very day it turned a vast mass of rock, at so sharp an angle that, despite the promptness and exertions of the four, The Columbus grazed it. Bob thought they were gone, but the blow was only a glancing one. The boat tipped dangerously to one side, and foaming water dashed over them all, but the stout wooden sides were not broken in. The Columbus righted itself, and away they went with the white water whirling about them. When they were fairly steady Obadiah Pirtle took off his cap and said to the boy:

"Bob, has my hair turned gray in the last five minutes?"

They had smoother going the next day, and in the afternoon they discovered another beaver stream, this time coming in from the west. Sam Strong marked it carefully on a rude map that he was making.

"We'll be back here, too, some day," he said, "if nobody beats us to it. I like to hope for the best, but I shouldn't be surprised if Carver an' his band were down in these parts somewhere. Carver's a good trapper, an' he's always ready, too, for any other business that's likely to pay. I believe that he's hand in glove with the Indians."

"I hope we'll never see him again," said Bob.

Sam was silent. He knew better than the boy the dangers of mountain and plain.

Occasionally when they tied up to the rocks, or in the coves, they tried fishing in the muddy water. They caught a number of fish, but they did not prove to be very good, and Bob greatly preferred the flesh of a second blacktail deer, which fell this time to the rifle of Obadiah Pirtle.

They had been on the river a week when the mountains sank down somewhat, and they floated between banks only three or four hundred feet high, covered with thin forest. The current was not so rapid, and they enjoyed a period of comparative ease, being released from the imminent fear of rocks and rapids.

Bob was sitting in the prow of The Columbus, leaning against the side. He had no particular duties just then, and he was in a half dreamy state, gazing upward at the blue sky which was soft with the breath of springtime. His gaze wandered to the banks, crested with green, and suddenly he sat up a little straighter in the boat. He looked again, thinking that perhaps he had been tricked by the imagination. But he beheld the same figure, that of a man standing by a tree at the very brink. Then he saw two more, three more, a half dozen, and they were Indians.

"Look! look!" he cried to the others. "There are warriors on the bank!"

Sam Strong shot a swift glance upward.

"So there are," he said, "an' they're goin' to do us harm if they can. Bill, you an' Obe hold the boat steady, an' lay low everybody."

Bob lay almost flat in the boat, but he held his rifle ready. They could now see the Indians. They were about a dozen in number, and their intentions were plainly hostile.

Something whizzed in the air, there was a streak, and a long feathered arrow struck in the stream near the boat.

"Bows an' arrows!" said Sam Strong, cheerfully. "They'll have to use something better if they catch us."

"Whiz! whiz!" went the arrows, striking in the stream, and some on the boat. One buried its barbed head deep in the wood, near Bob, and he shuddered when he saw it. He would rather have been struck by a bullet than by an arrow.

The boat was already moving rapidly, but Cole and Pirtle took the oars and increased the speed. The Indians could be seen running along the bank to keep pace. Part of them were now ahead of the boat, and were gathering at a place, where the cliffs

"As it shot through the mouth of the pass it took a foaming fall"

what difficult task, as the current still pulled, even at the shallow edge of the river, but, finally, they half-beached her on the sand, and tied her stoutly to some dwarf greasewood.

The four, when the task of securing The Columbus was finished, sat down on the sand, and drew deep, mighty breaths of relief.

"Hopin' for the best as I always try to do," said Sam Strong, "I was afraid of the worst when we came through that jug's mouth of a place, with all them Indians whoopin' an' yellin' an' fillin' the air with bullets an' arrows."

"I'd rather look back at it than forward to it," said Obadiah Pirtle, tersely.

"What kind of Indians were they?" asked Bob.

Sam Strong cut one of the arrows from the boat, and examined the sharp stone head critically.

"Utes, I should say," he replied, "an' it's lucky they couldn't get at us any better than they did. The river itself is mighty dangerous, but the banks are so high they mostly keep the Indians out of range."

They decided to remain where they were for the night, and they knew that they were absolutely safe from the Ute band. They were at the east edge of the river and the Utes were on the west bank. The Colorado now flowed between the cliffs high, steep and unbroken, and it was impossible for the warriors to cross it. They had so much faith in this protection that all four went to sleep at once on the boat, leaving no sentinel. Exhaustion gripped them so hard that none awoke until the sun was high the next day, and they decided to remain there until the following morning, especially as they wished to make a critical examination of The Columbus.

The good boat had passed the dangers wonderfully well. Her sides were scarred, where she had grazed the rocks more than once, but no cut was deep enough to require patching, and, the next morning, they set out again, with confidence in the boat and themselves increased.

Then followed a week of extreme danger and great wonders. Bob had scarcely credited to the full the tales of Sam Strong, but he found everything to be true. The river dropped down into a mighty chasm. All that they had seen before was merely the beginning. Now the cliffs, sometimes black basalt, and again red and yellow, rose far above them, so far that even if Indians had been standing on the bank they could not have been told from the shrubs that grew there. It might be a half mile or it might be a mile to the top. No one on the boat could tell.

Nor was the height of the cliffs the only wonder. The storms of the ages had carved them into strange and fantastic shapes. Bob's imaginative mind could make out towers and churches, vaster than any ever built by man, over which the light played in the most vivid fashion, now yellow, now red, now green, and all the blended shades.

All of them began to believe that the story of the subterranean river would prove true. The Colorado, sinking lower and lower, must finally plunge into the earth itself. Presently they might reach cliffs that had no break, no place where they could land, and carried on by the great torrent they must go underground with it. This thought was in the mind of every one of them, but none would speak it.

Their hardships increased also. One day they suffered five hours from a bitter storm of sleet and hail, from which they could not protect themselves, owing to the necessity of being always at the oars. The deep channel of the river, that immense slash in the mountains, seemed to serve as a sort of funnel down which the wind was drawn, shrieking with a power and ferocity that Bob had never heard before, and sending the hail and sleet like volleys from shotguns. Blood was actually drawn more than once from the hands and faces of the four. The river, too, was at its fiercest, demanding every exertion of eye and hand, and the time came when Bob tried to resign himself to death.

But resignation with the boy did not imply giving up. He still struggled at his oar, obeying all the signals of Strong, and after a long time the storm passed, leaving them cold, wet and stiff. Strong brought out a bottle from the stores and made every one take a big drink, but they were still in such a state that they managed The Columbus with difficulty.

Strong grew very anxious. In such a condition they could not fight forever against this ferocious river, and unless they found anchorage they must perish through sheer exhaustion. He compelled Bob, although the boy was very unwilling, to ship his oars, and crawl under the tarpaulin, while he sought for any sign of a break in the cliffs that would afford anchorage.

It was after nightfall when Strong's keen eyes, piercing the dark, saw another canyon entering the mightier one down which the Colorado flowed.

"Hurrah, boys!" he cried. "We've hoped for the best, an' it's happened. All hands to the oars now, an' we'll row up the tributary!"

They swung The Columbus into the second canyon, and found themselves on the bosom of a stream quite different from the Colorado. It was shallow and slow-moving, and when Bob dipped down with a cup he found its waters bitter with salt and brine.

It comes from alkali plains somewhere," said Bill Cole. "A river ought to be ashamed of itself for bein' as dirty an' bitter as this is, but anyway it's doin' us a good turn, an' we oughtn't to complain."

They rowed far up the tributary in the moonlight, but it was nearly midnight before they came to low banks and a good stopping place. There they built two great fires, and sat between them.

"I want to roast myself till I can't stand it any longer," said Sam Strong. "I'd advise you fellows to do the same, an' in the mornin' we'll hold a council."

The question put to the council was very simple: should they go on or turn back? Sam Strong laid down the premises succinctly. They had come hundreds of miles, and they had passed through chasms which must be a mile deep. They had located several good beaver streams to which they could come on future trips. The river would probably grow wilder the further they went, and The Columbus was not adequate for increased risks. As it was, the return trip by land would consume many weeks.

All voted reluctantly to go back, and they began the task at once. They rowed ten or more miles further up the creek, stopping only when the water was too shallow for the boat, which they pushed into some dense shrubbery growing at the water's edge, where it was completely hidden from any one, a yard away.

"We've got to leave the good old Columbus," said Sam Strong. "Maybe we'll find her jest as she is when we come down this way again three or four years from now, an' then she'll be of use."

They rolled up the skin tarpaulin and thrust it into the boat's little cabin. The oars were fastened aboard, and making of their ammunition and remaining supplies four packs, they bade The Columbus farewell.

"Good boat! Strong boat! She's served us well," said Obadiah Pirtle, sententiously.

"Yes, an' I'd like mighty well to go on a thousand miles further, if need be," said Sam Strong, the light of exploration shining in his eyes. "I'd like to be able to tell whether the Colorado goes into the earth or reaches the ocean above ground. Well, it can't be this time."

They now turned toward the northeast, every man carrying his pack, and they found the traveling over wild, rough ranges very slow and difficult. They had come at racing speed like a toboggan down an icy hill, but it was a heavy drag back, inch by inch. They were able, however, to examine the country, and Strong found further encouragement about beaver.

"We can find 'em in here for twenty years to come," he said.

They lived chiefly on the blacktail deer, which they found in abundance on the mountains, and now and then they killed a bear. As they advanced northward, Strong grew anxious about Indians. The country became more open, fit in many places for habitation, and he was sure that the tribes would not neglect such a region.

Strong was right. When they had been traveling about two weeks they saw a great cloud of smoke rising behind a hill to their left. They climbed the hill, and from the shelter of dense pines looked down upon an Indian village of forty or fifty skin tepees. Neither Strong nor Cole could tell to what tribe they belonged, and they did not stay to inquire into the matter.

"We'd better beat one of them masterly retreats Tom an' Porter are always talkin' about," he said. "We haven't got any river here to take us away from them warriors, if they should see us."

The Indians did not see them, and they continued their journey through country in which traveling was very slow. Often they did not make more than five miles a day, and it seemed to Bob that if he climbed one mountain ridge, he climbed a thousand.

They stopped sometimes for two or three days

to hunt or rest, and they utilized one of these occasions to make for themselves new moccasins of deerskin, which they needed badly. Bob had now become quite skilful in all kinds of work. He could sew deerskin with neatness, and moreover he knew how to shape and fashion it. Nearly all the clothing with which he had started from Omaha had disappeared, and he was arrayed in deerskin, which set off his tall, well-knit, active figure. His stature had increased to a considerable degree, and his strength remarkably, during his year with the trappers.

Another week of steady climbing toward the northeast passed, and they came into a country less mountainous, but in the main bleak and sterile. Trees and grass were to be found along the rare little streams, but there were long stretches of country, burnt with lava and absolutely bare. They found game along the streams only, and were compelled to be very careful with their resources.

"Beaver country lies north of here," said Sam Strong one evening when they camped by the side of a brook, so weak that it was barely able to trickle over the sand, "an' we'll strike forests, too."

"I'm glad of it," said Bob. "I'd like to have a little shade."

It had been very hot all the day, and the glare of the sun off the black lava burnt into him. Now he lay against a bowlder, seeking any coolness that the evening might bring.

"'It's a country that's known to trappers to some extent," said Strong. "They've come here several times from some of the border posts, an' Hudson Bay poachers have been in here, too. As our own grounds are private, we don't want to meet any of 'em, an' I'm hopin' for the best."

"So say we all," said Obadiah Pirtle, and a little later Bob fell asleep through sheer exhaustion.

CHAPTER XI

THE COMING OF CARVER

They entered the next day a more desolate country than any they had yet seen, a sea of lava without a trace of vegetation. As Strong remarked, they had to pass through the worst before they could get to the better. Bob glanced down at the hot, black slag that burned through his moccasins.

"This came from a volcano, somewhere," he said, looking at the rounded peaks far away.

"Volcano," said Bill Cole, incredulously. "I've been travelin' through the mountains most all my life an' I ain't ever heard of any belchin' out fire an' smoke and brimstone."

"It isn't that," said Bob, who had not studied his school-books in vain, "it never happened in your time, nor in your grandfather's time. That lava was probably thrown out a couple of million years ago."

Bill Cole laughed with the just scorn of a righteous man.

"You learned that from a book, Bob," he said. 'What happened two million years ago has never appened at all for me. It's jest a part of creation."

All that day the sun burned and blazed, but the ttest part of it was its reflection. The lava med to shoot it back with double strength, and b, although he drew his cap as low down as he could, was unable to protect his face and eyes from the glare. The lava not only grew hotter, but sharper. Despite every precaution, it cut through their moccasins, and their feet were bleeding.

Bob suffered severely. The sun stole his strength, and his head ached. His feet, swollen and torn, gave him great pain. His eyes, made weak by the fiery glare and the dimness, magnified the heat waves before him, but he saw, nevertheless, far mountains which looked dim and cool.

The boy would not utter a word of complaint. He tried to hold himself erect, and to walk with as firm a step as the others, but his head did ache horribly, and his tongue lay like a coal in his mouth. Sam Strong had been watching him with a look sideways, but none the less inclusive, and the frontiersman was a shrewd reader of the human heart. For a long time he said nothing. At last he remarked in a tone apparently careless:

"Well, I'm gettin' my second wind. It comes to some fellows quicker than it does to others, but that don't mean that it will stay the longest. Bob, suppose I carry that pack of yours a spell while I'm so fresh an' gay."

Bob glanced at his chief, and Sam Strong, stalwart, sunburned, the man of a thousand perils, actually blushed right through his brown countenance. The boy understood him and showed that he knew.

"You said, Sam, that I was to be a full partner in the furs," Bob replied, "and I'm going to be a full partner here on the lava, too. You're just about as hot and tired as I am, and your feet are as much cut up, too."

Sam Strong looked down at his moccasins. A red streak ran across each. Then he smiled, and his smile was half kind, half grim.

"Bob," he said, "I'm glad you gave me that answer. You are, as you say, a full partner in everything, an' I won't try to fool you. Come on now, an' we'll see who can walk on the hottest an' sharpest lava without flinchin'."

But it was only a narrow stretch of the lava desert, a spit thrust out from the main body between the mountains, and towards the middle of the afternoon the green slope showed nearer. At twilight it seemed to Bob that he could reach out and touch it, and when the sun was quite gone they were there.

They had reached the foot of the first slope, and in the light night it was the most beautiful mountain that Bob had ever seen. It was cool, shadowy and protecting, a kindly father of mountains. There were only dwarf pines about him, but they appeared splendid after the glare of the lava. His eyes became clear again, and his tongue no longer burned in his mouth.

Just over the first slope they found a beautiful little clear brook, flowing down from snows far away somewhere above the clouds. Bob started to rush for it, but the hand of Sam Strong, falling upon his shoulder, held him back.

"We won't drink it all up right away, Bob," he said, "just a few drops apiece, an' then we'll look to our feet."

They drank moderately of the water which was very cold, and then stripping off their moccasins, buried their feet in it. Bob felt a deep sense of refreshment flowing from his toes to his head. He lifted up his feet, let the water run through his toes, and then, thrusting them back again, laughed like a happy child.

"I ain't as young as you, Bob, an' I ain't laughin'," said Obadiah Pirtle, "but I enjoy it as much."

After a time they drank all the water they wanted and ate cold food from their packs. Then they lay on the ground, in their bare feet, and were happy. They repaired their moccasins by moonlight as best they could, and taking a night's sound sleep, went further into the mountains the next day. Coming to a likely valley, they agreed to separate and hunt for game, which they needed badly. A spring, bubbling up at the base of an old oak, was to be the point of return, and they started, all in different directions.

Bob bore towards the northwest and turned up a little canyon, well lined with oak and ash, pine and cedar. The coolness of the forest and the night's sleep had refreshed him greatly. Frequent bathing of his feet, both night and morning, in the cold water, had taken away the soreness, and he walked now with a strong and elastic tread.

It was a pleasant little canyon, two or three hundred yards wide, with frequent little pools of clear water, and a gentle slope to the enclosing ridges. Here one was almost sure to find game, and the boy's heart leaped with the desire of being the first to return to the camp with deer or wild turkey.

But the hunt led on. Search canyon and trees ever so well, he saw neither deer nor wild turkey. He was far from the camp now, three hours at least, and he neither saw nor heard anything. There was no wind, and the boughs of the trees hung motionless. The boy began to grow discouraged. He did not lose hope that in time he would find game, but his pride in being first would not be gratified.

The canyon turned suddenly almost at a right angle, and as Bob turned the angle, a thick clump of pines, he came face to face with a large man, dark of face and close-set of eyes. The man rushed out, seized Bob's shoulder in a powerful grasp, and began to laugh.

"Well, if it ain't the young sprout!" he exclaimed. "The boy that got away in Omaha with the others, when we lost the scent of the new fur country. What luck!"

Bob had recognized Carver in an instant, but he had hoped that the bully would not remember him. Now the hope was vain. What bad luck indeed! Carver showed his white teeth, while he still held a firm grip upon the boy's shoulder—he was a man of immense strength.

"It's quite sure," continued Carver, "that where you are the others are not far away. Now I knew that Sam Strong was headed for rich beaver streams, known to nobody else, and right there is where I want to go with my men. You will lead us, my boy. This is certainly my lucky day."

Bob was sure that the freebooter's band was not far away. He could see some distance up the canyon, but none of them was in view. He revolved rapidly in his mind some plan of escape. He must give a warning to his comrades, no matter how. But that fierce grip was still on his shoulder. The five fingers of Carver seemed to sink like iron into his flesh.

"Come, boy," said the man, "where are your friends and how far from here are those beautiful beaver streams? Not twenty miles, I'll wager, or I wouldn't find you wandering up this canyon."

"I will not answer either question," replied Bob with energy.

"You won't, won't you?" said Carver. "Well, I'll see that you do. There's an old saying that a bird that won't sing can be made to sing. Talk, I say!"

His fingers pressed right into the boy's shoulder, and pain shot all through him. A sudden passion of rage filled every vein of Bob's body. The passion and the pain together gave him a fierce impulse, backed by double his usual strength. He was held by the left shoulder, but doubling his right fist, he struck the man in the chest with great violence.

Powerful as he was, Carver's grip was torn loose, and despite himself he staggered back. The boy's anger was still at white heat, and now he swung his left fist also, this time full on the man's chin.

Carver staggered again, and fell upon his hands and knees. He remained there only a moment. With the blood dripping from his chin, but lithe and strong as a panther, he sprang to his feet. His rifle, which had been held in his left hand, lay on the ground, but his right hand flew toward the pistol in his belt. It stopped there.

Bob, with every nerve and sense keyed to the highest tension, had sprung back as Carver fell, and now when the freebooter rose he found himself looking into the muzzle of the boy's rifle, not more than five feet away.

"I won't tell you where my comrades are, and I won't tell you where the beaver streams are," said Bob. "I'm a bird that can sing, but you can't make me sing. Take your hand from that pistol or I shoot."

Carver was not a common man. He knew by Bob's eyes, full of excitement and anger, that he meant what he said, and he was too clever to give way to his own passion. His hand came away from the pistol butt, and exercising his great power of self control, he laughed lightly.

"It was a jest," he said. "Of course I didn't mean you any harm, boy. But we are beaver trappers, just like your party, and we ought to join you. Two are stronger than one. I wanted you to lead us to Strong and the others."

Bob looked down the sights of his rifle into the swarthy face and the close-set, cunning eyes. As the man smiled he looked at the long, white teeth which seemed to him to be sharpened as if they had been pointed with a file, and he was not deceived for an instant. The face of Carver made upon his mind an impression exactly like that of a mountain wolf.

"A man's face often lies, and you can see it when it lies," he said. "Yours is lying now. Turn square around at once and walk, or I shoot!"

Carver's face as he heard the words was ugly to see. All his evil passions, to be dragooned thus by a boy, flared forth upon it, but he turned without delay and began to walk away in the other direction. He was hoping that some of his followers would appear. His camp was not more than a couple of miles up the canyon, and one of them might come within sight at any moment. Rarely had his heart been torn by so fierce an anger. It was not endurable to be marched away in this fashion at the gun's muzzle. Black rage swelled the veins of his face. His hand stole again toward the pistol butt, but stopped halfway because he knew the boy with the rifle was watching.

A figure approached among the trees a hundred yards away. Carver, with savage joy, recognized it as that of one of his followers. The man saw his leader walking forward in seeming gravity and with measured step, and then he saw the figure now thirty yards behind him, covering him with leveled rifle. He was acute enough to know that the one with the rifle was a stranger and an enemy. He sprang forward, threw his weapon to his shoulder and fired.

Bob sent his own bullet at almost the same moment, but not at Carver. He could not fire into a man's back. He aimed instead at the man who had aimed at him. Neither bullet struck its target —the pulling of the trigger was too hasty—and

"As it was, Bob heard the bullet singing a little warning in his ear"

these two friends of his looked. He had never noticed before their great height and width, nor their fierce and terrible bearing. They were giants, well come to his rescue.

"It's Carver and his men!" he shouted, rushing toward them. "They want to raid our camp, and they tried to kill me."

Up flew the rifle of Sam Strong and a bullet struck one of the pursuing men in the shoulder. Carver and the three with him instantly fell back. It was one thing to pursue a single boy, but it was quite another to pursue him when two formidable frontiersmen stood by his side, ready to repel attack.

The two parties were now about five hundred yards apart, and stood for a moment or two looking at each other. Then Carver put a whistle to his lips and blew a long, shrill note.

"He's callin' to the rest of his people," said Sam Strong. "Well, we'll call to ours, an' hopin' for the best, I think he'll come, as there ain't but one of him."

He put his fingers to his lips and blew a note almost as loud as that of Carver's whistle. In three minutes they heard a rapid tread in the bush, and soon the lank figure of Obadiah Pirtle hove into view. His swift glance comprehended everything.

"Sorry I'm the last to get here," he said. "But I see that the real work ain't yet actually begun."

"No," said Strong, "nothin' much has been done yet, 'cept by Bob, here, though he ain't had time to tell me what that is, but I think we'll be busy soon. We'll drop back among the rocks."

The canyon was extremely rocky at that point and the four running in among the rocks, dropped down under shelter. Bob was still drawing long breaths, but they were growing shorter, and his lungs were refilling with fresh air. As he lay behind a high crag he briefly told the story of his encounter.

"They think that our beaver skins are stored close by," said Strong. "It's natural that they should think so, seein' that we're here. They expect to wipe out all but one or two of us, an' then make them that are left tell about the furs. Cur'us things, Bob, happen in these mountains, a thousand miles from nowhere, but hopin' for the best, I don't think they'll wipe us out."

"They're gatherin' in strong force," said Bill Cole. "See, the rest of his crowd have come."

It was evident that Cole was right, and that the shots had drawn all of Carver's force. More than twenty men were in the group that was now assembled about a thousand yards away, and in the clear, brilliant sunlight of the Western mountains Bob saw them very distinctly, all strong, sun-browned men, several of them halfbreeds, and two obviously Indians, but of what tribe Bob could not tell.

Carver stood a little in front of the others, and Bob could surmise his feelings. He had seen enough of him to know very well that he was, at bottom, a man of ferocious temper, and he must be raging over his temporary defeat by a boy.

"They'll spread out directly in a half circle," said Sam Strong, "expectin' to get at us that way, but I don't think they'll be able to do it."

Sam was a good prophet, as the freebooters, after a short conference, began to trail off, some to the right and some to the left, excepting Carver and four or five, who remained where they were.

"The party that turned off to the left," said Strong, "will climb up on the mountain side an' try to get our range, but as you remember, Bob, when we were on the Colorado, it's hard to shoot down at a man an' hit him."

Strong spoke quietly, but with a stern certainty in his tone that boded ill for the skirmishers on the slope. Both the leader and Bill Cole were watching the mountainside attentively. The intense burning light threw every rock, tree and shrub into brilliant relief. It seemed to Bob that he could see the convolutions in bark, on trunks a thousand yards away. His heart was beating rather fast, but he had become inured to danger, and he did not tremble. He lay close behind his rock, and was content to wait, having an abiding faith in his leader.

Something moved on the mountainside and a rifle flashed. The bullet struck only the unoffending earth, but another bullet, fired in return at the flash, sped true, and one wilderness outlaw lay down forever in the bush. Sam Strong's face was stern and hard as he thrust another cartridge into his rifle.

"Good shot, Sam," said Bill Cole.

The leader nodded.

"It'll hold 'em a while," said Obadiah Pirtle.

Everything relapsed into quiet, and the rays of the sun came down hotter than ever. Bob saw Carver and the men who had remained with him lie down on the grass, as if they would take their ease just out of rifle-shot, and he began to grow impatient. Waiting was getting upon his nerves. He wanted them to attack, if they were to do so, and have done with it. He moved a little from sheer restlessness.

"Careful, Bob," said Strong, "you're showin' yourself to them that are on the other side of the canyon."

Bob hastily drew back within the shelter of the rock, and not a moment too soon. A bullet, fired from the opposite side of the canyon, knocked up the earth where his knee had been. Both Cole and Pirtle fired in reply, but they did not hit their man. Nevertheless, he and his comrades were compelled to retreat swiftly.

"They won't try to get at us in that way again," said Sam Strong. "Too dangerous."

Strong was right again, and no other visible movement occurred for a long time. Then it came in a manner that they least expected. Carver walked deliberately down the canyon toward them, waving an old white handkerchief on the muzzle of his rifle. Strong expressed his frank astonishment.

"Now, I'd like to know what's at work in his brain," he exclaimed. "Comin' with a white flag. That means that he wants to talk to us. I'm hopin' for the best, but I hardly hope that he means to apologize. Anyhow, we'll let him say his say."

Strong came from cover and sat down on a rock in a comfortable position. Carver walked on boldly. Bob could not keep from admiring his easy bearing and air of confidence. It was quite evident that Carver was a man of quality, although the quality might be wicked. He came within about thirty paces, dropped his rifle stock to the ground, and leaned gracefully on the muzzle, old handkerchief and all.

"Hello, Strong," he said in quite a genial tone. "I've got a few things to say."

"You've got all the time there is to say 'em in," said Strong drily, "an' we're listenin', so go ahead."

"You're fur hunters and so are we," said Carver. "Good fur grounds and beaver streams ain't any too plenty now, as you know. But you and the fellows with you have made a big find somewhere in these parts. There ain't a doubt about it, and we want to be in on it. We're just bound to be in on it. Now, I lay it to you, fair and square. You take us in as partners, and we'll all divide even. You've just laid out one of my men, but I don't mind that. There'll be fewer to share. You need a strong party. Indians are troublesome, and are going to be more so. Few as you are you could never get back across the plains with your furs, even if you were so lucky as to reach the plains."

He paused as if he wished his words to sink in, but the face of the leader did not change a particle.

"That's our affair," said Sam tersely. "What's the other side?"

"The other won't be so pleasin' to you. It says that if you don't accept the first, we'll come an' take your furs. We're strong enough to do it, an'

I don't know of any law in these parts that will keep us from it."

"No, there ain't no law," said Sam, "'cept that of our rifles, an' I want to say that I've listened to you, Juan Carver. Now, havin' considered the question for all of half a second, an' speakin' for my partners, whose feelin's I know without askin', I've got to say that we choose rifles, hopin', at the same time, Juan Carver, that it won't hurt your feelin's."

Strong's tone was too decisive to admit of doubt, and Carver accepted it in a jaunty manner.

"A man always has his choice," he said, "an' you've made yours, though it's a bad one."

"I'm hopin' for the best," said Sam Strong.

CHAPTER XII

THE GREAT LAUGH

Carver walked back toward his men in the same graceful, careless manner. When he reached them he talked a moment with one, probably a lieutenant, and then disappeared further up the canyon, but the rest remained there on guard. Sam Strong removed himself from the rock where he had sat motionless throughout the negotiations, and laughed drily when he lay down upon the ground.

"Carver must have thought we were fools, when he made an offer like that," he said. "He knew that if we accepted it, we'd keep it an' that he wouldn't."

"What are we going to do now?" asked Bob.

"It depends a good deal on what they do. If the night comes on thick an' black we can slip away. Our packs are not more than two miles from here down the canyon. We can pick them up an' then light out for our real camp, where Louis and the two generals are."

Now came a long period of waiting and suspense that was very trying to Bob. Carver returned to the group in the canyon, but he made no movement, sitting down on the ground, apparently idling the time away. After two or three hours a little skirmishing was done, but it was at long range. The freebooters fired several shots, but they did not strike anywhere near, and Obadiah Pirtle fired one in return, which also found no target except the round earth. Then they relapsed into silence, and after a while Bob saw that the sun was setting. The dark haze spread slowly at first, and then so fast that the eastern mountains were gone, and the night was near. The four crept more closely together and held a council in whispers.

"It ain't our business to be fightin' a gang like that out there," said Sam Strong. "What we want to do is to be busy trappin' beaver. If we can slip away they'll spend all of a year roamin' 'roun' through these parts lookin' for us an' our furs, while we're far away gettin' more."

They decided not to make the attempt until after midnight. Carver and his men would naturally expect it earlier, and after long and disappointed waiting their vigilance would be relaxed.

"An' if they undertake to move on us we'll be sure to hear 'em, even if we don't see 'em," said Sam Strong, confidently.

Bill Cole and Pirtle seemed to agree with him, as they stretched themselves at ease on the ground, although Bob observed that each kept an ear to the earth. He had so much confidence in them that he fell asleep. He was awakened by a rifle-shot. But when he sat up with sleep still heavy upon him, Sam Strong told him that the shot had been merely a warning.

"They undertook to creep near," he said, "an' I fired at the sound. I didn't hit anything, but it was enough to make 'em go back, which was all we wanted."

Bob fell asleep a second time, and when he was awakened again it was the hand of Sam Strong on his shoulder that did it.

"We're ready to go, boy," he said, "an' it's makin' no noise that will do it if we do it. I'm goin' to lead, you come right after me, Obe follows you, an' Bill brings up the rear. It would certainly be a great joke on 'em if we slipped right away, leavin' 'em here holdin' the basket an' knowin' no different. If we all hope for the best together maybe we can bring off the joke."

"I'm hoping with you," whispered Bob.

"I'm hopin', too," whispered Obadiah Pirtle.

"Me, too," came the whisper of Bill Cole.

Without further words they slipped away along the mountainside, every one stepping so lightly that no sound arose as they passed. It was dark and the bush was thick, but Bob's pride was once more to the fore. If any one stumbled, or broke a stick under his foot, or made the bushes rustle, he was resolved that it should not be he who stumbled or broke a stick under his foot or made the bushes rustle. He was clever enough now to see how it could be done. He was careful to step exactly in the tracks of Sam Strong, who was only a yard ahead of him, and as he did not look back he did not know that Obadiah Pirtle and Bill Cole followed this example, not from resolution, but from long training that had become habit and intuition.

When they had gone a hundred yards or so Sam Strong suddenly stopped. It was long a matter of pride with the boy that he did not run into the leader, but stopped noiselessly and in time, with a clear foot of space between them. The two behind him stopped automatically. Sam Strong turned slowly and looked in turn at Bob, Obadiah and Bill. The moonlight, faint though it was, was sufficient at that short range to disclose his face. Sam Strong, frontiersman, grim veteran of a thousand dangers, was laughing. No sound came from his lips, but he was laughing with every feature. The corners of his mouth turned up, his eyes were all mirth, and even the tip of his nose seemed to take a jocund tilt.

"The joke is comin' off," he said in the softest of whispers. "The greatest joke these mountains have ever known is about to be played. I felt it in all my bones that it was goin' to happen when we hoped together for the best. Raise up about four inches an' look down there to the right."

They rose to the ordered height and gazed over the tops of some bushes into a little ravine that evidently led into the canyon. Bob's pulses jumped when he saw half a score of men, Carver at their head and rifles in their hands, stealing forward.

"They're ambushin' the place where we ain't," said Strong in the same soft whisper, "an' as many more, comin' from other points, are doin' the same. Well, luck to you, boys. You'll get to that spot without bein' shot. But by the great horn spoon, the joke is on you all the same."

His face contracted again in a great spasm of silent laughter, and the infection passed down the line. The corners of Bob's mouth crinkled up,

Obadiah Pirtle bent a little further forward and rubbed one hand appreciatively across his stomach, Bill Cole's eyes became like those of a child seeing his first clown at a circus.

Thus they stood motionless, while the attacking party filed by in the little canyon below them. Sam Strong cast a glance at the last man as he disappeared, and when the shadow was gone in the darkness, the leader dropped a heavy, sinewy hand over his own mouth. It was necessary. A great laugh struggling in his throat longed for vocal expression, and this was the only way in which he could keep it down. Not until he felt that he had acquired reasonable control did he take the hand away, and then he used it for making a signal to his comrades that they should move on.

Strong led a little higher up the slope of the mountain, crept another fifty yards, and the second time gave the signal to stop. Then he pointed through the bushes, and they saw another group of freebooters stealing upon the place that they had left. It was evident that the band of Carver were approaching it as the spokes of a wheel meet at the hub.

"The joke grows," whispered Strong. "By the great horn spoon, it is cert'nly the fanciest one that ever happened!"

The second detachment disappeared, stealing down upon the defenseless rocks, and when they were well out of sight the four sped swiftly along the mountain side. When they were a mile away they turned, descended into the canyon, passed by their camp, recovered their packs, and then leaving the canyon, entered the mountains again.

Now not a word was said. The marching was not so bad, as it was a fairly gentle slope, and their eyes had grown used to the darkness. Sam Strong led silently on one hour, two hours, three hours, until he came to a little hollow on the slope, where he stopped abruptly. The night had now lightened considerably, a good moon riding low in the heavens, and all the features of every face were visible to one another.

"Here we bust!" said Sam Strong.

"Let her rip!" said Bill Cole.

Sam Strong threw back his head, opened his mouth and shot forth a gigantic laugh, not a laugh of recent birth, a raw fledgling of a laugh, with only ordinary body and substance, but a laugh that had started four hours before, a laugh that had been nourished and vitalized every minute of that time, a laugh that was mighty, uncontrollable, that came rolling forth in wave after wave, every one higher than its predecessor.

Bill Cole and Obadiah laughed, too, and in zest and volume and true spontaneity their laughs were but little inferior to that of the leader. Then the three laughs united, harmonious, and making one note, swept along the mountainside and came back in a musical echo. Tears gathered in the eyes of the men, but they were happy tears. The three bent forward, but it was not with the weight of years, it was with the weight of mirth.

Bob laughed, too. He was compelled to do so,

but his was rather an undernote, a minor strain, as it were, in the grand diapason, and it was influenced somewhat by the laugh of the others, while theirs was strictly original, having its cause in the scenes that they had witnessed four hours before.

The grand united laugh swelled to the zenith and then began to sink. Its waves rolled up less violently, the echoes became softer, and then died away. Then all ceased, as if by preconcerted action, and looked at one another.

"By the great horn spoon, it was cert'nly worth it!" said Sam Strong. "To think of Juan Carver and his men ambushin' some cold rocks, an' we a dozen miles away. I couldn't hold that laugh in another minute."

"Nor me," said Bill Cole.

"Nor me," said Obadiah Pirtle.

Bob gazed at his comrades in some curiosity. They were certainly men of the wilderness, and their jokes were those of the wilderness. But he said nothing. He was too happy to be asking questions.

"In case some wanderin' Indian, coyote or somethin' else that don't like us heard our laughin' we'll move on a couple of miles an' then rest," said Sam Strong.

They walked the appointed distance, and found a pleasant place in a clump of pines where they slept, the four by turns taking the watch until noon. Then they decided to pursue the journey to their mountain home, as if nothing had happened.

"Carver hasn't the least notion which way we've gone," said Strong, "an' he can't trail us over mountains. So we'll march an' wish 'em joy with their hunt down here."

They now passed days of marching and exertion, but they were pleasant to Bob. There was much climbing over rocks and mountain ridges, and often it was mercilessly hot, but they were rarely far from wood and water, and they found abundant game. They felt so safe, too, that several times they turned from their line of march to look for beaver streams. They were successful in locating two, and Sam Strong marked them carefully on the map of tanned deerskin that he carried inside his hunting shirt.

"May need 'em some day," he said, tersely.

The journey still led peacefully onward, and to Bob it was like a long ramble, the most interesting trip that any one had ever undertaken. He had shot the rapids of the Colorado between mighty cliffs, more than a mile high—not knowing that others yet higher were below—and now he was returning through magnificent mountains, some of which no white man perhaps had ever seen before.

The boy's imagination was greatly stirred. Besides being a fur-hunter and man of arms, he was an explorer, too. He tried to surmise the height of the peaks, and he named the highest of them all Mt. Strong. A huge hog-back he called Cole Ridge, and the title Pirtle Crest was bestowed upon a singularly slender, but tall peak.

"It's good of you, Bob, an' mighty flatterin',"

said Sam Strong, "but them names won't stick. By an' by some feller from the East, wearin' big glasses an' carryin' measurin' instruments, will see our mountains, go back to the east, announce that he has discovered 'em, an' give 'em new names. Mt. Strong, Cole Ridge an' Pirtle Crest will fade right away like snow under the sun."

"That may be, but they will have been named right for a little while, at least," said Bob, loyally.

They crossed several rivers, mostly shallow and always cold, and on a beautiful golden day in late summer they reached their own creek and went up the little valley. It seemed to Bob that they had been away for ages, and he wondered if they would find the three comrades whom they had left behind alive and well. Some such thought was in the minds of the others, but they did not disclose it. Yet as they went up the valley they looked about very anxiously, lest they should see signs of a strange and hostile presence.

Everything was as they had left it, and as it should be. There was no smoke of an enemy on the horizon, no trail of a numerous band ran through the woods, there was no place where the camp of a war party had been. The very wind told of seclusion and peace, and at last they approached the good cabin that they had built the year before. The roof first came into the view of their knowing eyes, and then glimpses of the rough walls.

They saw no human being, but as they came nearer a most grateful odor assailed their nostrils.

"I've been hopin' for the best, an' it cert'nly has

come to pass," said Sam Strong. "That's the smell of a deer steak, bein' cooked by Louis Perolet. I'll bet, too, that the 'generals' are in there with him, an' as the window is wide open, we'll slip up to it an' see what they are doin' before we have ourselves announced at the front door by the butler."

They trod very softly, and gaining the window, listened.

"Now, as I was tellin' to you, Louis, seein' that you're a Frenchman an' ain't informed, at the Battle of the Wilderness old Grant came hammerin' down with 'bout ten hundred thousand men, expectin' to smash us to flinders, blow us away, eat us up alive, an' do a lot of other things sudden an' unexpected, but General Bob Lee was there, a splendid, big man, ridin' at the front of our army on a gray horse, an' when he saw old Grant an' his million comin' he looked 'round at his army, Gen'ral Bob Lee did, an' he says in a loud voice: 'Is Porter Evans here?' an' some one answers also in a loud voice: 'He is.' Then says Gen'ral Bob Lee: 'Forward march; let the battle begin', an' then we gave 'em the most awful lickin' that was ever give to one army by another army."

"Don't you believe him, Louis. That Porter Evans ain't fit to write history. His fancy is so bright an' hot it burns facts right up. At the Battle of the Wilderness we didn't let more than ten thousand rebels get away. I remember takin' one general with my own hands, an' him all covered with gold lace, besides so many colonels an' captains that I forgot to count 'em."

"*Mon Dieu,* how you two fellows brag, you Yankee an' you rebel! What was your Grant, and what was your Lee to the great Napoleon? With his valiant Frenchmen, *grands soldats*, he conquered all Europe, every inch of it. He had kings and queens to do—what you call it?—eat breakfast out of his hand every morning. He frowns in Paris, an' the next minute the Czar in St. Petersburg an' the King in London shake all over with fear. He smiles, an' the next minute there is not a cloud in all Europe, not one so leetle as my hand. He is sitting at his grand council with his councilors an' secretaries an' one dozen kings an' queens sharpenin' the pens an' pencils for him, when a boy rush in with a telegram. He open it an' read an' say: 'Excuse me for two days, I have to go out an' whip the Emperor of Austria'."

"But, Louis, there was no telegraph in those days."

"What, you think a poor, leetle man like you can get a telegram an' the great Napoleon not get one? You do not understan', Meester Tom Harris, that the great Napoleon was the greatest of all the great men the world has ever known."

"An' all three of you can lay down your arms an' surrender right here. Bless your ugly faces!" called out Sam Strong, suddenly thrusting his head in at the open window.

The three uttered cries of surprise, then of joy, and presently there was a mighty shaking of hands.

CHAPTER XIII

THE DEPARTURE

"I'm thinkin' that we arrived just in time," said Sam Strong, after the ferment had been stilled somewhat. "'Pears to me that the great Napoleon was jest about to wipe out all the rest of the world when we peeked in at the window."

"We'd have come back at him," said Porter Evans. "While me an' Tom here can't agree about the Civil War, Tom bein' so obstinate that he won't ever see the truth, we'd have united to down him. You did come just in time, just in time to save Frenchy."

Louis Perolet grinned. It was no ordinary grin. He had an expansive face, admirably adapted to grinning, large, white, even teeth, a wide mouth that stretched like rubber, and wonderful shining eyes. Now that expressive countenance was taxed to the utmost to show his joy. All his friends had come back sound and well, and the heart of Louis Perolet danced within him.

"Ah!" he exclaimed, "I am so glad to see you I go cook you more steak! I go cook you whole deer."

"Well," laughed Sam Strong, "we're just about hungry enough to eat one."

While Perolet prepared a grand banquet, they told of their adventures, and many long, deep breaths were drawn by the hearers as the narrative proceeded. Louis looked up from his fire in amazement when they told of rushing down the Colorado between cliffs of dizzy height.

"A river with banks a hundred miles high! What a wonder!" he exclaimed. "An' the great Napoleon never saw it."

Sam Strong laughed in unctuous delight.

"No," he said, "that is one of the things the great Napoleon missed. The banks were somethin' stu-pen-je-ous, Louis, but I reckon they weren't all of a hundred miles high."

The three who had stayed at home made angry gestures when they heard of Carver and his attempts, but they laughed also when Sam Strong told how the four had stolen away.

"That was cert'nly a good trick, Sam," said Tom Harris. "I can hear Carver swearin' now, when he an' his gang bore down on that hidin' place of yours, an' it as empty as a last year's bird nest."

Not much had happened in the canyon during their absence; as it was the summer season the men did no trapping, but they took an occasional bearskin. They had drawn little from their stores, living almost wholly upon game, and the horses had grazed on the meadows. There could be no doubt, however, that the beaver were still plentiful, and another great season of fur-taking was assured. The party, now reunited, would pass the remainder of the warm weather waiting for it.

Bob had enjoyed the great adventure, the trip down the sunken river, and the return through the high mountains, but he was glad to be back again in their pleasant valley, down the center of which ran the pleasant creek, with the pleasant meadows and woods on either shore. He renewed his acquaintance among the horses. Not one of them had died. All were as fat as butter, and Porter Evans and Tom Harris listened with deep content to his words of admiration.

"Yes," said Porter, "we've took good care of them. I'm a handy man among horses, an' by hard work an' stayin' reg'lar on the job, I've managed to teach Tom a little about 'em, too."

Tom Harris laughed scornfully.

"Port," he said, "you didn't know the difference between a horse an' an elephant till I showed you."

Not much of the summer was left, but they spent the remainder of it enlarging their cabin with another room, which they intended to devote wholly to the storing of furs. The completion of the task and the result gave them all great satisfaction.

"That's a fine, big house," said Obadiah Pirtle. "I ain't seen any other like it in these parts."

"Ah, eet ees the Versailles of the mountains," exclaimed Louis Perolet, triumphantly.

"Versy-y! what's that, Frenchy?" asked Bill Cole.

"Eet ees a grand palace, built a long time ago by Louis Quatorze, a great Frenchman, though not so great as the great Napoleon."

"We would say Versailles in this country, just as if that last syllable were spelled s-a-l-e-s," said Bob, "and we might as well name it Versailles, pronouncing it that way. Would you feel insulted, Louis, if we did so?"

"Not at all! not at all!" replied Perolet, proudly. "Eet ees the preevelege of other nations to name their attempts after the grand achievements of France."

So it became Versailles with the pronunciation of the last syllable as if it were spelled s-a-l-e-s, and now the second autumn was at hand. Again the forest reddened on the slopes; again a crisp sparkle came into the translucent air, and in the evening it was pleasant to hover somewhere near the glow of a fire. Now the trapping was resumed with great vigor and energy. They ranged further and further in pursuit of the beaver.

Heavy snows came later, and the winter was not so open as the preceding one had been, but they made snow-shoes for themselves, and still trapped with unfailing success. In such manner the cold months passed, filled with work, not untinged with danger because the mountain wolves were often numerous and always fierce, and when on long hunts the probability of snowslides was always present. But success, continued success, infused everything with a rosy tint, and the time seemed short to them all when spring came.

The snows broke up with a mighty pouring of water down the slopes. Their pleasant, peaceful creek became a raging torrent, and it was many days before it subsided into its old channel. Then the snow being left only on the crests and upper ridges, an important question was laid before the

Council of Seven, held in their Palace of Versailles in the spring of 1868.

The discovery of fine beaver streams, far down the Colorado, had turned in the minds of all the men throughout the winter. Some thought it might be better to cache the furs they now had in stock, go down to the new region, trap for another year, and then return to civilization, carrying at once the product of both territories. Others thought it might be the safer plan to go at once to the market with what they had, and then return direct to the new streams. Sam Strong inclined to the latter view, but he wished the whole party to be in agreement.

The session of the Council of Seven in their Palace of Versailles was long and arduous. Many astute arguments were produced on either side. The merits of the immediate return were shown, and so were those of the suggestion to go down the Colorado for another year. Shrewd trapping intellects were on either side, and so well did they debate that Sam Strong, President of the Council of Seven in their Palace of Versailles felt that the scales did not incline either way. With such a condition facing him he felt that he could not give any decision.

"We'll just wait a little while," he said. "Anyway it's too early to start. But we'll bale our furs, ready for the cache or the pony's back, whenever we do decide."

The work of packing took some time, and it was varied with an occasional hunt. One, by Bob and

Louis Perolet, took them far down the creek to its mouth at the river.

It was the warmest day that they had yet felt, with a pleasant southwestern wind and a sheer blue sky. The trees along the slopes and in the valley were bursting into green, and as they went along and the springtide rose high in their veins, Bob caroled lustily an old ditty that he had learned from Sam Strong:

"Railroad's too diggin'
Gamblin's too low,
If I go to stealin'
To Frankfort I must go."

The mountain ridges gave back the fresh, young voice in pleasant echoes, and Louis Perolet looked approvingly at his young companion.

"Eet ees good to hear you sing, Meester Bob," he said, "you do not have the wonderful voice, you would not make your fortune at the opera in Paris, but you have youth an' you have happiness, an' when I hear you sing so I have youth an' I have happiness, too. Now, Meester Bob, I hear Meester Sam Strong sing that song before. What does he mean by 'to Frankfort I must go'?"

"Sam is from Kentucky, Louis, and the penitentiary is at Frankfort, the capital of the state. There's a lot of deep philosophy in that song. He can't work on a railroad, it's too hard; gambling is not respectable; if he steals, off to prison with him, so he comes out here and turns trapper."

"Meester Sam Strong one smart man, fit to be a soldier of the great Napoleon."

Bob threw back his head and laughed joyously, and Louis Perolet, because he too was joyous, also threw back his head and laughed.

They had not yet reached the river, while this talk was going on, but in fifteen minutes more they were in the thick woods, from which they could look down upon the larger stream, and the Frenchman, uttering a sharp little cry, put his hand upon the boy's shoulder.

"Look, Meester Bob," he said. "Look down the river!"

Bob looked, and, far down the stream, he saw four moving dots that he knew to be boats. As he looked they grew larger. Drops of water, glistening like silver in the brilliant sunshine, fell from moving oars, swung by strong arms. Figures grew into outline, and he saw that each boat contained eight or nine men. Nearer they came, and the boy saw that while some of the faces were red most of them were white. One of the figures in the boat he recognized by the set of the head and the swing of the shoulders. It was no less a personage than Juan Carver.

Louis Perolet felt the boy's shoulder quiver under his grasp.

"Eet ees the wicked Juan Carver, ees eet not?" he asked.

"Yes, it is he," replied Bob. "I'd know him a mile away. He has come with the band to take our furs."

"Eet ees so," said Louis Perolet, "but remember, Meester Bob that he has not yet found us. The mouth of our creek is narrow. Eet ees hid also by bushes an' reeds, an' tall grass. They do not know that eet ees here an' they may pass. We will wait an' see."

Kneeling down in a thicket, where they could not possibly be seen from the river, the two watched, with beating hearts. If they saw the mouth of the creek and turned into it, as was possible, because along such streams the beaver was found, there was nothing for them to do but hurry to the cabin, give the alarm and arrange for the defense. But if they passed on—then time would be left for many things.

It is not often that every sweep of an oar is watched so eagerly, but Bob believed afterward that he saw every blade as it flashed. He could now see Carver distinctly. The man sat upright in the prow, a cone-shaped, broad-brimmed Mexican hat crowning his head. But he seemed to be looking straight up the stream, and the other three boats, with their hard-faced crews, followed straight behind him.

Bob drew an imaginary line, extending from the mouth of the creek to the other shore, and he measured the distance yet left between it and the leading boat. Allowing for the perspective of distance it was more than a hundred yards and alas! Carver could not but see!

Yet they went straight on up the stream, thirty yards more, forty, fifty, sixty, and then the boy's heart went down like a plummet in a pool. The leading boat checked its speed, and Bob was sure that it was going to turn, but one of the oarsmen had merely caught a crab. In an instant the full speed of the boat was resumed, and the others still came behind it in a straight line. Bob saw Carver turn his head, but he knew that he was rebuking the careless oarsman and was not drawn by the hidden mouth of the creek—at least not yet.

The sunlight seemed to grow more intense and brilliant. The bubbles that fell from the blades of the oars were now silver, now gold as the light fell upon them. Not twenty yards separated the boat of Carver from the imaginary line that Bob had drawn across the river. Now it was only ten, then the boat was upon it and passed on, the others still following in a straight line behind it.

A great sigh of relief burst from Bob, and Louis did not notice it because a sigh of about the same size burst from him also. The boats which had steadily been growing larger so long were now steadily becoming smaller at exactly the same pace, and to both Bob and Louis it was a beautiful sight to see—the gradual diminution of those boats.

"They didn't dream that we were here, that the beaver were here or that the creek was here," said Louis, "but that eesn't any sign that they won't come back to-morrow or a week from now. They are hunting all through this region an' we can't remain hidden. Een a great crisis the great Napoleon always did the best thing that was to be done, an' eemitating him we, too, will do the best thing that is to be done. We will rush back home an' warn Meester Sam an' the others."

They covered the long distance to their Palace of Versailles quicker than ever before, and found Sam Strong sitting before the door, scraping some fresh skins. The leader looked up when he heard their hurried footsteps, and a single swift glance was sufficient to tell him that they had something important to say. But he went calmly on, scraping the inside of a skin.

"We've seen Carver," said Bob, panting.

Sam Strong's eyes flashed, but he did not stop his knife.

"Where?" he asked, casually.

"On the river; he had a large party in boats, thirty at least. We were near the mouth of the creek, and we saw them coming up the stream."

"Are they in our creek now?"

"No, they did not see it. They passed on."

Sam Strong shut up his clasp knife, thrust it into his pocket, and sat up quickly.

"They'll come back some time or other," he said, "an' if we stay here long enough they'll find us. Our question is settled. We've got to leave at once for the plains, and our market. We can get ready and start to-night."

He put two fingers on his lips and emitted a shrill whistle. In a few minutes Bill Cole and Obadiah Pirtle came down through the woods, and presently Tom Harris and Porter Evans also approached. Sam Strong laid the case before them, and the decision was unanimous. They would go eastward, and their going would be immediate.

The horses were led from their corral or gathered

from the meadows. Most of them, having led a life of idleness and luxury so long, fought against lariat and pack, but the two "generals" soon reduced them to submission. The bales of furs were so numerous now that they and the supplies made a load for every horse. The trappers themselves intended to walk, at least until they reached the plains.

Then they dismantled Versailles as far as they could, hiding some things under stones, where wolf or bear could not reach them, and just at the twilight were ready for departure. It was with real sorrow that Bob regarded their big, comfortable cabin, the doors and windows of which they had secured tightly in order to keep out prowling wild animals.

"It's been a genuine palace, a real Versailles to us," he said, "and I hate to leave it."

"We may find it again some day just as it is, the seven of us just as we are," said Sam Strong, "leastways, by hopin' for the best, I feel that we will."

"Good-by to our home," said sentimental Louis Perolet. "It has sheltered us from many a storm. *Au revoir.*"

He took off his hat and waved it at the motionless building in the dusk. All the others did the same, and then turning their faces eastward, they trudged up the creek, the file of ponies, loaded with their riches, following close behind.

Bob glanced back once, but the stout log house was lost in the dusk. It was not until then that he realized fully the task upon which they had embarked. He was going back to fences, towns and many people. For the last two years this little world of the mountains was so sufficient to him that he never thought of the other, outside. He was returning with a sense of immense distance, not only in space, but in time and manners as well. But he resolved that he would not stay there. He had found companionship and satisfaction with these men. They, in a sense, had made him an equal, on the second and perhaps greater expedition far down the Colorado. He clutched his father's rifle more tightly, and with such brave comrades felt equal to any danger.

Their way led up the valley over the natural trail by which they had entered it, and for a long time they walked in silence save for the tread of the horses. The moon came out, the stars twinkled, and they saw clearly the ranges and peaks, and the slopes clothed with forest now turning green.

"There's one thing I hate about this," said Sam Strong, "an' that's to run away from a fellow like Juan Carver an' his crowd. By the great horn spoon, it would make my marrow jump to know that he was back there, sittin' in our palace, toastin' his feet on our hearthstone."

"Nevaire min'," said Louis Perolet, consolingly, "eet was the tactics of the great Napoleon to go away from a place when eet suited him, an' to come back again also when it suited him."

"I suppose you're right, Louis," grumbled Sam, "an' if we are followin' your Napoleon we are followin' the right kind of a leader. Some day I'll take a shot at that Juan Carver that will keep him from ever troublin' anybody else."

They left the creek valley after two hours of steady traveling, and entered a side cleft of the mountains, along which they led the horses for about two hours more, always rising. They encamped about midnight, finding it much colder than it had been in their valley, but for fear of a warning to possible enemies, they did not build any fire. The horses were all tethered, and the men rolled themselves in their blankets. The journey was resumed early the next morning, and for a week they went on without trouble or incident. Then they were compelled to stop a while to rest the loaded horses, some of which were growing footsore. Fortunately they found plenty of grass and water, and being in no hurry they took a rest of their own also.

They continued to follow in the main the trail by which they had come, and as they had an excellent sense of locality and direction, they were able to avoid difficulties that they had encountered before. For the last great range they chose the same pass that they had used on the outward trip. They knew now of one lower, but they avoided it, as Carver and his men, or others equally as dangerous, might be traveling that way.

"An' there's one thing I want to tell you, Bob," said Sam Strong, as they climbed towards the snow line, "if you see a nice, easy precipice to fall over don't you fall. There mayn't be enough soft snow at the bottom to break your fall, an' even if there was enough, you might never find us ag'in. Now, Bob, promise you won't do it ag'in, an' we'll all hope for the best."

Bob laughed at the banter which he knew was wholly good-natured.

"I give my faithful promise," he replied. "One exploit of that kind is enough for me."

There was plenty of snow in the heights of the pass, but they had a better knowledge of the way now. Here the loads of the horses became extremely heavy, and they moved at a very slow pace. Fortunately they encountered no blizzard, which was what they feared most, but every one felt immense relief when they descended the last slope on the other side, and now had before them only the vast rolling plains which extended to their destination, but which, nevertheless, swarmed with great dangers as they were soon to learn.

While they were in a pleasant valley, allowing the horses to recuperate after the great climb, a lone trapper wandered into their camp. He informed them that the war with the Cheyennes was still going on, that in fact it was at its height. Roman Nose and Black Kettle, their famous chiefs, had won some victories, and the passage of the plains was never more dangerous.

"An' it'll be all the harder for you because you carry such a load," added the trapper, glancing admiringly at the numerous bales of beaver fur.

"Yes, I s'pose so," said Sam Strong, "though I'm hopin' for the best."

"I know you won't tell me where you got 'em," said the trapper, "but you must have found some fine streams."

"You're right both ways," said Sam with a laugh.

"I think I'll go look for them creeks," said the trapper.

"All right," said Sam. "Creeks in the mountains are always free to them that can find 'em."

The trapper, an honest, open fellow, was as good as his word. He spent a night with them and departed the next morning on foot to look for the beaver streams.

"You just watch out for them Cheyennes," he called back. "They are buzzin' on the plains like hornets, an' they sting."

His words made an impression that stayed in Bob's mind.

CHAPTER XIV

IN CHEYENNE HANDS

They traveled many days, often at night in order to avoid the heat, as it was now midsummer, and their way led over the rolling swells with which Bob had become familiar two years before. They shot buffalo and antelope occasionally, but rarely turned aside to hunt, and never for more than a short distance. The grass turned quite brown under the strong sun, and the soil grew hard from the lack of rain. Nevertheless, they twice saw the clear trail of Indian ponies, and Strong and Cole reckoned that on each occasion at least one hundred warriors had passed. Obviously it was a time for anxiety, and all of them felt it.

Bob's lively imagination, impressed already by the trapper's warning, created a cloud before them, and this cloud was made of Indian warriors. It was not fear, it was merely his vivid brain that insisted upon making pictures. He had seen the Cheyennes once, and at close quarters, too, and he knew that they were formidable foes. He was continually searching the plains for a sight of the Dog Soldiers, rising under the horizon.

"These plains are so bright and they can see us so far," said Sam Strong, "that I'd like to ride through thick clouds all the way to the settlement. Still I'm hopin' for the best as much as ever."

They made several wide curves to avoid regions that seemed to be infested by the warriors, and the waning summer found them still on the plains in the Indian country, but down now towards the southeast. Barring the midday heat, the weather was good for traveling, as it had been very dry, and they were never forced to spread a tent. Game, previously so plentiful, now became scarce, and all of them pined for fresh buffalo or deer. There had been no sign of an Indian trail for more than ten days, and all agreed that it was safe to undertake a short hunt. Evans and Harris remained with the ponies, and the others went off in different directions. Since they had come upon the plains, and traveling had been easier for the ponies, they had been riding most of the time.

The country was rather more rolling than usual. Dip followed dip, and before they had gone five hundred yards Bob lost sight of the camp. Horses and men could remain concealed as long as they stayed in one dip, but when they moved on they could be seen every time they topped a swell. He saw the others in the hunt several times as they rose upon these crests, but as he rode further and further he lost sight of them entirely.

It looked like a game country, but he found nothing. There was not a sign of buffalo or deer or antelope. Not a Jack rabbit scurried away before him, but Bob retained his great pride. He would not go back to the camp with hands empty when they needed game so badly. If one only persisted one would always win, and so he rode on and on, not realizing how many miles he had gone.

He noticed at length that the ground was rising, and that before him lay the sharpest and highest ridge he had seen in many days. He had an idea that beyond this ridge was a shallow valley, likely to contain grass and better game, and his spirits rose sharply. He urged his pony forward at a greater pace, and he was soon at the crest of the ridge. Then he saw that he had made the greatest mistake of his life.

But he was right, too, in his original surmise. A shallow valley lay beyond the dip, and it did contain better grass, but instead of the game that he wished to see, there was a numerous band of Indian warriors, some in camp, with their ponies cropping the turf, and others on horseback, just returning from some point and about to start for another.

Bob instantly turned his horse about, hoping that he had not been seen, but his hope was in vain. A dozen of the mounted warriors shouted, and at once urged their ponies into pursuit, guiding them by a pressure of the knee, their naked bodies glistening in the sun, rifles and lances shaken by uplifted hands, in anticipation of this prize which had literally ridden into their arms.

Bob struck his horse and shouted to him. The animal flew across the swell. If he could only outride his pursuers, and warn his comrades, they might get away in time. But before he had gone twenty rods a great thought was born in the boy's mind. It was a compound of idealism, chivalry and gratitude. The warriors were coming so fast that he could never leave them out of sight. He owed all to these men who had taken him, a friendless boy, into their band. He had resolved over and over again that if the time ever came he would repay them. The time had come now, and a wild thrill shot through every vein as he began to keep the resolve of many days. There was a strain of high poetry and exaltation in his nature, and when he took the step he never flinched.

Bob gradually turned his pony towards the northwest, and soon he was riding directly away from his own camp. He might not save himself, but he could save Sam and the others. The Cheyennes were not yet within rifle-shot, and the miles were dropping behind them. He rode a strong and true horse, and he would lead them a long chase. He might even get away.

The boy heard occasional shouts behind him, but for a long time he did not look back. When he did at last turn his gaze he saw that he was followed by about twenty warriors, who were spread out in a concave line, enclosing him, or at least his line of flight, between horns, as it were. So far as he could judge, they had neither gained nor lost. Another mile and still they had not gained; a second and third mile and they had gained. There was not a doubt of it.

Now the boy bending somewhat in his saddle that the chance to escape trial shots might be better, prayed to kind Providence that it would not withhold its favors that day. He prayed that his horse might last, that the horse's rider might keep up his courage, and that both horse and rider might escape all shots.

Before him stretched low, blue hills, far away, and almost buried in a faint haze. He kept a straight course towards them, hoping that he might reach them and find forests there where one might hide, or at least find a better chance of escape. If only his good horse had sinews of steel! But surely horse had never responded better, as the flight was now long, and he had not ever faltered.

He heard a sharp report, and a bullet flew past him; a second, and his horse's ear was nicked. The first report came from a point behind him, but towards the right; the second towards the left. He took a hasty glance. The horses of the pursuing crescent were closing on him, and presently he would be within fair range.

Now the boy knew that all his prayers to Providence had been in vain. He would not escape. The low, blue hills had come much nearer, but they were not near enough. But whatever fate awaited him, he was sure that he had achieved his triumph. He had drawn the Cheyennes far away. Sam Strong and his comrades would escape. He had paid the great debt that he owed them. He felt anew that keen thrill of exultation. It was for a moment acute, penetrating and satisfying.

Crack! went another rifle, and then a second and a third. They did not touch him yet, but he saw the dust, flying from the dry plain ahead of him, where they struck. It was only a matter of time now when a bullet should reach him or his horse.

The Cheyennes knew it, too, and they set up a great shout of triumph which filled Bob with rage. He would make another desperate effort to escape from those enclosing horns, and he spoke persuasively to his good horse. He urged, he begged him to go faster. He entreated him to remember that he had no superior in strength and speed, and that it would be a disgrace to be overtaken by a lot of miserable Cheyenne ponies. It almost seemed to Bob that the horse understood. His head swayed a little from side to side, and his flanks heaved as he made a mighty effort.

They gained perhaps a yard, but another rifle cracked, and a great shiver ran through the horse. The next instant he pitched forward and fell. It was so sudden that Bob had no time to check himself and leap to one side. He shot over the horse's head, and ploughed along on his shoulder and side, although he managed to save himself from serious injury. But his rifle flew twelve or fifteen feet away, and when he sprang up again and stood erect, a Cheyenne, leaping from his horse, had already seized it and was waving it aloft in triumph. His belt also had broken as he scraped violently along, and with the pistol and knife in holster and sheath, it was lying out of his reach. Bob Norton stood erect, absolutely unarmed, with a chosen band of the Dog Soldiers of the Cheyennes in a circle around him.

The boy was bruised and his bones ached. The skin was torn off the back of one hand, and his shoulder and side were covered with the dry soil of the prairie, but he faced the silent circle with an undaunted eye. Another of the Cheyennes leaped down, secured the belt with pistol and knife, and in an instant was back on his horse.

The Cheyennes now gave no cry of triumph, nor did they address a word to the youth. They merely regarded him at a distance of eight or ten yards, motionless now on their horses, gazing intently as if he were some new and strange specimen of humankind who had come before them. Half of them carried long lances and shields. All were naked to the waist-cloth, and there was not one among them who was not a splendid specimen of a bold and savage race. Their black hair hung long, and the magnificent coronets of eagle feathers, their war-bonnets, waved lightly in the slight wind.

They were naked to the breech-cloth, and their lean, brown figures glowed with the tint of copper in the brilliant sunlight.

Bob's eyes were drawn at last by one warrior, as magnificent a figure of a man as he had ever seen. The warrior was of early middle age and of great stature. His face was large, and his mouth large, with thin, compressed lips. When these lips were opened they showed two rows of white teeth, as even and strong as those of a wolf. He had a great and splendidly shaped head, of which the most distinguishing feature was a long nose, hooked like that of an old Roman, and with fine nostrils. It gave him a look that was commanding to the last degree.

The chest and limbs of this magnificent savage

were powerful and covered with woven muscle. He was naked except for moccasins, a scarlet breechcloth adorned with little colored beads, and a cloak looped back from his shoulders. But this cloak was made of the skin of that rarest of animals, a white buffalo, and it had been so finely tanned that it was as soft as velvet.

Bob felt in his heart that this was the great chief, Roman Nose, and despite himself, he could not keep from feeling deference. But he looked directly at him.

The chief's eyes met his own in a steady stare, and Bob plumbed their depths. He read there ambition, malice, hatred of himself and of the race to which he belonged, but with it all a certain largeness, as if he could appreciate a foe who was his match. Bob met his gaze unflinchingly. When he was discovered he made one resolution which he had carried out, and now that he was brought to earth like a fox, with the hounds about him, he took another. He expected to die, and he would die as became one of the white race. He would make no cry for mercy. He would not utter a word, but if it were decreed for him to die there on the prairie, far from his friends, he would meet the end in silence.

But it was hard to feel even then that he had to die. The sunlight was brilliant, the plains wild and free, and the world seemed beautiful. The chief presently said a word or two to the warriors, and turning their horses with a pressure of the knee, they rode in a slow and silent circle about him, every man keeping his eye upon the boy who stood in their center. Bob's own eyes followed the commanding presence of the chief who seemed to dominate them all with a single glance, and unconsciously he began to wheel slowly with the wheeling circle.

Bob remembered afterwards that he suffered from a sort of spell, a kind of hypnotism. His fall and the strange action of the Cheyennes gave him a dizzy, vague feeling, as if he were in some mystic region of unreality. Around and around they rode, no one speaking, no sound whatever coming to the boy's ears but the light beat of the hoofs of the ponies, which presently became a monotonous rhythm, like the sound of the Hindoo's flute when he charms the cobra.

Bob noticed soon that the circle was widening. The warriors were thirty, forty, fifty, sixty yards away, and a little later they stopped. His eyes, in all this turning, never ceased to follow the chief, and he saw him now take one of the long lances from a warrior and lean a little over his horse's neck.

Bob understood. He would be speared by the chief in full flight. A deep shiver ran over him from head to foot, and his heart turned cold within him. Again he saw that it was a beautiful world, and that he did not wish to leave it. But he once more summoned up his resolution. He would show these fierce Dog Soldiers that he was as brave as they. He would not run, he would not try to dodge the unescapable lance, but he would stand up and face its point, praying to Providence, which had been unkind hitherto, to finish it all quickly.

He was thankful now that a veil was drawn before his eyes. His dizziness and the terrible tensity of his situation caused him to see but dimly. But he never ceased to look straight towards the chief, and he saw him raise his lance, shake it twice, utter a single, sharp cry and then gallop directly at him.

It was almost an impossibility to stand still. Only the boy's bewildered state enabled him to do it. He did not fully understand just then what was occurring, but he heard the hoof-beats of the horse like thunder in his ears; he saw the shining point of the lance, and the large, coppery face of the warrior who held it. Then he was forced to shut his eyes, but something seemed to whistle by his cheek and the hoof-beats thundered past him.

He opened his eyes and beheld the chief now on the other side of the circle, shaking the long lance. A low hum, a hum of admiration, came from the warriors, but Bob did not know then that it was for him.

The chief pressed his horse with his knees again, uttered that sharp, little cry, and a second time galloped down upon the defenseless boy. Bob now did not close his eyes. He seemed to have lost all feeling, all sense of what was happening, and he himself seemed merely a spectator at this strange scene upon the prairie. On came the horse, the chief threw the lance, its point passed within six inches of Bob's face, and the horse galloped by, so close that its hoofs threw dust upon him.

And that hum of admiration rose again, and this time louder. The chief turned and came back to the boy, but he walked his horse, and when he reached Bob he sprang to the ground and uttered a word or two of approval. Bob looked at him with an anxious, uncomprehending glance, and then sitting down upon the prairie, laughed.

It was the laugh of hysteria, and for a moment or two the Cheyennes did not disturb him. Then the chief motioned to him to rise to his feet. Bob rose and they bound his hands behind him. Then they helped him upon a horse, behind a warrior, the chief gave the word, and the whole band, after one long, thrilling whoop, galloped away over the prairie.

Bob had only the pressure of his thighs to hold himself upon his horse, but he was trained to that method of riding, and he did it without thought or conscious exertion. He knew that he was weak, and his head was yet dizzy, but he was not going to fall, and the rapid motion was beginning to revive him somewhat.

He never had the remotest idea how long they galloped, but they stopped at last in a shallow valley that contained a camp-fire and other warriors. Whether it was the original valley in which he had found them he could never tell, as his first glimpse had been too brief, but it was an intense relief to him to know that the journey was ended.

The warrior, behind whom he was riding, jumped off his pony and then helped him to the ground. But Bob, with his bound arms, was unable to stand. He collapsed from weakness and excitement, and sank down in a heap. The chief strode forward, cut his bonds, raised him to his feet, and gave him a drink of water out of a calabash. The boy leaned against the stump of a fallen tree and revived slowly.

When his eyes were clear he looked fixedly at the chief and his opinion did not change, that this was the great Roman Nose of whom he had heard so much. His eyes wandered from the chief to the warriors, who stood near, in numbers, regarding him. They had high cheek bones, straight limbs, and high, ridged noses. The warriors were clad in breech-cloths only, and moccasins, as the weather was warm, and they wore but few ornaments, generally strings of bear claws around the neck. Their hair was cut straight across their foreheads, just above their eyes, and a small ornamented plait hung down in front of each shoulder. The remainder, twisted with horse or buffalo hair, was divided into two large plaits which flowed over the back.

Squaws too came up and gazed at Bob. The Cheyenne women were notably inferior in physique and looks to the men. They had wide mouths, ugly noses and, in fact, all their features were ugly. They wore skin tunics, fastened with straps over the shoulders, and falling almost to the knee. They had ornaments of beads, shells, elk tusks, and rings and bracelets of brass. Their hair was long and flowing, not braided.

Bob was in a large temporary village of the Cheyennes, led by their great chiefs, Roman Nose and Black Kettle. Around him were the ten principal divisions of the two branches of the Cheyenne

nation, the northern and the southern. Their camp was a great circle, a mile in diameter, including at least six hundred tepees, or a fighting force of about twelve hundred warriors. The ten clans, or *gentes,* in their order of rank were:
1. Heviquésnipahis
2. Hevhaitáneo
3. Masikota
4. Omísis
5. Sutaío
6. Wotápio
7. Oivimána
8. Hisiometáneo
9. Oqutogóna
10. Hownówa

The ten *gentes* were also redivided into six warrior bands, every one with its own emblems and ritual. At the head of them stood the Hotamitáneo, or the famous Dog Soldiers, the ritual and instructions of whom had been given by a supernatural dog to their founder; hence their name.

Next came the Woksikitáneo, or Fox Men, who were called so because their leader carried ceremonial clubs, with the pendant skin of the fox. They were followed by the Himóiyogis, or Those With Headed Lances, because they carried lances of a very peculiar make. Fourth were the Mahóhivas, or Red Shield Owners, whose leaders bore shields painted red, with a pendant buffalo tail. Next to them were the Himatánohis, Those with the Bow String, who received their name because their leaders bore lances resembling a long bow in their shape. Last were the Hotáminasow, or Foolish Dogs, composed wholly of very young warriors, beginners in the art of war, who were not supposed to have much sense.

The tribes, or *gentes,* were ruled by forty-four chiefs, regularly elected at intervals of a few years. At each election forty new chiefs were chosen, while four older ones were selected from the retiring forty. These four were the head chiefs, and when they wished to call a council they sent around forty-four painted sticks to all the villages.

Such a council had been called recently, but Bob knew nothing of it, nor did he know anything then of the composition of the Cheyenne nation. He was destined to learn these things later. Now he was concerned about what was going to happen to him within the next few minutes.

"Vehoc" (Little Chief), said Roman Nose.

Bob shook his head. He did not have the faintest idea what "vehoc" meant.

"Strong boy. Brave boy," said the chief in English.

"Thanks," said Bob, who wished to deserve the Indian's praise. "I may be strong and I may be brave, but I'm willing to tell you, Mr. Roman Nose, that I'm just about played out."

"You go tepee," said Roman Nose. "We no hurt you—to-day."

Bob noticed the pause before "to-day," and he had to repress a tendency to shiver. But his life in the wilderness had taught him to make the best of the passing moment, and he went willingly with the two warriors, who guided him to a buffalo-skin tepee. It was a small place, with only a skin or two between him and the bare ground, but it was a haven of rest to one so tired and sore as he. He sank upon a wolf skin, and in some faint spirit of irony, waved a good-night to the two warriors who had brought him there.

"You drink?" said one.

"You eat?" said the other.

Bob roused himself at these words.

"Yes, an emphatic 'yes' to both of you," he said.

They did not understand his words, but the meaning of his tone was plain to them. They brought a calabash of good, cool water, and buffalo steaks freshly cooked. Bob drank thirstily and ate with a great appetite. Then he waved his hand to the warriors who had stood by, silent and impassive.

"It's really good-night this time," he said, "I'm just bound to go to sleep."

He had no idea how long it was until night, and he did not care. His own fate, too, had glided into the background. He was exhausted, and rest was the only mortal affair that concerned him much.

The two Cheyennes went out and closed the skin doors of the tepee. It was dusky now within the lodge, and the boy felt a great peace. He had eaten, he had drunk, and he had found rest. His comrades were up and away with their furs. Let the future look to itself; it could not bother him.

He doubled a corner of the wolf skin under his head, making a pillow. Then he floated off on the pleasant sea of sleep.

CHAPTER XV

A MODERN MAZEPPA

Bob was awakened the next morning by the lifting of the flap of his tent. A flood of sunshine poured in, and his eyes opened. Then a figure bulked large in the opening, and the captive stared at it in great astonishment. Both figure and face were familiar, but for a while he could not believe that what he saw was true.

Yet it was true. There was the swarthy face, the close-set eyes, and the pointed chin of Juan Carver. Moreover, he showed his teeth in a malicious smile as he looked at the boy.

"Yes," he said, "it is I, Carver, whom you neither expect nor want to see. No, I am not a prisoner like you. I am on the best of terms with the great chiefs, Roman Nose and Black Kettle, whom you will see here beside me if you will deign to take your eyes off my face."

Bob rose to his feet. Long sleep had steadied his nerves, and he resolutely stilled every tremor. The very presence of Carver made him more determined than ever not to show fear, nor to ask for mercy. He stepped out of the tepee, no one opposing, and stood in the sunlight, which was warm and grateful.

Carver had spoken truly when he said that Roman Nose and Black Kettle were with him. Black Kettle was somewhat shorter and darker than

Roman Nose, but he had all the bearing of a leader, and he, too, wore a fine robe made of light buffalo skin. Both chiefs carried shields of the stoutest buffalo hide, painted and decorated profusely with heraldic signs and a history of their exploits. In fact, nearly all the Cheyenne warriors whom Bob saw carried such shields. When Bob looked at them and bowed gravely he condescended to notice Carver.

"I should not be surprised to see you here," he said. "I know that you have all the qualities of a renegade."

As he thought of it, Bob saw that Carver's presence in the Cheyenne town was not at all extraordinary. He was a freebooter, and it would suit him to be hand in glove with the Cheyennes.

"Bad names don't hurt me," said Carver. "I am glad that the Cheyennes are my friends. Both Roman Nose and Black Kettle are old ones. I did not reach their village until last night, and when I found that you were here I gave them news worth knowing."

Bob's face fell. He knew that Carver had told the chief of his comrades and their treasure of furs. Carver, quick enough to make inferences, knew that Bob, when first seen, could not have been very far away from his comrades, and the fact that they were so well to the eastward proved that they were on their return to civilization, with a great taking of beaver.

Bob recovered his countenance, and said with an assumption of carelessness:

"I suppose that you are speaking of my friends. Well, I got lost from them, and I fancy that they are at least a couple of hundred miles further east by this time."

Carver looked at him closely, but Bob bore the scrutiny, without a change of feature.

"You may be telling the truth," said Carver. "We'd like mighty well to take that little train. I want the furs and the Cheyennes want the scalps, but I don't mind telling you that we have sent out scouts who have returned without them."

Bob felt a glow. His comrades had got clean away, and he had not made his great flight in vain. Carver, still watching him closely, saw him smile.

"We'll get them yet," said the freebooter.

"You'll never get them," said Bob.

"Vehoc," said Roman Nose, applying to Bob the word that he had used the afternoon before.

"What does he mean?" asked Bob of Carver.

"'Vehoc' in Cheyenne means Little Chief," replied the man. "Roman Nose rather admires you. He tells me that you bore yourself well when he rode at you with the spear."

"I thank him for that much. I like him a good deal better than I do you," said the boy.

"Well, as to that," said Carver, grinning, "Roman Nose is not exactly growing wings. While he admires your courage under one test, he expects to put it to another soon."

Carver's tone was full of malice, but Bob again refused to show fear.

"It may be so," he said, "and if it is so I will do

my best to stand it. But just now I'm hungry. Tell 'em I want something to eat."

Carver spoke to Roman Nose who seemed to have a sense of humor.

"Vehoc rather eat than have big talk," he said. "He eat here by ohe."

"'Ohe' means river," said Carver, "but ought rather to be 'ohec,' which is little river."

"So you have a river, have you?" said Bob.

"Yes, but as I said, it is a little one."

He pointed to a shallow stream, just beyond a fringe of cottonwoods, and Bob walked to its bank with his captors.

"Ehona," said Roman Nose.

Bob looked at him in doubt.

"'Ehona' means a stone," said Carver. "He wants you to sit on the flat rock you see there."

"Thanks for his courtesy," said Bob, and sat down.

There, good food, both buffalo and deer, and water were brought to him, and he ate and drank with satisfaction. Meanwhile the people came again to look at him, and there were many squaws among them.

Most of these women brought their work with them, and the work was of different kinds. The Cheyenne women, when they reached sufficient age, joined guilds like the labor unions of the white man, and when they became full members they were called "Moninico," which meant women who have chosen. One union made the tepees, that is the bare walls, another adorned them, another tanned and decorated buffalo robes, another moccasins and leggings, and there were yet other guilds, the work for every one being different.

The warriors who came to see him were mostly in pairs. This was due to the Cheyenne custom of a young man taking a "howi," or comrade, a friendship that endured through life, after marriage as well as before. Carver, who seemed to be much pleased with himself, told Bob more about the Indians as he ate.

"The Cheyennes are a great nation," he said. "The warriors are brave and skilful. They are organized, with their laws and their religion. The big tepee over there is their Council House. In it are the Four Sacred Arrows which are their holiest and most precious possession. Only the older men dare to mention them by name. On big public occasions they are brought out to be worshiped, but only by the warriors. No woman has ever been allowed to come near them, or to see them."

Bob was interested, despite himself.

"And these arrows are their guardian deities?" he asked.

"They are," replied Carver. "They used to carry them into battle to insure victory, but twenty-five or thirty years ago two of them were taken in a great conflict by the Pawnees, and have never been recovered. Two others were blessed and sanctified by the priests, and made to take their place, but the loss of the two original ones was the greatest blow that ever befell the Cheyenne nation."

Bob's interest continued, but he said to Carver:

"Why do you tell me these things?"

"I'm willing to make it as easy for you as I can," replied the freebooter, "until the time comes to apply the actual tests."

Bob thought that the man was trying to frighten him, and he turned scornfully away. Carver said no more, but left in a few minutes. Bob remained where he was, seated on the flat stone. The long, numbing process through which he had gone was now about finished, and he was fully awake to his situation. He was unbound, and his strength had returned, but there was no chance whatever of flight. The Cheyenne warriors and waspish, old squaws were everywhere about him. The great circular village was on both sides of the shallow stream, and the prisoner was at least a quarter of a mile from the nearest point on its rim. Whatever it might be, he could not escape this test of which Carver spoke so maliciously.

Bob did not doubt that it meant death, and he rebelled fiercely against the thought. Here was a great village with perhaps three thousand people in it, and they were all happy as human life went. The squaws went about their work, children were playing, the warriors mended their weapons or lounged in the sun. He alone was doomed. He choked, but looked down again at the river lest any one should see fear in his face.

After a while Roman Nose, Black Kettle, Carver and others came back to him. The two chiefs looked at him fixedly, and it seemed to Bob that there was a solitary gleam of pity in the gaze of Roman Nose.

"Come with us," said Carver, and Bob, rising without a word, went.

They led the way to the outskirts of the village, to a point on its rim facing the northwest, where the brown plains rolled away, swell after swell, to the horizon. A great crowd, silent, but watching intently, followed. When they stopped it was again Carver who spoke.

"We want to know from you," he said to Bob, "which way Strong and his party have gone. We expected our scouts to discover them last night, but they did not. Now you must tell us."

Roman Nose and Black Kettle nodded in affirmation.

Bob's figure stiffened. They must think him a child if he would help them, after the sacrifice he had made for his comrades.

"I do not know which way they have gone," he replied, "and if I knew I would not tell you."

"Perhaps you feel that way now," said Carver, "I've no doubt you do, but you may feel differently before many minutes. The bird that can sing will have to do it this time."

"I will not give you a particle of information that can help you," said Bob, quietly.

"There is the torture," said Carver in a tone of menace.

"Even so," said Bob, although he shuddered, "I still will not speak."

The two chiefs, who seemed to understand English, although they spoke it but little, at least to Bob, frowned. But Carver showed his sharp, white teeth, and smiled in his evil way.

"It will be the better for you if you tell," he said. "Put us on the track of Strong and the others, and you shall be spared. The chiefs promise it. You will not be released, at least not now, but you will be treated well. Look at this village; it is not a bad life for those who know the wilderness. Choose that or worse."

"I have nothing to say," replied Bob.

"Think again; think hard and you will find something."

"I have made up my mind," replied Bob, firmly.

Carver spoke rapidly to the chiefs in their own tongue, and they nodded their heads. Then he turned again to Bob. It seemed that the man had a sneering spirit, and some knowledge beyond that of an ordinary frontiersman.

"Indians are friends to their friends," he said, "but they are very bitter foes to their foes. Then, they have no use for milk and water. Now you are a foe, and since you will not speak they naturally turn to the torture, but by some chance a spark of mercy has lodged in the breast of Roman Nose. He has denied us the faggot and the stake, but he agrees to make a spectacle for his people."

Bob looked at him, but said nothing.

"The Cheyennes insist on amusement," said Carver, "and Roman Nose and Black Kettle, who are both statesmen, will give it to them. They are ready."

A warrior advanced, leading with a lariat a powerful mustang, one of the largest that Bob had ever seen, a wild and fiery animal, too, as the warrior, a strong man, was compelled to swing hard on the lariat. Four other warriors seized Bob and lifted him to the horse's back. Then they bound him, with his feet under the sides of the mustang, and his body bent forward on the neck and shoulders.

"Will you speak?" asked Carver.

"I know nothing to tell," replied the boy, "and if I knew I wouldn't tell you."

Carver said something to the warrior who held the horse. The man instantly slipped off the lariat and sprang away.

The mustang looked about for a few moments, and Bob could feel him trembling all over. Then he raced away towards the center of the village, and with a wild shout, mounted Cheyennes started in pursuit, striking with switches at the frightened and angry mustang. Squaws and children threw sticks and clods of earth at horse and involuntary rider as they passed.

Bob was made almost breathless by the wild gallop of the mustang, but he understood. He was to be chased about the village, and be scourged with switches and missiles for the benefit of the whole Cheyenne population. When he was finally taken from the horse he would be so broken that he would be glad to tell anything he knew.

The boy, bent far down on the horse's neck, could not see very well, but as the mustang galloped about he was conscious of a mass of brown, excited faces, and he heard a continuous shouting. He was struck now and then by a missile, but he did not feel the bruise.

It was great sport for the Cheyennes. There were worse things to which a prisoner could be subjected, but since those were denied them, this was acceptable. They chased the frightened mustang around and around the village meadows. At least fifty horsemen were following him now, the riders leaning forward for a cut with a switch at either the horse or the burden on his back.

Bob struggled hard to keep his senses, and by mere impulse he pulled continually at the thongs that held his arms. He sought also to ease his position and stop the intolerable jolting.

The sport grew wilder. Warriors, squaws and children thrilled with the excitement of it. Roman Nose, Black Kettle and Carver stood grimly by as the excited mustang galloped about, driven around and around by the horde. The numbness and dizziness that Bob had felt after his flight from the Cheyennes, came over him again, but he made a continued effort to keep conscious and remain in the easiest position on the horse.

A boy, somewhere in the horde, shot an arrow, more of a toy than anything else, but it struck the mustang in the flank, and stung. The horse, now insane with fright and fear, suddenly made a bolt directly through the ring of Cheyennes. People rushed to one side to keep from being trampled down, and the masses kept back the pursuing horsemen who sought now to catch the mustang and the prisoner that he bore.

But a slip had occured in the plans of Carver and the two chiefs. The mustang, freed for a moment from the goad of the switches and missiles, and seeing a clear space before him, made a rush for the plain. Two warriors on foot tried to seize him by the mane, but they were not quick enough and were compelled to leap back to avoid those trampling hoofs.

The mustang cleared the rim of the village and he saw freedom before him, the brown plain stretching away to the blue horizon, and nobody to torment him. He was in such a fever of rage, excitement and fear that his strength was the strength of three. He arched his back to make his burden lighter, laid back his ears a little, and ran with a speed worthy of the best mustang in all the Cheyenne village. The brown earth flew beneath his hoofs, and the gentle swells raced past.

Behind the mustang came a horde of mounted Cheyennes, eager now to repair the slip and to retake the prisoner. But they did not reckon with the full speed of the mustang. His involuntary rider, too, bent forward almost like a jockey, seemed to urge him to a faster pace.

Carver and the chiefs had mounted and pursued. Carver was raging, but a faint smile once or twice passed over the grim features of Roman Nose. Bob himself was dimly conscious of what had happened. The Indian village was behind him, but the knowledge brought him no great thrill. He was too much exhausted, too much numbed to feel it, but he was conscious that there was only space before him.

The Cheyennes shouted and sought to urge their horses to greater speed. The sound reached the mustang and increased his rage and fear. His strength, born of a great impulse, grew. His head was thrust out a little further, the sensitive ears quivered, and the long body, stretching itself for a faster flight, flew over the ground.

The mustang was gaining and the Cheyennes saw it. A little longer, and the gain was more decisive. There would be no chance for any warrior to throw his lariat, and Roman Nose gave the word to fire.

Rifles cracked and bullets sang by the mustang. One grazed his flank, drawing a little blood. It was like the touch of fire, and his indignant heart swelled to greater efforts. Right well that day did he prove himself a king of the prairie. He ran straight and true, there was no curving about which would enable his pursuers to gain upon him, but his head was always pointed to the blue horizon that hung over the northwest. The bullets still spattered around him now and then, but most of them fell short, and the sound of shots and shouts was further away.

The bullets yet came, but now all of them fell short. Nevertheless, the mustang did not decrease his speed. The burden on his back was quiet, not impeding him much, and he was as strong as ever. In his own horse heart he felt his triumph, and raising his head he neighed once. Then he sped on with renewed speed, and the Cheyennes and their horses sank into the prairie.

Bob came out of a period of unconsciousness and found that the mustang was walking. He heard no sound, but the steady hoof-beats. All his limbs and joints were aching, and the full weight of his body rested upon the horse. He pulled at one arm, and to his great amazement it came free from the thongs. It was cut, and he had probably been tugging at it for a long time without being conscious of the fact, but here it was free.

The surprising knowledge filled the boy with new life. The free hand and arm, at which he looked, were his own, and he could do great things with them. He began to pluck at the thongs holding the other arm. They, too, were loosened by and by. Then he remembered that he had carried a clasp knife in a small inside pocket of his coat. It was one that could easily have been overlooked by the Cheyennes, and when he felt tremblingly for it, he found it.

A few slashes released waist and legs, and then the boy, with a great and painful effort, sat up in the shape of a man on the bare back of the mustang. He was more like a bent, old man than a strong and active youth, but now he rode and was not merely carried.

He was very faint and weak, and he would have fallen to the ground, but the mustang's pace sank to the lowest and easiest walk, and he pulled himself together enough to take a comprehensive look about him.

The boy saw only the great plains, rolling away toward every point of the horizon, unbroken anywhere by a hill or a tree or a horseman. The Cheyennes were left far behind, and they would not be able to follow his trail on the hard, sun-baked prairie. He understood that he had escaped. By a miracle, as it were, he was out of the hands of his enemies. Their own trick, intended to torture and deride him, had turned upon them. He lifted his face to heaven and gave thanks. It was a face so dirty and begrimed that Sam Strong himself would not have known it, but for a few moments it was transfigured and glorified. Escaped and free! He raised his bruised hands and shook them in exultation.

Bob was so much occupied with the present that he took no thought of the future. He was proud of being able to keep his seat on the mustang, which now walked slowly on, his glossy, brown coat wet from head to heel with perspiration, his great eyes showing weariness, and a dim sort of inquiry as to what it all meant.

He was a noble mustang. He had been the largest, swiftest and wildest in all the Cheyenne village, and he had run a good race. But the victory won and the tormentors gone, he was very tired. He was conscious that his rider had straightened up, although he seemed to be more uncertain of his seat, but the mustang made no attempt to shake him off.

Bob leaned forward again and clutched the mustang's mane tightly. His weakness was coming back and the plains swam before him. But the long, coarse hair, grasped in his hands, sustained him and the mustang took no notice, merely walking on at a pace that did not seem to be much more than creeping.

The rider did not know how many hours passed. At times he saw clearly, and he knew that the country had not changed. At other times he seemed to be in a dream, and the faces of the Cheyennes came back to him. He awoke from one of these dreams with a shock, and saw that the mustang was standing still. The cessation from the slow walk had caused the shock, and the boy began to feel a great pity for the horse and himself.

They were together on the lone prairie, and he owed the mustang a mighty debt that he could not pay. The speed and strength of a dumb animal had brought him away from torture, and death to come. There was not an ungrateful fiber in him, and he leaned forward and patted the mustang on the neck.

"Good horse!" he said aloud. "Good old horse! The finest horse that ever was born!"

It may have been a mere coincidence, but the mustang stretched out his long neck and neighed. Bob felt at once that the relation of friends was established between them. He had spoken to the horse, and the horse had answered.

"Good horse!" he repeated. "I've ridden you long and hard, but it was from no choice of mine. Now you shall have the rest that you have so well earned."

He slipped from the horse's back to the ground, and he would have fallen on his face, but again he grasped the mane of the mustang and saved himself. The horse did not resent his fierce clutch, but turned his head a little and looked at him. Bob gazed into the great, dusky horse eyes, and it seemed to him that he read there a feeling akin to his own.

"You're lonely, partner," he said. "I'm sorry, but there's no other horse here, and it's just you and I. Come on, I don't know which way we're going, I don't know what we're going to, nor when we'll get there, but we're going."

He did not release the mane, and the mustang made no effort to pull away. So the two, now walking side by side, started again, the horse steady and upright, Bob staggering, but with one hand wound firmly in the long coarse hair that supported him.

But the boy could not last long. He had been through too much. The plains and the sky darkened before him, and he hung a dead weight on the mustang, which stopped.

I've come to the end, comrade," said Bob, patting the horse's head with his free hand, "and I won't burden you any longer. Go on; you'll find other horses somewhere on the prairie. I stop here."

He released the horse entirely and now, unable to support his own weight, he sank to the ground. He was so far gone in collapse that he did not even care to make any further effort. His spirit, at that moment, was one of resignation. But he raised his head a little, made a weak gesture to the horse, and repeated:

"Go on! I stay here!"

The mustang did not go on. He turned and gazed from great dusky eyes at his fallen rider, and, unless Bob was dreaming, he saw pity there. They *were* friends! They *were* comrades. The mustang came closer, and touched the boy's face with his nose, as if in a spirit of compassion. Bob felt that there was one who would not desert him. He could not rise now, but he reached up and stroked the horse's face.

"Just you and I!" he murmured. "Here I stay and here you mean to stay with me."

The darkness of the plains and sky suddenly turned to complete blackness, and he sank into a stupor.

When Bob came to himself he was lying upon his back on the prairie, and the twilight was coming. The horse still stood by him. He may have nibbled for a while at the burnt grass, but the sound of the boy's movement had brought him back.

Bob, weakened by his great nervous strain, felt a throb of emotion. This was indeed a friend as true as steel. He staggered to his feet, but all his muscles were stiff, and his bones were sore. Once more, he took the mustang by the mane, and there was no resistance.

"You've had a rest, good old horse," he said, talking to his comrade, because the mustang was then, in nearly every sense, a human being to him, "and I'll ride again."

He dragged himself upon the horse's back, steadied himself there, and then bade him go on as he would. The mustang, fully refreshed and once more the strongest of his kind, started at a long easy walk toward the East. The wind may have brought pleasant odors to nostrils, far more acute than those of man, or it may have been instinct, but the mustang not only knew where he was going, he knew also when he would get there, and what he would find when he arrived.

The easy, swinging walk that ate up ground so fast continued a long time. The twilight merged into the night, the moon and the stars came out, and the sky was clear and cold after the hot day. The coolness was refreshing to Bob, and he seemed to gather a little strength. He saw, finally, a thin, dark line on the moonstruck horizon, and he knew that it was trees. Trees, extending away to right and left, in that manner, indicated water, and he felt now, for the first time, that his throat and mouth were burnt.

The horse neighed, and broke into a trot. In another minute he was through the trees, and at the sandy edge of the shallow stream of clear cold water, from which he drank eagerly. Bob slipped from his back, and, kneeling down, drank beside him. Life flowed back into him as he drank up the living water, and, when he and the horse were both satisfied and he had rested awhile on the bank, he took off his torn clothing and bathed. It was soothing to his scratches and bruises, and, when he had dried himself, and put on his clothing again, he sought the softest place that he could find in the grass, which grew in length and abundance along the stream.

He was terribly hungry, but he tried not to think of it, and soon forgot everything in a deep, dreamless sleep, the slumber of exhaustion. He lay so still in the long grass that a man, ten feet away, would not have noticed him. But the mustang, seeking the softest clumps for his teeth, looked at him now and then, and it may be that the sense of comradeship was as strong in the horse heart as it had been in the boy heart.

The mustang after a while, with a long sigh of content, lay down and rolled a little, then became quiet and motionless. An hour passed, and a long weird howl came from the open swells. It was the cry of the prairie wolf informing his brethren that the odor of pleasant food had come to his nostrils. It is possible that his instinct, as good as that of the horse, had told him that the boy who lay sleeping in the grass was unarmed.

Wolf answered wolf and soon the hungry line drew near. Fierce eyes looked down among the trees, and lips crinkled back from sharp teeth. They could not yet see the figure of the boy in the deep grass, but the odor of food was strong and it drew them on with the greatest temptation that a wolf can know. They crept into the belt of trees.

The mustang felt that something was wrong. He rose to his feet standing almost beside the boy, and saw the red eyes and sharp teeth of the advancing line. He had seen such brutes before and he hated them. He did not move now, but his own eyes began to gleam as they had done, when he was first beaten and pursued by the Cheyennes.

The mustang, standing there in the moonlight, was a formidable companion. The wolves, with their eyes of preternatural acuteness, could see how the great figure was tense and drawn, ready to lash

"The great figure was tense and drawn, ready to lash out like lightning with those sharp hoofs"

"I see him," said Jack, "a horse without a saddle or a bridle, but he don't look like a wild horse. Anyway, as the wind is blowin' toward him, he has scented us long ago, an' he'd have been up an' away, if he'd been a real live mustang."

"It means somethin', shore," said Pete, "an' it's one o' the things that we've got to find out."

They rode forward warily, not wishing to alarm the lone horse, but he showed no fear. As they came nearer, he raised his head and neighed, and the horse of Pete replied in kind to his friendly salute.

"He's used to people, some kind of people. That's shore," said Pete. "Now I call this right strange. Whar such a horse is some kind of human bein' ought to be."

"There he is," said the sharp-eyed Jack, "an' he's dead. See him stretched out in the grass? A white man, too."

"Yes, I do see him," said Pete, rising in his stirrups, "but how do you account for the horse havin' no saddle an' no bridle? Mebbe it's an ambush, an' that's only a stuffed figger in the grass."

"It's real," repeated Jack, "and there ain't any ambush. There ain't a chance for any."

They rode forward among the cottonwoods. The horse moved a yard or two away, but showed no fear of them.

"It's a boy!" exclaimed Jack, "an' he ain't dead, by thunder! He's asleep. If he sleeps like that out here in the Indian country, how would he sleep in town in his little trundle bed!"

"He's been manhandled," said Pete, whose experienced eye had run over the prostrate form, "an' it's stupor as well as sleep."

He sprang down, and seized Bob by the shoulders.

"Here, wake up, young feller," he exclaimed. "The sun's risin' high, and it's time for you to go milk the cows."

Bob opened his eyes, and rose to his feet in bewilderment. It was some time before he could see clearly, and understood who had come. Then his thankfulness was great.

"White men, thank God!" he exclaimed. "You're friends! You can't be anything else!"

"Of course we're friends," said Pete. "Here, young feller. Steady! Steady! Don't you go to tumblin' over again. You must have been through a lot. I can see it. Here, Jack, your flask, quick!"

Something hot and fiery was poured down Bob's throat, and he stood erect once more. His weakness had really been due to excitement at the coming of the two white men, as his long sleep had largely restored his nerves. But his wild ride had come to a happy end, and he knew that he was now with those who could help him. He looked longingly at a little knapsack that the older man carried.

"I haven't had anything to eat since yesterday morning," he said.

"Then you must be hungry," said Pete, taking from the knapsack some bread and strips of bacon. "Set down thar, an' see if these will make any sort o' an appeal to your palate."

Bob sat down on the grass, and quickly proved that they made a most powerful appeal. The two men looked at him, with curiosity, but they yet refrained from asking questions. The mustang came near, and touched his nose in friendly fashion to that of Pete's horse. Pete's eyes ran swiftly over the mustang, noting his long, easy lines and powerful build.

"Fine horse, that," he said. "I wonder ef he belongs to the boy, an' I wonder why he ain't got on any saddle and bridle?"

Bob looked up from his bread and bacon.

"I belong to him," he said.

"Now I'll be smoked if I know what you mean by that," said Pete.

Bob smiled, rather wearily.

"I ought to belong to him," he said, "since he took me out of the Cheyenne village yesterday, brought me clean away from Roman Nose, Black Kettle and their people, and, for all I know, may have watched over me while I was sleeping here."

Pete and Jack showed signs of the liveliest interest.

"Tell us all about it, if you're ready," said Pete.

Bob began his story, the two sitting down on the grass beside him, that they might listen at their ease. But very soon they straightened up, and their lips parted, as the tale went on. Every detail of that wild ride was vivid in Bob's memory, and he told it from a full heart. The picture was full of color. It stood out complete, and like life itself, before the two listeners, who drew long breaths, when Bob finished.

"You're right," said Pete. "It's the mustang that saved you. But that long ride broke him to the use of man, while it didn't break his spirit. See, how he hangs around you."

"Good horse," said Bob.

"Since you've told us who you are and where you come from," said Pete, "it's only right that you should know who we are. This worthless young feller here is Jack Stillwell an' I'm Pete Trudeau. We're scouts for the United States army, an' Colonel George Forsyth with fifty men, scouts an' skirmishers too, ain't far from here. We're detached by General Sheridan to look for the Cheyennes, an' Jack an' me are on a little scout o' our own this mornin'. It's lucky for you as well as us that we found you, 'cause we know now that Roman Nose an' a big force ain't far away."

"Maybe you can lend me a saddle and bridle, a rifle and some ammunition," said Bob, "and then I can look for my own party."

But Pete Trudeau sagely shook his head.

"We kin lend you them things," he said, "but it won't do for you to go roamin' around now in search of your friends. These plains are alive with Cheyennes, an' you'd shorely be killed and scalped inside o' twenty-four hours. It's pure luck that's saved you so far. Ef your friends are smart, they've made off to the hills somewhar."

Bob looked about him helplessly.

"What Pete tells you is true," said Jack. "There's nothing for you to do but mount that mustang, and ride with us to Colonel Forsyth. You can find your friends later, an' you've got to choose between life an' death. It's life to go with us."

Stillwell spoke with the greatest earnestness, and Bob was impressed. But he meant to find his comrades some time or other, no matter how long it took him to do it.

"I choose life, of course, in preference to death," he said, smiling faintly. "If one of you can spare me a piece of rope or a rawhide, I'll catch my mustang and we can be off."

Trudeau had the rawhide, with which Bob made a rude kind of knot. He had no trouble in catching the mustang, which seemed to be tamed thoroughly, and he sprang upon his back.

"Now," he exclaimed, refreshed by the food, "I'll ride with you."

"We gallop at once to Forsyth," said Trudeau, "Your news about the Cheyennes is important."

They rode swiftly toward the north, the three of them, and they would have been stirrup to stirrup, but Bob had no stirrup. They kept close to the river, which broadened out considerably in places, but which was always shallow. Two hours, and they entered a little hollow among some cottonwoods. Bob saw soldiers walking back and forth, rifle on shoulder, and beyond them other soldiers. All were weatherbeaten and in faded uniforms. A straight, active and alert man, an officer by his epaulets, came forward at the sound of the galloping hoofs, and Trudeau and Stillwell sprang to the ground. Bob, feeling that he was not as much at home as they, remained on the mustang.

The officer glanced at the boy, and then turned his

attention to Trudeau and Stillwell, who had saluted respectfully.

"It appears that you found something," he said.

"Yes, Colonel," replied Trudeau, acting as spokesman by right of age. "We ran across this boy asleep in the grass. He escaped from the Cheyennes yesterday, and we knew from what he said that Roman Nose an' his whole force ain't far away."

The officer's figure became more rigid and a spark leaped up in his eyes. Then his face fell a little as he looked at his force and saw the smallness of its numbers. But in an instant his face glowed again, with pride in his little band, and perhaps with the thrill of coming conflict.

"Then there may be a meeting, Pete," he said, "and if so, we'll try to bear our part in it. Meanwhile, come with me. You, too, my boy, and we'll hear further details."

They sat by a small fire, and Bob told it all again.

"We've got to find that village or the trail, or it's people, if they've gone, no matter what the odds," said Colonel Forsyth. "It's what we've come out for."

Trudeau and Stillwell nodded.

"Are you willing to go with us, my boy?" said the Colonel, kindly.

"I am, sir," replied Bob, with emphasis.

"Then you're enlisted, Bob," said Colonel Forsyth, calling him by his first name. "Pete, you and Jack find him a saddle, bridle, arms and ammunition, and we'll march at once."

Bob was soon provided with all that he needed, and the trumpet sounded "Boots and Saddles." The little band of fifty mounted and rode out upon the prairie. Trudeau and Stillwell and Abner Grover, generally called Sharp Grover, a man of nearly fifty, acting as guides, were trying to make a reckoning of the direction in which the Cheyenne village lay. Bob confessed frankly that he did not know, but, by putting two and two together, they surmised that it was toward the southwest. So they left the Arickaree and rode over the plains.

Now Bob looked at his new comrades, and they filled his eye. Most of them were young, and most of them also had been soldiers in the Civil War, some on one side and some on the other, every animosity buried in the comradeship of the border. All were native born, except four, and one of these four, a young Irishman named Martin Burke who had served with the British army in India, soon attracted Bob's attention, showing all the proverbial wit and gayety of the Irishman. At least a half dozen of the men were graduates of Eastern colleges, bearing their share in the dangerous work of the border.

The second in command was Lieutenant Fred Beecher, nephew of the famous minister, and, although but a young man, already a veteran. He had received a bullet through the knee at Gettysburg and he walked lame the rest of his days, which were not long now. By the side of Lieutenant Beecher rode First Sergeant William McCall, a man who had risen to the rank of general in the Civil War, had passed out of the army, when the great volunteer force was disbanded, and who now reappeared upon the plains in this humble rank, but faithful and devoted.

There were others with whom Bob was soon to become well acquainted. Louis and Hudson Farley, father and son, serving together, and considered the best shots on the plains, Mooers, the surgeon, and more.

Every man carried a repeating rifle, with six shots in the magazine and one in the barrel, a large revolver, 140 rounds of ammunition for the rifle, 30 for the revolver, and a large, strong hunter's knife. Every one had rations for seven days, already cooked, in his haversack. Four pack mules bore picks, shovels, camp-kettles, four thousand rounds of ammunition, medical supplies, salt and coffee.

It was a gallant band. None finer could have been found anywhere, and, since Bob could not be with his own comrades, he was glad to be with these. The air rushed swiftly past as they rode onward and the tide of life rose high. He was by the side of Stillwell, who was scarcely older than himself, and the two were already fast friends. Martin Burke, a yard away, hummed Irish tunes under his breath, and the two Farleys, father and son, rode knee to knee.

"This is something like it, isn't it Bob?" said Jack Stillwell.

"It beats riding alone, tied on the back of a mustang," said Bob with so much sincerity, that Jack laughed.

"That's behind you," said the young scout, "but

we may have something that will keep us jumping, before us. Colonel Forsyth is not the man to turn back."

"No, I think not," said Bob, looking at the compact active figure of the leader, swinging easily in the saddle.

Bob soon became as much interested as his comrades in the quest, and he, too, scanned the brown soil for signs of a trail. He tried, also, but without success, to remember the direction in which he had come, examining every swell in the hope that he might remember some familiar sign. But it was too much like a dream, and a sleep without a dream for him to pick out landmarks from such obscurity.

"You're sure that none of it comes back to you?" said Colonel Forsyth.

"I wish I could bring it back," replied Bob, "but I can't. I'd know that village if I saw it, but whether it's north, east, south or west from here is more than I can tell."

Colonel Forsyth did not upbraid him because he could not answer. Instead, he regarded the boy more than once with sympathy. The commander, as Bob noticed, seemed to be regarded with great affection by his men.

The day was brilliant, and as it was the middle of September, there was a breath of coolness in the air. Bob drew deep breaths, and his happiness increased. He was naturally optimistic. He had been through so much, and he had been harried so much that it was like heaven to be free again, with fifty brave white men around him. He did not fear the whole Cheyenne nation now, and he had a firm belief, too, that Sam Strong and the others were somewhere in advance. The three scouts now led, Colonel Forsyth was just behind, with Bob by his side, and, after them, came the cavalrymen in a close group. The scouts suddenly reined in their horses, and the others automatically did the same.

"What is it, Sharp?" asked Colonel Forsyth eagerly.

"See, sir," said Sharp, pointing to the ground.

Bob looked down too, and there, imprinted across the plain was the broad trail of many unshod horsemen. The boy's heart throbbed when he saw it, and so did that of every man in the company.

In that expanse, vast and silent save for themselves, the trail was like a living thing. There it was, standing out on the brown soil, wide, vivid, and full of significance. It told Bob in words that must be understood that here the Cheyennes had passed, many warriors, hundreds and hundreds, hunters of men, with the fierce war chiefs, Roman Nose and Black Kettle at their head. This was the tale the trail told.

Colonel Forsyth examined it long and carefully, and his face was at once eager and anxious. He looked from the trail to his men, and he counted to himself the fearful odds. The trail led on before, but it was so wide that one had to go aside to see its farther edge. The Commander rode a little apart, and beckoned to Grover and Stillwell.

"How many warrirors would you say have passed here?" he asked.

"I reckon that countin' people of all kinds, about four thousand people have rid on this trail," replied Grover, "an', figurin' on the usual basis, that means about fifteen hundred warriors. What do you say, Jack?"

"That's about as near it as human calculation can come," replied young Stillwell, with emphasis.

"And we are only fifty," said Forsyth. "Well, General Sheridan sent us out to find the Cheyennes, and whether we're fifty or five thousand, we must find them. Isn't that so, boys?"

"It's so," replied the two scouts together.

"Do you think the men understand it?" asked Colonel Forsyth.

"Every one of them," replied Grover. "They read this trail like print."

"And they are not afraid," said Forsyth, looking at his troops with pride. He turned his horse and faced the little band, which drew up in a compact body, and saluted. Bob instinctively drew his mustang back until he rode in the first line. He now felt himself a member of this little force, as he had felt himself a member of Sam Strong's party, and he was accepted as such.

Colonel Forsyth raised his hand, and there was complete silence, save for the heavy breathing of the men.

"My lads," said the officer, in a firm, clear voice, "every one of you has seen this trail and every one of you knows what it means. Pretty nearly the whole of the Cheyenne nation has passed here, and their fighting men, if they should turn on us, would outnumber us twenty to one. But we follow! Do you understand that? What I wish to know is, do you follow with willing hearts?"

Fifty throats roared out, "We do!" and Bob shouted with them. He was carried away by excitement, and its impulse. He was as ready as any of them to gallop forward against twenty or thirty to one, or, if need be, against fifty to one.

"That is all, my lads," said the Colonel quietly. "Sharp, you and Jack and Pete lead on."

The three guides started up the trail at a trot, and the men, still in a close group, followed them, all looking closely as they rode to saddle and girth, rifle and pistol. The blindest novice could not mistake the trail. It stretched on, broad, obvious and menacing, mile after mile.

Moreover, other signs soon multiplied. Now they saw an abandoned tent pole lying by the trail, and then another. Farther on were fragments of buffalo meat, pieces of clothing, old moccasins, feathers from war-bonnets and other fragments, such as an army might leave behind on its march. It was evident that the Cheyennes were not seeking to hide their trail. "It looks as if they were defying all the white forces, doesn't it?" said Stillwell to Bob, who had dropped back by his side again.

"Yes, they're telling us to come on if we dare," said Bob.

"The Colonel dares," said Stillwell tersely and Bob felt a certain pride in it. He could see, too, a visible increase in his own importance and Pete and Jack accepted him as comrade.

The afternoon waxed and waned, and there was the trail yet before them, as broad, and as menacing as ever. It was impossible to tell how old it was, but the guides surmised that the Indians had a lead of ten or twelve hours. Sunset was at hand, and, to the great vexation of Colonel Forsyth, mists and vapors from the southwest promised a dark night. The promise was soon fulfiled, and in another hour they could not see fifty yards ahead of them.

It was impossible to continue the pursuit until morning, and they went into camp, if blankets and the bare prairie can be called a camp. But Bob did not think it so bad. He had the companionship of the men, and they found enough buffalo chips for a fire, over which they cooked bacon and made coffee.

The food and drink heartened them wonderfully and, although they put out the fire as soon as the cooking was over, the effect of its warmth lingered. Grover, Trudeau and Stillwell were off on the plain, scouting in the darkness. Bob would have gone with them, but Colonel Forsyth detained him, in order to ask further details about the Cheyennes. The younger officers also were allowed to sit by and listen.

Bob recounted again all that he had seen in the Cheyenne village, and he dwelt much on the figure of Roman Nose.

"A great chief," said Colonel Forsyth, "a dangerous and a worthy enemy. And the crafty Black Kettle is not much inferior to him. You have met him face to face, and maybe we will have the chance too."

The scouts came back, after a while, and reported that nothing could be found on the prairie. There was no danger of a night attack, and the men could sleep easily until the morning.

Colonel Forsyth uttered a sigh of satisfaction. He knew the value of peace of mind and a night's rest. He put a friendly hand on Bob's shoulder and said:

"Go to sleep as soon as you can, my boy, because we march early in the morning."

Bob drew his blanket closely about his body, pillowed his head upon the haversack which had been given to him as part of his outfit, and closed his eyes. Weariness had come back upon him. Some of the effects of the wild ride, bound upon the back of the mustang lingered, and he began to wish again for absolute rest.

He felt now, for the first time in days, the complete luxury of peace, the peace of both the body and the mind that rebuilds. Within this ring of brave men he took no thought of the Cheyennes, and the gentle wind that blew over the plains was as soothing as the sound of faint and distant music. He heard the tread of a horse now and then, the rustle of a trooper, seeking a better position for his body, and then he heard nothing. He was sound asleep and he did not wake again until the clear note of the bugle called to him to rise.

Food and coffee were served, and then the fifty remounted. Among all the horses there was none more tractable than the mustang. Bob raised himself in his stirrups, and searched the rolling plain with his strong, young eyes. He could see nothing. It was as bare as it had been the day before. Young Stillwell rode up by his side.

"You don't see anything, Bob," said Stillwell, "but that don't mean that you won't see anything. I'm <u>thinking</u> that the trail will grow pretty hot before the day is over."

"If it means a fight I hope to do my share," said Bob. "I've been in battle with the Cheyennes already."

"I've fired a lot of good metal at 'em," said Stillwell, "and they've fired a lot at me, but it's all in the job. Come on, Bob."

Bob spoke to his mustang, and the powerful horse leaped forward, his compact, muscular body taut like steel wire, and his spirit alight. Bob shared his eagerness. A second night's rest had driven away the last traces of his collapse and he was ready for anything. Jack Stillwell glanced at him approvingly.

The trail seemed broader than ever. It looked almost as if a buffalo herd had passed that way and Grover announced presently that two other parties had joined the great band.

"Never mind," said Colonel Forsyth, "we still follow."

He shut his lips tightly together and rode directly behind Bob and the three scouts, and, behind him, the troop rode as one, every man knowing to what he was riding, and no man flinching.

The trail veered after a while and once more they saw the Arickaree. Then it ran on for hours by the side of the river. They halted a little after noon, for a short rest and to water the horses, and when they resumed the pursuit Grover said to the commander that he did not think they would overtake the Cheyennes that day.

"They are movin' pretty fast," he said, "an' while the trail is growin' warmer it won't be warm enough by nightfall."

The hot sun began to cool, the afternoon passed its zenith, but the band rode on, now in silence. The trail wound along the south bank of the Arickaree, forty or fifty yards from the stream, among thickets of alder, willow and wild plum. Just as they had passed one of the densest parts of these thickets, the river made a bend, and, as they rode through a narrow gorge, they saw a pleasant valley, two miles wide, and a little longer, well grown in grass. On the south side, the land made a gentle incline down to the Arickaree. But on the north it stretched away in a level expanse for nearly a mile, the valley there ending abruptly against a line of bluffs, about fifty feet high.

Colonel Forsyth gave a signal, and the whole troop stopped, looking into the valley. He was troubled. He feared that he was going to face very great odds, and he was worried, too, by the scarcity of his provisions. Except the food in the haversacks everything was gone save a small quantity of coffee and salt. The horses had depended on grass, and the valley before him was full of it. Perhaps it would be best to camp here.

As he looked, his eyes fell upon an island in the

middle of the stream, a peculiar little island, about a hundred yards long, and perhaps half as wide. It had been formed of sand, accumulating around a gravelly rift at its head. It was seventy or eighty yards from the shore on either side, but at this time of the year, most of the distance was sand. The water in either channel was not more than fifteen or twenty feet wide, and about half a foot deep.

Long sage grass covered the head of the island, in the center grew a thicket of alders and willows to the height of about five feet, and at the foot stood a lone, young cottonwood. The Colonel's eyes wandered away from the island and then he gave the command to ride into the valley and camp. Bob thought the Colonel was going to have them camp on the island, but instead he chose a place opposite it on the mainland.

The Colonel himself saw to the making of the camp and the posting of the sentries. Every man was directed to hobble his horse, and to see that his lariat was knotted right. He was ordered also to drive his picket pin firmly into the ground, and before lying down for the night he must see that it was still right. He also gave detailed instructions in case of surprise. Every man was to seize his horse's lariat with one hand and his rifle with the other. He was then to stand by his horse to prevent a stampede, a thing greatly to be feared in their situation.

Bob, after he had tethered the mustang, walked to the edge of the river and looked at the island. The sun had set but some of its last red rays lingered over the island tinting its sand and the alders and the willows and the lone young cottonwood as if with blood. A chill wind blew out of the west, and the water in the river looked dark and cold. A strange shiver, a premonition, as it were, of an event tremendous, ran through every nerve and vein of Bob's being, and he knew that it was the island, or something about it, something mysterious and uncanny. He looked so long at it that he seemed to see an ashy vapor rising from its sands, and, angry at himself, he dashed his hands before his eyes to drive it away.

"What's the matter, Bob?" asked Stillwell, who had seen the gesture.

"Nothing, at least not anything real. That island there was putting a spell on me, and I was seeing all sorts of things."

"I don't see anything but a spit of sand."

"And I don't now, either."

"Well, you'd better get to sleep."

"I want to stand my share of the watch."

"You don't have any share. The Colonel says that a fellow who has ridden a horse barebacked, and at a gallop, two or three hundred miles without stopping, can't play sentinel, for at least a week afterward."

Bob was forced to acquiesce, and again wrapped in his blanket he sought sleep on the bare ground. It came quickly enough, but it was not so sound this second night. He awoke at some unknown hour, though the moon was shining, and, sitting up, looked over the camp. About him were the motionless figures of the men, deep in slumber. Further away were the figures of horses, and beyond them, the sentinels, with ready rifles, watching every point of the horizon.

But Bob's eyes came back to one point, drawn there by a sort of hypnotic spell. It was the island, the reach of sand, upon which the moon was shining. But the sand, instead of turning to silver in the moonlight, turned to ashen-gray. It was a cold and forbidding expanse and half-awake, half-asleep, Bob felt, for the second time, the premonition of something tremendous. But he shut his eyes and resolutely sought sleep again.

When he awoke it was only faint dawn, just three fingers of pale gray in the east, but he felt that he had sleep enough and he sat up, letting his blanket drop from him. He saw an erect figure just beyond the last row of figures and he recognized Colonel Forsyth. The leader of the little band was on guard. Beyond him stood another man, the young scout, Jack Stillwell.

It was Bob's first intention to join them, but he refrained. They might not want him. He sat a little longer, and the slim strip of gray in the east broadened to a band. The band turned from gray to silver and from silver to an edge of flaming red, the first herald of the sun. Bob was still looking at the Colonel and the scout, and he saw both of them make a sudden movement, as if they had seen something unusual. They were staring at the crest of a low hill that lay some distance beyond the camp.

Bob, acting partly on impulse and partly on Sam

Strong's training, leaned backward and put his ear to the earth. He heard distinctly a soft, regular sound and he knew it. It was the beat of horses' feet. He sprang erect, with a single motion, and he saw Stillwell bring his rifle forward with his finger on the trigger. Bob sprang to the Colonel's side, and then, although erect, he could hear the soft thud of hoofs. He knew that the Colonel heard it too, as he held in his hand his drawn revolver.

The dash of scarlet in the east turned to a blaze. Suddenly above the crest of the hill appeared the tips of waving eagle feathers, and then several mounted Cheyennes, phantom-like and gigantic against the first sunrise. He knew that they were the famous Dog Soldiers, and he knew too, that others must be near. Stillwell fired instantly at one of the warriors and sprang back shouting the alarm.

"Up, men! Up! The Cheyennes have come!" cried Colonel Forsyth, and instantly the fifty men were upon their feet, rifles in hand, the frightened horses held firmly by the lariats.

The mounted Indians appeared upon the brow of the hill, and the whole band galloped straight toward the group of white men, their robust bodies glistening in the morning light, and the long feathers in their hair streaming out defiantly. Some of them carried shields of buffalo hide, upon which they beat with a loud, rolling sound like that of drums.

"Steady, men! Steady!" said Colonel Forsyth. His men raised their rifles, and Bob, who was just in front, raised his also, but the Cheyennes suddenly veered, and charged around the flank of the whites, shouting the war-whoop with all the strength of their voices.

"Look out!" cried Trudeau, "they're trying to stampede our horses!"

The Cheyennes, bending low in their saddles, rushed the horses and pack-mules gathered behind the camp, intending to sweep them all away, and leave the little command on foot and practically helpless. But the soldiers ran forward and fired upon them rapidly. Grover, Trudeau and Stillwell, reckless of the return fire from the Indians, dashed forward to save the pack-mules and Bob followed them. A Cheyenne fired at him from under his pony's neck and missed. Bob did not fire back, because his hands were now occupied with his own struggling horse.

Then one of the Cheyennes uttered a short, sharp shout, and the band, turning about, galloped away at top speed. They had not created a stampede, but they carried with them two of the pack-mules loaded with stores and two horses that had not been picketed properly. Young Stillwell fired again at them, as they rode away, and a feathered warrior, throwing up his hands dropped backward from his pony to the plain where he lay still. There were other scattering shots, but the rest of the band galloped out of range with their prizes. Some of the soldiers started to follow, but the Colonel ordered all to saddle and bridle their horses instantly, and stand fast.

The swift charge and the swift retreat passed in a minute or two, while the daylight was still showing in the east, and had not yet appeared in the west. Bob was almost dazed by its rapidity. He stood, holding the bridle of the mustang, while a little cloud of dust, kicked up by the hoofs of the ponies, drifted over them.

He looked through the dust as through a mist, and an army of red horsemen seemed to rise out of the plain. The line stretched far to right and to left, and every man was bent forward a little over his horse's neck, like those who ride to the charge. The boy's heart gave a great jump, and then every nerve tingled and throbbed. The first band had been mere raiders. This was the Cheyenne army.

"Look! Look!" cried Grover, standing beside his commander. "All the Cheyennes have come!"

It was true. The great Cheyenne force had turned upon its own trail, and now it approached the little white band from all sides. Besides the horsemen in front, other Indians, some on foot and some mounted, were pressing forward along either bank of the river. Just in front of the red line, where the Indians were massed, a gigantic man sat on a great mustang. This man's appearance was ferocious and impressive to the last degree. Feathers and plumes, woven into a great gorgeous braid, swung from his hair. His face was covered with war-paint, red and black in many designs, even to the nose, which was large and curved. The head was crowned with the war-bonnet, a magnificent ornament of large colored feathers, with two short, black buffalo horns projecting from it, at the temples. He was naked save for his moccasins and a broad scarf of blood-red about the waist.

The man sat perfectly still on his horse, and regarded the group of white men with a gaze that expressed hatred and triumph. He was like one who had long sought a foe, and who now held him in the hollow of his hand. Bob thought that he had never seen anything more impressive than this startling apparition. But he knew the man.

"Roman Nose!" he cried.

Every white eye was instantly turned upon the chief, but he yet sat motionless, gazing upon them with that look of malignant triumph, the certainty of victory to come.

CHAPTER XVII

LITTLE THERMOPYLAE

Bob saw the great chief raise his hand, and then a wild cry burst from a thousand throats, a savage cry, so instinct with hatred, ferocity and triumph, that every man shuddered. Then the whole Indian army swept forward, horse and foot, more than twenty to one.

Bob felt himself recoiling as if an irresistible mass were rushing down upon him, but in a moment he checked himself. The white men stood now in a circle with their horses behind them in the center. But the deadly muzzles of their rifles faced in every direction. Bob was between Trudeau and Stillwell and Colonel Forsyth was only a few yards away. The boy, although he stood motionless, was tremendously excited. The little pulses in his temple were beating furiously, and the charging horde came on in a red mist. Nevertheless he heard amid all the fierce yelling from hundreds of throats the low "steady! steady!" of the commander, an insistent undernote. All the time, the rising sun was pouring a flood of golden beams down upon this wild scene of the Western plains.

Nearer came the red horsemen and the thousands of hoofs beat like thunder. It looked to Bob as if they must all be trodden under foot. He saw through the clouds of dust, always tinted red, the wild faces of the warriors, their curved noses, and their white teeth, from which their thin, red lips were drawn back. He looked for Roman Nose. He did not see him, but he chose another, a large warrior who also wore a magnificent war-bonnet and who was in the very front of the charging red line. The trigger of his rifle fairly burned against his finger, but Colonel Forsyth had not yet given the command to fire, and he dared not pull it. Nearer they came, and it seemed that in another minute the Indians would be upon the troopers. Then the Colonel shouted: "Fire!" the single sharp word rising above the roar like the crack of a pistol-shot.

Fifty eager fingers pulled trigger at once. The little circle of men was rimmed around with fire, and a cloud of smoke at once arose. But it was a deadly circle. From every point it emitted singing metal, as the men loaded and fired as fast as they could. Their bullets crashed into the masses of charging Cheyennes. Ponies and riders went down. Warriors fell as if smitten with a thunderbolt. Horses, screaming with pain, galloped about the plain. Dust and smoke mingled, and heavy with odors and vapors, floated over them all.

Bob aimed directly at the big warrior with the eagle beak, when he pulled the trigger. When the rifle flashed he saw the warrior no more. After that he fired at whatever was nearest. The little pulses in his head were beating more furiously than ever, and he was scarcely conscious of what he was doing, but he did not flinch. He remembered afterward that he could still feel Trudeau at his right and Stillwell at his left, while the commander stood as before only a few yards away.

The crash of the rifles was so steady now that it was like the roll of thunder. Mingled with it, the unbroken yelling of the Indians and the drum of hoofs beat upon the boy's ears, with such regularity that he became unconscious of sound at all. The troopers seldom shouted, but aiming low, sent their bullets straight to the mark. Bob saw the head of a pony almost in his face. He fired at it and the pony fell. Other ponies appeared through the clouds of dust and smoke but they too went down, and no wild horseman broke through the white ring.

Bullets struck in the ring also. Men were wounded but they hid it for the time, and kept their places in the defense. Bob felt something hot searing his side, but he knew that he was merely grazed and he forgot it the next moment. Then he became conscious of the great shouting and firing, but it was because both were decreasing and becoming irregular. The clouds of smoke and dust lifted, and showed the Cheyennes in retreat, the ground between the foes sprinkled with dead horses and fallen warriors.

The little band of fifty—though not fifty now—uttered a great shout of exultation. That invincible front of fire had beaten off the entire Cheyenne army—for an instant. The Cheyennes were sullenly withdrawing out of rifle range, but Colonel Forsyth knew well enough that the attack would soon come again, and that they could not beat it back a second time, standing there in the open plain. His quick mind was at work and it was working well. He glanced toward the island, and he saw that the water would form a defense against a charge, or at least help.

"Come, my boys," he said, "we will fight from the island. Move toward it, as fast as you can, but do not break your ring."

The firing and the shouting had ceased, and in the silence his voice was like thunder to Bob. Then he heard Trudeau murmuring under his breath: "A good move; it's our only chance."

The ring, as even and orderly as a Macedonian phalanx, protected by the fire of their best marksmen, went swiftly toward the river, the frightened horses dragged with them by the lariats, the men carrying also their wounded and their dead. It was a perfect movement, which only the bravest of veterans could have executed at such a terrible moment. In an instant they had reached the shallow water, in another they were in it, and in a third they were on the sandy island.

The Cheyennes, when they saw the retreat, rushed forward and began to fire again from every point of vantage. They leaped from their horses, and took advantage of every inequality in the earth. They swarmed among the reeds and willows on either side of the river bed, and poured in a storm of bullets. More men were wounded. Several horses were killed and fell into the water, while the others were so terrified that it took half the time and strength of the men to hold them.

But the troopers were upon the island and Forsyth

shouted to them to dig, dig for their lives. Bob understood when his heels sank in the soft sand. Half the men were at work already, while the other half, forming a ring about them, were returning the Indian fire.

The men were scooping up the sand, some with their hands, some with empty tin cans from the mess, but most with their hunting knives. Bob took out his own knife and he and Stillwell began to dig a hole.

"It will be a good place for us, dead or alive," said young Stillwell with grim humor.

Bob dug furiously and threw up the soft sand in a shower, while Stillwell arranged it all around the hole in the form of a breastwork. The sand seemed to go down to an unlimited depth, and it was so soft that the hole sank fast. Bob could not tell anything about time, but eight or ten minutes must have passed, when Stillwell shouted to him:

"Up with your rifle, Bob, the Cheyennes are about to charge again!"

All the men threw down the tools with which they had been digging and seized their weapons. Some of the horses had been tethered, but in the hurry the others were left to shift for themselves. But many holes had been dug, and many mounds of sand had been thrown up. The island, with its band of water on either side, and its sand protection, was a different place from the open plain. Stillwell sprang down by the side of Bob in the hole that they had dug, and the two on their knees were sheltered almost completely.

"Let 'em come, Bob, my boy," said Stillwell, the fire of battle flaming in his veins.

"Yes, let 'em come," said Bob, peering down the sights of his rifle, the barrel of which lay on the wall of sand.

The Cheyennes needed no invitation. They were coming fast enough, and from every side they swarmed toward the island, continuously shouting the war-whoop, and firing their rifles as they charged. The skirmishers in the beds of reeds also pressed closer and these were now the most dangerous. Picked sharpshooters, they sent the sand flying in little puffs. One puff struck Bob in the face, and it stung like small shot. He and Stillwell turned their attention to these wasps and their bullets sang among the reeds.

But the majority of the troopers, at the command of Colonel Forsyth, fired at the charging hordes of horsemen, and sheltered by their mounds and ridges of sand, they were able to break the lines, shooting down warriors and ponies alike. Now a great crowd of Indian women and children appeared on the bluffs, at the back of the valley, and added their shouts to the uproar.

The Indians charged to the very edge of the water, but they paused there in the face of the withering fire from the island, and then breaking, retreated rapidly out of rifle range, followed by the derisive cheering of the island's defenders.

"Twice we've licked 'em," exclaimed Jack Stillwell, joyfully, "but they'll come again. Hurt, Bob?"

"Not touched," replied the boy, "but I'm hot,

and my heart has been pounding like a drum. Good Heavens! What's that?"

A wild scream of pain, more terrible than a man could utter, made them both jump. It came from a wounded horse, and presently two more joined in his shuddering cry. Several had torn loose and were running up and down the island. Others, mortally wounded had broken away, only to fall dead beyond the stream, and while the main attack had been repulsed, the skirmishers among the reeds turned their aim from the defenders to the horses which could not be protected from their bullets.

"It's all up with them," said Stillwell. "We can't save 'em. Our good horses have to go."

The rifles cracked fast among the reeds and horse after horse was struck.

"Turn them loose!" commanded the Colonel, and the men quickly obeyed, first securing their food and extra ammunition. Even then many of the horses were shot down as they galloped across the Arickaree. Bob approaching his mustang, and careless of a chance shot, took him by the mane.

The boy's heart was full of sadness. He had a genuine affection for this horse which had saved him, but he knew now that he must let him go, or see him slain almost at his feet. The mustang thrust out his head, and muzzled his hand. Bob's heart was rent again, but it was no time for waiting. A bullet struck in the sand at his feet. Another grazed his buckskin coat.

"Farewell, good horse!" he exclaimed. "Now go!"

He struck the mustang smartly on the side with his rifle-barrel, at the same moment slipping off the bridle. The horse galloped down the island, looked a few moments at the water, crossed it with a few bounds, and then stood upon the open plain.

Several of the withdrawing warriors fired at the mustang, but their bullets merely knocked up the dust about him. He stopped, and looked scornfully at them. Two more shots were fired at him, and then he broke into a run across the plain, which was encircled by the Indian line.

Bob jumped back into the pit with Stillwell and the two watched the mustang, whose fortunes had assumed a wholly human interest for them. The splendid beast galloped on toward the Indian line.

"They'll kill him," said Bob.

"Since they missed him first, it's more likely that they'll try to catch him now," said Stillwell. "They'll see that he's worth having."

Three or four of the best mounted Cheyennes galloped forward, and threw their lariats. But the rope missed his head every time, and slipped along his smooth side to fall fruitlessly on the ground.

"Good horse! good horse!" repeated Bob. "They haven't got him yet."

The mustang went straight on, tore through the Indian line, the lariats whistling about him in vain, and then galloped at full speed toward the bluffs, the disappointed Cheyennes firing at him two or three shots that fell short. Presently he reached a crest out of range, looked back a moment, shook his long mane, and then with a final burst of speed, disappeared over the hill.

Bob laughed aloud in his pleasure.

"They could neither take nor kill him!" he exclaimed. "I was fond of that mustang, Jack. I ought to have been, as he saved my life."

"He may have been a wild horse once, and it's likely that he'll become one again," said Stillwell. "He's fit to be the head of a great herd."

"I hope so," said Bob, "and since he's got away, we'll take it as a good omen, and reckon it as a sure thing that we're going to get away too."

"Right enough," said Jack cheerfully. "Of course we'll get away. There ain't more than a million Cheyennes around us, but with our sand pits here, we could beat 'em off if they were two millions. Listen to that, Bob! We haven't been shooting for nothing."

From the bluffs back of the battlefield came a long, high-pitched wailing sound. It was the women and children mourning the dead warriors, most of whom had been carried away by their comrades and their horses. It was inexpressibly sad to Bob, and for the moment he felt sympathy for the Cheyennes.

"Fighting is hot business in more ways than one," said Stillwell, and one of the hot things that it does to you is to get up a thirst. The Arickaree is a cool, clear stream, and I'm bound to have some of it, right away."

"Don't you try it," said Bob. "It's too dangerous. Those fellows in the reeds would pick you off when you bent down for the water."

"I don't intend to do any bending down," said Stillwell. "I'm going by underground, and you're going to help me."

All the men during the lull in the fighting were busily scooping their burrows deeper, and Stillwell, using a broad tin plate, set to work digging a shallow trench toward the river, which was only a few feet away. He lay almost on his side, and made the sand fly fast. Bob helped him with his hunting knife, and as they pulled forward eight or ten feet in the trench, the sand grew damp. Then the cool water oozed up and the two drank greedily, one from a can and the other from the plate. It was like nectar to their parched lips and throat, and they did not neglect to take a plentiful supply back to their comrades.

"Lucky thing for us," said Stillwell, "that we've been cooped up with a river full of good water all about us. We're likely to need it in our business before this thing is over. Look, there's Roman Nose!"

The great chief had ridden again to the brow of the low hill, and just out of rifle range, sat there looking down at the devoted band on the island, the blazing sun showing every bright feather in his magnificent war-bonnet.

"He's planning," said Stillwell, "as sure as shooting. I'll bet that he's as mad as a hornet, through and through, because we got upon this island, but he expects to get us out of it, all the same. Now I wonder what's turning in that cunning Indian brain of his?"

Colonel Forsyth was also wondering. He lay in a sand burrow by the side of his surgeon, Dr. Mooers, and closely watched his formidable antagonist. The dust had settled back to earth, the smoke had lifted, and everything could be seen clearly. The commander felt in his heart that an attack more determined and savage than either of the others was about to be made. He feared, too, that it would be accompanied by more craft, and he looked sorrowfully at his little band. The wounds were numerous, and several men lay dead in the sand. But there was no thought of surrender in his mind. Little mercy could be expected from the Cheyennes, and he would not have asked it, even had there been a chance. He and his band were resolved to die there, to the last man if need be.

"Look well to your rifles, boys," he said, "and see that all the cartridges are in."

Their rifles were the best of the time, and they knew that their lives depended upon them. Bob counted the cartridges in his to see that all were in place, and also surveyed the pistol in his holster. The water had refreshed him greatly, and Stillwell gave him a strip of bacon to chew.

"You may not be able to taste it at all," he said, "but it will hearten you up and give you strength. I've saved another strip for myself."

Bob followed his advice, but as the young scout said, he could not taste the food. Meanwhile the Cheyennes were gathering for a greater effort than ever. The chiefs assembled for council on one of the low bluffs within sight of the island, and their great war-bonnets glowed in the sun. Roman Nose was there, so was Black Kettle, and so were chiefs from all the clans, the Dog Soldiers, the Fox Men, Those-with-Headed-Lances, The Red-Shield-Owners, Those-with-the-Bow-String, and even the Foolish Dogs. There was with them, too, a white man, a freebooter, no less a person than Juan Carver; but Roman Nose was the great dominating personality. He had been successful for two years in his war with the whites, and he did not mean to fail, now that he held Forsyth in the hollow of his hand.

Bob could distinguish Roman Nose at the distance, and he felt that the coming charge would be far more formidable than either of the others. Roman Nose, not sparing his own men, would hurl the Cheyenne army directly upon them.

The little band finished its last preparation for defense. The saddles from the dead or injured horses were piled in rows on the mounds of sand. Everything that could serve as a shield against bullets was put in place, and then they waited.

The sun never ceased to shine with the utmost brilliancy. Only tiny white clouds dotted the blue of the heavens. In the transparent light it seemed almost possible to distinguish the features of the women and children on the bluffs, watching them to see the warriors destroy the white force to the last man.

The council of the chiefs was over. Bob could see them going away, and the Cheyenne skirmishers, advancing directly in their front, opened fire. It was not a headlong charge of horsemen now, but the slow and careful approach of sharpshooters who, lying almost flat on the plain, crawled forward and sent in a bullet whenever they caught sight of any portion of a trooper's body. The warriors, who had never left the cover of the reeds and willows, also resumed their fire, and the island, low, flat and bare, was swept by bullets.

Only their burrows in the sand saved the troopers, and raising themselves just enough to take aim they returned a careful and deadly fire. It was the order of Colonel Forsyth that no man was to pull trigger until he could draw a bead on his target, and despite the smoke, many a bullet struck true.

Stillwell was watching the advance intently, noting the white puffs of smoke on the plain wherever a Cheyenne fired, and he was puzzled.

"This can't be the main attack," he said to Bob. "Their riflemen may cut us up a lot, but I don't believe they mean to rush us in front. Look at that! Some of those fellows in the reeds have reached the end of the island. Keep close, Bob! Keep close!"

Several of the most daring of the Cheyennes had actually crawled through the reeds and water and effected a lodgment on the upper end of the island, where they hid in the sage, and from that ambush fired upon the troopers.

Colonel Forsyth was lying in one of the sand pits, within five feet of Bob and Stillwell. He was almost flat upon his side, firing with the others, but low as he lay, the bullets from the daring warriors on the island began to patter around him.

"We've got to clean those fellows out," said Stillwell. A Cheyenne rifle flashed, and the young scout instantly fired at the flash. A warrior, uttering a cry, sprang convulsively into the air, and fell back out of sight.

"One's gone," said Stillwell, "but more are left, and I tell you, Bob, they're mighty dangerous. Good God, why don't the Colonel keep down!"

Colonel Forsyth had risen and was walking around among his men, encouraging them, telling them to stand fast, that they could yet beat off the Indians. Bob looked at him, the only upright figure on the island, and saw him stagger. Bob knew that he was hit, and his heart sank.

The Colonel clapped his hand to his thigh where the blood was already running through the cloth of his trousers, and then sank down again in the sandy trench. The shot was seen by all the men, and they cried out, wishing to know if he were alive. Although suffering acute pain, as the bullet had ranged upward in his right thigh, he replied cheerfully that he was all right, and as the last word left his lips, another bullet struck his leg half way between knee and ankle, shattering the bone. But the indomitable man roused himself again and cried encouragement to the others. A third bullet passed through the crown of his felt hat, ploughed under the skin of his head and fractured his skull, a piece of the bone being taken out a month later. Surgeon Mooers was mortally wounded by his side.

But this dauntless commander did not lose either consciousness or courage. With these terrible wounds he propped himself up on his elbow, called to his men to fight on and, taking a rifle himself, fired at mounted Indians, who were now approaching from the front. With such an example no trooper could falter. Forsyth bleeding from his three great wounds, in spite of everything kept his faculties clear in this terrific moment, and directed the battle.

The Indian force steadily crept forward, wrapping themselves around three sides of the defenders, and sending in the bullets faster and faster. Man after man, despite the protection of the sand, was hit, and some were killed, usually dying without noise in the pits that they had dug, and the least exposure of an arm or a shoulder was sure to bring a bullet. Now the warriors redoubled their shouting, and from the bluffs a horde of women and children increased it with a great chorus.

It seemed to Bob that the final charge must come the next moment, and he did not see how it could be held back. Unconsciously he resigned himself, and he was glad that he was not to die in the darkness and alone.

"They'll rush upon us in a minute," he said to Stillwell.

"Not so," replied the experienced young scout. "They're not going to charge us in front. You don't see Roman Nose there. You don't see any of the big chiefs there. Now I wonder how they're coming at us. But they'll come sure."

Bob slipped new cartridges into his rifle, and peered again through the bank of smoke and dust. His eye swept entirely around the circle and rested upon one point from which no attack had come. There his gaze was fixed, and with a convulsive start he straightened up in the pit.

"Here they come now," exclaimed Stillwell. "Look, Roman Nose himself leads."

Five hundred red horsemen, Roman Nose at their head, rode up the bed of the river which was very low. Just behind Roman Nose were Black Kettle and all the chiefs, and on the flank an old medicine man, as brave as any of the chiefs, led. Every man in that wild army was stripped for battle, naked save for the breech-cloth, moccasins and war-bonnet. They held rifles and pistols in their hands, and they urged their horses forward with their heels. The sunlight, for here the air was clear of smoke and dust, floated down on them, and lighted up their features, the high cheek bones, the curved beaks, and the bare arms and shoulders, lean, sinewy and powerful.

The great mass of red horsemen halted for a few moments at the mouth of the narrow gorge through which the force of Forsyth had come the day before, and then the two forces looked at each other, the little white band half hidden in the sand on the island, and the chosen Indian warriors, more than ten to one.

It was a sight that Bob saw many a time afterwards in his dreams, so tense, so vivid, etched so strongly against the background of blazing sunlight, that it was real again.

There for an instant sat the gigantic figure of Roman Nose on his horse, general, warrior, worthy leader of a savage army. He turned a single glance toward the women and children who stood in thousands on the low line of bluffs. Then he raised his right arm and waved his hand to them, like a Roman gladiator saluting the multitude. When they saw the gesture they replied with a vast shout of joy that rolled in echoes up the valley and beyond. It was a cry so full of ferocity and the savor of triumph that the two youths lying together in the sandy hollow could not keep from shuddering.

Roman Nose turned his gaze back from the Cheyenne nation to the little white force on the island. He seemed fairly to rise upon his horse as he clenched one fist in the white man's fashion, and shook it fiercely at his foe. Then he threw back his head, clapped the palm of his hand across his mouth, and uttered the most tremendous war-cry that ever passed human lips. It pierced the air like a rifleshot, then swelled in volume and filled the whole valley. Before the terrible echoes died, the deep note of a bugle, captured from some trooper, sounded above all the battle that was raging elsewhere, and with one tremendous shout the five hundred rode for the island.

"Now, Bob," shouted Stillwell, "shoot as you never shot before! This is the real attack!"

Bob knew already that it was the crisis, and so did every man among the fifty who yet lived. They whirled about, ignoring for a moment the sharpshooters in front, and faced the charge, the indomitable commander himself, who could scarcely move, lying against the sand and raising a revolver.

A wind cleft still more the banks of smoke and dust, and the entire mass of horsemen was revealed, the sand flying in showers beneath the beating hoofs. By the power of will and the concentrated energy of the moment, Forsyth raised himself on the sand and gazed at the rushing host, Roman Nose still several paces in front.

There was a sudden lull in the firing from the plains, as if the sharpshooters had risen up to see. The women and children on the bluffs sank into silence. Forsyth watched for a few minutes longer, and no man fired. Then he uttered the single sharp syllable that every one understood:

"Now!"

CHAPTER XVIII

THE CHARGE OF ROMAN NOSE

When that single monosyllable, "Now!" shot forth, the men in the pits raised up a little and pulled trigger, so close together that there was only a single crash. But every rifle was aimed true, and a hole was torn in the Indian line, men and horses going down together. The Cheyennes, great warriors, did not falter, and the magnificent Roman Nose led as before.

The dismounted Indians on the flanks resumed their fire, but the defenders of the island took no notice of them. Their eyes were never turned from the horsemen. They were a dauntless band, sunbrowned, nearly all wounded, but their hands were steady and their eyes alight with the flame of battle. Forsyth lay upon his back in the sand, unable to move, but despite it, sending bullets from his revolver. A second time they pulled the trigger and a third time, and always the bullets went low and to the mark. The air was full of whistling metal. Riders and horses struck down disappeared from the line, but others took their places, the mass closed up and never for an instant ceased its charge.

"Can we ever stop them!" exclaimed young Stillwell, and Bob echoed his words. The Cheyennes were rushing their horses now through the shallow water and would soon reach the island, carried on by their own courage and the fire of their daring leader. On the island more men were slain by the rifle-fire of the Indians which now came from every point, and others received fresh wounds, but those who still lived pulled the trigger with fiercer energy. It was all a red whirl to the boy, a terrible medley of fire and sand and water and smoke, pierced by the mingled crash of shots and shouts. Despite his danger and the fierce excitement of the moment, he could not withhold admiration for the courage of the Cheyennes, and above all for the daring of their leaders.

The Cheyenne chief was still in the van. His powerful horse came on with great leaps, and Roman Nose riding without a saddle sat far forward on the bare back. His knees were under a horse-hair lariat, wound around the animal's body, and he held the bridle firmly in his left hand. He grasped a heavy repeating rifle in his right hand, and now and then he whirled it aloft as he galloped down upon his enemy. Fearless of death, no more magnificent figure was ever seen upon the plains.

"Fire at Roman Nose!" Bob heard Stillwell shout. He raised his rifle in obedience to the impulse, and then he turned his muzzle upon some one else. He did not know why he shifted the rifle, but he was always glad of it. Others were not moved by the same feeling.

Roman Nose had already reached the island, riding at a gallop directly down upon the rifle pits. The medicine man who led the flank had been killed, but the other chiefs were close behind him.

"He will ride over us!" exclaimed Bob.

Stillwell's only reply was to pull the trigger of the rifle aimed directly at the chief. Several others fired upon him at the same time. Roman Nose leaped convulsively upward and then sank back on his horse. The rifle dropped from his outstretched hand to the ground. His great body swayed, darkness quenched the flame of his eyes, and he fell to the ground, dead, pierced by half a dozen bullets.

A cry of grief and rage rose from the Cheyennes when they saw the death of their best chief, but the charge did not stop. Swerving their horses to one side, or leaping them over his body, they rode to the very edge of the rifle pits, but the fire swept them away. More chiefs went down. Horses, riderless or wounded, galloped here and there and spread confusion among them. The thrice-wounded Forsyth, lying on the ground, never ceased to direct his men. The Indians were so close now that even an excited marksman could scarcely miss.

The charge, one of the bravest and most dramatic ever made, broke on the island. The fire from the rifle pits was so fast and so deadly that the Indians, their great leader gone, gave way at last and galloped back, carrying with them the bodies of most of their fallen chiefs. A great cry of grief rose from the multitude beyond, and then came a lull like that which had preceded the charge. It was broken for Bob by the exultant cry of Stillwell:

"We've won! We've won!"

The boy was gasping. He was so much excited by the charge, the conflict and the tremendous picture he had seen that he could not speak. He was conscious that the Cheyennes had been driven back, but he did not feel the full reality of it. His eyes, his ears and his throat were full of the mingled reek of smoke, dust, sweat and burnt gunpowder. He was about to choke, but at last he managed to say:

"Have we really fought them off?"

"Not a doubt of it," said Stillwell, joyfully, and then he added with emphatic admiration, "But that was a great charge. I never expect to see its like again. If Roman Nose hadn't been shot from his horse they might have ridden over us."

"Down, men! Down!" suddenly cried Forsyth with all his energy, and the troopers obeyed just in time, throwing themselves flat on their faces in the rifle pits. The swarm of Indians on foot among the reeds and alders and willows swept the island from side to side with a rain of bullets, volleys that had been withheld before for fear of hitting their own charging horsemen.

The fire was so fierce that the brave Lieutenant Beecher, despite the protection of the sand, was mortally wounded, and others received fresh hurts. But the best of the white riflemen began to pick off the Indians among the bushes, and gradually cleared out this deadly ambush. Then the shots ceased, the smoke lifted, and the battle stopped for a time.

Colonel Forsyth, white from the loss of blood, raised himself feebly on the sand and looked around at his men who now crawled again from the pits. A faint smile of mingled triumph and pity passed over his face. He was victorious so far, but the cost was great. His own dead were too numerous. Not more than six or seven in the whole command were without serious wounds. Heroic as had been the charge, the defense had been more so.

Stillwell and Bob seized the tin cans and began to bring water from the trench that they had made, giving it to the men who were hurt the worst. Others, skilled from long experience, began to bind up hurts, while others brought forth fresh ammunition and looked to the rifles and revolvers, knowing that there would still be full need of them.

Two of the troopers attended to the wounds of Colonel Forsyth, who was now extremely weak. But his intelligence and energy were as great as ever. He could not stand on his feet, but he had them remove him into an easier position, and while they were swathing him in numerous bandages, he was studying the Indian position.

Bob lay on the edge of his sand pit, gasping for breath, and scarcely yet understanding that it was all real. It had been like the passing of a terrible dream. Three or four Cheyenne warriors lay so close to him, shot dead from their horses, that he could have reached out and touched them with his rifle muzzle. Not far beyond were a dozen more, and for a distance of nearly half a mile, coming to the island and leaving it, was a broad trail of slain warriors and horses. Sometimes they were strewn along in single file, and then they lay in groups. Once more Bob paid his silent tribute to Cheyenne valor. As the boy looked he saw the body of Roman Nose. The great chief lay flat upon his back, his dead eyes staring up at the heavens, now blue again as the rifle smoke floated away. The splendid warbonnet was still on his head, and the heavy repeating rifle lay by his side. He had died as he would have chosen, leading the fiercest charge red men ever made.

"Will they come again?" asked Colonel Forsyth of the oldest scout, Grover.

The veteran shook his head.

"Not that way," he replied. "I never saw its like before, an' I never expect to see it again, but they mean to get us yet."

The women and children, on the bluffs, within plain view of the island, maintained a wailing chant that rose and fell, but never ceased. It was a mingling of sorrow and anger, inexpressibly wild and savage, and it got upon Bob's nerves. He could see the figures upon the bluffs, leaping up and down, and he knew that he and his comrades could expect no more pity from them than from the warriors.

The warriors themselves were not noiseless. They rode around and around the island, but out of range, shaking their fists, brandishing rifles and lances, and uttering savage cries.

"They are telling us what they are going to do with us," said Stillwell, "and the things are so pleasant I won't repeat 'em to you, Bob."

"Let 'em shout," said Bob. "They haven't got us yet."

"That's the talk," said Stillwell. "There, they're drawing off! I guess they're going to have a big talk."

Although the dirge of the women and children still rose and fell, the shouts of the warriors gradually ceased, and they rode in a great body toward the gorge, whence they had issued for the charge. There they remained for a long time consulting, and the band on the island rested, although troubled, now and then, by sharpshooters.

The troopers ate a little food, and attended to the wounds of one another as best they could. They also threw up their banks of sand higher, but they suffered much from the sun, which poured fiery rays directly down upon their unprotected heads. It brought fever into their veins, but they were thankful now, for another reason, that they had been able to reach the island. Besides the defense that it gave them, plenty of good water was at hand for the taking, and they took freely. Bob and Jack bathed their faces, and all the others did likewise.

There was little sound on the island. Martin Burke hummed old Irish songs under his breath, but only the two youths heard him. In one rifle pit the elder Farley lay dying, and by the side of him, his son, hiding a severe wound of his own, held his hand, and listened to his last words. In the pit, with the triple-wounded leader, lay the dying lieutenant and the dying surgeon, one on either side. In every pit men eased their hurts. Upon all beat the pitiless sun, and great black birds began to wheel overhead.

Bob rested himself against the bank of sand, pulled the brim of his cap down over his eyes, shaded as much more of his face as he could with one arm, and remained motionless. Gradually his nerves sank into quiet. His eyelids drooped, although he had no desire to sleep. He merely sank into a strange sort of apathy, lulled now by the wild and weird wailing from the bluffs. Stillwell also did not move, although he continued to watch closely the mass of warriors at the head of the valley.

The sun shone in dazzling rays upon these warriors, showing their war-bonnets, their rifles, and their naked bodies, a savage group, stirred wholly by primitive emotions. A little wind sprang up, and blew away the last of the smoke and vapors that hung in the valley. Then Stillwell turned to Bob.

"I think they're coming again," he said.

The boy said nothing but raised up a little and pushed his rifle forward on the sand. Forsyth saw too, and called to all to be ready. The tremendous shout of the Cheyennes once more clove the air, and the valley thundered, as half a thousand horsemen, again galloped toward the island, the eagle and heron feathers in their war-bonnets trailing out behind them, their fierce brown faces bent forward over their horses.

At the same instant swarms of skirmishers in the bushes and reeds began to fire on the flanks of the island, but the defenders, as before, paid no attention to them. Their fingers burned on the triggers, but they waited until Forsyth should give the word. He cried "Fire!" long before the charge reached the island, and, once more, the hail of metal beat upon the wild horsemen. One volley followed another, so swift and deadly, that at a hundred yards the Cheyennes, lacking now the fire and passion of Roman Nose to lead them, broke and fled, leaving many more of their dead upon the ground.

Towards twilight they made a third attack that was beaten back in the same fashion, and then while the women still wailed, the warriors formed a great camp, in a ring about the island, but beyond the range of those rifles, which had cut down so many of their bravest warriors. Forsyth knew now that a close siege would be maintained and that, unless help came,—of which there seemed to be no chance —all the valor of his men would be as nothing.

Twilight was now at hand. The day was closing upon one of the most remarkable scenes of valor ever witnessed upon the American continent. Both white and red had done as much as man could expect. The sun set in a sea of fire, throwing its last rays across the fatal plain. Here and there lay the bodies of fallen warriors. The mournful wailing came from the bluffs again. Then the sun vanished and after it came the gray of early night. A low wind rose and blew sadly.

The defenders came forth from the rifle pits and counted their wounds which were enough to supply two or three to every man, and they bound up their fresh hurts received in the last two attacks. The evening breeze was cool on Bob's forehead, but he walked in an unreal world. It seemed impossible that he could live after all the fire and tumult of the day. The island had been torn by thousands of bullets, and had it not been for the sand pits, not a man would have escaped.

The boy's heart throbbed. The roaring was still in his ears, and the night seemed weird and unearthly. He ate and drank with Stillwell, and then slowly came back to the earth. Trudeau and several of the best sharpshooters kept watch while the others rested, but the Cheyennes maintained their distance for the present. Lights by and by leaped up on the bluffs, but the mournful wailing still came. On the island they were wholly in the gray darkness, which did not hide the defenders from one another, but which rendered them invisible to the Indians on the plains.

The wind by and by rose a little and began to moan. But there was dampness in it as it touched Bob's face, and the fever left his veins. His temples, too, ceased to throb, and the sand no longer burned when his hand lay against it. The gray of the night turned to black, and the Indian fires on the bluffs shone through it like stars. The wind rose yet higher, and the dampness in its touch increased.

A low rumble came from the far southern horizon, inexpressibly solemn after the day's terrible strife. All the men heard it, but none spoke. It is likely that they felt the same awe that was in the breast of Bob. They were now but little more than the grains of sand beneath them, as they lay there on the tiny island in the vast wilderness.

The far rumble came again and was repeated, a little closer and a little louder. Lightning flared on the dim horizon, and the wind moaned without ceasing.

Drops of rain struck the men. They turned their

faces upward to meet them, and were grateful for the cool touch. The rumble of the thunder ceased and became a crash. Then the lightning cut with such vivid strokes across the sky that the whole valley swam in its glare, disclosing the island, the shallow river, the grassy plain with the dark bodies of the dead lying thick upon it, and the hills beyond, crowned with the Indian fires. Then the darkness closed in again and the rushing rain came.

None of the white men cared how long the rain fell, but it ceased by and by and the moon and stars sprang out. Then troops of wolves, drawn by a hideous instinct, came down from the hills. But the same instinct would not let them come within range of the rifles, and they stood at a distance, howling in a terrible lupine chorus.

"How are you feeling now, Bob?" asked Stillwell at last.

"Better," sighed the boy. "Things are beginning to look real to me again. If only those wolves and women would stop howling."

"I've come back to earth myself," said Stillwell. "I've had a lot of Indian fighting, and I've been in some hot corners before, but I've never seen anything like this, and I hope never to see anything like it again. I don't understand how any of us ever came out of it alive."

Bob said nothing, but he felt a deep thankfulness. He was presently called with some others by the commander who thanked them for their bravery and tenacity, and encouraged them to endure still more. Forsyth lay against a mass of bandages with one

blanket under him and another over him. Bob
regarded him with wonder and an admiration that
grew always. An ordinary man would have been
dead already of his wounds, but Forsyth still lived
and still commanded.

Bob volunteered to watch through the night with
Trudeau, Stillwell and a half dozen more. He
pointed to the fact that he was one of the five or six
who had escaped without wounds, and the Colonel
consented. Then he and Stillwell, now close comrades who seemed to have known one another for
years, went back to their sand pits where they talked
in low tones as they watched.

The night darkened again, but their eyes became
so well used to it that they could see the fallen horses
and the plain, and the outline of the bluffs beyond.
There the fires burned all through the night, and the
mournful wailing did not cease until late.

After midnight some of the Cheyenne skirmishers
crept along the plain and fired a few shots, but they
flew wild, and the sentinels did not think it worth
while to reply. Most of the others slept so heavily
that the reports did not awaken them.

The two, wrapped in their blankets because the
night was chill, ceased to whisper by and by, and
sat almost motionless in the sand pits. The wind
rose a little and came with a wailing sound up the
bed of the river and among the reeds. But on the
island scarcely anything stirred. Deep exhaustion
reigned there. The cold moon looked down on an
island which might well have been taken for an
island of the dead. Colonel Forsyth, wrapped in

his blankets, sank into a stupor, but he roused himself from it at dawn which came on crisp and cloudless, showing the Indians still in a circle about the island, but out of rifle range. The siege had begun.

Forsyth made preparations for a long and desperate defense. A circular breastwork of sand was thrown up entirely around this little camp. In the center they dug a well, an easier task than it would seem as the cool waters rose in the sand when they had gone down a few feet. They also cut strips from the slain horses, not knowing to what straits they might arrive for food.

Their tasks occupied the whole morning, and the Cheyennes made no demonstration save an occasional distant rifle shot or a defiant whoop from a warrior well out of range. These things were the merest trifles to them now. The afternoon passed in the same way, the second night came, and then it was Bob's turn to sleep. His nerves were so well rested that he did not awake once during the night. While he slept the Cheyennes crept up and carried off most of their slain, including Roman Nose and the medicine man. The soldiers heard them, but did not seek to interfere.

The second day came and the horse meat could not longer be eaten. Other food was too scarce to withstand a long siege, and unless help was brought it became evident that sooner or later they must fall into the hands of the Cheyennes. Valor could avail nothing against starvation. But the dauntless soul of Forsyth, suffering from his terrible triple wounds, still would not despair.

"Somebody must get through to-night," he said, "and go to Fort Wallace for help. It is a desperate chance. Who will take it?"

"I! I! I!" shouted half a score, Bob among them. But Forsyth chose the two scouts, old Pete Trudeau and young Jack Stillwell.

"You have had the most experience outside of Grover whom I must keep with me," he said, "and you are the most likely to succeed. When do you think will be the best time to creep out, Pete?"

"To-night along about midnight," replied the scout. "I think it is going to be dark. What do you say, Jack?"

"You're right," replied Stillwell. "If we can't get through then we never will, but we're going to get through."

They made their preparations in the afternoon, merely an increase of cartridges, a little more food in their wallets, and they were ready. Then the night came, cloudy and dark as Trudeau had predicted. All accepted it as a good omen. But the two men waited until midnight when, hearing no noise from the Cheyennes, they decided to start. Stillwell had selected what seemed to be the most dangerous plan. He intended to cross the river and go directly towards the bluffs where the main Indian encampment lay. It was his theory, and Colonel Forsyth approved of it, that the Indians would be less vigilant on that side. He and Trudeau would cross the plain, crawling on their stomachs, and then pass over the bluffs by the side of the Indian encampment.

It was Bob's night on the watch, and he was one of those who saw the daring scouts leave. His heart was filled with admiration for both, and he gave a strong farewell clasp to the hand of his good friend, Jack.

"We'll be back, Bob, and we'll bring the troopers with us," said Stillwell, confidently. "You can look for us."

He and Trudeau dropped silently over the earthworks and crawled along the sand. Bob followed their dark figures for a little distance as they crept on the edge of the island, and then he lost them in the further darkness. Listening intently he heard a faint splash or two in the water, but he neither saw nor heard anything more.

The boy was now beside the Colonel, and the two waited a long time, dreading to hear the sound of shots or of exultant yells, telling that the two scouts were slain or taken. The minutes dragged, a slow chain.

"They are across the river now," whispered the Colonel. "When I close my eyes I can see them lying almost flat, crawling across the plain."

Bob said nothing, but he never took his eyes off the camp-fires, shining through the darkness, which showed where the bluffs stood. Trudeau and Stillwell were going straight towards those lights.

"They must be at least three hundred yards away now," whispered the Colonel. "Do you hear anything, Bob?"

"Not a thing, sir," replied Bob, "except those coyotes howling away off there to the north."

"Brave lads! Brave lads!" muttered the Colonel. "They must have gone a quarter of a mile now. What do you think, Bob?"

"I should think so, sir," replied the boy.

"You are sure you don't hear anything—any sound of a struggle?"

"Nothing at all, sir, but if I have your consent I will creep a little way along the sand and listen."

"Do it."

Bob stepped over the earthworks, and then lying almost flat upon his face pushed himself along until he reached the river. There he lay with his ear to the sand, but heard nothing save the faint ripple of the water. He could now see objects on the opposite shore more distinctly. Presently his eyes made out the figure of a dead horse, and then that of a warrior huddled up, lying as he had fallen.

While he stared, trying to read in the darkness the whole story of the plain, he saw two moving shadows. Gazing at them long and intently, he saw that the shadows were men, and for the first time he felt despair. Trudeau and Stillwell, finding the way closed, were creeping back, and no help could ever come.

The figures advanced, and as they came closer they were outlined more clearly against the bank. Then the war-bonnets and naked shoulders showed that they were not the two scouts, but Cheyenne warriors creeping forward. Bob crouched closer and slipped his rifle in his hands until a finger rested on the trigger. Then he marked an imaginary spot. If they reached it he would fire.

The two warriors veered a little, and Bob let his rifle drop upon the sand again. He would not fire. The Cheyennes were now beside the dead warrior, lying in his cramped-up position. They suddenly straightened up, and when they did so they bore the body between them. Running swiftly, they carried it off for burial or the funeral pyre.

Bob waited a little longer, and still seeing and hearing nothing returned to the earthworks.

"The plain is quiet, sir," he said to Colonel Forsyth. "I can't detect a sign of a disturbance anywhere."

"It is good," said this man who could move but little, but who could command well. "I should judge that they are at least a half mile away. Watch those lights."

They watched them. A half hour—an hour passed, then a second hour and then a third. All the time the lights burned steadily and did not shift. It was after three o'clock in the morning when Colonel Forsyth moved slightly on his blanket.

"Now I can go to sleep," he said. "Trudeau and Stillwell are through, and we shall be saved."

CHAPTER XIX

THE AMAZING FLIGHT

While Colonel Forsyth and Bob watched and listened long at the bank of sand, Jack Stillwell and Pete Trudeau were creeping forward on a task so thickly bestrewed with dangers that the chance of ever achieving it seemed but slight. They had left the island, they had crossed the river, lying in its wide bed, and were now advancing toward the very bluffs on which the Indian camp lay.

The leader in this daring venture was the boy, Jack Stillwell. He was superior in intelligence to his older comrade, Pete Trudeau, and Colonel Forsyth recognizing it, had given him the instructions, and had told him that he must make Trudeau follow his judgment. But Trudeau himself willingly took second place, and followed the brave and handsome youth who was destined in later days to become a judge and man of large affairs in Oklahoma.

The two, after emerging from the sand bed of the river, lay for a few minutes flat upon the plain, their rifles close by their sides, listening intently and looking for enemies with eyes trained by the wild life of the border. They heard low sounds and then a pattering of light feet.

"That's coyotes, isn't it, Pete?" said Jack in the lowest of whispers.

"Coyotes and the big timber wolves, too," replied

they had never been. Jack Stillwell passed his hands before his eyes as if he would sweep away a mist or veil. Used as he was to the wilderness, he was oppressed by its ominous loneliness, and their own position on a narrow strip, between life and death. But he could shut his eyes and see the faces of his comrades, especially that of the gallant youth, Bob Norton, who had become such a good comrade of his. He and Trudeau must get through! They must save the heroic little band that had made such a tremendous fight against more than twenty to one.

Jack turned his eyes away from the island and toward the bluffs, where lights burned and where even after the third day the wailing of the women for their dead still arose. It was a singular weird chant, and it contained a threat as well as grief. It got upon the nerves of the older man.

"Jack," whispered Trudeau, "don't you think we'd better turn back and try to escape up or down the bed of the river?"

"No," replied Jack. "They'll be keeping a double watch there, and we could never get by. If we make it, Pete, and we're going to make it, we must take a road they won't expect us to choose."

He resumed the slow crawling on hands and knees, and Trudeau, obeying the superior will, followed. Jack led straight toward the lights and now, both to right and left, they saw the figures of Cheyennes passing. Never did men need a dark night more, and fortunately the early promise held good. There was a little moon, but heavy clouds were continually floating before it, and the whole surface of the plain was in deep obscurity. They hoped that as long as they lay so close to the earth they might pass. Both were in great fear lest Indian dogs should scent them and betray their presence, but this danger did not yet develop itself. The two heard the stamp of the Indian ponies, and an occasional neigh, and they saw squaws bringing fuel for the fires, and the dark outlines of skin tepees that the Indians had pitched on the bluffs. Then they rested once more and tried to pick out the place for their passage.

Jack noticed at last a dark spot in the bluffs, and he was convinced that a dip or depression between the hills lay there. The fires burned both to right and left, and he could account for the hiatus on no other ground. He felt sure that it was the road by which they must pass, and he touched Trudeau's arm lightly.

"Don't you think that's our path, Pete?" he said, pointing to the dark space.

"If we are to find any, that's it," Trudeau whispered in reply.

Both now remained flat and still, longer than usual. Their knees and elbows were sore from so much creeping, and since they were upon the Indian camp they must choose the way well. If the chance failed there would be no other.

"Now, Pete," Jack whispered at length, "we'll make the try."

They scarcely crawled; they lay almost flat on the ground, dragging themselves forward by a series of muscular contortions like a snake, and making no noise. They heard voices, the crackling of dry wood in the fires, and the death chant of the squaws.

There was a sudden growl, and an Indian cur, shooting out of the darkness, leaped like a wolf straight at Jack. But Trudeau, reaching straight up, grasped the dog by the throat and compressed it between two powerful brown hands. Another growl had arisen into the cur's mouth, but it died behind his teeth, and then the fierce human grip permitted no more to come.

A warrior heard the growl and stopped, but not hearing it a second time, walked on. A cur snapping at a bone and yelping at another cur was common in an Indian camp, and the warrior, dismissing the incident from his mind, looked with vengeful glance toward the island where the white foe lay hidden in the sand. He did not know that the greatest of all opportunities was almost within reach of his hand.

Jack saw the warrior, and his fingers slipped forward to the trigger of his rifle. But he made no movement, and his glance turned back to Trudeau and the dog. Pete lay flat upon his side, and his great brown fingers were sunk deep in the hairy throat. The powerful muscles in his arms rose under his sleeves as he poured all his strength into them. The dog kicked, tore at the earth with his hind paws, shuddered and then was still. Trudeau loosed his grip and laid him upon the ground. The dog was quite dead.

"You did that in great style, Pete," whispered Jack, "and it saved us. Come on."

They were a long time in making the short distance that separated them from the dark space between the bluffs, and both rejoiced when they saw that their guess was correct. The bluff dipped down there, making a sort of sunken ridge, covered with short bushes and too rough for a camp.

Although low fires burned on either side not many yards away, they believed that they could pass through the depression. At least they must try. Stillwell still led, and they entered the little pass, moving scarcely more than a yard a minute. When they reached the shelter of the bushes they paused at least five minutes. From where they lay they saw the fires quite well, and the Indians sitting or standing beside them. They even heard words, some of which they understood. The warriors were speaking of their losses, and of their confidence that they would yet secure the foe whom they encircled. Savage and implacable, they had no thought of giving up.

Stillwell slowly led the way again. The bushes were at once a help and a danger. They covered their bodies, but a rustling among them might draw the Indian's gaze. Now the two scouts exercised every precaution known to the most skilful of borderers. Neither put down hand or foot until he saw that it would rest in a place that gave forth no noise. It was painfully slow, it was hard to be so patient, with warriors all about them not twenty yards away, but they held their nerves under control, and never sought to increase speed. They even dared to rest more than once, lying still for five minutes at a time, and from the covert of the bushes, surveying the

Indian camp about them. It was a full hour before they traversed the length of the little ravine between the bluffs. Then they found themselves on the far side of the Indian camp, and outside the circle. But they did not stop until they had gone several hundred yards beyond the lights, where they lay among some bushes and held a brief and whispered conference.

"I think we'd better get out now and make a break for it," said Trudeau. "Let's trust to our speed."

"Don't think of it," Jack replied, earnestly. "The main camp's behind us I know, but the country for miles is bound to be swarming with their scouts and skirmishers, and we've got to be all the more careful now because it won't be long till dawn."

Trudeau, as usual, gave up to his younger comrade, and they continued to crawl on hands and knees, soon finding that their action was fully justified, as Cheyennes, both on foot and horseback, passed them, and they saw one fire in a little grove where several Indians slept and two others watched.

The country here, luckily for them, had a considerable growth of bushes, and as long as they remained on hands and knees they were not likely to be seen, unless the enemy came very close. But the crawling was horribly monotonous, and was growing quite painful. Their knees were bruised, and every joint was stiff and sore. They were compelled to take a long rest among some willows, and there they ate scraps of food that they carried in their haversacks.

While they ate they saw the east lighten, and the

aspens and willows began to whiten and quiver. Then, as the world turned slowly, the great sun swung into view, the white lights turned to red, and the wild plains were suffused with its glow. In six hours of crawling they had come three miles, and the day showed more clearly than ever that they still had need of the utmost caution. A half dozen bands of Indians were in sight, and the smoke of camp-fires rose straight in front of them.

"It's crawling again for us," said Stillwell.

"It looks like it," said Pete, ruefully. "I guess, Jack, that if we ever get through with this it'll be hard for us to rise up and walk like men."

"That isn't our worst trouble," said Jack. "Practice will bring it back. Come on, Pete, and we'll see which of us is the better crawler."

The grim competition lasted all the morning. Again and again the temptation to stand up and walk like men was almost overpowering, indeed it would have been overpowering for Trudeau, but Stillwell resisted for both. Twice he pulled the older man down and encouraged him continually, justifying the confidence that Forsyth had put in him, despite his youth. Throughout the long, terrible hours they were never out of sight of Indians. They saw them on foot and on horseback, in little parties and alone, and at intervals they heard the distant sound of rifle-shots coming from the island through the thin, clear air.

The Indians were so numerous, even beyond the bluffs, that it seemed now as if they could never pass. Trudeau spoke despondently, but Stillwell, despite the sinking of his heart, would not let a word of discouragement escape him.

"We've just got to do it! We've just got to do it, Pete!" he said with energy.

The sun was brilliant and intensely clear, making all objects conspicuous, and they could not relax caution for a moment. Their soreness and stiffness increased. Their knees now were cut and bleeding, and their backs ached. The sun, too, beat down upon them. In the afternoon they came to the divide that separates the Arickaree from the Republican River, and here Stillwell saw a wash-out around which sunflowers and tall grass clustered thickly, forming a dense screen. He was so tired that he could scarcely move, and he saw that Trudeau was almost in a state of collapse.

"Pete," he said, "let's creep in here and rest the remainder of the day."

"I don't have to be asked twice," said Trudeau.

They slipped in through the grass and sunflowers, rearranging the latter behind them so carefully that no sign of a trail would be shown, and then lay down panting, but thankful, in the little sandy wash-out.

It was a close, snug place, and they remained in it all the afternoon, hearing at intervals rifle-shots about the island, and now and then when they peeped through the tall grass, seeing Indians riding about the prairie.

Stillwell grew very anxious. He knew that time was precious as diamonds, but he did not dare to move from the wash-out until night had fully come.

Both he and Trudeau awaited eagerly the advance of the twilight, and then the heavier darkness of the night. Before the moon could come up they slipped from the protection of the grass and sunflowers, and started erect like men.

"I can walk again, Jack," whispered Trudeau, "and I'm a man, not a monkey."

The youth laughed softly in the darkness.

"It does feel good to stand on one's own feet," he whispered back. "Come on now, Pete. We've got to make the most of the night-time. I hope it will stay dark as it did last night."

His hopes were fulfilled. When the moon came out it was veiled in vapors and shed but little light although enough for them to see the way, which le through bushes and now and then across a ravin. It was also sufficient to disclose to their watchful eyes numerous Indian trails, and they knew that the time had not yet come when they could relax their caution a particle.

Before midnight clouds began to gather and the moon was hidden. A wind, damp to the touch, blew with a sad, sighing sound out of the southwest. Low thunder rolled, and now and then the lightning flared across the prairie.

"I hope we won't have any storm," said Stillwell. "It would hold us back."

"There won't be much rain," said Trudeau, weather-wise with the experience of many years.

The wind presently blew a little harder, and a slant of rain came, but it soon ceased. Then the low thunder rolled again, and the lightning flared fitfully, but neither lasted long, and the two scouts, messengers now, went on as swiftly as they could. They were going toward the south, and about an hour after the rain passed the two, by the same impulse and at the same moment, sank softly down among the bushes where they lay flat against the earth.

A war party of Cheyennes, at least fifty in number and mounted, was passing. There was enough light now to disclose their painted faces, their warbonnets, and their naked bodies. They rode in single file, and not one spoke. The unshod hoofs of their ponies made a low measured beat as they passed.

"They're going to the island to take part in the siege," whispered Jack. "Bob and all those fellows will surely need help as soon as we can bring it."

Two hours later they passed another Indian band of about the same size, and again they lay hidden among the bushes while it passed.

Dawn came a second time, and to their alarm they found that they were on the outskirts of a great Indian village, probably the one which furnished the warriors who were attacking Forsyth. They had come so close to it in the darkness that they could not retreat in the day. They saw many lodges, and warriors, women and children were everywhere.

Jack and Trudeau thought themselves lost, but the eyes of the boy, always extremely quick, alighted upon a small swamp, that is, a patch of tall grass growing out of water.

"Come, Pete," he exclaimed, "we've got to hide

in there. It's great luck that we haven't been seen already."

They slipped into the swamp and went to its very center where they sat down to their waists in the grass and water. Here they could not be seen from the edge of the swamp, but they could hear the many noises of the village, the squaws talking, the barking of dogs, the whistling of boys to the ponies, and even the tread of warriors passing the little marsh. About ten o'clock a party of mounted Indians stopped and watered their horses at its edge. The two hidden scouts could hear the horses as they swallowed.

Jack and Trudeau scarcely breathed until the horses finished drinking and the men rode on. Then they looked at each other, two strange creatures with their heads and shoulders projecting above the water, but hidden in the grass.

"Do you think we'll ever get through, Jack? Do you think we'll ever get through?" asked Trudeau, something weak and plaintive appearing in his voice.

"Of course we will," replied Jack, showing a confidence that he scarcely felt. "Think what a fine rest we can get, Pete, while we're here with nothing to do but sit in the water."

The day was warm, but they were so long in the water that they began to grow cold. Jack felt the chill creeping up his body, but he did not dare move. The slightest noise might attract the dogs, and Pete could not choke them all to death before they gave the alarm. At noon they ate scraps of food again, and then they waited for the long afternoon to pass.

The chill and the tension became so great that they were forced at last to take the chances and move a little. They even dared to straighten up in the grass and stand erect for a minute or two. When they sank down again they felt much better.

Their third night came, and cold and stiff they crept out of the swamp. It was some time before they could stand erect with ease, and men less resolute than they would have given up. It was now a pain to exert the mind as well as the body, but they rubbed their wrists and legs until the circulation was restored, and then, haggard and wan, their wet clothing streaked with mud and their eyes red from watching and loss of sleep, they took up once more their flight toward help.

They passed around the village without being seen, and with a new strength that came from hope, fled onward at a pace that would not have seemed possible in men who had endured so much. They were not able to travel the entire night, as the strength of both, particularly Trudeau's, began to wane again. Feeling that they must take the chances, both lay down after midnight, and at once sank into a deep slumber.

Jack was the first to awake, and it was dawn. He sprang to his feet, but saw nothing alarming, and then he awakened Trudeau. Before them lay open plains, and as they believed that they had now left the Indians behind, they resolved to travel by day. Time, be it repeated, was more precious than diamonds, and the lives of their friends might turn on a single hour. They agreed to risk it, and set off at a good pace across the plain.

The sun rose, flooding the land with the usual sharp, clear light. They had been walking more than an hour, and just as they were about to top a swell Jack seized Trudeau and pulled him down in the grass, falling himself at the same time by his side. A party of at least a dozen warriors were coming straight toward them, but had not yet seen them. Yet, it seemed that they were now surely lost.

But Jack Stillwell was one who never gave up hope. A few yards to the right he saw a patch of weeds, and he and Trudeau at once crept into it. Then they made a discovery. In the center of this patch lay the skeleton of a big buffalo, long since dead, but with some of the skin hanging upon it, and all the bones intact and upright. Men in desperate case often do desperate things, and do them quickly. Jack Stillwell and Pete Trudeau at once crawled inside the ribs of the buffalo, and lay, side by side, in that extraordinary hiding-place. They did not dare move, but they peeped between the ribs and pieces of skin, and saw the Indian party go on. They rejoiced, but too soon. Other Indians, mounted and apparently scouts, appeared. This seemed to be a post for sentinels, and they were constantly coming and going. The singular hiding place of Jack and Trudeau became an equally singular trap, and there they lay.

The Indians often came as near as twenty yards. One came within fifteen yards and sat there on his horse a full hour, examining the country in all directions. He was a fine warrior, entirely naked save for moccasins and war-bonnet, and he carried a magnificent lance. While the Indian's side was turned toward the buffalo, Trudeau softly pressed Jack's shoulder with his hand.

"What is it, Pete?" whispered Jack.

"Somethin' else is in here with us."

Jack listened and heard a faint, soft sound that made the blood grow cold in every vein. A rattlesnake, before them, had taken up its abode in the skeleton of the buffalo. They did not know why it had remained quiescent so long, but now it was moving.

It is probable that no men have ever been in a more terrible position, one so dangerous, and at the same time so full of horror. They could see but little, a chance blow would not do, and the slightest noise would attract the attention of the Indian warrior.

They lay still for a while—how long they could not tell—in a sort of paralysis, and then it was Trudeau, the weaker of the two, who saved them. The lives of many people may turn upon absurd things, and now the fortune of a campaign was to be decided by a chew of tobacco. It would be doubly ridiculous, if it were not true.

Trudeau was of the old type, and he always carried tobacco with him. Now he had a quid in his mouth, and he was chewing vigorously for consolation and strength. Lying upon his side and one shoulder, he faintly saw the snake near his feet, coiling, and raising his head to strike. Perhaps it was impulse, an inspiration of the moment, but old Pete Trudeau spat a stream of bitter brown tobacco juice straight at the venomous head. It struck full and true. Blinded and dazed the rattlesnake uncoiled and slid swiftly out of the skeleton.

Pete lay back exhausted, and Jack, himself, was dizzy with the relapse after such tension. The Indian, on his horse, never moved. Trudeau, by and by, raised up a little and began to talk to himself. Jack tried to quiet him, and presently he understood what had happened. Trudeau's mind had become affected for the time, by one tremendous ordeal after another. He was tired now, he said, of crawling and hiding. He wanted to fight, and he meant to fight. He would not stay where he was forever, even if all the Indians that ever lived were out there. Rage steadily rose and grew in his breast, and he meant to take vengeance.

This was the most terrible moment of all for Jack. In the lowest of voices he tried to soothe Trudeau and make him see reason. It was a sort of mental struggle between them while the Indians rode outside, but the valiant youth conquered. Under his soothing words the rage of Trudeau began to abate. He ceased by and by to mutter, and lay still for a long time.

They did not move until dark. Then they came forth, a sorry sight, but still uncaptured, and still zealous for their mission. They found a pool of cool water near, and when Trudeau drank from it and bathed his face, his mind regained its balance.

They traveled all night without meeting any more

Indian parties, and with their experience of the day before fresh in their minds, they meant to hide the next day, but a pale, yellowish sun rose in a fog, so dense that one could see but a little distance. The sun did not dispel the fog, and they pressed on through it. About an hour before noon, they saw through the haze, two mounted figures near them on the prairie. The eyes of Jack Stillwell, yet strong and alert, recognized the uniforms of the United States Army.

"Soldiers!" he cried.

Then he and Trudeau rushed forward.

CHAPTER XX

A LIGHT IN THE DARK

The morning of the third day came, and although little was said in the island camp, the spirits of the men were better. All felt sure that Trudeau and Stillwell had got through the Indian lines, and that some time or other, help would arrive. It was now their task to hold out as long as food and life lasted. Another reduction was made in the rations, and they found it necessary to bury the bodies of the horses in the sand.

Bob, that afternoon, fell into a fever caused by the excitement and the great strain. For a little while he was unconscious, and he babbled of Sam Strong and his old comrades, of trapping beaver, and of shooting down a great river between cliffs a mile high. In the cool of the night he revived, and was much ashamed of himself, but the others laughed at his apologies. Almost every one in his turn, suffered from some sort of delirium or other, but they were so hardy that nearly all of them began to recover fast, although their wounds were sufficient to kill ordinary men. Colonel Forsyth was one of the worst hurt of them all, but his courage never flinched for a moment. In fact, he cut the bullet from his thigh himself with his own razor which was in his haversack, and with its removal, began to improve fast.

That night they sent out two more messengers—Donovan and Pliley—for help, in case the first two should fail, and Forsyth dispatched by them a letter to the commanding officer at Fort Wallace, written with a pencil on a leaf from his memorandum book. He gave details of the battle and said that he could hold out six days longer. Donovan and Pliley slipped away in the darkness and the rest settled back to waiting again.

The Cheyennes maintained a continual stalking of the island. Their sharpshooters, by night and by day, crept forward and sent bullets at the breastworks. The men were compelled to be very watchful, but they did not often fire in return, reserving their strength and ammunition for another charge, if one should be made. But as the time passed and the Indians did nothing but skirmish, Colonel Forsyth became convinced that a grand attack would not be made again.

"They think starvation will do the work," he said, "and it would if our messengers had not slipped through their lines."

He did not waver in his belief that the scouts had succeeded and Bob shared his faith. If they had been taken it would have been the Indian nature to have exulted over it and to have shown some sign, but none came from the bluffs. The lights still shone there at night and often by day they could see the Indians moving about on the plain out of rifle range, but nothing occurred to indicate any change in the siege.

The fourth day, the fifth and the sixth passed

with the same constant sniping of the skirmishers and the same incessant watchfulness on the island. It was so tense a life, so singular in all its aspects, that Bob fell again into a state of unreality. It seemed to him that he had been there forever. His range was limited to a circle of sand ten yards across. The people with whom he lived, and the only ones whom he knew, were a few men, brown as leather, carrying many gun-shot wounds in tight bandages. Their sentences were few and short. Conversation was as restricted as their home on the island.

The spell was deepest at night. Then he would sit long with his rifle across his knees and look at the river. It was a shallow stream at low water, not more than a foot deep now, but it hemmed them in like an ocean. No one sought to pass beyond it. Under the moonlight it took on aspects of death which it had not. Then its surface was dark, breaking into little crinkly waves here and there, and his attentive ear magnified the sighing of the wind among the reeds into a gale. Then he would grow lonesome, longing for Stillwell, and above all for Sam Strong and his old comrades.

The Cheyennes, despite all their losses, seemed to regard the troopers as their sure prey. Sometimes they came out on the plain and derided the defenders. One morning, a large and very fat Cheyenne appeared beyond what seemed to be safe rifle range, and began to make derisive gestures. He was entirely naked, and his actions continued so long that the troopers, whose nerves were not in a good state, began to grow angry. They did not wish to be ridiculed by an unclothed savage.

Colonel Forsyth shared in the annoyance. After carefully surveying the distance, he called the best three shots in the band and gave to them three rifles which would carry about four hundred yards further than the others. These rifles had sights for 1200 yards, but he directed them to aim well over the sights at the dancing Cheyenne and fire together, at his signal. It was a long chance, and Bob watched eagerly for the result.

"Fire!" shouted Forsyth.

The three rifles cracked together. The fat savage leaped into the air, fell upon his face and lay there stone dead. But no one of the three marksmen ever knew which slew him. After that the Cheyennes kept further away and taunted less.

The seventh day passed and the rations were reduced in size again. Men spoke less than ever. They were lean and wasted with hunger and disease, wounds and watching. But there was still no thought of surrender. The little island was yet ready to spout fire at any moment, should the Cheyennes rush forward to attack, and knowing it, they refrained. The long list of great warriors, Roman Nose at their head, gone to the happy hunting grounds, told them too well that waiting was their only road to success. Yet the snipers never ceased to worry the island, by day and by night.

The eighth day was at hand and Bob felt that unless help came soon it would come in vain. He was reduced greatly in weight, and his strength was declining, but all the others were in the same condition. The food, with the utmost possible saving, could not last more than two or three days longer, and that would be the end.

The eighth day passed, and Bob sat much of that night with Colonel Forsyth, who trusted him and treated him like a young cadet. He did not seek to hide from the boy the full gravity of their situation.

"Trudeau and Stillwell will make for Fort Wallace, which is about a hundred miles from here," he said. "It would not take them so long to do that distance, even on foot, but as the country is swarming with Indians they will have to travel by night. I think we can expect the troops in three more days."

Bob was not so sure now. When he thought over the immense difficulties, it scarcely seemed possible that the two scouts could get to Fort Wallace. But he said nothing and he had grown so used to danger and death that his feelings were blunted. His decreasing confidence did not make his heart throb any faster. Then the Colonel himself fell into silence. He lay upon a blanket with a little heaped-up sand for a pillow, as he was not yet able to stand. His figure was wasted almost to a skeleton, and his face was as white as death. His head was swathed in wrapping after wrapping, and his legs, lying useless, were also clothed in bandages. But his eyes, deep and fiery, shone out from the white and sunken face. Bob looked at him with admiration, wonder and affection. He had not believed that any man could endure so much, and yet, shot to pieces, he still lived and led.

The Colonel by and by fell asleep, and a soldier, himself wounded, softly spread a blanket over him. Bob rose, walked over the noiseless sand, and softly dropped outside the earthwork. There he lay down on the sand, and looked up at the moon and the great stars dancing in the blue. It was a silent and peaceful moment. The Indian snipers were at rest, for the time, and as the boy lay there, the spirit of hope crept once more into his mind. It could not be that they, who had endured so much, that they who had done deeds, seemingly impossible to mortal man, should fail and die obscurely on that little island of sand in the western wilderness.

After a while, he crept to the edge of the river. It did not now look dark and menacing, but flowed slowly, with the faintest of soft, singing sounds. The bubbles that broke on its surface were tinted silver in the moonlight. He looked toward the bluffs where the light from the Indian camp had never gone out, and then his eyes passed on to another point on the horizon, hitherto always dark. But it was not dark now. A light like that of a torch twinkled there for a few moments, and then went out. It reappeared again presently, but for not more than a minute. In a quarter of an hour it showed for a third time and then no more, although he watched a long while.

Bob did not know what the brief and fitful light meant, but he accepted it as a good omen, and when he crept back inside the earthwork, hope was stronger within him than it had been at any time since the first day. He slept well and saw the dawn of the ninth day, brilliant with sunshine, and cool with the touch of early autumn. Then the morning moved on, with the usual slow procession of hours, and the fitful shots of the snipers.

Bob sat at the earthwork, gazing at the bluffs and the far circle of the horizon. He was very still. He had learned in the last few days the Indian virtues of patience and of rest, when work was not needed. He was so much at ease that he let his eyelids droop, and soon a soft, sweet sound came to his ears. The wind among the reeds! No, it was not that, because no wind was blowing, and the sound came from another quarter.

He shut his eyes again, because he had an impression that he could hear better with them shut, and the soft, penetrating note came again. He knew it now. It was the far call of a bugle and he sat up as suddenly as if an electric shock had shot through him. He opened his eyes and looked off toward the point where he had seen the fitful light of the night before. Something was moving on the brown slopes, indistinct figures that came forward in the sunlight, until they looked like horses and men.

Others saw, at the same time, and a deep cheer came from all left of the fifty. The troops, in strong force, were advancing. Already they were marching upon the plain, and the Cheyennes, breaking up their camp with great speed, were preparing to retreat.

After his share in the great cheer Bob became dizzy. The relief coming after that long and tremendous strain was so great that the earth reeled.

He steadied himself against a mound of sand, and as his eyes cleared, looked again at the glorious sight, the troopers galloping across the plain toward the island, waving their hats and shouting now, and the Indians sullenly withdrawing.

Then came an extraordinary spectacle. Living skeletons crawled out from the holes in the sand. Bandaged heads, arms and shoulders showed over the earthwork. All were pale or white of face, ghastly and sunken, from which looked eyes preternaturally enlarged. The graves had literally given up their dead.

The rescuers, with a shout, galloped through the stream and then stopped, gazing in amazement at the few gaunt figures that had so long held off the Cheyenne nation. But Jack Stillwell threw himself from his horse, rushed forward and grasped Bob by the hand.

"We've come, Bob, my boy! We've come!" he cried. "This is the command of Colonel Carpenter that we found at Lake Slater, and you're saved!"

The troopers were off their horses now, bringing both food and medicines, and hearing the wonderful tale of Forsyth's great defense. While their horses drank from the stream they looked curiously at the little island fortress, the burrows in the sand, the shallow well, and all the desperate shifts and expedients to which the defenders had resorted.

For the first time in nine days Forsyth's men walked freely about the plain. Some scattering shots had been fired by skirmishers as the relief came up, but the Cheyennes seemed to have enough, and now, with their women and children, were far away, waiting to fight again at some other time and place. Over the good food that the troopers brought, Jack told Bob of the thrilling passage of Trudeau and himself through the Cheyenne lines.

Bob listened breathlessly to the extraordinary narrative, one of the most remarkable in the history of the plains. He followed all their adventures as they crawled night and day, as they hid in the washout, in the marsh, and at last in the skeleton of the buffalo, and he uttered a laugh, half of relief, half of amusement, when Trudeau once more put to flight the terrible rattlesnake with a stream of tobacco juice.

"The two mounted soldiers we met," concluded Stillwell, "were carrying despatches from Colonel Carpenter's command, which was then at Lake Slater, only fifty miles from our sand island in the Arickaree. That was tall luck, as I don't think we could ever have got to Fort Wallace in time. The two soldiers galloped to Colonel Carpenter, he came as fast as he could, and here we are."

Such was the extraordinary and truthful story of the rescue, and it kept Bob's eyes sparkling with excitement and amazement. The wonderful defense of the island had been crowned by an equally wonderful escape of the two men through the Indian lines in search of rescue, and young Stillwell did not seem to be much the worse for his extraordinary adventures. Donovan and Pliley also, had made their way through the lines, and they returned later.

Bob revived rapidly. His youth, great strength

A LIGHT IN THE DARK 317

and elasticity served him well. In a day or two he was as well as ever in all respects. On the second day he and Stillwell rode on borrowed horses to examine the country in a wide circle about the island. The Cheyennes had disappeared completely, evidently in search of easier victims elsewhere, and they had no fear of ambush or other attack.

As they rode they came to a small valley, not far from the field of battle, and the eye of Bob was attracted by an object among some small trees. They hastened forward to investigate, and they saw a wigwam, constructed with great care from freshly tanned buffalo skins of the finest quality. The two dismounted, opened the door of the tepee, and then they started, awed by what they beheld.

In the center of the tepee on a heap of brush lay the body of a magnificent savage, the body of a man six feet three inches high, with mighty shoulders and chest, and the features of a great Roman in bronze. The body was wrapped in buffalo robes, and by the side of it lay a beautiful repeating rifle, revolver, tomahawk and knife.

Bob, in the faint light, looked down upon the features of the great chief, Roman Nose, whom he knew so well, and his feeling of awe was succeeded by one of respect and admiration. The Cheyenne had fallen fighting for his people and their hunting grounds, and he had fallen like a hero, leading the warriors to the charge.

"We'll leave him here, Jack, just as he is," he said to Stillwell.

"We'll fasten the door tight so the wolves can't

get at him," said Stillwell. "The Indians have embalmed him in their own way and the body will rest here."

They made the lodge secure, and then reported what they had found. Others went to see it, but the body of the great Roman Nose was not disturbed, being left in all honor as the Cheyennes themselves had placed it.

The little army was now ready to move again and Bob was confronted by an important problem. Sam Strong and his comrades had never left his mind, and he must find them. But it was the most difficult of all things to do in the vast expanse of the west. Diligent inquiry among the soldiers indicated that no party of trappers had passed to the eastward along any of the known lines of travel. Cheyennes, Sioux and Arapahoes were so thick everywhere that in all probability they were still hiding in the hills, awaiting a chance.

"You can't go alone hunting them, Bob," said Stillwell. "Why, if your scalp were nailed down and riveted with copper it wouldn't stay on your head more than forty-eight hours. From north to south thirty or forty thousand warriors are wandering about, eager to snap up any stray white."

"I'm afraid your're right," said Bob. "It's hard to decide what to do."

"Why don't you enlist with Custer? This war is going to be pushed, and he's the man who will push it. With him you'll have more chance to find your friends, because they'll naturally make for a strong force of soldiers as soon as they hear that it's near."

The suggestion appealed to Bob, and he decided to offer his services to Custer as soon as they reached him. Meanwhile he bade farewell to Forsyth, destined, despite his terrible wounds, to live many years more and become a general. Then he and some others rode into Custer's camp not long after the Battle of the Arickaree, and Bob frankly stated why he had come. Custer looked at him with interest.

"And so you are one of that little band who made the great defense on the island in the Arickaree!" he said. "It was a marvelous achievement."

Bob blushed at the high praise.

"I was there by chance," he said. "I did not really belong to Colonel Forsyth's command."

"I have heard all about it. You were a hero with the others. I shall be glad to take you. We need lads of strength and courage like you, and since you are riding a borrowed horse, the United States will quickly furnish you with another."

Bob's heart warmed within him. He liked the commander, who himself was a very young man, under thirty, and an hour later was enrolled in the service for the campaign that Custer intended.

CHAPTER XXI

A-HORSE WITH CUSTER

Bob now spent several weeks riding about the plains with Custer and his men in search of the Cheyennes who were still raiding everywhere, causing great loss of life, cutting off emigrant trains, hunters, and detachments of all kinds. Now and then they overtook and defeated small bands, but the great force kept out of their way. It was known definitely that since the death of Roman Nose, Black Kettle was head chief, and he was proving himself a general of ability. It was also rumored that he was helped by a white man, and Bob had no doubt that it was Carver.

Bob never failed to inquire of every one whom they met of news of Sam Strong and his friends. Nobody had heard anything. It became a certainty that they had not reached civilization, but that was all. So the boy, as he rode with Custer, continued his quest, and he could not have carried it on in any other way. The life itself was not without its compensations. He was well treated, and the companionship was good.

The autumn advanced. The brown grass was dead to its roots. Then fierce winds blew out of the northwest, and often they had an edge of hail or snow. But the country, through which they now rode, was wooded in part, and they nearly always encamped at night in groves where they could find plenty of fuel. There the troopers built fires high, and gathered in a circle about them, while their brethren, the horses, stood in another circle just behind the men. Often the snow would blow about them, and the horses would come still closer, reaching over and touching the men with their noses. The friendship between man and horse was exceedingly strong, the result of close association, and of the service that each did for the other. Bob remembered with feeling the splendid mustang that had carried him out of danger, but he did not wish to have him with him now. He was glad that the great horse had gone to take his true place at the head of some wild herd.

They came one evening in a light snowfall to a dense wood along a shallow stream, and Bob, who was in advance with the scouts, pointed to the trees on the branches of which roosted a great throng of splendid, bronze turkeys. The hunters at once became busy, and shot all that they could possibly eat. That night they had a feast. The fires were built higher than ever, the men congregated about them, and as it was known that no enemy was near, Custer allowed them to sing and talk as much as they pleased, while the turkeys were roasted or broiled, and the savory odors penetrated every corner of the dark woods.

It was a night that Bob will never forget, the roaring fires showing the tree trunks, filing away in the distance, the hundreds of soldiers with their brown or ruddy faces, and the feelings of courage and friendship that pervaded everything. It reminded him of evenings with his old comrades, only this was on a much greater scale.

They had been short of rations, and he ate turkey as heartily as any of them. Afterwards he sat a while, listening to the laughter and the songs, and then, wrapping himself in his blanket, he lay down under an oak tree. He dozed for a while most pleasantly, body and mind relaxed into a soothing and peaceful state. The soldiers and the fires wavered before him, and beyond both he could just see the backs of the horses, basking also in the genial glow. He thought vaguely of the many things that he had seen, and he wondered with equal vagueness to what end all this marching would come. Then he dropped into a sleep that was deep and without dreams. Others presently wrapped themselves in their blankets, and they, too, were soon in a sleep as sound as Bob's.

The next day the whole force, encouraged and refreshed, resumed the march, traveling here and there among the hills and on the plains in search of the Cheyennes, Bob also seeking for some trace of his lost comrades of whom he never despaired, although it was now weeks since his capture by the Indians. His confidence in Sam Strong, Bill Cole and the others was so great that their taking or destruction by the Cheyennes seemed impossible to him.

Bob's earnestness and efficiency, his willingness at all times to help gave him a high place in the regard of the young commander, Custer, who attached him to his personal staff, and because of merit, favored him in many ways. The fact that Bob's father had fallen in the great Civil War also caused Custer's heart to warm towards him, and he sometimes talked to the boy of the long struggle, particularly of the mighty battle of Gettysburg, where Custer, then scarcely more than a boy, had proved himself a brilliant cavalry leader.

"Two of my friends, Porter Evans and Tom Harris, were there," said Bob. "One was on one side, and one on the other, but that fact seems to make them like each other all the better, though they never agree about the result of that or any other battle."

"It's a way the boys have," Custer said, "but it does no harm. Out here on the plains we have veterans of either army, and they are all fighting well under the old flag."

"I've found my best friends here in this wild country," said Bob.

"The wilderness breeds friendship," said Custer. "Men are compelled to rely upon one another."

The weather now increased in coldness. All the signs betokened an extremely severe winter. Snow and hail were frequent, but the fierce winds, coming off the vast reaches of plain, were the worst. They cut to the bone, and many of the men made skin masks to protect their faces. An ordinary leader would have gone into winter quarters, but Custer resolved to defy winter itself, no matter how terrible it became. The ravages of the Cheyennes had been so severe, so many people had been killed in the last two years, and there had been so much devastation of all kinds that he was not willing to give them another chance. With his regiment, the Seventh Cavalry, he pressed the hunt anew.

It was now the last week of November, and winter was in full blast. The regiment, led by friendly Osage Indian guides, hit upon a trail so large that they believed it to be that of the main Cheyenne band under Black Kettle. All the men woke to new life at the news, and they pressed forward, hoping that they would now find their elusive foe, and compel a battle.

But their bad luck pursued them. About noon the skies became overcast. Heavy, solemn clouds marched in battalions, fused into one great mass, and then began to pour forth snow. To make it still worse, the wind arose and the storm was blinding. The trail, of course, was quickly lost, and then it was as much as the men could do to keep in touch with one another.

As the afternoon waned the storm increased in violence. The regiment rode forward, a little army of white phantoms. Men and horses were robed in snow from head to foot. It was impossible for any man to keep clear of it. As fast as they shook off one white coat it was replaced by another, and they soon gave up the effort.

As time passed the storm only deepened. The air was filled with whirling, white flakes, driven fiercely by the wind, and they could not see more than two or three hundred yards ahead. But they did not complain. It was only one such incident in the long story of the American army on the border, fighting for generations in the lonely wastes against a brave and crafty foe, obscure battles of which the world heard but little, but which were marked by courage and devotion equal to any shown on great fields like Gettysburg or Chickamauga.

Bob was near the head of the army, just behind General Custer, who closely followed two Osage Indian guides, Little Beaver and Hard Rope, and several times he turned to look back at one of the most remarkable sights that he ever beheld, nearly a thousand figures wrapped in snow, riding silently on, not a man speaking, not a horse neighing, every soldier bent well forward to protect his face from the storm, while all the time the shriek of the wind across the plain was full of menace. They rode, too, through a country of which they knew nothing, wholly uninhabited, except by a savage foe who might at any time lay a well-planned ambush for them. It was a time and situation when even the stoutest heart could find abundant excuse for going into winter quarters and awaiting a milder season to make war.

But Custer had no thought of turning back. It was his intention now to reach a point on Wolf Creek, about thirteen miles from his fortified camp, which he had called Camp Supply, and he still hoped to make it before dark, but the two Indian scouts suddenly stopped and looked at the general. Custer read bad news in his eye and he half guessed its nature but he asked of the nearer:

"What is it, Little Beaver?"

"The snow took the Cheyenne trail from us," replied the Indian, a fine tall warrior, "and now it has done more. We have lost the way to Wolf Creek. Hard Rope and I have talked it over and we tell you the truth. We do not now know which way Wolf Creek lies. What does the yellow-haired chief wish to do with us?"

The Indian spoke with resignation, but Bob who heard the words knew that the pride of both Little Beaver and Hard Rope was deeply hurt. Custer, although his disappointment must have been great, did not rebuke them. He had now the hearts of the friendly Osages, and he knew how to keep them.

"The storm hides all the country from us," he said, "and where you, Little Beaver and Hard Rope, have failed, all other men would fail too. It is no fault of yours."

The eyes of the two Osages flashed with gratitude, and they bent their heads in a sort of proud salute, although they said nothing.

"But," resumed Custer, cheerfully, "where man's own senses have failed, maybe something that man has made will help us."

He drew from his pocket a little compass, studied it carefully, and then announced that Wolf Creek lay not many miles almost directly ahead. Little Beaver and Hard Rope, who looked curiously at the singular little instrument, bowed their heads in submission. It was not for them to question the white man's magic or to feel hurt because it knew more than they.

The soldiers, who had been sitting silently on their

horses, letting the snow beat upon them, raised their heads and silently resumed the march. Bob kept near Custer, and now two white scouts rode with him, one on either side. They were California Joe, a famous veteran, and a brave young Mexican, named Romero, but whom the troops always called Romeo. Bob, in the easy fashion of the border already called him Romeo too.

"Romeo," he asked, "did you ever hear of a man called Juan Carver? He is half of your race."

Young Romeo's eyes darkened.

"I've heard of him," he replied, "and I have seen him too, Senor Bob. He is half American, half Mexican and all bad. He has led a band to raid the beaver grounds either for himself or the Hudson Bay Company, and he will do any evil thing that he can if he may gain by it. I know that he is with the Cheyennes now."

"I knew that he was," said Bob. "He's an able man, and he's probably helping Black Kettle."

Late in the afternoon they came to Wolf Creek, Custer's pocket compass leading them aright, and made camp in some thick woods along the stream. They managed to clear away a good deal of the snow, and to build fires, but the night was trying in the extreme. It snowed hard, for a long time, and then turned bitterly cold. Had they not been able to reach the firewood along the creek, many of them would certainly have frozen to death. None slept long and they were careful also to see that their horses shared in the heat of the fire.

Morning came, the skies were clear and the snow

ceased to fall, but it lay on the ground nearly two feet deep, and a bitter wind blew out of the north. The trumpet sang boots and saddles, and the men mounted, casting, despite themselves, reluctant looks at the fires that they were leaving behind.

"Where are we going now?" asked Bob of California Joe.

"I don't know," replied Joe, "but I know where we ain't goin'. We ain't goin' to no warm house; we ain't goin' to crawl in on top 'o a feather bed under a pile of covers; we ain't goin' to any nice, little town, where you can hear the girls play the pianners, we ain't goin' to do none o' them soft, sweet things; we're jest goin' to march, poundin' two feet o' snow an' mebbe runnin' across a crowd o' howlin' Cheyennes that will give us the picnic o' our lives."

Bob laughed. In the company of hundreds of brave men, he felt cheerful, despite every hardship.

"Isn't that the kind of a picnic that we're looking for?" he asked.

"So it is; so it is," said California Joe, "but I never before had to look so hard for a scrap, through snow up to your neck, with the mercury a hundred degrees below zero, an' the wind blowin' a thousand miles an hour."

Bob laughed, feeling sure that California Joe, despite his much grumbling, would be in the thick of the fray when they found it.

But they did not yet find it. Several days passed, and they were still ploughing around in the snow and cold, sometimes on the plains and sometimes through forests, crossing shallow creeks and rivers that were frozen fast in the ice. The Osage scouts and trackers, in particular, Little Beaver and Hard Rope, showed the greatest courage and devotion, but the deep snow seemed to have covered up all trails, and their skill and energy availed nothing. Custer still refused to go into winter quarters, and continued the hunt. Game was abundant. Buffalo and deer were everywhere, from which fact the scouts drew the inference that the Cheyennes were resting in a hidden camp, with plentiful stores of food.

Various bodies of scouts were sent out, including one under Major Elliott that went toward the south, and the main body of the army, moving on, came to the wide and shallow stream of the Canadian River, the crossing of which was long, difficult and dangerous. The heavy wagons containing the supplies broke through the ice, and the teamsters, in order to keep the horses to their duty, were compelled to leap down in the freezing flood, and pull on the lines, or put their shoulders to the wheels. Many of the cavalrymen helped them, standing waist deep amid the water and the floating ice. It was an extraordinary scene, typical of the great American wilderness and the heroism with which it was won.

Nature could not have provided a sterner aspect, the leafless trees, coated with ice, the bleak desolation of the rolling plains under that great pall of snow, the wide sullen river, filled now with broken ice, and the grim, silent men whom Custer ever drove on and who were always willing to go. Custer himself rode back and forth amid the ice, encouraging and helping.

It took nearly the whole day to get all the wagons across the dangerous flood. Just as the last of them was drawn upon the further bank, they heard the soft crunch, crunch of swift hoofs in the snow and Major Elliott and his scouting party galloped up. Bob knew from the look on their faces that they had news, and he heard the Major's words when he saluted and addressed Custer.

"We have struck an Indian trail, sir," said Major Elliott. "At least one hundred and fifty warriors and their ponies have passed since the last snow fall. I suspect that it is a returning party of hunters."

"If so, it will go straight to the big Cheyenne camp, wherever it is, and we follow," said Custer.

Custer, full of youthful fire and enthusiasm, organized the pursuit with amazing rapidity. The soldiers, who had been wading in the water, exchanged their wet clothing for dry from the wagons, and eighty men, with the poorest horses, were detailed as a guard for the wagons, which must advance with relative slowness. The rest, eager, all their toils and privations forgotten, galloped off, Bob as usual with his friends, California Joe and Romeo. They had started twenty minutes after receiving the news.

"It makes me feel young again," said California Joe. "I don't know that I'm fond o' fightin' as a reg'lar diet, but when I'm lookin' for a fight I'd just as soon find it as keep on lookin' for it till I froze to death."

Bob was serious. He had a sensitive, impressionable nature, and in Forsyth's great defense of the island in the Arickaree, he had seen what war could be. Still, he was relieved to know that they had found the Indians and that in all likelihood the campaign would come to an issue. He looked to his rifle, and felt of the pistol in its holster.

Custer, in his eagerness, was at the very head, with Major Elliott and the two Osages, Little Beaver and Hard Rope. The Major had left a party of his troops on the trail that he had discovered, and Custer, turning to the southwest, galloped toward that point as fast as the deep snow would allow. It was now late in the afternoon, and the sun cast a glowing red tint over the white wilderness. It was weird, like a portent of great events and Bob felt, in every bone of him, that the time had come.

California Joe and Romeo, who had been exchanging low comments, sank into silence. The snow flew in showers beneath the rapid hoofs of the command, which left a broad, deep trail behind it, but the speed was not diminished. The sun, with a last blaze of red sank into the prairie, and then they struck the path of the Indian band. They found that the troops left there by Major Elliott had gone on, and they followed.

The night was at hand, but it was not dark, and the white gleam of the snow helped also. Even had it been dark they could not have missed a road, broken through snow nearly two feet deep. Evidently the Cheyennes did not suspect the nearness of the white army, and California Joe and Romeo began to talk about surprising them.

"The watchfulest men in the world are caught off guard some time or other," said Joe, "an' it may be our chance."

About 9 o'clock in the evening they overtook the detachment, left by Major Elliott, and now the whole force was united, 800 strong, experienced, brave, on fire with zeal, and led by a great captain. But Custer, eager as he was to strike his evasive enemy, now became watchful and cautious. They had already come long and far, and he ordered his men to take a rest of an hour.

"The General is right," said California Joe to Bob, who was now burning with impatience. "Of course, I know how it is. When you think you've got your game in range you want to shoot, but our horses are nigh pumped out, and we need to steady ourselves."

"It is surely so," said Romeo, twisting up the ends of his curly, black mustache. "It is well to have the calm nerves before you fight, and then to fight like a Cortez or a Pizarro."

The young Mexican, brave and courteous, a master of the craft of wood and plain, was a general favorite with the army, and now Bob watched him with interest and admiration, as he prepared for battle. After curling up his mustache in a satisfactory manner, Romeo carefully arranged the red silk handkerchief around his neck, and smoothed down his beautifully tanned buckskin hunting shirt and leggings. He caught Bob's eye and said earnestly:

"If I fall, I wish to fall like a gentleman, clad properly and with everything in order. It will be a great comfort to me."

California Joe laughed softly.

"Mighty little you'll know about it, Romeo," he said, "but I ain't criticisin' you, though, by gum, you're the finest dandy I ever saw on these plains."

Romeo smiled in supreme satisfaction.

"Ah, California Joe," he said, "you pay me the great compliment. Some day when I am rich I shall go far down to the City of Mexico. I shall wear the magnificent suit of red velvet, with a broad and flowing red silk sash around my waist. I shall have the broad-brimmed black hat, with a single immense red plume. Great jewels, diamond, ruby, sapphire, emerald, will glitter all over me like stars. The king of the bull fighters will be but a shadow beside me, and all the beautiful senoritas will be at my feet."

"They'll be struck plum' blind by your splendor," said California Joe, grinning in admiration at the vivid picture that Romeo had drawn.

The two relapsed into silence, and Bob was silent with them. In fact, the whole army was silent, save for the occasional low words of a trooper, and the soft crunch of horses' feet in the deep snow. The men were dismounted now, that their horses might rest too, but they stood beside them and held the reins.

The night was very cold, although Bob, in his excitement and anticipation, did not notice it. But on the eve of battle the feeling of unreality came over him again. It was a phantom army standing there in the icy moonlight on the vast, unpeopled plains, and he was a phantom himself. The cold increased, and the wind that came now and then, cut like a knife. An icy crust was forming on the snow.

Custer gave the word to advance at ten o'clock, and a deep sigh ran through the whole army. But it was a sigh of relief; it was like the unleashing of a hound, eager to move forward. The troopers sprang into the saddle and the stern command of silence was passed all along the line. No one knew how near the enemy might be.

The two Osage scouts, Little Beaver and Hard Rope, led the way on foot, fully four hundred yards in advance, their moccasins making no sound on the snow, their brown figures flitting forward like ghosts. Then in a little group, came about a dozen more Osages, California Joe, Romeo, the rest of the white scouts and Bob. About a third of a mile behind them, in order to keep the noise of so many hoofs from being heard by the Indians, rode the army, Custer at its head, with Major Elliott, Captain Whittaker and other important officers beside him.

They did not move very fast. The surface of the snow on the trail had frozen after the Indians had passed, and now it broke with a crackling sound, faint when one horse made it, but steady and insistent when eight hundred made it together. It was impossible to avoid it, and as the alert ears of the Cheyennes might hear it some distance, Custer did not dare to go faster than a walk.

This crackling sound, at times almost a tinkle, was not unmusical, and it was soothing to Bob's excited senses. He was not apprehensive. He had full confidence in Custer and his army, and he was proud to be riding there in this group of brave and loyal scouts.

They rode on, hour after hour, mile after mile, in the snowy desolation of the wilderness. The moonlight faded, brightened and faded again. Little Beaver and Hard Rope still led with sureness and precision, keeping their distance of four hundred yards ahead of the others. At times, when the moon darkened, their figures seemed to fade away, and only the keen and accustomed eyes of the scouts saw them. But they were always there.

"It's a long trail," whispered California Joe to Bob, "but I think these Osages will take us to the end of it."

It was now far past midnight, and Bob responded in an excited whisper:

"Look! Little Beaver and Hard Rope have stopped!"

The two Osages were standing motionless in the trail, but were looking back toward the little group of scouts, who rode forward quickly.

"What is it?" asked California Joe.

"Me don't know," replied Little Beaver in a soft tone, "but me smell smoke."

Hard Rope nodded in confirmation. Bob sniffed, but could not smell anything. Neither could California Joe, nor Romeo, nor any of the scouts. Custer, Wittaker, Elliott and other officers came up, and they could not detect an odor, either. But they did not lose confidence in the two Osages; the wonderful keenness of their senses had been tested too often. When Custer himself questioned them the Osages still remained absolutely sure.

"Me smell smoke," repeated Little Beaver, and Hard Rope nodded again in confirmation.

"If they say they smell it, they smell it," said Custer, "and the Cheyennes are somewhere near. Now, Little Beaver, you and Hard Rope go on again, but Whittaker, you and Elliott caution the troop to be quieter than ever. Maybe we can strike the Cheyennes before they see us. The snow and the great cold will keep them close to their lodges."

The slow advance was resumed, the two Osages once more becoming shadows that led silently on. Bob's heart began to beat a little livelier tune. He was quite as confident as Custer that the Osages had made no mistake, and that the great moment was at hand. His own little group did not say a word, and Romeo, satisfied that his costume was correct in every detail for battle, ceased to preen.

Little Beaver and Hard Rope decreased speed again. Bob saw the two shadows moving slowly, and yet more slowly, over the white snow, and soon they stopped, remaining upright, motionless, waiting for the group of scouts, which Custer and several of his officers had now joined, to come up. They were no longer shadows, but were now two bronze statues, silhouetted against the gleaming snow. The second stop was about a half mile from the first. When Custer reached them, Little Beaver looking up

said quietly and without any change of countenance:
"Me told you so!"

He pointed, with a long brown forefinger, to a small, dark spot beside the trail, but well inside a patch of timber. Custer, his officers and Bob followed the pointing forefinger, and saw the embers of a small fire. It had never thrown out more than a faint smoke, but in the cold, absolutely pure air of the night, the two Osage trackers had smelt it at a distance of half a mile, and had identified it, without the shadow of a doubt in their own minds.

"Isn't it wonderful?" whispered Bob to California Joe.

"It's wonderful, an' it's true," California Joe whispered back.

"What does this little fire mean?" asked Custer of the Osages.

Little Beaver and Hard Rope looked around in the timber a while, before answering. Then they told Custer that they had reached the edge of ground used by the Cheyennes for herding their ponies. Beyond lay a considerable open space, a fine, large meadow when not covered by the snow, thickly surrounded on all sides by timber, hence making it easy for the boys to hold the ponies there. Some of the boys undoubtedly had built the fire for warmth, and the great Cheyenne village could not be more than two or three miles away.

Custer drew a long, deep breath when Little Beaver told the terse tale, and the others also felt their blood leap.

CHAPTER XXII

THE BATTLE OF THE WASHITA

Custer, always quick and decisive, instantly arranged his plan. He would go forward himself with the two Osage trackers and see, for the sake of absolute certainty, if the Cheyenne village was at hand. The others would follow very slowly. When he announced his plan, the general glanced at the group about him and caught Bob's appealing eyes. He knew very well what it meant, and Bob's youth and the great efficiency that he had shown moved him.

"Well, come along," he said. "You have proved yourself a good boy and a useful one, and you may be of help now."

Bob instantly rode forward by the general's side, and California Joe and Romeo cast envious, but not jealous looks at him. Romeo gave his mustache another and more ferocious twist, and then waved his hand to Bob, in a gesture of brief farewell and many good wishes.

The two Osages on foot, moved forward for the third time, the young general and the boy on horseback following close behind, none of them speaking, and the footfalls of the horses making very little sound. They went forward about two miles, the road dipping down between ridges, and at the top of every ridge they stopped, both to look and to

THE BATTLE OF THE WASHITA   339

listen. When they came to one a little higher than the others, Little Beaver, who was in advance, suddenly crouched down on the snow, and Hard Rope, who was just behind him, at once did the same. The general and Bob stopped their horses.

"What is it?" asked Custer in a whisper.

"Heaps Injuns down there," replied Little Beaver, pointing toward a valley, which lay to their right, partly shut in by timber. Bob, whose eyes naturally keen, were trained now by experience, saw, through the timber, a great dark group of large animals. They were at least a half mile away, and he took them to be buffaloes. Custer, looking intently at them, was of the same opinion, and he turned again to Little Beaver.

"Why do you think Indians are down there?" he asked.

"We heard dog bark," replied Little Beaver.

Neither the general nor the boy had heard anything, but they already had ample proof of the wonderful acuteness of the Osage senses, and Custer knew that Little Beaver and Hard Rope were to be trusted absolutely.

"Suppose we go forward a little further," whispered the general.

They advanced about a rod, and then stopped to listen. Presently both the general and the boy heard the faint sound of a dog's bark in the heavy timber to the right of the herd. "Ah!" uttered Custer softly, and then, following the bark, came a sound, singular for the time and place. It was a low tinkle, very soft and sweet, but penetrating in the still night.

"That little bell on a pony," said Little Beaver, "and down there you see the great herd of Cheyenne horses."

So that was what the general and the boy had mistaken for buffaloes! Not the slightest doubt could exist any longer. There were the Cheyenne ponies, and the Cheyenne village was bound to be close by.

"Come Bob," said the general, "we'll go back now for the others. Little Beaver, you and Hard Rope stay here and watch."

The two Osages, without a word, crouched down, remaining silent and motionless, while Custer and Bob rode back to the group that contained the other scouts and principal officers. The whole army had halted a few hundred yards back of this group. The officers took off their sabers and laid them on the snow that their rattling might not be heard, and rode back to the crest of the hill, where Little Beaver and Hard Rope had been left. Thence, they looked long at the herd, and also saw a few lights twinkling among the trees beyond. There the Osages located the Cheyenne village.

All were convinced, and they rode back to the point where they had left their sabers, which they regained. Then they held a council, to which Bob and the scouts were admitted, a council between midnight and morning, in the snow and ice of a vast wilderness. Custer decided to surround the village and attack at daylight. He divided his army into four detachments. Two moved off at once, making a circuit of several miles, in order to gain the far

THE BATTLE OF THE WASHITA 341

side of the village, where they were to attack at different points. An hour before dawn the third should move up toward the right, where it was to charge at the signal. The fourth, under Custer himself, remained on the hill, from which the discovery of the village had been made, and would attack from that point. Little Beaver, Hard Rope, Bob, California Joe and Romeo remained with Custer.

Theirs was the hardest part, as they were compelled to sit absolutely quiet and wait. Bob had never felt such hours as these before, sitting on his horse in the darkness and in the cold, which was growing more intense, fearing at any moment that their presence would be discovered, and the alarm given, before the circle of steel was complete. The boy's hands grew stiff in his buckskin gauntlets, and the men, who were dismounted and standing beside their horses, were not permitted to stamp their feet to keep them warm, or to walk back and forth for the sake of circulation. Some of the officers, wrapped in huge overcoats, lay softly down on the snow and slept. But Bob had neither the ability, nor the wish to sleep. He looked steadily down into the valley, where the dark figures of the ponies were growing plainer, and several times he heard the sweet, penetrating tinkle of the bell, taken, doubtless, from the horse of some slaughtered emigrant.

The Osages, under Little Beaver and Hard Rope, who were chiefs as well as incomparable trailers, collected in a little group on one side, under the low branches of a tree, and presently Bob learned from California Joe that they had become uneasy.

Now that the Cheyennes were found the Osages feared that, with their great force, they would be more than a match for Custer's army. Custer learned of it and he did not upbraid them, but he whispered to California Joe:

"Will the Cheyennes put up a big fight?"

Bob saw the weather-beaten face of the scout become very serious.

"Yes," replied the veteran, "they will. You can depend on that, general. Mebbe we've bit off more'n we can chaw."

"We'll see about that," said General Custer, firmly.

"I'm with you to the end, general," said California Joe quietly.

Very little was said after that, and the icy hours trailed slowly away. Bob saw afar in the east a faint, grayish tinge. The dawn was coming, and with it the attack. His heart gave a great leap. Custer awakened the officers who lay wrapped in their overcoats on the snow. They sprang to their feet, and all thought that they had been discovered by the Cheyennes, because they saw a sudden, beautiful light, as if from a great fire.

"What on earth is it?" asked Bob in a whisper of California Joe.

"Look! a star!" said Joe.

It was a brilliant morning star, fleeing before the dawn, and, seen intensified and magnified through the atmosphere of the plains. In a moment it faded, and all understood. The Cheyenne village was still in ignorance.

THE BATTLE OF THE WASHITA 343

"Forward!" said Custer, and the stiffened figures of the men became elastic once more, as the blood bounded through their veins. They rode down the slope, and reached the outskirts of the great herd of ponies, which was stretched out, hundreds and hundreds. The dawn was growing stronger.

Custer, Bob, California Joe and Romeo were now in the lead. Just behind them, at Custer's command, came the mounted regimental band, the leader holding the cornet to his lips.

The tops of many tall white tepees rose out of the morning mists, and from many of these tops plumes of smoke shot up. But the presence of the army was still unknown to the Cheyennes. For once the cunning and craft of the white man, had outwitted the cunning and craft of the red. Bob could scarcely believe it. Every pulse in him was leaping wildly.

Custer was turning in his saddle to give the leader of the band the word to play "Garryowen," which was to be the signal for attack, when a single rifle-shot came from the village. The Cheyennes, not dreaming of attack in such terrible weather, were lying close in their tepees, but one warrior now saw the coming foe, and fired.

But the signal was given. Forth from the band came the famous, old air, loud, clear and sweet, singing over the whole village. Up sprang a sun of uncommon splendor, filling the valley with winter gold, gleaming across the skin lodges and on the tawny stream of the Washita which ran through the Cheyenne town.

The men uttered a tremendous cheer, and from

three points in the ring about the town came the answering cry. The other three detachments had come up at the exact time, and the circle of steel was complete. High above the band rose the fierce pealing note of a bugle, and then, with Custer waving his sword aloft, and his long, yellow hair floating out under his hat, they charged the village, the great winter camp of the Cheyennes, containing fifteen hundred or two thousand warriors.

But surprised, though they were, at the dawn of a winter morning, the Cheyennes, Dog Soldiers and all, fought with a courage worthy of their brave and powerful nation. The men rushed from the tepees, rifle in hand. Many of them sprang into the river, breaking the ice, and, standing in the water waist deep under the shelter of the banks, poured a deadly fire upon the advancing army, replying to the cheers of the cavalry with defiant shouts of their own. A small body, seventeen in number, leaped into a rocky depression, where they lay down, protected from the white fire, and sent in bullets rapidly. A formidable force reached a deep ravine, within the limits of the village, and the hail from their rifles was deadly. The women and children, perhaps having confidence that the white troops would not fire upon them, remained in the lodges and began singing the death song, a wild, wailing chant from hundreds of throats, that never ceased during all the fury and tumult of the battle, rising over everything like the solemn despair of a Greek chorus.

Despite all the advantages of the surprise, the army of Custer was faced by a powerful and formi-

THE BATTLE OF THE WASHITA 345

dable foe. The alert Cheyennes, trained by lives of incessant danger, now took advantage of every opportunity. In addition to those already in shelter, they hid behind trees, rocks and bushes, which were thick in the village, and added to the defensive fire which was now fast increasing in volume. At intervals they sent forth their defiant war-whoop.

Bob, carried away by the excitement of the moment and the intensity of feelings so long held in leash, was shouting with the shouting cavalrymen, and urging his horse to a gallop. But a line of fire seemed to blaze directly into his face, as a thousand Cheyenne warriors pulled the trigger. He heard the whistle of bullets, the low cry of men, and the wild scream of horses as they were struck. He saw men plunge suddenly from the saddle and fall into the snow where they lay still. He saw horses without riders break from the line and gallop away in the smoke that was now rising fast, but he saw also the yellow hair and waving blade of Custer just in front of him, and he followed where the leader led.

The first charge of nearly a thousand cavalry was irresistible, and the Cheyennes were driven in toward a common center. The circle of steel wrapped the village around, and closed tighter and tighter. Custer seized the lodges, and the women and children, who still kept up the terrible death chant, were prisoners, but the warriors were not. They were in great force, wherever cover could be found, and the troopers were falling under the bullets of the red marksmen. The huge cloud of smoke rising from so many rifles helped them. They knew every inch of the ground and the soldiers knew none of it. Their yells of defiance became yells of triumph because many of them now began to believe that they would not only drive off the white foe, but destroy him.

"We've bit off a lot," Bob heard California Joe say, but the veteran showed no signs of discouragement, firing slowly and only when he had picked his target. Bob also fired, but he was confused by the great volume of sound, the shouting, the crash of the rifles, and the dense smoke that was now enveloping the whole village and making all things obscure. The snow was trodden into slush under the horses' feet, and particles of it kicked into his face stung like shot. More than once he thought that he had been hit by a bullet, only to find that it was a ball of snow or a piece of ice.

He did not know, in all the confusion and obscurity, that the advance had ceased. The ring of steel seemed to have tightened as far as it would go. It had now met a body that would not yield. Bob felt a sinking sensation. Were they to be beaten, after having executed so complete a surprise? Then he heard Custer give an order to dismount, and he leaped from his saddle. Some of the men dropped to the rear, holding the reins of the horses, but Bob was not designated as one of them. He remained in the front line, on foot now, feeling that he was better able thus to continue in the battle.

"Sharpshooters!" cried Custer, and he rapidly detailed men to pick off the small body of Cheyennes who had taken refuge in the rocky depression, and were doing deadly execution. As long as these Indian marksmen stung their flank no battle could be won.

Bob, California Joe and Romeo were in this force, and Bob noted with surprise that the brave, young Mexican was still a dandy. His clothing seemed to have escaped all the snow and slush, and the pointed black mustache still curved up beautifully at either end.

"Down flat!" cried California Joe, and every man threw himself face forward in the snow which almost buried them. Then they began to creep toward the Cheyennes, holding their fire, while the battle whistled and thundered on either side of them. Bob was humane, but the odor of the smoke and burnt gunpowder entered his nostrils and he felt all the passion of the hunter. For the time he was as eager as any of them to get at the Cheyennes in the rocky hollow.

California Joe looked back at his creeping band.

"Don't any of you dare to pull trigger 'till I say the word," he called, commandingly.

Bob glanced along the line. All the faces were fierce and eager. The snow and the cold were forgotten. The rifles were held well forward, ready for a shot when the time came. The rest of the battle, which was always increasing in volume and ferocity, was wholly forgotten by every one of them.

They reached the side of a little knoll, and crawling cautiously to its crest, they could see the heads of the Indians in the smoky hollow. Bob detected, through the film of smoke and vapor, the feathers of war-bonnets, and black eyes, as hot with the fire of battle as any of those in California Joe's band.

"Now," said California Joe, "lay low an' pick your men."

Bullets struck among the Indians in the hollow, so long immune hitherto. Several of their best warriors were slain before they knew whence the fire came, and then they turned their attention from the main army to this new danger. A deadly duel ensued, but the sharpshooters of California Joe were too much for the Cheyenne marksmen. Although two or three of the whites were slain and several wounded, they never ceased to send bullets, aimed with a sure eye and firm hand, into the hollow. The Cheyennes at last looked around for flight, but they knew that the moment they rose from the hollow they would be swept away by the fire from the main army, so they stayed there, fighting the sharpshooters of California Joe, and died where they lay to the last man. Their bodies, seventeen in number, were found among the rocks after the battle. Then California Joe and his band, Bob with them, turned to other work.

The main body of the troops, relieved of the terrible fire on their flanks, pressed farther in. The white sharpshooters from all sides poured a perfect storm of bullets into the ravine, where the big Indian force lay. The Cheyennes there stood it long, but broke at last. They leaped to their feet and ran up the ravine, leaving half a hundred dead behind them. They renewed their fire from other points, while that of the warriors hidden under the banks of the river had never ceased for a moment, and the doubtful battle still surged to and fro.

It was now ten o'clock, and the combat was three hours old. The brilliant sun now and then made its way through the clouds of smoke and mist rising from the snow, and in one of these rifts Bob saw Indians collecting on a knoll below the village. He instantly pointed them out to General Custer, who viewed them with great alarm, although he did not let his face show it. If a second strong force was coming up, could his men withstand them?

At that moment Romeo ran up and explained the presence of the warriors on the knoll. He knew a dozen Indian languages, and he had learned from a squaw in a lodge that only two or three miles below them was another great Indian village occupied by Arapahoes under their head chief, Little Raven, Kiowas, under their head chief Satanta, and some Comanches and Apaches who would undoubtedly come to the relief of their hard-pressed brethren, the Cheyennes.

Bob, who now remained close to Custer, as an aide, heard the words, and he knew their full import. The combat with one Indian army had been fierce enough, what would it be with two? But he did not feel any deep depression. The excitement of the moment would not permit. He merely watched the General to see what he would do.

Custer knew the value of time. Once more the bugle sounded the charge, and the circle of steel pressed in with a force that was irresistible. The riflemen leaped down into the river and cleared out the Indians lurking under the bank. The four detachments, charging with the greatest fire, met in the center of the village, and the Cheyennes were beaten before their kinsmen had made up their minds to attack.

At this critical moment, Major Bell, the quartermaster, cutting his way through the Indian lines, arrived with a great supply of fresh ammunition. A tremendous cheer greeted him, and, with replenished belts the army wheeled to meet the second Indian force.

Custer was thorough. Two hundred of his men were detailed to tear down the lodges and set them on fire, first having brought out the women and children. The task was quickly done, and a vast column of smoke and fire shot up where the Cheyenne village had been. Outside, the squaws and children kept up the terrible wailing death chant, that had never been broken for an instant.

But the battle itself sank for a few moments, while the white army faced the new foe, who was gathering his forces for the attack. California Joe brought word that the head chief, Black Kettle, had been found among the slain. Though not as great as Roman Nose, he had been an able chief and a valiant warrior, and he had died fighting for the hunting grounds of his people. Bob had caught two glimpses of a white man who he was sure was Carver, but the wily freebooter disappeared each time in the confusion.

When the great fire from the burning tepees rose,

THE BATTLE OF THE WASHITA 351

the rage of the Indians rose with it. Those Cheyennes, who had broken through the lines and the Kiowas, Arapahoes and others outside, rushed forward to a new attack. The deep snow in the village was trampled into a slush, red for wide spaces. The smoke hung in heavy banks, which a stray wind now and then lifted, and revealed the two armies, white and red, firing along a long, curving line, creeping rather than standing, but always coming closer.

Bob was thoroughly possessed by the fury of the conflict. He had abandoned his horse, long since, to the little body of troopers detailed for this service, and keeping with California Joe and Romeo, he was at the point in the line, where the Indian attack was fiercest. But Custer was not waiting for the Indians. He also was attacking, pressing forward his men who now fought on foot, taking advantage, in Indian fashion, of every shelter afforded by rock or bush or swell of the ground. Meanwhile, he held many of the Cheyenne warriors prisoners, all their women and children, and a herd of fifteen hundred ponies.

Noon came, and despite the cold, the men felt parched and burnt from the long struggle which was yet far from a decision. Another hour passed, and then another, and both sides stood firm, neither able to advance further. Custer now was consumed with anxiety for his wagon train, with its escort of eighty men, which he knew must be coming up, and which was likely to come straight into ambush. His own losses, moreover, were heavy. The gallant Major

Elliott and nineteen men had been ambushed and all killed. Many more were killed elsewhere, and there was a great swarm of the wounded, although all of the latter, who could stand, yet fought.

"Will we beat 'em, Joe? Will we beat 'em?" gasped Bob, who was covered from head to foot with snow and mud.

The old scout paused a half minute before replying, and then he said very gravely:

"I said we'd bit off a lot, mebbe more'n we could chaw. We've got iron jaws an' we've been chawin' hard an' long, but I don't know yet. By the great horn spoon, Bob, them Injuns fight well, as they gen'ally do! We don't know what would have happened if old Roman Nose had been alive an' kickin'."

California Joe was right. The North American Indian, always a formidable foe, full of courage, skill and tenacity, was fully justifying on that day his title as a great fighter. The warriors, although surprised in their tepees, had held a powerful white force, led by a great captain, at bay for more than eight hours.

But Custer was now preparing for a supreme effort. The mellow notes of the bugle sang over the desperate field, and the whole army was quickly formed into a hollow square with the prisoners in the center. It was no longer necessary to hold the Cheyenne village, because there was no Cheyenne village to hold. As soon as the square was complete the bugle sang again, and then the army rushed with its full weight upon the second Indian force, many of the remounted cavalry charging, saber in hand.

THE BATTLE OF THE WASHITA

The Indians fired one volley, two volleys, three volleys, and then, as the troop still came on, they could stand no more. They broke and fled in all directions, leaving their dead behind them. Custer, waving his sword, did not permit his men to stop, but continued the chase, pursuing the Indians to the second village, taking that also, and scattering Cheyennes, Arapahoes, Kiowas, and all the rest in one wild rout.

The Cheyenne nation was practically destroyed, but it went down to ruin fighting with a valor worthy of any race. The great battle of the Washita was over, and the Indians had suffered the greatest defeat in their history beyond the Mississippi, but the white army was exhausted. The men threw themselves down among the tepees in the second village, and some of them sank into a stupor. The surgeons were busy with many others, and the rest still stood to their arms.

Bob also felt this great temptation to sink down and lapse into forgetfulness, but he resisted it, and looked with a sort of dim wonder back over the great trail by which they had come. He saw the smoke still rising from the Cheyenne village, and here and there in the trodden slush dark spots that he knew to be bodies. On the distant hills stood brown figures, those of the defeated Indians, but they no longer fought. They were merely looking sadly at the scene of desolation and ruin.

Not a shot was fired now, and the silence, after such a continuous crash, was heavy and oppressive. The huge bank of smoke, made by so much firing, lifted, but coils and eddies of vapor still rose from the ground. The sun in all the brilliancy of mid-afternoon, presently scattered the smoke entirely, and poured down a torrent of vivid, golden light that disclosed all the terrible field, the trodden snow, the fallen men, white and red, the slain horses, and the columns of smoke that still rose from the burning ruins of the first village.

"Well, we've won, boy," said the voice of California Joe in Bob's ear, "but, by the great horn spoon, we know we've had a fight. It was a case of pitch and toss for about eight hours, an' I don't min' tellin' you now, Bob, that I thought more than once we'd be singin' our last little death songs. Even Romeo here has lost all the gilt off his clothes."

It was true. The attire of the young Mexican was stained in many places with snow and mud, and in one with red. He took a look of dismay at himself, blushed through the olive of his cheeks, and hastily began to make repairs.

Bob turned away from the scene up the river, the great trail of battle that they had made. He did not know which way he was going, but he was tired of looking upon the marks of combat, and the fallen. He was weak, and he saw dimly. His eyes were stinging with the smoke, and the lodges, the soldiers and the wintry landscape wavered before him. Suddenly he fell to trembling, and California Joe, who was watching him, clapped a strong hand on his shoulder.

"Hold up, Bob, my boy!" he cried. "Here, come in this lodge and sit down a bit!"

They entered a lodge of buffalo skin. Everything showed signs of a hasty flight. There were two couches of buffalo robes undisturbed. Dried herbs hung from the skin walls, and in one corner was a heap of jerked meat. In another lay an old musket.

"Just you spread yourself out here for a few minutes," said Joe, indicating one of the couches or pallets, and the boy, without protest, stretched himself on the buffalo skins. Then the dimness passed away from his eyes, and his nerves ceased to tremble. Oh, the deep, intense luxury of rest at such a time! Moreover, the battle and its ruin were hidden from him. He saw only the walls of the tepee and California Joe, sitting on the other pallet and hugging his knees in pleasure.

"This ain't the finest house in the world," said California Joe, "but I'm glad to be here, come safe through what I reckon was the terriblest Injun battle ever fought."

Bob was fully restored in fifteen minutes, and then he sprang up from the pallet. California Joe joined him, and they went outside. The sun had already passed the zenith of the quick winter day, and far off the twilight was darkening, while the cold deepened. The soldiers had lighted fires, and were beginning to cook their scanty supplies of food. Romeo was already helping them, and Bob and California Joe joined in the task.

The fires brought warmth, comfort and cheer, and the steadily darkening twilight hid the sanguine field that they had left behind them. To the right the women and children and the captured warriors were gathered in a dark mass with troopers, rifle on thigh, riding incessantly about them.

Bob, now that his strength and spirits were back, was assailed by a fierce, ravening hunger, and when the time came he ate like one who had not tasted food in a week. Then he drank cupful after cupful of black coffee. He was ashamed of himself presently, but when he saw that the others were doing the same, he resumed his congenial task.

Night came, clothing the valley, but not obscuring the circle of red light where the fires burned. Custer was still extremely anxious about his wagon train, and at ten o'clock he took up the march again, despite the darkness. But before going he set fire to the second village also, and it burned for a long time, a pillar of light behind them.

The march was kept up for four hours, when they encamped again in the valley of the Washita, and Bob, wrapped in a coat, slept on the snow till dawn. He rose to see another brilliant day, and shortly after they resumed the march a dark line appeared on the hills. Custer was the first to see it, through his glasses, and he gave a little cry of joy.

It was the wagon train, coming up through the deep snow, and its very slowness had saved it. Had it been able to move faster the Indians about Custer would certainly have destroyed it.

The whole army advanced swiftly, met the train, and there was great rejoicing and congratulation. Ample supplies of food, ammunition, medicines and fresh clothing were at hand, and the spirits of the men rose to the zenith.

CHAPTER XXIII

THE LONE SEARCH

The army, still holding its captives, moved slowly and encamped again the second day on the banks of the Washita. Despite the slain and the large number of wounded, it was in excellent condition, and since the wagon train had come, it would have been in condition to fight another battle had there been need of it. But there was no need. The power of the Cheyennes was shattered, and they would not be able to raise their heads again for years. They would never be able to raise them as high as they had once held them.

But for lone, white wanderers, or those in small numbers, the plains would be more dangerous than ever throughout the winter, because the scattered Cheyennes, Arapahoes and Kiowas, without villages now, would be wandering everywhere, eager for revenge. Yet, the knowledge of these facts did not keep down a resolution which was forming in Bob's breast.

He must find Sam Strong and his old comrades. Two buffalo hunters who came in that morning reported rumors of a little band of troopers, hidden somewhere among the hills to the southwest. Bob believed from the first that these were his friends, and he was quite sure now that if he had not come with Custer he would never have obtained this news.

He was encouraged, too, by what he considered a good omen. Among the spoil of arms, picked up in the Cheyenne village, was the rifle that he had inherited from his father. Bob happened to see it in the hands of a trooper, who readily exchanged it for the weapon that the boy carried. Such omens as this decided him. He would brave all dangers, and start at once.

He went to General Custer and told him of his plan. The young commander looked around at the vast wilderness, deep in snow, and infested with wandering warriors burning with hate of the white man. Then he looked at the brave youth for whom he felt a real affection.

"Don't do it, Bob, lad," he said. "This may be a false rumor. Besides, if your friends are in hiding somewhere, it is likely that they will come out safe in the spring. I'm afraid that inside of a week your scalp would be hanging at the belt of some vengeful Cheyenne. Stay with me. You have the making of a good soldier, and you shall be an officer on my staff."

Bob flushed with pleasure, but his resolution was not shaken.

"I thank you, General, I thank you from my heart," he said, "but I belong with these men whom I wish to seek. I'm used to the wilderness now, and I know its ways. I must find them."

Custer glanced at him and read his spirit in his firm eyes and chin.

"If you feel that way then you must go," he said. "Remember that the horse on which you ride is your own, and take all the ammunition and other supplies you can carry. The United States Government owes you at least that much."

Bob thanked him. The general gave his hand the warm clasp of sincere friendship, and turned away to his tent. Bob speedily made ready, and dozens of the men, who had fought with him in battle, came to tell him good-by. Many believed that it would be a good-by forever.

Most notable among these were California Joe and Romeo. The young Mexican was again the perfect Spanish dandy, fit to thrum on the guitar under the window of some senorita, far down in the warm valleys of Mexico. Never had he ruffled it more bravely. The plume in his hat had taken a fresh curve, the red sash around his waist was looped in jauntier folds, and not a speck of mud or snow disfigured his velvet costume.

"Good-by, Senor Bob," he said, "I am sorry to see you go. You have fought with Senor Joe and me in the great battle of the Washita. You would do better to stay and be a soldier. Ah, Senor Bob, you lose your life alone on the great plains, and it is not good."

Genuine tears stood in the eyes of the emotional, but brave, Romeo. Bob was grateful to him.

"I shall never forget the time when we fought side by side, Romeo," he said, "and I hope that you won't either."

"What you want to do, Bob," said California Joe gruffly to hide his Anglo-Saxon feelings, "is to keep a mighty good lookout, an' if you see any human bein' that acts suspicious, shoot first. Then, after you've put a bullet through his head, ask him whether he's a friend or not."

Bob laughed, partly to hide his own feelings, and then took the reins of his horse in hand. At that moment, two men rode up and greeted him joyously. One was old and the other young. They were Pete Trudeau and Jack Stillwell. Bob was full of delight to see them again and he took their coming as a second good omen.

"And so, Bob, boy, you've been distinguishing yourself again," said Stillwell. "Not satisfied with being with Forsyth, in the great fight at the island, you've come with Custer and licked the whole Cheyenne nation."

"I did just the same, Jack, that a thousand others did," said Bob. "We had to fight for all we were worth, or be wiped out. There wasn't any choice."

"I believe you, from what I've heard," said Stillwell admiringly. "You're having your young life, Bob, crowded with about as much action as it can hold."

But both he and Trudeau looked very grave when they heard of Bob's expedition. They did not believe that he could ever succeed, and tried to dissuade him, but, as before, he was unshakable in his resolution. Nevertheless, he waited an hour or two, as they were the bearers of dispatches, and returning, would ride with him some miles. Bob was glad of their companionship even for a short distance.

When they were ready the three rode away, the

boy in the center, and the soldiers knowing why he went, gave three great cheers for the brave youth. He looked back, lifted his cap in reply and let his eyes linger for a few moments on the scene outspread before him, the line of wagons, the files of soldiers, the dark mass of captives, and encircling all, the white world of untouched snow, which seemed to stretch away into infinity. He had found many good friends among these soldiers. He knew the great work that they were doing in the obscurity of the West, and he hoped to meet them again.

The three glanced back several times from the crest of the swells, and it was some time before they completely lost sight of the army, but it sank into the plain at last, and they were alone with the snow. After that they rode on more than an hour in silence. Then Stillwell asked:

"What are your plans, Bob?"

"I'm going to ride straight for the range of big hills down there, and I believe that I'll find Sam and the boys among them. I've food enough for two weeks, and I've got two big blankets rolled up here on my saddle."

"The blankets will do against the cold," said Trudeau, "an' I don't think you'll lack for food. You're sure to run against buffalo long before the two weeks are up. I'm hopin' you won't run against Cheyennes too."

"I'm willing to take the chances," said Bob bravely, and they rode on another hour in silence. Then the time for parting came, as they must go toward the east, while he went southward. They shook hands, said a few words only, although these were very real and very earnest, and then a single horseman rode through the snow into the south. The other two stopped presently, and sitting motionless, watched him until he was out of sight.

Bob, at the first parting from these good friends, felt an overwhelming loneliness. That was why he did not look back, but as he crossed swell after swell, and became used to the desolation, his spirits returned. He was strong and enduring. He had passed through great dangers. He had come wholly unharmed from the thick of two long and desperate battles, and one who had been so fortunate might hope for much. He had a good horse under him, a good rifle at his back, and he knew wild life. What more could he ask?

The boy's spirits rose fast, coming up from reserves of great strength in his nature. He whistled a tune, the gay lilt of which was heard only by himself, and his horse, sharing his high courage, raised his head and neighed once. The cold had moderated somewhat, and the snow was no longer covered with a crust of ice. The going was fairly easy, but Bob did not urge the horse beyond a walk, knowing that he must husband his strength, as without him, he would be lost on the great snowy plains.

He maintained his course throughout the day, always scanning the horizon with great care, for wandering bands of the defeated Indians. But his great safeguard lay in the fact that the sunlight was intense and brilliant, and he could see a horseman miles away. Despite his vigilance, no black speck appeared upon the horizon, and he rode all through the brilliant afternoon without interruption. Towards night he began to think of a place for a camp, and marked a dark line, on his left, which his skilful eye told him was trees.

He turned his horse toward the timber and approached cautiously. While the trees would afford shelter for him, they would afford shelter for the Indians also, and one must choose his bed well before sleeping in it. Bob relied to a certain extent upon his horse, a trained army campaigner, likely to shy at the presence of Indians, but the horse gave no sign of alarm, and just at the coming of the twilight, he entered a fine grove of oak, ash and cottonwood, which stretched for an indefinite distance along both sides of a broad but shallow creek. The plains could offer no more inviting place for a camp, and to one as hardy as he, it seemed good. The creek was frozen over to the depth of several inches, but he broke the ice and drank and his horse drank after him. The snow among the trees was not deep, and Bob scraped away large places, revealing grass yet alive, of which the horse ate eagerly, then pushed his nose through the snow on his own account for more.

Having provided first for the faithful animal that carried him, the young horseman then provided for his own comfort. He found a little secluded arbor, as it were, in the thickest clump of trees and cleared away all the snow. By this time the sun was gone and it was quite dark, with the cold increasing fast.

Satisfied that a little smoke would not be seen in the night, he gathered a heap of dead wood and lighted it with matches. He never suffered the blaze to rise much, but it threw out a great heat which warmed him through and through, and gave him a feeling of comfort, even luxury.

The grass around the fire thawed and then dried. The boy drew pemmican and army biscuits from his stores, and sitting on one of the blankets, with the other wrapped around him, he ate and felt a great content. The horse satisfied after his grazing, also came over and stood by the fire, basking in the heat. His great, mild eyes like those of the boy expressed content.

Bob knew that he was taking a certain risk by sleeping there without a sentinel, but it must be taken if he would preserve the strength to continue his long search. By and by he put out the fire, smothering it in snow, and then searched the woods for some distance, in either direction. There was no sign of an enemy, and coming back to the dry place in the thick shadow of the clump, he rolled himself from head to foot in the two blankets. He stretched himself at full length on the ground, and luxuriously contemplated the stars for a few minutes. Then he dropped into one of the deepest and pleasantest sleeps of his life, never stirring until the daylight came.

He rode all that day slowly, but without a break, eating his brief noonday meal from the saddle. It turned somewhat warmer and the snow began to melt, making it more difficult for his horse on account of the deep slush. He camped the second night on the open prairie, and only his blankets saved him from the raw, wet cold. Toward the middle of the third morning he saw a dark, blue line which one less experienced might have taken for a low cloud, but which he knew to be the foot-hills. Once again his pulses took a great leap. His comrades, these men who had done so much for him, would surely be there.

He was anxious to urge his horse to greater speed, but he knew that he must spare him, in all that snow and slush, and they went on at the same slow, steady walk. The air was so thin and so intensely bright that the blue line did not seem to grow any stronger or more distinct. But Bob was not discouraged. He knew that the hills were yet far off, and that he could not possibly reach them until late the next day.

In the afternoon he saw dark, moving specks which came nearer, and which proved to be buffaloes, nosing through the snow for the short grass which winter had not killed. They were uncommonly tame, indicating that they had been hunted but little, from which Bob drew a cheerful omen, feeling sure that very few Indians, perhaps none, had passed that way. It was pleasant also to see his dinner on the hoof, if the supplies he carried should become exhausted.

He was fortunate enough to find another creek, and more thick covert of trees for his third night, but he did not build a fire. He had an idea that, as he approached the hills, he was more likely to be in the vicinity of wandering Indians in search of shelter and refuge.

He fastened the horse to a bush in the very darkest shadow, and lay down himself, under another bush, where in the night he was not visible to the best eye ten yards away. It was not very cold now, and with one blanket beneath him, and the other wrapped around his body, he was warm enough. He did not fall asleep for at least an hour and he woke again about midnight. The night had now cleared and a full silver moon and many bright stars were shining. The horse was standing peacefully by his bush, and for all Bob knew, was asleep on his feet.

The boy would have gone back to sleep also, but his roving eye caught a pin-point of light far down the stream. He remembered the brilliant morning star that they had seen just before the dawn at the Battle of the Washita, and he believed at first that he was now deceived in the same way, but a longer look convinced him that it was a real earthly light, probably the flame from a fire.

It might be Sam and the others, and for a moment his heart beat high at the thought, but the next moment, cold reason told him he must be wrong. It was not at all likely that they would yet come down into the plain.

The boy, knowing that a fire at such a time and place must have some great significance, resolved to investigate it. He saddled the horse in case he should have to take a sudden flight, rolled up the blankets tightly, and tied them to the saddle. He patted the intelligent animal on the nose and said in a whisper that he would soon be back; the horse might not understand the words, but he would the stroke of the hand. Then, with his finger on the trigger of his rifle, he stole down among the trees toward the light.

It was a windless, quiet night. The restless airs of the plains were still for once, and the leafless boughs of the trees did not move. The creek broadened as he advanced, and seemed to have a fair depth. It was filled everywhere with ice, broken up by the thaw, and moving slowly. The forest seemed to extend back at least a quarter of a mile, on either side.

Bob kept his eyes fixed on the light, which burned steadily and grew larger as he advanced. He was quite sure now that it was the flame from a fire. He had gone about a half mile, when he stopped suddenly, and despite all his experience and self control shuddered violently.

The boughs of the trees above his head contained many long, dark objects, and he knew what they were. He had come to an ancient Indian burying ground. Perhaps the mummies swinging from the boughs were the very ancestors of the warriors who had fallen on the Arickaree and the Washita, and this most certainly was *not* a good omen.

He steadied his nerves and continued his advance toward the light, coming near enough now to know absolutely that it was the flame from a camp-fire. It was obscured, at moments, by dark figures passing before it, and these figures must be men. Many would have turned back now, but Bob's resolve to see who these men were increased in strength. There was the barest of chances that they might be Sam Strong and his comrades, and every probability that they were hostile Indians. In either case he wished to know.

Bob stalked the camp-fire. The snow was so soft now that it gave back no sound at all, and there were bushes in plenty. He was soon near enough to see that the camp-fire was large, surrounded by perhaps thirty men, and as he lay down in the snow and drew his body yet closer, he perceived that three or four of these men were white, the rest being Indians, mostly of the Cheyenne nation, but with four or five Arapahoes and Kiowas.

The boy, lying in the dark, and with his body almost covered by the snow, saw that the principal figure among the white men was that of Juan Carver. He sat where the full light of the fire fell upon his somber face, and in the luminous glow, he looked very cruel and very powerful. Evidently he had come out of the battles without a wound.

The three other white men belonged to the band with which Carver had expected to take the beaver skins from Sam Strong and his comrades. The rest, Bob supposed, had either been killed or had wandered away. The fire threw out much heat, and Indians and white men were grouped about it, enjoying the warmth. Bob surmised that they had made a night march, and that the fire had just been built. Carver was talking to one of the white men, and judging from the deference paid to him by both white and red, he was the leader of the party.

Bob, feeling secure in his snowy ambush was extremely anxious to hear what was being said, and he gradually crept closer. All the horses were on the far side of the flames and there was no danger from them. He was soon within fifteen or twenty yards of the fire, lying among the thick bushes. There he had the reward of skill and daring. Carver and another of the white men finally rose, walked toward an open space in which their blankets were spread, but did not cease their talk.

Bob did not catch all the words, but he caught enough to make a connected story. Carver and the Indians, refugees from the Washita, also had heard the rumors that a party of trappers were hiding in the hills, with a rich store of furs, waiting a chance to get through to civilization. Bob heard Carver twice say the word "Strong" and he could not doubt that his comrades were beyond the low, blue line that marked the beginning of the hills. Carver and this strong band were seeking them also, and now his obligation to reach them was all the greater.

He remained quite still, while Carver and most all the others lay down to sleep, in a circle about the fire, leaving three Indians and one white man to keep the watch. Then he began his slow retreat. He was so careful about it, that it was twenty minutes before he was well beyond the circle of the firelight, and could safely rise to his feet. But after that he sped back to his horse, mounted, rode out upon the plain, and making a wide curve around the hostile camp, advanced as swiftly as the snow would allow, toward the hills.

CHAPTER XXIV.

A MIRACLE

Bob turned back into the timber towards morning. He deemed it wiser to risk a chance of encounter with Indians there than to remain in the bright sunlight on the open plain, where any one could see him for miles. Besides a wary man, alone in the timber, would be likely to see an enemy first and there would always be a chance to hide.

He took his breakfast in the saddle and as he advanced, the snow became thinner, melting rapidly under the rays of a fairly warm sun. None of it was left on the boughs, and the creek was beginning to rise, under the influence of the innumerable streams that poured into it from the thaw. Bob surmised that this creek entered the hills, passed through into the mountains, and probably flowed into some river on the other side. Its valley offered a path, easy for his horse, and all the more likely to take him to his comrades, who would surely seek some warm valley, containing flowing water.

The dim, blue line of the day before now became high and dark, a ridge of hills, shaggy with pine and cedar, and beyond them were white summits and crests, which showed where the ridges sloped up into mountains. Bob was sure that he could reach them before dark, and he was equally sure that Carver and the Cheyenne band were far behind him.

A MIRACLE

That night's start of six or seven hours was a great thing, and might prove the salvation of more than one man.

At noon he gave his horse a rest of more than an hour, bathed his face and hands in the icy creek, and walked vigorously up and down, in order to take the stiffness from his limbs, caused by so much riding. When he sprang into the saddle again it was with renewed vigor. Throughout the afternoon he saw great quantities of game, buffalo and deer, which had sought the shelter of the forest, and many wolves lurking about, in the hope of pulling down the weak. The wolves often were so bold, or were so hard driven by hunger, that he was tempted to take a shot at some particularly ferocious haunter of the timber, but he did not dare, because of those whom he knew to be behind him.

At dusk he reached the first slopes, and he was glad to see that the plains and cedars were very dense, but with a fairly good trail leading into the hills by the side of the creek, which was now a foaming torrent. He continued as long as the light made travel safe, and then turned aside into a narrow valley like a cleft, which cut through the hills. He did not know how far it went or to what it would lead him, but he could not afford to camp beside the creek, because the Cheyennes would certainly come that way. He went fully two miles, and then he was somewhat surprised to find the trail leading into a wide valley which, as nearly as he could make out in the moonlight, seemed to be two or three miles square.

It was now about midnight and thoroughly exhausted with twenty-four hours of riding, watching and supremest tension, he stopped among the trees that fringed the valley, tethered his horse, leaving him saddled, took the usual refuge among his blankets, and in five minutes was asleep.

Bob's awakening was sudden and alarming. He heard a terrified neigh and sprang to his feet just in time to see his horse break the lariat, and gallop off wildly down the valley. All this he saw through a great, white veil, because the snow was pouring down as if the bottom of the very heavens had dropped out. He also saw rushing directly upon him a great dark, heaving mass, a herd of buffaloes in a panic.

Bob's action was partly due to quickness of mind and partly to impulse. He had slept with his rifle, rolled in the blankets beside him, and when he sprang to his feet it was still in his hands. Now, with the blankets still hanging about his shoulders, he ran swiftly to one side, endeavoring to secure the slope on the right. It was fortunate for him that he was strong and active, as the need of speed was heavy upon him. It seemed to him that he felt the breath of the leading bulls on the back of his neck, and the thunder of their hoofs was a deafening roar in his ears. He slipped once on the first slope, but remembering at the same time to cling to his rifle and blankets, regained his feet and ran, with all his might, reaching the crest, as the black herd thundered over the place where he had been.

The buffaloes seemed to be frantic with terror,

either of the storm or some force behind them, and they plunged, with irresistible force, down the narrow ravine into the valley. The weaker members of the herd, driven to the outside, were pushed up the slopes, and Bob found them coming dangerously near to him. For further protection he climbed a huge oak tree and sat down in a low fork. There he was in no danger of being trampled, although he might freeze to death.

He made himself as easy as he could in the fork, drew the blankets as closely as possible around his body, and watched the buffaloes go by. The buffalo is subject to panic, and he believed now that they had been attacked somewhere else by Indians, possibly by the warriors who were with Carver, and that the sudden coming of so great a snowstorm had added to their terror.

It was not a large herd, two or three thousand, perhaps, and they were not long in passing. Bob watched the last big, black form disappear in the driving veil of snow, and then he took thought of himself. He was in a serious case, perched in an oak, in the wild hills, his horse lost, his friends far, his foes near, and the snow coming down so fast that it seemed to crowd the air.

He dropped to the ground and tried to get his bearings. But he knew nothing, except that before him lay a large valley into which the buffaloes had gone. The great trail that they made was quickly covered by the falling snow. In the east was a yellowish blur, which told that the sun was rising, but the sun itself was invisible through the mass of sullen clouds.

Bob was in great doubt. He might stay among the trees and find some sort of shelter there, but it would lead to nothing. On the other hand, it might be that his friends had taken refuge in some such valley as this, and he decided at last to enter it, and cross it if possible. When he fell down the cliff in crossing the pass, he had taken the boldest course and won. He might succeed again. At least, if he needed food the buffaloes would be there, and he had his rifle.

He left the trees and entered the plain, plunging forward over rough ground, through the snow, and unable to tell much about the region into which he was coming. The falling snow was so dense that when he looked back he could no longer see the trees. He kept manfully on, trying to maintain the direction in which he had started, but not at all certain about it. Fortunately the cold was not great, and the exercise made his blood circulate freely.

He expected to cross the valley in an hour or two, but he did not come to any trees, and he thought that he might be walking in a circle. There was no way in which to tell, and he stuck to his task, going forward without stopping, until he thought it must be noon. Then he stopped, crouched down in a little hollow and drew the blankets over his head. Most of his food supplies were gone with the horse, but with a hunter's precaution, he had put some pemmican in his belt, and now he ate eagerly. Then he rested a while, but he was afraid to stay long, and transferring the blankets from his head to his body he started again.

A MIRACLE

Bob fought the snow all that afternoon without coming to a forest. He passed several clumps of bushes and every time he was tempted to seek some sort of shelter among them, but always he successfully resisted the temptation, knowing that it would not do to yield. The afternoon passed in such struggles, and then, the yellowish, pale sunlight showing dimly through the veil of snow, began to fade. In its place came a whitish darkness that filled the boy's soul with apprehension. One could not live forever, unsheltered in such a storm. The night was at hand, the snow was not abating, and he was becoming so weak from his long exertions that he could not keep his feet another hour.

He stood still for four or five minutes, trying to choose a course, like a mariner in a storm. Then his weakness grew great upon him, but he thought that he saw off to the left a dark line which might be trees. At least hope put trees there, and summoning his last reserve of strength he walked toward the dark line.

As he came nearer, he was quite sure that he could discern the outline of boughs, and then he became aware of peculiar noises, something like groanings or gruntings, and he dimly saw darker figures under the dark trees. He could not tell what they were because he was staggering now with weakness, and besides he did not care. He was so weary of the eternal snow that he was ready to walk straight into an Indian camp, if it was there.

He reached the trees, and saw what had made the noises. Many of the buffaloes were lying under them, evidently having sought such shelter from the storm, and near the edge of it, some of the biggest were lying in a group, surrounded by the deep snow, but keeping one another warm.

The buffaloes continued their groanings and heavings, but did not stir from their places, when Bob came near. They shook the snow from their manes and looked at him with great, red, incurious eyes. Perhaps some instinct told them that he was harmless, that he too merely sought shelter.

The boy, the blanket drawn around his shoulders and falling down around him like the folds of a tunic, stood regarding the group of big bulls, at a distance of less than a dozen feet. He was in a haze, and the animals, that he would have hunted so zealously another time, were now like tame cattle to him. They were more. They were sympathetic friends, friends in need. He could see it in their mild, incurious eyes. Man and beast had come together at last in a common brotherhood.

The boy was wholly without fear. Some of his reasoning faculties were atrophied for the time, but primitive instincts were strong within him. He walked boldly forward, and touched one of the big bulls, lying well under the trees, and close to some bushes. The animal, apparently, made an effort to rise, but sank back in his bed of snow and lay quite still.

Bob surmised that the buffalo was hurt, that in the mad rush into the valley a leg perhaps had been sprained too severely for him to move after he had lain down and it had become stiff.

"The buffalo, hurt and weak, no longer tried to move"

once by the skin of the grizzly bear that he had shot, once by a wild horse that had become tame, and now by a crippled buffalo. Since a miracle had intervened in his behalf, he must succeed. Bob was not superstitious, but all these circumstances seemed to him an omen, powerful and propitious. As they had intervened in his favor at the most critical moments of his life he must succeed. Hope leaped up with mighty impulse.

CHAPTER XXV

THE FINAL SETTLEMENT

Back of Bob was forest, extending for an indefinite distance along the slopes of hills and mountains, and he was quite sure that Sam Strong and the others were in this maze. It would be his wisest procedure to find some small stream and follow it. That course might also lead him to his lost horse.

After a breakfast of pemmican, he went down through the edge of the forest to what seemed to be its lowest point, making his way with difficulty through the deep snow, but he was rewarded with the discovery of a brook that he had no doubt ran into the creek. He undertook to follow this to its source, and he found that it led upward through an extremely narrow ravine. He went against the stream four or five hours, making perhaps ten miles, and then came upon a little plateau clothed in forest. Here he was so much exhausted that he sank down on a fallen log, ready for a long rest. The long rest did not come because a voice powerful and penetrating hailed him with these words:

"Hold up your hands! Tell who you are! And be quick about it!"

Bob knew that voice. Its tones filled him with delight, and he felt moreover an overwhelming sense of triumph, because he had succeeded in the face of such tremendous obstacles. He threw both hands as high above his head as they would go, and shouted:

"My name is Robert Norton! I come from many places, and I'm looking for six rascals, Samuel Strong, William Cole, Obadiah Pirtle, Louis Perolet, Thomas Harris and Porter Evans. Have you seen them?"

"By all the stars! and the sun! and the moon, too! if it ain't the youngster, alive an' kickin'!"

Sam Strong made a rush through the snow, seized Bob by the hand, and nearly wrung it off in the violence of his joy.

"Is it you, Bob? Is it really you?" he exclaimed. "An' did you come on the edge of the storm? Are you sure you ain't no ghost, slippin' aroun' to ha'nt us?"

"No," replied Bob, exuberantly, "I'm no ghost, but I did come in on the edge of the storm. Where are the others? Are they alive? Are they well?"

"They're alive, an' if they ain't well I don't want to see 'em when they are well. They're eatin' their heads off in the stall at a rate that's somethin' tre-men-jeous. I s'pose if they was real well they'd eat up a whole buffalo herd, hoof an' horns. Now, Bob, boy, I've always been hopin' for the best, but I sca'cely hoped for this."

He wrung Bob's hand again, and then the boy said:

"I believe, Sam, it was a miracle that saved me last night, and maybe it was another miracle that sent me here. I'll tell about it after I've seen the fellows. Where are they?"

"Back in our shack in the woods. We hunted for you, days an' days, an' at last had to give you up. Then we started ag'in for the East, but the Cheyennes were so thick on the plains that we had to come here in the hills, an' hole up for the winter."

"The Cheyennes are in these hills, too," said Bob, "but I've come ahead of 'em an' I think I'm in time. I'll tell that, too, as soon as I reach the others."

Sam Strong repressed a start.

"Come on," he said, and led the way to the thickest part of the woods, in which Bob presently saw the outlines of a rude cabin.

"We didn't build as well as we did back there near the Colorado," said Sam, apologetically, "because we wasn't expectin' to stay as long. All we needed was a shanty. But all the boys are inside, an' the horses are in the woods back of us."

He pushed open the rude door and said simply:

"Boys, here's Bob; he's come back ag'in!"

Bill Cole dropped the rifle that he was polishing. Louis Perolet dropped the fish that he was cooking. Obadiah Pirtle dropped a moccasin that he was repairing, and an elaborate discussion on the Civil War, conducted with some heat by Tom Harris and Porter Evans, was dropped in the middle of a sentence. The five sprang to their feet and made a rush at the boy. They overwhelmed him with handshakings, and then pushed him to the fire where he might thaw out.

Bob's joy, like that of the others, was exuberant and bubbling, but he did not spend more than fifteen minutes in impulsive question and answer. In that time he told briefly of the two great battles through which he had passed, and listened to their expressions of wonder. Then he said:

"A band of Cheyennes, with Carver and two or three other white men like him, are in these hills, not far away, looking for us. I have seen them myself, and they may come up the valley as I did."

"Tell us all you know about it, Bob," said Sam Strong, instantly becoming the quiet, resolute and resourceful leader.

Bob told everything. His imaginative mind painted all the details vividly, and they understood clearly what they must expect. Sam Strong quickly made his decision.

"Ef they come," he said, "they'll come up the ravine that you followed, Bob. It's the only possible way in here, through such deep snow, an' they'll have to come slow. 'Stead o' waitin' for them to attack us, we'll go meet 'em. Like as not, they'll come along to-night, plowin' through the snow, an' what with an ambush an' a surprise, it'll be plum' funny ef we don't beat 'em. Does my plan seem proper to you, boys?"

"General Lee hisself couldn't have arranged better," said Porter Evans.

"It's exactly what General Grant would have done," said Tom Harris.

"Since you two mighty captains agree with me," said Sam Strong, "I reckon there ain't nothin' more to be said. Bill, you an' Obe take your rifles, go straight to the mouth of that pass an' watch. The rest of us will be there at sunset, ef you don't bring us an alarm before then."

Bill and the Maine man went forth at once, and the others began to prepare fresh ammunition, all except Bob, who was compelled to rest on a pallet of skins. Strong would not let him work, and he became reconciled to his enforced rest when told that he must recover his strength for battle.

They had abundant cartridges, as they had used very few in the winter, and when the long shadows began to fall across the snow in the west, they went forth, resolved, in the words of Sam Strong, to make an end of it.

"We're tired of bein' chased aroun' by Cheyennes an' fellers like Carver," he said, "an' want to go about our business, which is trappin' an' sellin' the proceeds."

As they had the sunset light to guide them, it did not take them long to cross the plain, and when the twilight was fully come they were signaled by Bill Cole and the Maine man. The two were hidden behind some big trees, where they had a view of the pass for a long distance. The narrow way was now filled with deep snow, and no one could come through it except slowly. The steep sides were impossible, as any attempt to climb them now would bring down an avalanche of snow. Sam Strong surveyed the position with delight.

"It was jest made for us," he said. "Why, Bill, standin' here, we could drive back an army."

"Certain," said Bill Cole. "We could drive back two of 'em. Do you think, Sam, we ought to put our own army on both sides of the pass?"

"No," replied Strong. "It'll be better fur us to stick together. Then, whatever happens to one of us will happen to all, an' there won't be no divisions of any kind."

"Reckon you're right, Sam," said Bill.

They settled down in a close group and waited, speaking rarely, and then only in whispers. They had brought their blankets along in order that they might be warm and their sinews elastic when the time came for battle. These blankets were wrapped closely about them, and each huddled figure looked shapeless in the darkness.

Bob had seen so much now of Indian combat that his imagination was not lively, as he sat there with his friends in the pass, awaiting the advance of the Cheyennes and Carver. The joy that he felt at the reunion carried over, as it were, and the coming event cast no shadow.

There was a yellow half moon and it tinted the snow. The pass itself seemed to have a sort of golden glow. A timber wolf howled at the crest of a hill, but the huddled figures behind the trees filled him with terror, and he would go no further. He howled again, and fled to the higher hills. The huddled figures paid no attention.

It was half way between twilight and midnight, and the moon was fading, but the seven could still see clearly anything that might move in the pass. They saw nothing, but Sam Strong held up a warning finger.

"Listen!" he said.

They heard a faint crushing sound.

"Their footsteps in the snow," said Sam. "They're comin'."

Bob strained his eyes down the pass, and a dark face emerged into the moonlight, then another and another, until the whole band of the Indians, with Carver and his friends appeared, laboriously toiling through the snow, in which they sank to their knees at every step. The moon at that moment seemed to shine at a new angle and its rays fell full upon them. As they drew near Bob saw that their faces were eager and hideous with the passion for blood and revenge. Whatever compunctions he might have had about firing upon them from ambush, were dissipated now. He and his friends, for the sake of their own lives, must use the advantage they held.

"When they come opposite that fallen tree, fire," whispered Sam Strong. "I'll count, but I'll count only one."

Bob drew an imaginary line across the snow, and pushed his rifle forward a little. He saw that all the Indians carried their rifles well in advance, and that they were looking eagerly up the pass. He had no doubt that they had obtained information from some wandering warrior of the presence of the band.

"One!" said Sam Strong in a sharp, tense whisper.

Seven rifles were fired so close together that they made but a single report, and all the leaders of the Indian band went down in the snow, while the others gave forth a shout of consternation and rage. Before they could recover, the seven poured in another volley.

Overwhelmed by the surprise, which had in it also a strong element of superstitious terror, since the attack seemed to come like a thunderbolt from heaven, the Indians rushed back down the pass.

"After 'em!" cried Sam Strong, "but keep behind the trees where they can't see us! We must hit 'em as they run, an' they'll never come back!"

He led along the slope, and they shot rapidly at the running Indians who were now in a state of absolute panic. Bob and Sam were in advance, firing as fast as they could reload and pull the trigger. Neither, in the excitement of the pursuit, noticed that a dark figure detached itself from the mass and climbed the slope.

Bob was farthest down the incline, and he had just emptied his rifle when the dark figure, pistol in hand, came face to face with him.

"You don't escape this time!" said Juan Carver, raising his pistol and aiming at the boy.

Bob, paralyzed at the sudden appearance of the freebooter, was unable to move. The face of Carver blazed with triumph. He, at least, would find revenge. But as his finger moved toward the trigger, Sam Strong hurled himself upon him. The pistol was fired, but the bullet went upward, and the two men writhed in a powerful embrace.

Bob, recovering his power over himself, drew his own pistol and ran forward. But he could not use it. The two men, almost equal in strength, went down in the snow, and whirled over and over. He heard hard breathing, muttered cries, and the crunching of snow. Then they rolled toward the last edge of the slope, and Bob himself uttered a cry. The snow gave way and the two, still locked fast in each other's arms, shot down in a white avalanche into the pass. The sliding snow moved for a minute, and then the boy, looking down, could neither see nor hear anything.

"They're both killed!" exclaimed Bob in horror.

"We'll see," said Bill Cole.

All the surviving Indians had disappeared, fleeing in such terror that they would never return again, and Bill did not consider it worth while to bother about them any longer. He and the others carefully climbed down the slope, and stood in the deep snow at the bottom of the pass. But they saw nothing.

"Now, I wonder where Sam is," said Bill Cole in much alarm.

"Here!" replied a voice, weak but confident, and a white figure, rising out of the depths, stood erect.

"Sam!" they exclaimed joyfully and together.

Then they added:

"Where's Carver?"

"There," replied Sam, pointing to the place in the snow from which he had arisen, his voice very solemn. "He's dead. I think that, as we rolled down, his head hit a rock which mine didn't."

It was true. Carver's skull was fractured, and he was quite dead.

"Providence must have been watchin' over me

THE FINAL SETTLEMENT

as it was watchin' over you last night, Bob," said Sam Strong, and his tone was devout and grateful. "I'm always hopin' for the best, and often I get better than I deserve."

They took the body of Carver from the snow the next day and gave it Christian burial.

* * * * * * * * *

Bob and his comrades remained in the hills until the winter broke up. His lost horse, driven by the instinct of companionship, joined the others, saddle, blanket and supplies still strapped on him, and Bob soon reduced him to order.

The snow melted, the trail became good, and they went down into the plains, taking a straight course to the northeast. Fortune was with them, and they met no more Indian bands, but they passed many troops, and Bob saw again all his old friends, Jack Stillwell, Pete Trudeau, California Joe, and the young Mexican, Romeo.

When their furs were sold and the money was put where it would be safe, Sam Strong asked the question:

"What is to become of this band?"

"It's goin' to the new beaver streams you an' Bob an' Obe an' me found away down the Colorado," said Bill Cole.

"Is that so?" said Sam Strong to the Maine man.

"I reckon it is," replied Obadiah Pirtle.

"I know eet ees," said Louis Perolet. "The great Napoleon, after making one brilliant campaign, would make another."

Tom Harris and Porter Evans joined in the general approval.

"An' you, Bob?" said the leader.

The boy's eyes were shining.

"We're bound to go to those new beaver streams," he said.

That was where they went.

THE END

Printed in Great Britain
by Amazon